MARRIAGE OF INCONVENIENCE

KNITTING IN THE CITY BOOK #7

PENNY REID

WWW.PENNYREID.NINJA

Made in the United States of America

Print Edition: January 2018

ISBN: 9781635763508

DEDICATION

The end is always a beginning.

PART I

WHAT HAPPENS IN CHICAGO, STAYS IN CHICAGO

CHAPTER ONE

Marriage: The legal union of a couple as spouses. The basic elements of a marriage are: (1) the parties' legal ability to marry each other, (2) mutual consent of the parties, and (3) a marriage contract as required by law.

Wex Legal Dictionary

Kat

"WHAT DID YOU just say?"

My sharp question earned me a sharp look from Ms. Opal. She eyed me from across the room. Mouth pinched into a disapproving pucker, my coworker's gaze lingered on the cell in my hand. Ms. Opal didn't do this often—send me disapproving looks— just whenever I spoke too loudly. Or laughed. Or smiled. Or showed any emotion.

None of which I did with any frequency.

"Sorry," I said to her, even though my sharp question hadn't been directed to Ms. Opal.

It had been directed to the person on the other side of my call. The unexpectedly disastrous, panic-inducing call.

I heard a chair creak, and then he repeated, "He's planning to have you committed."

"Please wait," I whispered, dipping my chin to my chest, allowing my hair to fall forward. Blocking my face from Ms. Opal and anyone else who might walk through our shared space, I whispered, "Let me call you back. I'm at work."

Uncle Eugene huffed, the sound ripe with impatience. "At work."

"Yes. At work. As in my job."

"Your job." His words were as flat as matzo.

"Please give me five minutes. Thank you," I said on a rush.

Not waiting for his response, I ended the call and clutched my cell to my chest. I stared unseeingly at the dark, solid wood surface of my desk while trying very, very hard not to FREAK THE FREAKITY FREAK OUT!

Oh God, oh God, oh God. What am I going to do? Why now? Why—

"Kat?"

I stiffened, instinctively straightening my spine, and managed a raspy, "Yes, Ms. Opal?"

I sensed the older woman hesitate, and felt her disapproving eyes move over me. I was familiar with this look of hers. It was the kind of look I imagined mothers gave their kids during teenage years. The kind of look parents everywhere administered to children when they were *acting like a fool*, as I sometimes caught Ms. Opal muttering under her breath.

Struggling to paste on my polite smile of perpetual calm, I glanced at the older woman. We'd been working together in the same space for going on five years and I'd grown accustomed to her pointed looks, usually. But today, as Ms. Opal lifted her eyebrows and narrowed her eyes, my throat tightened and my cheeks heated.

I was officially off-kilter.

Discovering one's cousin wishes to send thee away to a nunnery will do that. And by nunnery, I mean a mental hospital. And by send away, I mean lock away forever.

As far as coworkers went, I liked Ms. Opal a lot. I appreciated her exacting nature. We were the two highest-ranking administrative employees in the firm, and we worked well together. She was no-nonsense, dedicated, and never gossiped. The woman was always five minutes early and fully prepared for all meetings. Sometimes I thought she liked me too, like the time she came back from vacation and discovered I'd organized the copy room according to her preferred design. She hadn't given me a pointed look after that for a full six weeks.

Presently, she cleared her throat. "I need a few number-ten envelopes from the supply closet. Will you please retrieve them for me? I'll cover your desk."

Startled, I stared at her. She was still giving me a pointed look, but even through the wild jungle of my panic I recognized that it wasn't a look of disappointment. She seemed concerned.

"Yes. I will."

"Thank you."

"You're welcome." Forcing myself to nod, I stood from my desk. As my chair made a clumsy scraping noise against the floor, I darted out of our shared office. It wasn't until I was three cubicles away from the supply closet, and one of the senior architects gave me a weird side-eye, that I realized I hadn't stopped nodding or clutching my phone.

It didn't matter.

Maybe nothing mattered.

Maybe not even cheese mattered.

Ceasing my inane nodding, I redirected my attention to my sleeve, fiddling with the buttons in order to avoid eye contact. I then pulled at the keys attached to my waist and unlocked the closet. Once inside, I shut the door behind me and flicked on the light, hoping none of the staff architects had spotted my mad dash.

Architects were like junkies around office supplies, insatiable. I didn't understand their preoccupation with mechanical pencils and graph paper, especially since all their work and renderings were done using computer models. Regardless, we could never keep either in stock.

I once had a junior architect buy me a fruit basket for a packet of highlighters. I felt like saying, *Dude. Anyone can buy highlighters. Just go to an office supply store.* Instead I wrote her a thank-you note.

Staring at the screen of my phone, I pushed past the rising tide of fear and redialed Uncle Eugene's number.

He picked up the phone immediately. "Hello?"

"Hello," I said. Waited. When he was quiet, I added, "It's me. It's Kat."

"Yes. I know."

I waited again. When he said nothing else, I asked, "What am I going to do? Please tell me what to do."

"You don't have many options." He sounded grim, but then he always did. I appreciated his consistency.

Eugene Marks wasn't really my uncle. He was my family's lawyer, but I'd known him since I was a kid, and he'd always been nice to me. Grim, but nice. The bar had been set so low by my blood relatives, to the extent that Uncle Eugene had been my favorite person growing up. I always remembered his birthday with a hand-stamped card and an edible bouquet of mostly pineapple. Pineapple was his favorite.

"Please, tell me my options." I paced within the small closet.

"Fine. First option: you allow your cousin to become the guardian of your person and your property. He will promptly commit you, take control of your inheritance when the time comes—specifically, your controlling shares in Caravel Pharmaceuticals—and you may spend the next several years institutionalized. He'll have control of your accounts and finances, therefore you'll have no funds legal representation."

See? Grim, right?

"Please explain to me how any of this is possible. I've been— voluntarily—going to counseling for just over two years now. I earned my GED, and my AA all on my own. Now I'm putting myself through the part-time business program at the University of Chicago, main- taining a 3.9 GPA while working full time."

"Yes. Even though some of those actions will work in your favor, it won't be enough."

"Please explain."

"Firstly, you aren't ready to lead a multi-national pharmaceutical empire."

"I agree. Of course I'm not ready." I kept my tone calm, firmly dispassionate. "But I have been flying there two weekends a month, haven't I? I've been meeting with you, the board, learning, preparing. As far as I know, the board is happy to vote my father's shares as a collective until I reach thirty-one. That was the plan we all agreed to two years ago, and I've done everything asked of me."

"Except quit your job and move back to Boston."

I shook my head. "We've already discussed this."

What I didn't say, what I hadn't admitted to anyone, was that I didn't know if I'd ever be ready to move back to Boston, to assume the role I'd been born into. I'd been stubborn, stalling, putting off the inevitable, because just the thought of living that life, living in that empty mansion, sequestered from the real world, filled me with misery.

"Caleb has never been a proponent of the plan. He believes the shares should reside with the family, not with the board." Eugene's reminder was unnecessary.

Whenever I saw my cousin, he mocked me, told me how I'd failed my family, and how I'd never be capable of leading the company. He's say I was too shy. Too inexperienced. Too timid. Crazy like my mother. His favorite taunt was that I could snap at any time.

I wasn't shy. He mistook my silence for timidity. I saw no reason to converse with people I didn't like and the truth was I didn't like him. Just thinking about the weasel made me want to throw spoiled milk on his weasel face. And then heft loaves of maggoty pound cake at his weasel face. And then rotten tomatoes. And then drown him in a vat of sewage. And then bring him back to life just to burn him in a dumpster full of dead rat carcasses . . .

I might have unresolved anger issues.

That said, on the bright side, dealing with weasel-like Caleb and his weasel face had forced me to become more assertive. The intensity of my desire to prove him wrong was 49% of the reason why I'd stayed the course over the last two years.

"Whether that . . . Caleb is pleased with the plan or not makes no difference," I seethed through clenched teeth, acknowledging the uncomfortable spike in my blood pressure for what it was, an uncharacteristic display of emotion. "I am Rebekah and Zachariah's child. He is not."

"Yes. But Caleb is your closest living relative. Well, closest relative who is not institutionalized."

I had to swallow my sorrow before I could respond. "How is that relevant?"

"He will make the case that you, like your parents, are unstable."

"Again, please explain to me how he can make a case that I'm unstable."

"Because he will, and he'll win. He'll use your voluntary dilution of responsibility—handing over voting control to the board—as proof of your instability."

"No—"

"Try to look at this from a judge's perspective. You are the sole heiress to the single largest privately held pharmaceutical fortune in the world, which employs over one hundred thousand people across four continents. You choose to be a secretary in Chicago and haven't accepted a single cent from your family in over seven years. You can't just be 'stable.' Your mental health must be above reproach, because there's too much at stake."

"Begging your pardon, but I'm not *just a secretary*." I seriously, seriously despised it when people called secretaries and administrative professionals *just a secretary*. Being a secretary was a multitasking marathon, a daily gauntlet of making everyone happy all the time. "I am the executive assistant to the CEO. Not taking money from people doesn't make me crazy, but I will point out that I do allow reimbursement for my travel expenses to and from Boston."

"Family history is not in your favor. Your mother—the last heiress in your position—was diagnosed with schizophrenia shortly after your birth, close to the age you are now. She was in and out of treatment facilities until she was committed by your father when you were five. You were hospitalized as a teenager for a suicide attempt and diagnosed with bipolar disorder—"

"I didn't try to kill myself and I definitely don't have bipolar disorder. I've been seeing a therapist—"

"You refused treatment at fifteen and ran away from home. You lived on the streets for almost three years. You have a history of illicit drug use, engaging in promiscuous and risky behaviors—"

"That's not—" My face burned brighter.

"Again, you've refused to move back to Boston. You've refused help from your family."

I snorted at this—another burst of uncharacteristic emotion—because bitterness burned my throat. By "family," he meant Caleb. Help from my "family" was no help at all.

"All of this has been well documented by your cousin, and I know he has a parade of witnesses to support this version of events."

An agitated laugh tumbled from my lips and I clamped a hand over my mouth.

Okay.

I was really losing it.

I needed to calm down.

I told myself to calm down.

"I have witnesses, too. I have friends here, people who will speak to my character and stability."

"But you won't have access to the *funds*. You won't have money to pay a legal team to fight this because—as I said—he will have control of the accounts as your guardian. We can try to stay ahead of Caleb, start shifting the money under your control now, but at this point it will be too late. The wheels are already in motion, the accounts will be frozen."

"But you're the trustee! You have control of the—"

"I won't. It's too late."

"What do you mean it's too late?"

Eugene hesitated, finally saying, "Trust me, it's too late."

9

I struggled with my composure. "Fine. It's too late. I don't like this option."

"I didn't think you would." His chair creaked again. I was going to have to call his assistant about getting that chair oiled.

"What is my next option?" Proud of the deceptive calm of my voice, I released a slow exhale.

"Option two: you execute a medical power of attorney pre-emptively to someone close to you, but your cousin will definitely contest that appointment."

The panic began to recede, finally. This was good news. "Oh. Okay."

"Not okay."

"Why? That's better than option one."

"Yes, but not by much."

"Why not by much?"

"At best it'll only buy you some time. When I say Caleb is motivated, I mean he is motivated. He's not going to stop until you're under his thumb. Voluntarily assigning someone your medical power of attorney is basically admitting you're not mentally competent to make your own decisions. Most judges will agree that a family member has priority and is better suited in this role than a friend selected by the incompetent person. Plus, you would be subjecting this friend to intense scrutiny and litigation."

I stopped pacing. "What about option three?"

"Which option is that?"

"You tell me." There had to be an option three, because neither option one or two were acceptable.

He was quiet for a long moment, and then said very, very grimly, "I assume you are considering the transfer of your shares to Caleb? A buyout?"

My gut response was, *hell no*. Not only was Caleb a terrible cousin, I was convinced he was a terrible human. For the last several months, whenever I visited Caravel headquarters and reviewed division earnings, I'd always left with a creeping notion that something wasn't right. The numbers added up, but they were too good to be true.

Profits were soaring with Caleb as the CEO, which meant the board was ecstatic. Yet, the sudden sharp profit margin concerned me. We'd had no new properties come to market in five years, spending in drug development was down, and I'd identified obvious inefficiencies in our clinical trials subdivisions. Vague revenue reports from several of the most lucrative divisions culminated in a nebulous sense of anxiety about executive operations.

What would become of my grandfather's company under Caleb's tenure if left unchecked?

Whereas my brain and heart asked, *Why not? Why not walk away?*

I didn't want the responsibility. I'd never wanted it. No one—especially not father when he was still fully cognizant—believed I was capable of it. Even on my best days, I doubted myself in the extreme.

Why not just wash my hands of it? Walk away. Live a normal life.

Eugene didn't wait for me to respond. "I discussed that option with him, suggested a buyout of your shares. He . . . did not appreciate the suggestion. Firstly, he doesn't have the money. As you know, the CEO's compensation package is capped at five million, inclusive of pay-for-performance and share options. That puts him at far less than his contemporaries. Secondly, he said he wouldn't pay you a single cent, that he's taking what's rightfully his. As he put it, 'what I'm owed.'"

"Hypothetically speaking, not that I'm considering this," I hesitated, choosing my words carefully, "couldn't I just sign it all over? Free of charge? Just give it to him?"

"The bylaws disallow that. As the controlling shareholder, bylaws require you be compensated at least one hundred and ten percent the average stock price of the last two years, and current stock is at an all-time high."

Well, there went that idea.

Despite the suffocating lump in my throat and tears pricking my eyes, I was able to whisper, "Eugene, there has to be another option. Talk to me. Give me some hope. What can I do?"

His chair creaked once more, this time giving me the impression he'd been struggling to find a comfortable position. "There is one more option."

"What? What is it?"

"Do you have a boyfriend? Or a girlfriend?"

My eyes flickered over the neatly organized shelves of office supplies, my brain stuck on the word *boyfriend*. "What?"

"Are you seeing anyone?"

I thought about retorting with, *"Other than a string of enormously substandard first dates last year, which make me question the solvency and continued relevancy of the male portion of the human species, no. Not anyone of note."*

Or, *"How the heck am I supposed to find someone to date when I have work, school, and flying to Boston twice a month for heiress lessons?"*

Or, *"Do you really think it's wise or even possible for me to date anyone when I know eventually what I'll become? What they'll have to put up with?"*

Instead, I replied, "No. Why?"

"You could get married."

"Married?" Panic resurged, causing me to shriek, "Eugene! I can't get—" I stopped myself, swallowing, endeavoring to breathe. Breathe. Breathe . . . *Calm down.* "Sorry for my outburst. I apologize."

"Caleb could try to contest a marriage, this is true." Now he sounded less like his grimly pragmatic self and more like he was trying to soothe and pacify; this alteration in his voice did not help my mood. "But his chances of success are minimal, especially if you marry immediately."

"I am not irrational, Eugene. You do not need to use that tone of voice with me."

"Fine." He sighed, and when he spoke again he sounded like good-old grim Eugene. "In the absence of a valid medical power of attorney by a mentally competent person, your spouse would be the default for all medical decisions. Therefore, it's not as though you signed anything over or admitted—or even implied—mental incompetence. In the eyes

of the law, the bond of marriage typically surpasses all other relationships, familial or otherwise."

"Married." Now I definitely couldn't breathe. I was dizzy. I needed
to sit down. Spotting a stack of printer paper, I lowered myself onto the
top ream.

"Yes. Married."

"This seems implausible." Married? What a ludicrous suggestion.
"This isn't a movie, Eugene. Sorry, but I do not believe people just *get
married* to protect themselves from greedy family members' nefarious
scheming."

"Yes. They do. People get married to avoid being deported, to
obtain a green card, to avoid testifying in court, to secure medical
insurance or other tangible benefits, and—yes—even to avoid greedy
family members' nefarious scheming. It's why marriage fraud is
against the law."

"Marriage fraud? Are you suggesting that I commit a crime?"

"No, I cannot suggest you commit a crime. That is completely
unethical and I could be disbarred."

My head was spinning so I lowered it between my legs. The last
thing I needed was to faint in the supply closet. "But you can break
attorney-client privilege with Caleb and warn me about his intentions?"

"I was just one of seven lawyers present during Caleb's last visit to
Sharpe and Marks. Your family's estate employs the firm, and you are
the sole beneficiary of your father's estate. I have—personally—been
on retainer, paid by your father since before you were born, since
before Sharpe and I founded the practice."

"I thought you were retiring."

"I will be next month, for the most part, with some exceptions. The
most notable exception being Zachariah Tyson. I hold your father's
power of attorney and I'm the executor of his estate, the trustee. I have
fiduciary interest in carrying out your father's wishes. You are Zachariah's sole beneficiary. Caleb assumes too much. I have no reason to
believe Caleb is ignorant of my freedom to discuss estate matters with
you, at my discretion." If I didn't know better, Eugene almost sounded

like he was grinning. "Nor have I identified any cause to clarify this point with him or any of my colleagues—including Sharpe."

Spoken like a true lawyer.

He continued, "As long as you intend to make a life with the person you marry, it's not marriage fraud. If you marry immediately, Caleb's request for guardianship will look like a reaction to your marriage rather than the other way around."

"You're serious."

"As my billable rate."

Darn. "I see."

I lifted my torso, placing my elbows on my knees; my forehead fell to my hand.

"Again, you would have to intend to make a life with this person. Kathleen, this has to be someone you've known for a while. Trust that Caleb will have him—or her—investigated, how long you've known each other, etc. He may try to invalidate the marriage."

Tears of frustration stung my eyes. "What if I don't know anyone I can ask?"

Wait.

That wasn't exactly true.

I did know someone. My good friend, Steven Thompson. I'd known him for two and a half years and I loved him dearly. He was my plus-one whenever I had a business function, or went shopping, or wanted to go see a play.

"Kathleen, I'm not exaggerating." Eugene cut into my thoughts with more grimness, more urgency. "There has to be someone you can ask, and not a stranger or a casual acquaintance. Because, this is it. This is your only hope. This is the only way. But it is *by far* your best option. The chances of invalidating a marriage in situations such as these are very slim. The chances of Caleb—as your cousin— becoming your guardian are therefore also very, very slim. Sorry to break it to you, kid, but you need to get married, the sooner the better."

I lifted my eyes heavenward, wanting to ask, "And just how does one propose marriage to a person in a situation such as this?"

Oh, hey. I know you're gay, but my family thinks I'm crazy. Marry me, maybe?

"Let me reiterate, this person must be someone you trust implicitly because . . ." He paused, and when he spoke next his voice was laced with uncharacteristic urgency. "Caleb will try everything, even bribery, threats, everything. Please make sure he or she knows what's expected."

"Please explain to me how can I do that when even I don't know what's expected."

"You misinterpret my meaning. Don't ask a friend who might have feelings for you. We don't need that kind of complication. Let them know a platonic, trustworthy affiliation is what's expected for, by my estimation, at least five years."

I shut my eyes. Eugene didn't need to worry, because Steven definitely didn't have feelings for me. I didn't have a choice. I had to ask Steven. If Steven wouldn't marry me, I didn't know who I would ask.

Maybe Marie? Marie was a good friend from my knitting group, and—more importantly—the only other single friend I had.

That's not true.

Ms. Opal was also single; her husband had died a few years ago . . .

Am I really considering this? Asking my widowed coworker to marry me? Am I this desperate? Think of what you would be asking of her!

Whoever agreed—if anyone agreed—I knew Caleb would not hesitate making both our lives a complete hell.

How can I ask this of anyone?

I cleared my throat of sentiment and asked, "How soon?"

"With your father. . . you need to move fast." I listened as he took another deep breath, palpable worry turning his tone a new, troubling shade of bleak. "Kathleen, please, please listen and understand. This blindsided me. I wish I could've given you more warning, but this *will* keep you safe. Getting married today wouldn't be too soon. We'll . . . talk soon."

Eugene ended the call and it felt like I'd been tossed off a cliff. Numbly, I glanced at the screen of my phone. We'd been talking for twenty-three minutes. Twenty-three minutes was all it had taken to completely scramble my world.

My phone was almost out of battery.

I hastened to call Steven. He didn't answer and I cursed, turning off my phone before it went dead. I then indulged in five more minutes of allowing myself to feel. Then another five minutes of hiding within the closet of despair while I collected myself.

When I stepped out of the supply closet, I had Ms. Opal's number ten envelopes. I was also calm, cool, and focused.

I was on a mission. I would hold myself together until that mission was complete, and that mission started with finding Steven.

Both Steven and I worked in the Fairbanks building in downtown Chicago; he worked on the top floor, I worked on the fifty-second.

Steven had a fancy job title at Cypher Systems—a corporate security firm—that translated to a senior accountant type of position. We'd been introduced by my friend Janie, a member of my knitting group (except she crocheted). Janie used to work with me at the firm, but she'd been let go when her ex-boyfriend's father pulled some strings and had her downsized.

It had all worked out, because that's how Janie met her husband, Quinn Sullivan.

Anyway, that's a long, convoluted story with very little relevance on what was happening today.

Steven worked for Janie's husband's company and we all worked in the same building, that's the important part. Moving on.

Wearing my detached resolve like armor, I tucked Ms. Opal's envelopes under my arm and took the elevator to the lobby. Cypher Systems headquarters was on a secure floor and a keycard was needed to access the level. My plan was to ask the security guards to call Steven's desk, and then have my friend escort me to his office where we would talk.

So I can propose marriage.

Acutely nauseous, I placed a hand over my stomach and walked out of the elevator doors as soon as they opened to the lobby. But then I stopped as soon as I saw who was standing at the security desk.

Dressed in all black, looking the definition of ruggedly gorgeous, was the man of my dreams. Literally.

It was Dan.

Dan the Security Man.

My façade slipped.

I did not appreciate his ability to discombobulate me by merely existing.

Daniel O'Malley was second in command at Cypher Systems and my . . . my . . . Honestly, I didn't know how to describe him.

We'd almost had a thing, but I'd messed it up before anything real could happen. He was *that guy.* That guy I'd been successfully avoiding ever since I messed everything up. That guy I'd known for years and against whom all other men were compared.

Basically, I lusted him.

Before I'd ruined my chance, I used to frequently wish I were someone else. *Anyone* else. Maybe someone who'd grown up in a middle-class, two-parent household. With a family dog rather than a pack of German shepherd/wolf hybrids who ferociously guarded the gates of my grandparents' compound in Duxbury.

And a mother who tucked me in at night with a kiss, rather than a billionaire heiress who hid me in the second attic in the east wing from the imaginary clown in her head for a week and a half when I was four.

And a father who took me to baseball games instead of having the house butler drop me off at boarding school when I was five and never visiting me. Or allowing me to go home to visit instead of me running away one too many times and being expelled.

But enough charming and hilarious anecdotes from my childhood, let's talk about Dan.

As I looked at him, standing behind the lobby security desk talking to one of the guards, I hesitated. The call with Eugene had left me off-kilter.

The last time I was off-kilter and within Dan's proximity, my brain had suggested topics like, *Talk about the weather.* My mouth had translated 'weather' to mean, *hurricanes are a type of weather, let's talk about death by drowning.*

Did I want to interact with Dan while off-kilter?

No.

No, I did not.

But what choice did I have? It was almost noon. Eugene had been adamant, time was of the essence. Hurriedly, I made a mental list of subjects that were off limits—basically, anything gross, illegal, or morbid—and propelled myself forward.

Dan was scanning the crowd in the lobby as he talked to his subordinate and his stare passed over me once. He immediately did a double take and, unsurprisingly, I was ensnared.

My steps faltered. Through sheer force of will, I recovered. But not before the expected eruption of awareness in my stomach and tightness in my chest.

However, given my reason for being in the lobby—my mission to thwart Caleb's attempts to have me committed for the rest of my life—disregarding the flustering sensations was relatively easy. Or maybe I was just getting really good at ignoring my emotions. Whatever. Either worked.

Time is of the essence. Steven. Marriage.

Dan stepped away from his employee and positioned himself at the edge of the high counter. Dark brown eyes—that always seemed alight with mischief—swept down and then up my person, as though conducting a quick assessment of my physical well-being. I ignored that too, determined to keep our interaction as perfunctory as possible.

But then he said, "What's up, Kit-Kat?"

Oh.

Darn.

I gulped a large quantity of air at the unanticipated use of the old nickname, knowing I'd pay for it later. The price would be ruthless hiccups. But for now, the gulping swallows helped.

The way Dan twisted his mouth to the side lent him an air of amusement without actually smiling. He was adorable.

I hadn't spoken to him in a long while. His chestnut hair was longer than its typical close cut and it was styled expertly, back and away from his forehead. Or maybe he'd been pulling his hands through it. Either way, it was an exceptionally good look for him.

We'd seen each other in passing, at Janie and Quinn's apartment, in the lobby of this building, but this was the first time we'd traded words in six months. This was the first time he'd called me Kit-Kat in over two years, since before he started dating Tonya from accounting on the seventeenth floor.

"Sorry. Hi, Dan." I gave him a tight smile. "Sorry. I just wanted to ask—"

Dan shifted closer and dipped his head, like he couldn't hear me, and I caught a trace of cologne, just the faintest hint of something expensive and masculine. His new proximity set my heart racing. Inexplicably, I felt like crying.

But I didn't. I wouldn't. I never did.

Clearing my throat, I started again. "Sorry. I don't mean to interrupt."

His mouth did curve then, a slow spreading smile that usually would've made me forget what I was doing, because I loved this smile.

Dan didn't have perfect teeth. They were a little crooked, like he'd never had braces, and maybe one or two had been cracked during a fight or while playing sports, and then capped. The dentist had done a great job with the repair work, but I suspected the reason Dan rarely showed his teeth when smiling was because he was self-conscious about it. That meant, when he did show teeth—like now—it was because he couldn't help himself.

To me, his real smile was wholly genuine, devastatingly charming, and absolutely perfect.

Also perfect, his nose. It had been broken at least twice and was bent just slightly. His shoulders were also perfect, big and wide; how he moved paired with his stocky frame reminded me of a boxer, capable of both brute strength and remarkable grace.

His neck was also strong—but not in a disconcerting way—and provided the perfect pedestal for his exquisite jaw, which was perpetually shaded with a twelve o'clock shadow. Every so often, when he turned his head, I'd catch a tantalizing glimpse of swirling, black tattoos peeking out of his suit shirt.

But his lips . . .

No words could adequately describe the flawless beauty of his lips.

He was rugged everywhere that I could see, except for those lush lips.

I wanted to bite them.

"You're not interrupting," he said, gaze warm and a little lazy, eyelids at half-mast. Dan leaned closer, lowering his voice. "How can I help?"

Marry me.

Internally, I shrank from the unbidden thought. *Holy wish fulfillment, Batman.*

In the next moment, it occurred to me that Dan was recently single, having split from his longtime girlfriend—the aforementioned Tonya from accounting on the seventeenth floor—just two months ago.

When I'd first discovered they were dating, I'd been devastated and ate $47.31 worth of cheese in one sitting. While crying. I cried on my cheese. It was a sad day.

But when I'd discovered they'd split, I went home, did my laundry, did my homework, *didn't* cry, and answered work emails while steadfastly refusing to obsess about it.

Presently, I was staring at him, unable to speak, as the idea solidified in my brain.

Marry me . . .

The dangerous notion dug its claws into my fragile yet safe plan and tore it to shreds. Shaking my head, I cursed myself for approaching Dan while I was like . . . this. Already feeling all the feelings, I was vulnerable and I *hated* feeling vulnerable.

Seeing Dan just compounded everything; it made me contemplate crazy, grasping-at-straws ideas. I should've waited until he was gone.

Not helping matters, with each beat of my heart the words chanted between my ears, *Ask him. Ask him. Ask him. Ask him.*

Dan's grin waned after a time. And then, after more time, his grin reappeared. He was looking at me like he thought I was funny. Or cute. Or maybe both.

"Kat?"

"Yes?" The single word was strangled, but I was profoundly proud of myself for managing to say it.

Another flash of teeth framed by his alluring lips before asking gently, "How can I help?"

"Oh, sorry. I apologize. Thank you." *Stop apologizing. Stop. Apologizing.*

Some people have curse jars.

I had a "sorry" jar.

I also had a "thank you" jar.

Believe it or not, I'd been much better over the past year, but —*gah!*—something about Dan made it worse. He was dangerous. His sexiness was a hazard. To my soul. I required distance.

Taking a full step backward, I unnecessarily tucked my hair behind my ears—one of my practiced maneuvers for stalling—and infused my tone with controlled aloofness. "Excuse me."

At my withdrawal, Dan's warm smile fell away and his eyes narrowed as they flickered over me, now assessing.

"I'm trying to get ahold of Steven," I said, my voice now even.

"You called him?"

"He's not answering his phone and now my cell is dead." I took two deep breaths before continuing with renewed detachment, "I was hoping I could ask one of the guys to call his desk."

"He's at my place." His tone was no longer gentle, but now impersonal and business-like, mimicking mine.

"Your place?"

Dan scratched his neck, glancing over my head. "He's working from my place today. He's watching Wally."

"Oh." An automatic smile tugged at my mouth. I couldn't help it. Even in my present state of distress, the mere mention of Dan's dog improved my mood. He had the world's most adorable canine. A lab/terrier mix with expressive brown eyes, floppy ears, and short black fur—except for a white patch around his mouth that made him look like he was always smirking.

"Steven has been helping me out for the last month, working from my place a few days a week." Dan pulled out his cell. "You wanna use my phone?"

"No, thank you. But I appreciate it." I glanced over my shoulder, out the lobby doors to the street beyond, debating my options. I couldn't ask Steven to marry me over the phone, and definitely not in front of Dan. It was a conversation that required an in-person meeting. "Thank you, but I'll try to reach him later."

Would later be too late?

"Or, you know, maybe bring him lunch."

"Pardon me?" My eyes darted to his. "At your place?"

I'd never been in Dan's apartment before. The urge to snoop would be strong, but I would overcome it. What I might not overcome was the desire to discover what brand of cologne he wore. Sniff it. Write it down. Buy it for . . . reasons.

"What's wrong with my place?"

"Nothing at all. But, you don't mind?"

"Don't be ridiculous. Why would I mind?" His voice rose, just a smidge, and his eyes seemed to harden.

"I don't want to—"

"What?"

"Take advantage."

"You never do." Dan shrugged, but there was something odd about the gesture as well as his tone, a strange tension in his shoulders. Abruptly, he lowered his eyes to the marble floor, took a deep breath through his nose, and then lifted his chin once more. A new, fastidiously polite smile now in place, his gaze was cool and remote. "He'll be there all day. If you want to talk to him in person, you should go."

I hesitated.

"It's no big deal." He said these words softly, his gaze dropping to my hands, and that's when I realized I'd been twisting my fingers. "Seems like you got something weighing you down."

I balled my hands into fists and hid them behind my back, and then immediately felt like a dolt for doing so, especially when the number ten envelopes almost slipped from their place under my arm.

But I also managed to say, "Thank you. I appreciate it."

Dan continued to inspect me, his eyes growing sharper. "Are you sure there's nothing I can do to help?"

Again, the unbidden *marry me* whispered through my mind and I rolled my lips between my teeth, cutting off what I knew would be a small but hysterical-sounding laugh.

Shaking my head, I backed away. "No, thank you. No. Nope. Have a nice day."

Turning from Dan, I power-walked back to the elevators and punched the button for the floor of my office. I needed my wallet. I needed to give Ms. Opal her envelopes and inform her that I had a family emergency, and let my junior administrative staff know I would be gone for the rest of the day.

Just before the elevator doors closed, I hiccupped. Loudly. Violently. Lifting my eyes as I covered my mouth, I found Dan watching me. He hadn't moved from his spot by the desk, and a painful squeeze constricted my heart just before I hiccupped again.

A tempting but completely impractical thought whispered through my mind. Another, W*hy not?*

This time, *Why not Dan?*

I sighed, leaning heavily against the wall of the lift, and rubbed my hairline where a tension headache was now forming.

Dan O'Malley was a good guy. A great guy. Because I avoided him, we hadn't talked much, especially after what happened between us in Vegas.

But we'd known each other for over two years and he'd always been kind. He'd always taken great care of our overlapping circle of friends. He was the kind of guy who'd give someone in need the shirt off his back, and then offer a beer and a place to stay. If I asked him to help, there was a real chance he might agree. He was just that good.

And yet, a marriage of convenience to the man of my dreams? *That* sounded like a nightmare.

CHAPTER TWO

Marriage fraud: A marriage of convenience entered into purely for the purpose of gaining a benefit or other advantage arising from that status.

WEX LEGAL DICTIONARY

Kat

MY VIOLENT HICCUPS persisted, even while waiting for and grabbing takeout from Steven's favorite sushi restaurant; even while walking along the long stretch of North Michigan Avenue enjoying the summer sun; even while trying to come up with an alternative—any alternative—to marriage.

I'd held my breath several times. Likewise, several times, I'd been convinced the hiccups had passed, only for them to sneak up like a ninja and strike when least expected.

Unexpected hiccups were the worst, mostly because of their volume. My hiccups sounded like a shrill gasp if I wasn't careful to keep my mouth closed. A few people eyeballed me as I walked, as though attempting to determine if I were in distress or just a weirdo making truncated shrieking sounds.

I supposed it was a mixture of both: I was in distress; I was a weirdo making truncated shrieking sounds.

Thankfully, my diaphragm decided to take a chill pill about two blocks from Dan's apartment. Aside from the hiccups, the walk had been good for me, calming. Once I'd accepted my fate, that marriage was the most expedient and efficient answer to my conundrum, I'd prepared a speech, hoping it would help Steven make the right decision.

I had to ask, I didn't feel I had a choice, but I didn't want him to feel pressured.

Dan's apartment building, which was owned by Cypher Systems, was situated in New East Side. The structure had views of Lake Michigan as well as the green space—including Millennium, Daley, and Grant Parks—all the way to the Field Museum to the south.

Because Quinn's company owned the apartment building, and because he was particular about security, several employees and individuals associated with Cypher Systems also lived there.

For example, Cypher Systems provided the security detail for my friend Elizabeth's famous comedian husband, Nico Moretti. Nico and Elizabeth lived in one of the penthouses. Janie and Quinn lived in the second penthouse on the same floor. Sandra—another member of my knitting group—and Alex—her hacker husband who worked for Quinn —lived on the floor below the penthouse level, the same floor as Dan and my friend Steven.

A very friendly doorman I recognized as Charles, who looked more like an MMA fighter than a doorman, grinned when I came into view. "Where is everyone meeting tonight?"

"What?" I stopped to converse with him; I had no way to enter the building without Charles opening the door.

"Isn't your knitting group meeting tonight?"

"Oh. No. That's on Tuesdays."

"Right. That's right." Charles gripped the large door handle, waited a moment for it to scan his prints, and held the door open for me, winking as I walked past. "See you later, Kat."

I gave him a polite nod, unable to stop myself from adding him to my list of potential marriage candidates.

Obviously, first I have to find out if he's single.

Scrunching my face at myself, I struggled to shake off the desperate turn of my thoughts.

Once inside, I sent a short wave to Lawrence, the concierge—*he's married*—and crossed to the elevators. Lawrence returned the greeting as he unlocked the controls. Soon I was on my way up to Dan's floor, berating myself for fanatically cataloguing the relationship status of every person I encountered.

I practiced my speech on the short walk down the hall to Dan's apartment, knocking on the door as I debated how much money I should offer Steven for his trouble. I wanted to pay him for his trouble —because it *would* be trouble—but I didn't want to pay him so much it might unduly influence his decision one way or the other.

Ten million dollars might be too much, for example. I wanted Steven to marry me because he wanted to help and because he was freely willing to accept the trouble Caleb would rain upon us, not because of the money. I didn't want him to feel trapped or coerced.

I resolved to call Eugene and ask his opinion regarding the appropriate dollar figure just as Steven opened the door.

"Kat." He wore a surprised yet welcoming smile. "Are you here for me?"

"Yes. Dan said you were here."

"You spoke to Dan?" Steven's gray eyes widened with obvious expectation and excitement as he stepped back from the door, motioning me in. "Tell me everything."

"It wasn't like that. You know he doesn't think of me that way." I hesitated for a split second, and then I walked into the entryway of Dan's apartment.

"Maybe because you avoid him."

"You know why I avoid him." My attention was distracted by the pictures on the wall. "I needed to speak to you and Dan told me where you were, that's all."

My stare snagged on a black and white photo of Dan and Wally, when the dog was just a pup. He was holding the little bundle tucked in a jacket, cuddled to his chest, and Wally was licking his face. Dan wore a look of complete adoration and joy.

Oh my heart.

I sighed.

As though on cue, I heard a dog bark, followed by a whine and scratching.

"You've been here less than thirty seconds and you're already bursting bubbles." Steven shut the front door, huffing as he walked farther into the apartment. "Come on in, Debbie Disappointment. I need to let Wally out of the bedroom."

"Why is he in the bedroom?" I tore my gaze from the photo and followed Steven.

"He growls at people he doesn't like and runs after people he does. When Alex stops by, Wally tries to follow him out. It's better to keep him in the bedroom whenever someone comes or goes."

The short hall opened to a large living room with floor-to-ceiling windows showcasing the parks and lake. I only tangentially noted the comfy leather couch and wood furniture decorating the space, mostly because I was trying my best not to notice anything. This was Dan's apartment, and I wasn't present by invitation.

Least I forget, proposing marriage to Steven while simultaneously and thoroughly warning him of potential dangers was my goal.

"I brought you lunch," I called after my friend, setting the bags of takeout on a granite bar that separated the kitchen from the living space. "Sushi from Mai Tai."

"Okay, then you're forgiven." His voice reached my ears just before Wally bounded into the room, making a dash straight for me.

I squatted, grinning, and opened my arms to receive him. The first thing he did was lick my face and I laughed as he danced excitedly in front of me, enthusiastic tail wagging almost knocking him over.

Rubbing behind his ears and turning my head to avoid additional doggy kisses, I looked to Steven as he re-entered the room. "Forgiven for what?"

"Forgiven for not asking Dan out. He's been single for something like two months. The time has come to stop avoiding The Security Man."

I stood, still scratching the spot Wally seemed to love. "Steven."

"Kat." Steven crossed his arms, giving me his *bitch, please* look.

Whenever Dan came up in conversation—but especially over the last two months—Steven would not-so-subtly push me to do something about my feelings. My friend knew all about my two-and-a-half-year crush, though I hadn't yet told him what happened between Dan and me in Vegas. Steven hadn't asked and I hadn't volunteered.

We didn't have time for this conversation. It was already past noon. If we were going to get married as soon as possible—which was tomorrow—we needed to go to the Clerk of the Court and obtain a marriage license *now*.

No use beating around the bush, best just to be out with it.

"Listen, I need—I need you to consider a request for your help." I pulled off my coat, tossed it to the couch, and walked to my friend. I grabbed Steven's hands. "I received a call today from Uncle Eugene, you know, my father's lawyer? And, Steven, this is serious."

His demeanor immediately sobered and he tightened his hands around mine reassuringly. "Tell me."

"You remember my cousin Caleb?"

"Yes. The pharma bro who is one evil deed away from becoming a real-life portrait of Dorian Grey."

"That's the one. Well, you know how my dad is getting worse? Caleb is trying to obtain guardianship of me—and my property."

"Why would he do that?"

"He wants control of the family's shares, which—if he succeeds in his bid for guardianship—would be his as soon as I inherit."

"But, honey,"—Steven shook his head, clearly confused —"your dad's condition has been pretty stable, hasn't it? When is the last time he even recognized you? Isn't that why you've been flying to Boston, to visit your parents, learn the ropes, so you'll be prepared when the time comes? I thought the doctors said you had years."

I did my best to faithfully relate the majority of my conversation with Uncle Eugene to Steven, the bulky burden of reality resettling on my shoulders as I recounted the facts. I repeated Eugene's assessment of the situation. I didn't cry. When I felt close to tears, I walked to the couch and sat, crossing my arms over my stomach and working to separate myself from the moment.

But when I arrived at the most crucial part—the part about needing to get married—Steven interrupted me.

"Oh my God. Are you going to ask Dan?" His mouth fell open, his gray eyes circles of excitement.

"What? No! Not Dan. You."

Steven recoiled. "Me?"

"Yes. You."

I'd surprised him. He looked horrified. His eyes darted between mine for several long seconds, and I knew.

He was going to say no.

My face fell to my palms. "Darn."

"Oh honey." He placed a hand on my back and rubbed.

"What am I going to do?"

"Lamb chop," he began gently. "I can't say yes. I'm . . . seeing . . . someone."

This news had me sitting up straight. "You are? But—this is great. Who? And for how long? Why didn't you tell me?"

He'd never admit it, but Steven had been hoping to meet someone for a while.

"Not long." He wouldn't meet my eyes.

"Do I know him?"

"Maybe." Flicking his wrist, Steven batted my question away. "But we can discuss all that later. And, listen, if you can't find anyone else, I'll do it, okay?"

"No. No way. I can't ask you to do that."

"Nonsense."

"Steven—"

"What are the requirements? Besides marrying you, what will this person have to do?"

"Uh, let's see." I searched my memory, describing Eugene's warnings about Caleb, and then added a few stories from my recent visits, during which Caleb had been particularly awful.

"You need someone impervious to threats and bribery." Steven tugged at his bottom lip.

"Yes. Someone I trust, obviously. Someone I've known for a while. Preferably someone who isn't interested in me *at all*. That would only complicate matters."

"Well, I check all those boxes. Plus, I'm magnificent. I see why I'm your first choice." He gave me a small smile. "But let's think. Why don't you ask one of your gal pals? Which one of you knitters isn't married?"

"I thought about asking Marie."

Steven shook his head. "I don't think so. Isn't she involved with that professor guy?"

"Who?"

"The hot nerd who lives next door to Fiona and Greg."

"Matt Simmons? I don't think so."

"Think again. I spotted them out shopping together at the Hugo Boss store. She helped him pick out ties."

This was news to me. "She did?"

"And a man doesn't ask just anyone to help him pick out ties." His tone was thoughtful as he stared off into space.

"Damn it." I rubbed my head again. I felt like I'd been rubbing my head all day. "There's got to be someone."

"Yes. There is." Steven moved his gaze back to me. "And it's the most obvious someone."

I squirmed in my seat, my heart doing another round of *ask him, ask him, ask him.*

He grabbed my hand, as though to preemptively keep me from fleeing. "All right. Enough is enough. I can't believe I'm going to ask this—you know my feelings on the sacredness of Vegas—but you have got to tell me what happened between you and Dan at Janie's bachelorette party."

I winced. "You don't want to know."

"Did he take the hot dog bus to taco town?"

"What?"

"The sex, Kat." Steven rolled his eyes. "Did you have the sex with Dan the Security Man?"

"No. No, much worse." My words were anguished, because the memory tormented me.

"In my imagination, literally everything is worse than having the sex with delicious Dan,"—Steven pushed my shoulder—"so you're going to have to be more specific and tell me what happened."

"Does this place have any cheese?" I craned my neck, searching for the fridge.

"No cheese until you tell me what happened."

"Just once I would like to be the person that wanted to go exercise when they had a bad day, and not eat a block of cheese for dinner."

"And I want Hugh Jackman's body."

"You could if you lifted weights."

"No. You misunderstand. I don't want to look like Hugh Jackman. I want his body." Steven gave me an unapologetic shrug, and that plus his cheeky words made me laugh.

"Good, a smile." He patted my leg. "Now tell me what happened in Vegas, 'cause it obviously didn't stay there."

"Fine." I tugged my hand from his, suddenly too exhausted to dodge his questions. "I was drunk. If you recall, Sandra spiked our drinks that night, she misunderstood or didn't realize it was absinthe. I don't remember much after that until I woke up in bed next to Dan the next morning. I was in my underwear and so was he."

"Oh! Do go on." Steven leaned in.

"I assumed we'd slept together." I peeked at my friend. "And that made me so very, very sad."

"What? Why?"

"Because I didn't remember it. I'd promised myself that those days —of getting drunk or high or waking up next to someone, not remembering much from the night before—were behind me."

Steven's look of confusion dissolved into one of patient under-standing.

I'd told Steven about my teen years, about how I'd tried to "live life to the fullest," or what the world plus my fifteen-year-old brain told me living life to the fullest meant. Convinced I'd eventually become my mother, I wanted to spend what limited time I had left doing everything, feeling everything, experiencing everything. And when I was too shy to try things on my own, I'd turned to the inhibi-tion-loosening powers of alcohol and drugs.

But by seventeen, I was so tired. Tired, dissatisfied, remorseful, and miserable.

We traded stares for a few seconds, and then Steven gently nudged my knee. "So what happened next?"

I glanced at my hands, at the pale pink polish I'd applied last night. It hadn't yet begun to chip. "Since I assumed we'd slept together, I told Dan to,"—I glanced around the apartment, not able to meet my friend's eye as I continued on a rush—"I told him to look for the condom because I didn't usually remember using one, and I wanted to make sure we had. He asked me something about what I meant by 'usually.' And then I basically admitted that I'd had a bunch of drunken one-night stands."

"And what did he do?"

I rolled my eyes at myself, because the memory still stung. "He couldn't get out of the room fast enough, but not before he told me nothing happened between us. That I'd puked, and he'd stayed to make sure I was okay. But that nothing had happened."

"So why were you in your underwear? Why didn't he leave you in your clothes?"

"The dress I'd been wearing smelled like smoke and vomit. I assume he removed it because of the smell."

"Hmm. I guess that makes sense."

"So, that's it." I glanced at my friend and found him frowning thoughtfully. "Can we get back to the problem at hand? I can't believe I'm asking this, but what do you think about Charles? The doorman. He seems nice."

"Charles?" Steven's expression told me he was either confused or constipated. "I'm not finished talking about Vegas, because that doesn't seem like Dan. I've never known him to be judgmental. Generous? Yes. Adorable? Bossy? High-handed? Loyal? Yes, yes, yes, and yes. Judgmental? No."

"It was more like,"—I shook my head, struggling to find the words —"he was disappointed. Like he'd expected me to be one way. Who I actually was, who I am, disappointed him."

"I'm sorry, but that's still an assholeish thing to do. So what if you've had one-night stands? That shouldn't make any difference. I bet he's had one-night stands. Why should he care who you've slept with?"

"I get it. I do. I'm—"

"Don't you finish that sentence unless the next words out of your mouth are, 'I'm sexy and fabulous, he'd be lucky to peel my grapes while wearing a loincloth.'"

My mouth formed a rueful line. "No. I do get it. The drugs, the stealing and shoplifting, living on the street, thinking only about myself. Sometimes I run into my old friends, the people I used to run with. They love that lifestyle and still thrive in it. Most of them, not all, have no responsibilities, no mission in life other than to get high and get laid. I can't judge them because I've been there, and I know why I thought it made me happy for a time, but I wouldn't want to be involved with any of them now. What I want now is so different."

"Better."

A familiar frustration made my throat tight; whenever I tried to explain this, explain my perspective on my past, I never felt like I had the right words. It was easy to sound like I hated the person I was, or that I was ashamed of my decisions. The world told me I should be ashamed. I hated certain parts of myself, some of the memories, and I was definitely ashamed of the stealing, though I'd worked hard to make restitution.

But everything else? I'd made mistakes. Big ones. Small ones. And I was trying to learn from them.

Choosing my words carefully, I focused my attention on the

window behind him. "I don't think it's fair of me to say that what I want now is *better* in general. I can't speak for other people, what brings them fulfillment. What I can say is, for me, it's better. I'm happier."

"See? This is what I'm talking about. All this wisdom." He made a sweeping gesture to my whole person. "How can you still have a thing for someone who walked out on your amazingness? Why haven't you moved on from him?"

A twinge of guilt and doubt had me pulling at the wrist of my cardigan. I was speaking as though I was an authority, but in truth I still had issues. Additionally, I had no experience with monogamy, only hopes for it. Hopes that it would help me rewrite the intimacy script I'd drafted in my head, leading to a healthier—for me—future.

"Anyway,"—I needed to get us back on track—"whatever his reason for leaving that morning, he left. After that, he's never looked at me the same."

"What do you mean?"

"Before Vegas, I felt sure he was interested. He used to give me . . . sexy eyes, you know?"

"I don't know. So complete is your dedication to avoiding the man, I've never seen the two of you in the same room. But I get what you mean. And then after Vegas?"

"He stopped. He's always been really nice, polite, friendly. But he's never looked at me the same."

"Maybe you haven't given him a chance?"

"No. The way he looks at me now, it's like he's either overly polite, or irritated with me, like I annoy him."

"And you've never talked to him about it? About what happened in Vegas?"

"No, you know how I was."

"*Was?*"

"Come on, I'm not nearly as shy as I used to be."

"Correct, you're not as shy. You're just exponentially more rigid and controlled."

"That's not true. Since I started seeing Dr. Kasai, I'm much better."

"Fine. You're much better. Please do go on, because you were just telling me how you never spoke to Dan about what happened between the two of you in Vegas."

I ignored the sarcasm in his tone. "As you know, Dan started dating Tonya a few months later."

"She's nice." Steven paired this with a reluctant smile. "I like her."

"I know. And she's smart. And really pretty." I nodded, my heart hurting because my affinity for Tonya had been one of the worst parts of Dan dating her. I'd liked her before they'd dated, while they'd dated, and still, after they'd broken up.

"And she makes those lemon bars for the building's Christmas party." Steven pushed his bottom lip out in a little pout. "I hope she makes them this year. I always bring a bento box to stash them in and take extra from the tray."

"She gave me the recipe." I grimaced. "I·don't know why he broke up with her."

"I have some suspicions." Steven straightened in his seat. "But, oh well. He did. That ship has sailed. Which means he's single and ready to mingle. Plus, I want to set her up with Carlos."

I chuckled, mostly because it was all I could do in the face of crushing anxiety about my future. "I need to get married. I have to find someone to marry. Eugene said I need to make this happen as soon as possible, which means I need to find someone today, go to the courthouse this afternoon, so I can get married tomorrow."

Steven regarded me, tapping his chin with his index finger. "Hmm . . ."

"*Hmm* what?"

"Do you think—and this is purely hypothetical so don't freak out—if you explained the situation to Dan, asked him to marry you, he would?"

I didn't answer, because I didn't want to lie. It would probably be horribly embarrassing, but he'd probably say yes if I explained how dire the situation was. My nausea returned just thinking about it.

"You're not helping." I glared at my friend.

"Oh, but I am. You said yourself he's not interested in you, and didn't your uncle Eugene say he wanted you to marry someone trust-worthy? Someone you've known for years? Someone who wouldn't complicate things with icky feelings? If you're so sure Dan doesn't think of you 'in that way,' then why not?"

"Steven."

"Kat. Think about it. He's actually perfect for the job." My friend gave me the impression he was talking himself into this idea in real-time, as we sat on the couch. "Dan won't care about Caleb's threats, and Pharma Bro won't scare him one iota."

I stayed silent because Steven was absolutely right. Just the thought of Caleb trying to intimidate Dan was laughable. The stocky security executive's reaction to Caleb's threats would almost be worth the abject humiliation of asking Dan for help.

Almost.

But not quite.

Steven was still speaking, ". . . hilarious. And deserved. Have you ever seen *Road to Perdition*? It would be just like that, but with less trench coats and hats. Also, Dan will be impervious to bribery. He has enough money already. He'll be impervious to it all—"

"Yes, but *I'm* not impervious to *him*." My face crumpled and I covered it with a hand.

"Oh, lamb chop." He placed his fingers lightly on my shoulder and I shrugged them off.

Taking three deep breaths, I stood from the couch, moving out of Steven's reach. Wally followed, standing from where he'd been curled next to my feet.

I spoke when I was sure I had myself under control. "I'm sorry. I still like him. A lot. Even after he left me in Vegas. Even while he dated Tonya. I avoided him *because* I like him so much. Do you really think it's a good idea for me to ask the guy I haven't been able to move past in two years to fake-marry me?"

"Yes. I do." Steven also stood, reaching for and holding my shoul-ders, forcing me to meet his eyes. "Honey, you're out of options. And even if you weren't, I think it's the best idea I've had all month. And that's saying a lot because I just bought a gorgeous new rug."

I shook my head, but before I could offer new objections, he cut me off. "You said it yourself, you haven't been able to move on from Dan. Honey, that's nuts. It's not normal, as an adult, to be hung up on a guy for over two years and never do anything about it."

"What do you want me to do about it?"

"Stop avoiding him. Marry him. Confront the situation. Think of this as killing two birds with one stone. He'll be impossible to avoid. Once you actually *know* him, then you'll let go of this super unhealthy fascination with a man who, yes, is very hot, and nice, and funny, yada, yada, yada, but who isn't worth your unrequited affection. You can move into the safe and neuter-feeling friend zone."

"You realize this suggestion makes absolutely no sense."

"You realize this suggestion is genius."

I groaned, moving farther away, wanting to pull my hair out. Wally again followed, shadowing my movements and wagging his tail. "I don't have time to debate this with you. I need to—"

"Then I have a proposition. You ask Dan, today. Wait for him here. When he gets home, ask him. Tell him the minimal amount of information required to get the importance of the situation across. If he doesn't immediately say yes, if he hesitates *at all*, then I'll marry you."

"Of course he's going to hesitate."

Steven held his hands up. "Then I'll marry you."

"And what about your boyfriend?"

"I'll talk to him tonight. He'll understand, or I'll make him understand. I hope. Don't worry about it."

"No. No. That's not fair—"

"Like I said, you ask, and if the words out of his mouth aren't an immediate, 'Yes. Let's do this,' even if he pauses for a moment to deliberate, then tell him it was an early April Fool's Day joke, call me, and we'll go to the County Clerk's office tomorrow."

"Steven."

"Trust me. I insist."

I didn't respond. I couldn't. If I tried to speak, I had a feeling I'd end up screaming instead, and I didn't want to do that.

Swallowing my pride, I nodded. My lungs were on fire.

I would wait here for Dan. I would ask him to marry me. It would be humiliating. In the end, I had no doubt Steven and I would be the ones getting married.

CHAPTER THREE

Mental incapacity. 1 :an absence of mental capacity. 2 :an inability through mental illness or mental retardation of any sort to carry on the everyday affairs of life or to care for one's person or property with reasonable discretion.

MERRIAM-WEBSTER DICTIONARY

Dan

"WHAT DID YOU just say?" I checked my watch again. I didn't have time for this shit.

After ten on a weekday. I was running late on one of the rare nights I'd get to sleep in my own bed. Steven needed to get home.

We were at the East Randolph Street property, on the north side of Millennium Park. Our main office was downtown, but we'd moved the data center to the apartment building a few months ago. Since Cypher Systems owned the whole building—and controlled all access points and ports in or out of it—Alex, Quinn, and Fiona believed the apartment building was the more secure option.

So here we were, in the apartment building where I lived, working late into the night, and I hadn't yet had a chance to go home. Unbelievable.

Quinn glanced over his shoulder, giving me a look. "I said bring a Tonya. It's a couple thing."

I crossed my arms, returning his evil eye. "Tonya and I split."

Quinn did that thing, that stupid thing where he waved his hand in the air like he was shooing away a bug. "I know."

This was a stupid thing he'd been doing since we were kids when he didn't want to talk about something. What did he think? That I wanted to talk about this shit? I needed to go. Now.

"Why do you want me to bring Tonya?"

"I meant *a Tonya*." Again with the hand wave. "Bring a Tonya."

"Bring a Tonya?" I scratched the back of my neck, not following. "You mean someone who looks like Tonya? Why does my date need to look like Tonya?" Checking my watch again, I rubbed my wrist. Steven hadn't called, but I didn't like being this late. Unfortunately, more and more over the last month, this had become the norm.

"I don't care what she looks like as long as she knows how to act at these things." More hand waving. "Like Tonya."

Ah. I got it. *Okay. No biggie.*

But if he thought he could give me the impatient hand wave, then that was my cue to annoy him. "You're going to bring up my ex-girlfriend and that's all I get?"

"What?" His tone clipped, he glared at me.

"The least you could do is offer me tea." I shrugged, sniffed. "What if I'm still emotionally unstable about the breakup?"

Alex made a sound, like he was trying to hold in a laugh.

Quinn wasn't laughing.

"Hey, I have feelings." I mimicked his stupid hand wave. "We were only together two years, but—"

"No, you weren't," Quinn grumbled.

"Yeah, we were. We hooked up just after New Year's, and—"

"You weren't together. You were passing time."

"She had a toothbrush at my place." I was pushing the issue for no reason, but something about his easy dismissal of Tonya pissed me off.

It also made my neck itch. My neck only itched when I felt guilty about something.

"So?"

"So, toothbrush residence-sharing equates to a serious relationship. Everyone knows this." I didn't know who I was trying to convince, him or me.

"That's bullshit. You were never serious."

Of course, he was right. We were never serious. "Fine. But, again, in my defense, we were together for only two years."

"*Only* two years?" Quinn glanced at the back of Alex's head. "Two years is a long time."

"No, it's not." I shook my head.

"Yeah. It is." Quinn nodded his head.

"No, it's not. Two years is long enough to be infatuated with a person, sure. But definitely not long enough to know whether something is real, or whether it'll last."

Quinn's frown of annoyance became a glare. "Are you fucking with me right now?"

"I agree with Quinn." Alex said this without turning from his computer. By computer, I mean a wall of monitors and shit that buzzed.

I caught myself before rolling my eyes. "You always agree with Quinn, Chachi."

Alex pivoted completely around in his chair and glared at me. I tried to glare back but I swear, the kid's glare was unnerving as hell.

"Don't call me Chachi."

"Fine. Fuck you. I'll call you Joanie."

His unnerving glare intensified and my phone buzzed. Pulling it from my pocket, I checked the screen, and then did a double take, growing sick to my stomach.

Mom: *I assume you're dead since you can't be bothered to call your mother on her birthday. Tell Quinn we'll send flowers to the funeral home since we don't know where to make a donation in your name. I hope your mourners aren't allergic to calla lilies.*

Love, Your Mother, who gave birth to you after 42 hours of labor.

Mom: *Call me. If you can spare the time.*

"Who's that? What's wrong?" The kid sounded like he was on high alert.

I closed my eyes, muttering under my breath, "Fuck a fucking duck."

After moment of inspecting me, Quinn said, "It's his mom."

I opened my eyes. Quinn was wearing his little shit-eating grin. It was so little; someone who hadn't grown up with him would need a magnifying glass and some really good light to spot it. But I'd known him since either of us could remember.

"Oh." Alex turned back to his wall of buzzing shit without another word.

Quinn stepped closer to me and lowered his voice. "You didn't call her?"

"No, I didn't fucking call her." This was a disaster. I was dead. She was going to murder me with guilt. Speaking of which, my neck itched.

His freaky blue eyes moved over me. "I called my mom this morning."

"I know." The shithead.

Quinn's mother and my mother shared a birthday. That meant we always reminded each other to call our mothers every year on their birthdays. Even though a few years back Quinn went through a period of time where he didn't call his mom at all—because they weren't talking to each other—he'd still remind *me*.

"I reminded you this morning. I reminded you during lunch. Janie said she sent you a text."

"I know that too, fuckface."

Janie was Quinn's wife and currently hugely pregnant with their first kid. She was also on bed rest for some kind of medical something, which made Quinn crazy. Quinn had been taking this crazy out on me.

Additionally, I'd been doing all his travel plus mine, which meant I usually didn't know if I was coming or going.

Meanwhile, he'd been spending more time with his hot wife, probably also driving her crazy.

I'd planned to call my mother this afternoon while checking in with the team at the Fairbanks building, but then Kat Tanner had shown up. Basically, I'd had difficulty concentrating on much after that.

Kat Tanner was . . . fuck. I didn't even know how to describe her.

She was that girl—that idealized, wicked-smart, wicked-nice, wicked-hot girl—you knew all your life, from pre-school to high school. At first she had you convinced that she had no fucking clue how fucking amazing she is. She was humble, kind, salt of the earth, good people. You watched her with her friends and thought, fuck, she's a goddamn diamond. Even her laugh sounded amazing.

Let me explain. I'd never had what some people call "a type." I loved all women. I loved looking at them. I loved talking to them. I loved them talking to me. Didn't matter young, old, tall, short, chunky, thin, red, brown, blue, gray, I have a steadfast admiration for females.

That might be because my mom was a super lady, basically raised all us kids on her own while my dad wasn't around much. A career Navy guy, he was deployed more than he was home, but that's not why he wasn't around.

My love of women might also be because my sisters were angels, whereas my brother was a worthless piece of shit. Sure, my sisters had their dramas, but those dramas were mostly caused by undeserving men who mistreated them.

Whatever. Women were fucking amazing, I loved them all, and I'd dated all kinds.

But I'd never felt the shitty feeling in my chest until I met Kat Tanner. Like I couldn't draw a full breath when she was around. Actually, scratch that. I couldn't draw a full breath sometimes when I simply thought about her.

Why her, I didn't know. Could be her pheromones did strange stuff to my pheromones, messed up my endocrine flow, or Chi. Whatever.

Could be, I just really liked the way she looked, her dark thick hair, her big brown eyes, how her lips were the exact shade of the roses in my grandma's garden, her skin's olive tint, the way she walked, the curve of her ass, how she looked down and always sounded a little guilty when she laughed. Whatever. It was everything.

But then I found out she was some kind of frickin' billionaire heiress.

So I thought, *Hey, she doesn't make a big deal about it, why should I?* So what if I grew up on the other side of the tracks? So what if I was in and out of jail and gangs when I was a teenager? So what if I have a GED instead of a high school diploma? So what if I never went to college, and meanwhile she'd gone to University of Chicago for some fancy degree?

People were just people when you got down to it, right? No biggie.

But then I woke up next to her one morning in Las Vegas, after holding her hair the night before while she threw up, only for her to tell me she's not into monogamy.

For the record, I had nothing against polyamory. I had an aunt on my dad's side who lived up on a compound in Vermont. Aunt Becks had, like, three lady friends and six gentleman friends—that's what my mom called them—something like that. They all seemed to get on just fine with each other for the most part. Shit, she'd lived there for twenty years and she'd always seemed happy.

When I was old enough to understand her lifestyle wasn't typical, I'd asked her why she was into it. She'd said something similar to what Kat had said that morning in Vegas: "I've never been very good at monogamy."

My father's family hadn't been any more or less dysfunctional than my own, and none of us had chosen the polyamorous lifestyle. My brother had, but it was different. He just dicked around with a bunch of different crazy women who didn't know he was dicking around; not the same thing as a consensual committed relationship with a bunch of different sane people.

But that kind of lifestyle wasn't for me. Knowing myself as I do, I wouldn't be able to stomach seeing some other guy or lady touching the woman I loved. Furthermore, I'd probably beat the shit out of that other guy.

I wouldn't beat the shit out of the lady, though. Likely, I'd give her a seriously dirty look.

But that's just me.

So, yeah. I saw Kat this afternoon after not talking to her for six months. Seeing her reinforced the fact that she was still a goddamn diamond, and she still gave me that shitty feeling in my chest. We'd talked briefly. As usual, she couldn't wait to get away from me. Afterward, I'd been distracted and irritable, and I hadn't called my mom on her birthday.

Quinn's smile spread. He tried to hide it by clearing his throat and covering his mouth with a fist. "You want me to call your mom? Tell her you're on assignment, out of the country?"

"I'd have to be on Mars, resurrecting both JFK and Bing Crosby from the dead, for her to give me a pass. Short of that . . ." I shook my head. *Fucking disaster.*

He hesitated for a second, then asked, "Is your dad in town?"

"No." And that was all I was going to say about that.

Even though my father had retired from the Navy some years back, he was still never around. To say he and my mom had a complicated relationship was an understatement. The long and short of it was: he had a kid—my brother Seamus—by another lady who he loved, that lady left him and the baby, and my mom stepped in, raised Seamus as her own, and my dad had been so grateful.

So damn grateful. The only problem was, gratitude wasn't the same thing as love.

"I could tell her you were doing something for Janie and the baby."

"No." I groaned. "That would only make it worse, give her a chance to point out you're married and giving your mom grandkids." And I wasn't.

"There's got to be something she wants." His face was now sober. "Diamond earrings?"

Quinn remembered the last time I hadn't called my mom and the tempest of ignominy and shame that she'd rained upon me.

I'd been seventeen and in jail. She didn't care that I'd had no possible way to call her. She didn't care that I'd taken the fall for Seamus. She didn't care that I'd bribed a guard an ungodly amount of cash to have flowers sent, along with her favorite perfume. She didn't care that I'd organized her party and to have the rest of my siblings—including Seamus, who, let me point out again, should have been in jail in my place—take her to church, make her cake, and treat her like a goddess.

I hadn't called; therefore, I was Judas the Betrayer. I'd take fire and brimstone over Eleanor O'Malley's unrelenting, passive-aggressive guilt squall any day of the week.

May God have mercy on my soul.

Quinn shrugged. "Let me know if I can help."

"I need a miracle." Exhaling my frustration, I turned and left without another word.

Glancing at the screen of my phone, I re-read her message as I walked out of the room and down the hall. Pressing the button for the elevator, I decided I couldn't call her and tell her I'd forgotten. That was not an option. So I ran through the list of things my mom wanted the most, ranked highest to lowest:

Me getting married and settling down.

Me giving her more grandkids.

Me moving home to Boston and buying a house on her street.

Me going to stay for every major holiday for the rest of my life.

Me asking her advice about every major decision for the rest of my life.

Four of the five weren't possible. They just weren't. The first three because they were impossible for me to do within the next twenty-four hours, and the last one wasn't going to happen because I wasn't a helpless asshole.

Number four would have to do it. I'd pledge at least five years of holidays as penance. So be it.

Plus, I was going to have to make up a lie about why I hadn't called yet, and it was going to have to be good. If I told her the truth, that I'd forgotten, it would legitimately hurt her feelings. There was nothing I wouldn't do—including lie, cheat, and steal—to avoid hurting my mom's feelings.

Getting on the elevator, I pressed the button for my floor and leaned against the cushioned velvet wall, tired. So damn tired. I couldn't wait to sleep in my own bed.

But first things first. I'd apologize to Steven and then spend some time with Wally while I called my mom.

As soon as I opened the door to my apartment, I called out, "Hey, Steven. Sorry I'm so fucking late. Quinn has me doing this fucking thing with the corporate division, and those fancy fuckers need more hand-holding than my one-year-old nephew. I swear, I thought that Townsend douchebag was going to ask me to jerk him off."

I pulled at the tie around my neck, grateful to remove the noose. Laying the tie over my jacket, I tossed both to the chair in the entry-way, frowning at the darkness.

And the silence.

"Steven?"

No answer. But then a lamp switched on someplace in the family room, the light spilling into the hallway as I unbuttoned my collar and the top three buttons of my shirt.

And where the hell was Wally? Typically he waited by the door, ready to lash me with his whip of a tail.

Wally was always a bundle of energy whenever I came home. Didn't matter the time of day, he'd wag his tail so hard sometimes he'd knock himself over. I'd adopted him when he was only six weeks old. Now he was four, but I swear, he still acted like a puppy, loved to be held.

My boy was a good-sized dog, a Labrador/terrier mix—plus some other stuff, I was sure—so the best kind of dog, with the best person-ality traits from each breed in his ancestry. Smart, friendly, gentle and patient with kids. I was convinced that dog had a sixth sense about things, especially people.

For example, Wally didn't like Seamus. Every time he'd come around, Wally would growl and bark, didn't want Seamus touching him.

He knew my brother was a nasty fucker. You could tell a lot about a person based on how they interacted with animals. I didn't trust people who didn't like dogs; they're not my people. How could you dislike dogs? They're the best fucking thing about this planet, with hockey, sex, and a good Irish whiskey taking places two, three, and four.

Plus, dogs were loyal. There's nothing more loyal than a dog. Probably because they had their priorities straight: food, sleep, and chasing shit.

But enough about my awesome dog, for now.

Unbuttoning the right cuff of my suit shirt, I strolled into the main room. "Steven, again, I'm sorry about being so late. If I—"

Holy shit.

I stopped short, rocking back on my heels, staring like a dummy at the wholly unanticipated image of Kat Tanner rubbing her eyes as she ungracefully stood from the couch. And Wally lifting his head from where he'd been curled up next to her.

"Kat."

"Hi, Dan."

I was dreaming. It was the only explanation. I was already asleep and this was one of my fantasies, because Kat was the only woman who'd consistently starred in my dirty dreams.

This was a dream. I almost crossed the room and kissed her. But I didn't, because Wally was there. Wally had never been a star player in my fantasies, and I believed that made me 100% normal.

Wide-eyed, I stared at her, having no words. If my sisters were here, they'd have a field day, seeing me tongue-tied and brain-dead.

Luckily, she filled the silence as Wally jumped off the couch and rushed to me, as though just realizing I'd arrived. *What a stinker.*

"Steven let me in. He said I could wait for you. I hope you don't mind."

"No," I said too fast, but it was already out and there was no taking it back. So I cleared my throat and tried to sound less like some loser, eager for her company. "No, I don't mind." I bent to pat my boy and take a damn minute to compose myself. "Is Steven still here?"

"No. He left at six. He offered to take Wally, but I thought—and I hope I didn't overstep—I thought since I was here and waiting anyway . . ." She gestured to my boy. His tail beat an enthusiastic rhythm against my leg as though Wally knew a beautiful woman was talking about him.

He trotted back to her and rubbed his head under her hand. She immediately patted him and rubbed his ears. Wally sighed like he was in heaven.

Lucky dog.

"I hope that's okay," she repeated, looking guarded.

But then, she always looked guarded.

"Yeah." I nodded, waving away her concern. "Yeah. Makes sense." I sounded winded. My chest was doing that shitty thing where it felt too tight, or too full.

Not helping matters, she looked gorgeous. Her hair was a mess, a sexy mess, mussed from sleep, big and poofy, falling over her face and shoulders. Her eyes were drowsy and her clothes were rumpled. I liked her like this, so different from the starched-shirt façade from earlier in the day.

Get a fucking hold of yourself, Daniel. Obviously she needs something. She didn't wait here all day so she could hump your leg.

But the thought that she'd waited for me, and might need something *from me*, was almost as intoxicating as if she'd actually come here to hump my leg. To put it plainly, I wasn't about to turn either request down.

"So, uh." I tried to take a deep breath. I couldn't. "Is there something you need?" I walked to the bureau to put some distance between us. She was too close. Four feet with anyone else was fine and dandy. Four feet with Kat, alone in my apartment, was suffocating.

"I . . ." I heard her take a breath. Then another, louder this time.

I glanced over my shoulder, found she was holding herself, her arms tight around her middle. That made me frown.

"Okay. Okay." She nodded, obviously talking to herself.

Finally, my stupid brain moved beyond the shock of seeing her, her being here, and all the clutter of hopes and dirty dreams her presence inspired. I looked at her. I really, fucking looked.

She was scared.

A jolt of alarm had me crossing to her before I could check the instinct. Holding her shoulders, I angled my chin to catch her eyes.

"Hey, what's wrong? Are you okay?"

"I need your help."

"What's wrong?"

"It's . . . it's—I can't believe I'm going to ask you this." She exhaled a laugh, sounding a little guilty, like always.

"You need money?"

"No." She shook her head adamantly. "No. I'm actually here to offer you money."

I let my hands drop and backed up, lifting my chin. The fact she was here to offer me money landed like a blow. Or at the very least, it felt like a papercut. It stung.

Sure, we weren't close, but we were friendly. At least, I thought we were. You don't pay friends, it was the eleventh commandment, right after not coveting thy neighbor's cow.

Thou shalt not covet cows. Oh yeah, and don't offer to pay your friends either.

Dropping my chin, I tried not to glare at her. But I'm pretty sure I did.

"I don't want your money. You need something, just ask."

"It's not that simple."

"It is that simple. It's the ABC's of friendship, Kat."

She looked a little startled. "We're friends?"

Ugh. Fuck a duck.

Then she took a small step forward, and she looked *hopeful.*

Ugh. Fuck another duck.

"Yeah. 'Course we're friends." I wiped my hand across my mouth, then shoved it in my pocket.

What I didn't say was . . . a lot.

She was twisting her fingers again, like she'd done today in the lobby. "What if I pay you—"

"How about this. Why don't you tell me what you need first? Then we'll discuss the money after. Okay?"

She hesitated, then nodded, her breath coming faster. "Okay, okay." Again, I got the impression she was speaking to herself. "I can do this."

Another spike of alarm had me wanting to touch her again, but I didn't. From the look of it, whatever was bothering her, whatever brought her here, must've been a big deal.

I tried to keep the worry out of my voice, gently prodding, "Start from the beginning."

"The story is too long. Can I just—." She paused to swallow, her eyes pleading. "Can I just tell you the end?"

"Fine, tell me the end."

She was really freaking me out here.

"I need . . ."

"Yes?"

Her chin wobbled. "I wouldn't ask if it weren't an emergency."

"Anything. It's yours. Just ask. Please," I begged.

I swear, this woman. My heart was beating a million miles a minute. She clearly had no idea the kind of power she had over me. Or maybe she did, and this torture was on purpose.

"Dan."

"Kat."

She reached into her pocket and took out a small velvet box. Her hands were shaking as she opened it, revealing two plain gold rings. One was thicker and bigger, obviously meant for a guy. The other was small, for a woman's finger.

Does she want me to pawn them?

I glanced between her and the box, waiting.

"Dan. I want . . . will you marry me?"

CHAPTER FOUR

Legal Guardian: An individual who has the legal authority (and the corresponding duty) to care for the personal and property interests of another person, called a **ward**. Guardians are typically used in three situations: guardianship for an incapacitated senior (due to old age or infirmity), guardianship for a minor, and guardianship for developmentally disabled or mentally disabled adult.

WEX LEGAL DICTIONARY

Kat

DAN WAS STARING at me, but he wasn't looking at me.

His eyes were unfocused and it was obvious he was looking inward. But it was in that way people do when they're either trying to make sense of a nonsensical situation, or they're trying to figure out how best to extract themselves from dealing with a crazy person. Or both.

My heart plummeted even though it didn't have a long way to go. I hadn't allowed myself to hope. Even when I'd left briefly to buy the rings, I'd done so assuming I'd be marrying Steven. Not Dan.

This had been a kamikaze mission, with the same chances of success as racking up an enormous credit card bill and expecting to pay for it by winning the lottery.

Never a solid plan.

But I'd promised Steven. What was a little humiliation in exchange for a fake marriage? I would owe Steven. I would owe him big time, a debt I'd never be able to repay. Pride would matter very little if my cousin became my guardian.

Looking at Dan's handsome face as he stared through me, I almost laughed. The idea of him agreeing to marry me for *any* reason was the ultimate delusion of grandeur. Right up there with discovering I was adopted (never going to happen, I'd had two DNA tests already . . . just to be sure); or winning a Nobel Peace Prize for knitting; or learning Doctor Who was real and I would be the next plucky companion; or finding out cheese had no calories.

Ridiculous.

I did laugh. At myself. A small, breathy little laugh. Not a hysterical laugh. I didn't laugh hysterically. I was always very careful to never do anything in a hysterical way.

At my laugh, his stare refocused on me, but his expression was unreadable. "When would this need to happen?"

I gave him a tight smile. "Forget I—"

"I'm guessing as soon as possible?"

"A month ago wouldn't be too soon." *Whoa. Was that my voice?*

I sounded impressively calm, even for me. But then, I was calm. Why wouldn't I be? The hard part was over.

Thank him for his time, and then leave.

"Okay, well—"

"Shh."

I reared back an inch. "Shh?"

"Yeah, I'm thinking."

I opened my mouth to respond, but thought better of it, and instead turned to grab my coat.

"What are you doing?" He glanced between my jacket and me, his expression shaded with irritation. "I'm trying to think here. Hold still."

Again, I opened my mouth to respond. Before I could, he invaded my space, gripped my shoulders, and walked me three steps to his couch.

Dan guided me to a sitting position. "Stay there."

"Dan—"

"I know a guy." He gave my shoulders a quick squeeze, his eyes wide and serious.

But his mouth was not serious. It hooked subtly to one side and—entranced—I stared at his lips.

Stop staring at his lips and listen to his words.

What was he suggesting?

Was he suggesting . . .

Did he know someone who he thought would want to marry me? Perhaps some gentleman who was a professional marry-er? Whose job it was to marry desperate heiresses, perchance?

"You know a guy?" My voice cracked.

Dan didn't answer, but his subtle smile turned into a real one as he straightened and pulled his phone from his pocket.

I thought I heard him mutter, "He'll do it."

Twisting the hem of my coat, I struggled to speak through my panic.

And, being honest here, it wasn't just panic I was feeling—about Eugene's phone call, about having to ask Dan to marry me, about everything—it was also a little hurt. I knew Dan had moved on from any romantic feelings he may have had for me years ago. He'd moved on in a big way.

But his enthusiastic willingness to have me marry *this guy he knew* hurt my nutty, neurotic little heart. It didn't make sense; it was especially wackadoodle that I had any anxiety to spare over hurt feelings considering my present dire circumstances. But there it was.

"Dan, I appreciate—"

Dan held up a finger. "Luis. This is a secure line? Good. I'm calling in the favor."

Calling in the favor? What had Dan done for this guy? Donated sperm? A kidney? Bone marrow?

Unable to sit still, I stood and placed a staying hand on Dan's elbow. His gaze flickered to mine and he slid his arm back, entwining our fingers. He brought the back of my hand to his chest, just over his heart.

My stomach did a summersault. I tried to ignore it and mostly succeeded.

"Listen, I need a marriage certificate backdated to a month ago. Don't worry about—what was that?"

I stood close enough to hear the man on the other side of the call ask, "Is the couple married yet?"

"No."

"Will they get married?"

"Yes. But it needs to look like it already happened."

"No problem, man. I'll need social security numbers, passport if you have it, birth certificate, current address, and a few other things. I'll send you a list."

Dan released a breath, giving me a quick smile. "Great. Give me the list and I'll pull it together."

I couldn't keep up. I also couldn't form thoughts and words now that he was holding my hand and pressing it to his chest. We were standing so close, he smelled so good, and apparently I was married a month ago.

"So how real does this need to look?" the man named Luis asked.

"Airtight." Dan gave me a meaningful nod, his eyes sober. "As real as you can make it."

"We have cameras at the courthouse. Your couple needs to come tomorrow and get the certificate. Then come back later, maybe next week, and see the officiant. Make sure you're wearing different clothes. We can splice the tape to a month ago and change the time stamp."

"We'll do that."

"Mr. Lee will officiate. He always wears the same damn suit every day." Luis chuckled. So did Dan.

I did not chuckle. I didn't understand what was happening.

"We'll make it look like they came in to get the certificate and then waited until the next day to get married. Video evidence should take care of any doubt about the legitimacy of the date."

"Great. I owe you one."

"No, man. I still owe you ten. I'll text the list. Have them come see me tomorrow, we'll get it sorted."

After short salutations, Dan ended the call and gathered a deep breath. He stared at his phone's screen for a long moment, like he was deep in thought.

I stopped breathing. I was having one of those out-of-body experiences people spoke of. Nothing made sense.

What just happened?

"Dan," I ventured, my voice sounding very far away to my own ears.

His name on my lips drew his eyes to mine. I glanced at my hand where he held it pressed to his chest. He followed my eyes, then released me, giving me the impression he hadn't realized he'd taken my hand to begin with.

Stepping away, he pulled his fingers through his hair and shook his head. "I'll let Quinn know I need to skip the New York trip tomorrow morning, but Betty can reschedule that. Then we'll need to find a day next week. I go to London tomorrow afternoon. We can change that flight to leave from Chicago, but I won't be back until next Thursday. I guess Friday could work . . . "

"Dan. " I wasn't going to let my brain draw any conclusions that weren't independently and explicitly verified by the man standing in front of me. I would not allow myself to go there. I would not. *I will not.*

"And I just had that suit made," he continued thoughtfully. "What size is your finger?"

"Dan." My voice was even further away now, and I could barely hear it over the beating of my heart.

"Yeah?" He glanced at me, biting his bottom lip, his hands on his hips.

"I'm sorry, but who am I marrying?"

His eyebrows jumped and his eyes widened to their maximum diameter. "Me, of course."

A short breath of wonder escaped my lungs, my knees not quite steady, as tears of ALL THE FEELINGS stung my eyes. I covered my mouth with a shaking hand and stared at him.

And then I lost control.

Rather, for the first time in a very long time, I ceded control to emotion and instinct. Launching myself at him, I encircled his neck with my arms and held tight. He felt like a life raft. Like a strong, steady, safe harbor in the tempest of the last twelve hours. Or maybe in the chaos of my entire life.

"Thank you. Thank you so much. Thank you, thank you, thank you."

"Hey." His arms came around my middle and he returned my embrace. "No big deal, okay?"

"No big deal? I cannot thank you enough. I owe you ten. I owe you a hundred. I owe you infinity."

With each of my words I felt Dan stiffen a little more, until he disentangled himself from my grip and pushed me slightly away. "Kat, you owe me nothing."

"I do. I owe you so much. Like I said, I will pay you. I'll give you anything you want."

"Helping you is reward enough, okay? I don't want your money. Or anything else."

I got the vague sense he was frowning at me now, but I couldn't be sure. I couldn't see him, not really, not through the enormity of what I was feeling. It was like being pardoned.

He'd given me my life back—or he was about to—my safety and my freedom.

How could he not see?

I owed him everything.

* * *

DAN WAS TOO TIRED to discuss any details—he looked exhausted—so I insisted we save the long conversation for another time.

Dan, in turn, insisted on driving me home. He used one of Cypher Systems's company cars and brought Wally along for the short ride. During the drive, we decided to meet at the County Clerk's office tomorrow, where Luis worked, after Dan's morning meeting across town. The plan was to obtain the marriage license. Then, we'd go back next Friday late in the afternoon—once he returned from his business trip—for the ceremony, mostly just to get it on video with the Cook County judge at the Marriage and Civil Union Court.

In the meantime, Dan's friend would make it look like we'd already done the deed a month ago.

Wally seemed content to sit in the back of the SUV at first, but as soon as Dan turned left on North Michigan Avenue, the sneak made his move. I didn't suppress my delighted laugh at Dan's attempt to return the dog to the back seat. My lack of inhibition was likely a by-product of enduring shock; I still couldn't believe Dan had agreed to marry me. I just . . . I just could not believe it.

As much as possible, I encouraged Wally to lay on my lap. He was much too big to be a lapdog, so he ended up with half his body on my legs and the other half on the floor next to my feet. Dan gave us both a disapproving side-eye, but—again—I was too preoccupied to care.

I was distracted during the car ride. I was distracted as I waved goodbye, while I climbed four flights of stairs, and when I entered my studio apartment. My brain didn't focus until I plugged my phone in to charge and checked my messages. Eugene had called and left two voicemails.

The first was to check on my progress finding a spouse.

The second was a warning.

"Kat, this is Eugene again. Caleb sent over the preliminary list of witnesses he plans to use in his petition for guardianship. I'm going to email it to you. A large percentage of the individuals are men he claims you were intimate with. A few he has noted as suppliers of illegal substances or witnesses to acts of petty crime and theft. Unsurprisingly,

he also included the team of specialists who diagnosed you as bipolar when you were a teenager. One woman in particular is of concern. She alleges she sold you drugs—specifically, ecstasy and heroin—as recently as last month. More important, I need to talk to you about having your future spouse sign a prenup. I should have brought this up earlier today, I apologize for this oversight. I've taken the liberty of sending you an initial draft. Obviously minor changes can be made, but I advise against revising the section related to inheritance and community property. Please call me when you have a chance."

I didn't sleep well that night. At Dan's apartment I'd been so focused on the miracle of him agreeing to my proposal—without explanations, without terms, without assurances—I'd been too overwhelmed and grateful to recall the reasons why I hadn't wanted him to be the one to marry me.

I'd never touched heroin. I might have been reckless, but even at fifteen I'd been afraid of addiction. Caleb was a terrible human. If my cousin felt justified finding some woman to lie about me buying drugs last month, to ruin my life, then what would he feel justified doing to Dan?

What about Dan's family and friends?

Could I ask Dan to do this? Should I? But if not him, then who? Could I put Steven through this torture? Ugh. I was thinking in circles. Lest I forget, very soon Dan would know almost everything about my history.

As I tossed and turned, I reminded myself that he already knew about the drinking and some of my other choices. I'd confessed that much in Vegas, right before he walked out the door.

Soon he'll know it all. Then he'll change his mind.

I glanced at the clock next to my bed. It was just past two in the morning. The omnipresent weight over my heart had grown heavier. I rubbed my chest.

By the time my alarm sounded at 4:30 AM, I'd decided a few things:

1. I would not marry Dan until I felt confident I'd provided enough information for him to make a fully informed decision. He needed to

understand what kind of person he was helping. He needed to know about my family. He needed to know what he could expect from Caleb. After going to the Clerk's office this morning, I would suggest lunch so we could talk. During lunch, I would spell it all out. That would give him enough time to halt the backdating of the marriage certificate if he changed his mind.

2. Also during lunch, I would insist that I pay him for his time and trouble. But I was not going to bring up the prenup. How could I? He was putting himself on the line for me. Having him sign a prenup would be like taking out an advertisement in the *Chicago Tribune* and announcing that I didn't trust him.

3. I needed to call my therapist. Whenever I began thinking in circles, I knew it was time for a check-in.

Therefore, I called my therapist first thing and left a message. Next, I messaged Eugene and informed him I would need access to a large quantity of liquid assets as soon as possible. On autopilot, I showered, applied makeup, and did my hair. And then I texted Steven and told him the news.

He responded almost immediately.

Steven: *OOOHHHHHHHHHHHHH MMMMMYYYYYYYYYYY GGGGOOOOOOOOODDDDDDD!!!!*

I laughed at his antics, but he wasn't finished.

Steven: *I want all the details. Call me. And pics or it didn't happen.*

* * *

WHILE SITTING ON THE L, I composed a list on my phone of my most egregious sins, along with important events, dates, and people from my past. Typing the list required the entire thirty-minute train ride. When I arrived at my building, I re-read the items on the elevator, surprised when I found I'd also typed, *I eat too much cheese* without realizing it.

I didn't delete the entry. If we were going to marry, he should know about my queso obsession. It was a problem.

I sent an email to the executive team, the administrative staff, and the senior architects right away, letting everyone know I would be taking my lunch from 10:30 AM until 1:30 PM, but would be working two hours early and staying late to make up the time.

My boss, the CEO, was out of town for the next two weeks, on a business trip in Helsinki, so I knew she wouldn't care. When Mrs. Opal arrived, she didn't bring up my strange behavior from the prior day or my modified schedule, instead settling into her desk promptly at 7:20 AM and getting down to business.

Work was uneventful, but I was distracted. I must've checked the clock on my computer seven hundred times and almost jumped out of my chair when my cell phone rang at 9:34 AM. It was Eugene. I didn't answer, opting to text him instead.

Me: I'm at work. What's going on?

Eugene: He needs to sign the prenup.

Me: I don't think that's appropriate.

Eugene: Have him sign the prenup.

Me: I'm already asking a lot of him. It's not appropriate.

Eugene: I'm serious.

Me: He's very trustworthy.

Eugene: I don't care if he's Moses, he will sign that prenup.

Eugene: Kathleen. Assure me you will have him sign it.

Eugene: YOU MUST NOT GET MARRIED UNTIL HE SIGNS IT

Reading his last text, I couldn't quite swallow. I'd never known Eugene to be a shouty-caps texter. Before I could respond, my phone buzzed. He was calling me again.

Flustered, and therefore handling my phone like it was a hot potato, I turned it off and tucked it into my backpack. Returning my attention to the pivot charts on my computer screen, I endeavored to decipher what I'd been trying to accomplish before his interruption.

I couldn't. I was basically useless for the next forty-five minutes, sorting and resorting data, waiting for ten thirty to arrive. Thank goodness it was Thursday and I'd have a chance to catch up on work tomorrow and over the weekend.

Finally, *finally* it was time. Locking my computer, I was in the elevator by 10:31 AM. Lost to my thoughts, I didn't see or hear the man in the lobby calling my name until just before he caught me by the elbow.

"Kat. Kat—hey, wait."

Startled, I tugged my arm from his grip and turned on him. I'm not going to lie, my first panicked thought was that Caleb had arrived and I was too late, that his goons had come to collect me and lock me up.

When I saw who it was, I relaxed, releasing a self-deprecating laugh as my heart slowed. "Stan."

Stan Willis. One of Quinn and Dan's most trusted guards. He wore a black suit, black tie, and white shirt.

"Hey. Dan sent me to drive you." He spun a ring of keys around his finger, his eyes moving over me as though to ensure I was unharmed. "Didn't you hear me? Are you okay?"

"No, sorry. I was distracted. I'm fine. Sorry." I fiddled with the buttons at my wrist, taking a moment to compose myself; Eugene's text messages must've aggravated me more than I thought. "Please. Lead the way."

Stan gave me another concerned once-over, then complied, walking slowly toward the exit and checking over his shoulder a few times to make sure I followed. "The car is right out here."

He led me to a black SUV parked directly outside the building; it reminded me of the one Dan had driven last night. Stan opened the door to the back seat for me. Soon I was settled and he'd pulled into traffic. Feeling eyes on me, I glanced at the rearview mirror and found him studying me from the driver's seat.

"Hey, is your phone off? Dan said he tried to call but it went to voicemail."

"Oh. Yes. It is." I reached my hand into my backpack, but then thought better of it. If I turned it on then I'd be hitting ignore on Eugene's calls.

"Don't worry about it; I'll just let him know I got you and we're on our way."

"Okay. Thanks." I turned my attention to the window, allowing my hair to fall forward to block me from any further inspection.

My long, thick, dark hair was my favorite feature about myself for exactly this reason; it allowed me to easily hide my face—and therefore my expression and thoughts—at will. It was like wearing a veil but without making an archaic, Miss Havisham-esque fashion statement.

If there was one literary character I didn't wish to imitate, it was Miss Havisham. Maybe also every Edgar Allen Poe character ever. Except the Raven. That bird was cool.

Sooner than expected, Stan was pulling up to the County Clerk's office, stopping in a loading zone and jumping out to open my door. Before he could, I'd opened it myself, spotting Dan standing on the steps talking on his cell.

I gathered a deep breath through my nose, balling my hands into fists to combat jitters as I hungrily devoured the sight of him. I needed to look my fill before he spotted my ogling. Truly, I needed to work on subtle ogling. I was not at all good at it.

Dan stood in profile, one hand in his pocket, the other holding a phone to his ear. He wore a white T-shirt, jeans, and brown boots, and looked absolutely delicious. Absolutely. Delicious. I say delicious because my mouth began to water as though a platter of fancy French fromage had just been placed before me.

Dan turned, and I sensed he was about to look my way, so I dropped my eyes to the sidewalk.

At that moment I heard Stan shut the door behind me and sensed him take a step backward. "Hey. I'll drive you back to Fairbanks after, okay?"

"Yes. That's great. Thank you." I gave him a quick smile, gathered a bracing breath, and lifted my chin to meet Dan as he approached. *Here we go.*

He still held the phone to his ear. Reaching me, he mouthed, *I'm sorry* while rolling his eyes and slid his hand into mine, entwining our fingers.

I shrugged and shook my head quickly, hoping to communicate that he shouldn't apologize. Together, we climbed the steps to the courthouse and through the gilt-edged art deco doors.

It took my eyes a moment to adjust to the interior, but Dan seemed to know exactly where we were going, guiding me down a short hall until we came to a security line.

"Hey, listen. I have to let you go. I have to go through a metal detector and I don't think they want me on my phone in here." He gave me a tight smile, nodding as he listened to the person on the other end of the call. "Okay. Okay. Uh-huh. Okay. Yeah. Bye."

Closing his eyes briefly, he dropped the phone from his ear and ended the call, releasing a low sound of frustration.

"Is everything all right?" I thought I sounded pretty good considering he was holding my hand.

Let me repeat that: Dan O'Malley was holding my hand. We were holding hands.

I could've died happy in that moment, and that probably made me a complete wackadoodle. Clearly, I couldn't stay focused around this man. I should've been anxious about the list I'd be sharing over lunch. I should've been worried about my malicious cousin and his array of lying witnesses. I should have been thinking of ways to adequately express my gratitude for what Dan was doing.

But instead, I was thinking about how very, very nice his hand felt in mine, and mine in his, and how strong and big it felt, and how it made me feel like I . . . belonged. Here. With him.

Wackadoodle. Not to be confused with a *wackjob.* One is fun and fancy-free, the other is nasty and malicious.

"Yeah. Fine." Dan glanced toward the metal detector and heaved a sigh. "I'm going to have to call him back when we're finished."

"It's okay. Thank you so much for taking the time and I'm so sorry to—"

"No more apologizing." His eyes cut to mine and his frown intensified. "And stop thanking me."

"I don't know if I can."

"Well, you're gonna, or else I'll start charging you a tax." His expression turned matter-of-fact. And also—if I was reading him correctly—a little teasing.

"A tax?"

"Yeah." He smirked, lifting his chin. "Every time you apologize you have to . . . uh . . . ." His eyes narrowed.

"I have to what?"

"Shh. I'm thinking. It's gonna be good though."

I rolled my lips between my teeth so I wouldn't respond with, *Define good.*

Turning away, I shook my head at myself. And shook myself.

What was I doing? Teasing? Or flirting? Flirting was not an option. Flirting might send him running in the opposite direction, calling the whole thing off. Or it might catapult us to awkward level ten. Thousand. Awkward level ten thousand.

Do you want to make things worse?

Before I could answer any of those questions, we had to separate as we came to the bag check. I left my backpack on the belt and walked through the metal detector. Dan followed, slipping his hand in mine once more, waiting for me to grab my bag before moving us to the reception desk.

As we approached, his cell rang. Visibly frustrated, he released me and pulled out his phone, checking the screen and answering it.

"Just a minute," Dan said to the person on his cell. Moving the phone away and to the side, he lowered his voice and said to me, "Ask for Luis De Capo. He's expecting us."

I nodded once and approached the woman at reception when she waved me forward; Dan stood off to the side, talking on his cell.

"Hi."

"Birth certificate?" She barely looked at me.

"Sorry. We're here to see Luis De Capo." I fiddled with my bag strap. "He's expecting us."

"Yes. Okay—he's at the end of the line. Go ahead." She indicated to a long, high counter with areas separated by black privacy screens; I turned my attention to the last cubby. It was the only one without a line.

Walking to Dan, I tilted my head in the direction the receptionist had indicated and he nodded, falling into step next to me. Moving to the counter, I spotted a man sitting on a stool working at his computer.

"Hello?"

He turned his head at my greeting, giving me a surprised but welcoming smile. Then his eyes moved beyond me to Dan and he abruptly stood.

"Hey. You're here."

"Sorry, Luis. All the emergencies are happening today." Dan gestured to his cell as he tucked it in his back pocket, giving the man behind the counter a wan smile.

"No problem. Are you . . ." The man named Luis looked between Dan and me. "Are you the ones getting married?"

"That's right, we—" His phone rang. Again. "Fucking helpless motherfuckers. Can't do a single fucking thing on their own," Dan growled, pulling out his phone as well as two folded pieces of paper, placing them on the counter. "Shit, I gotta take this. Here's our info. I'll be right back."

Luis watched Dan move some steps away, then shifted his gaze to me; his eyes were wide and full of wonder. "I had no idea."

"Pardon?"

"Congratulations. This is so great." Luis beamed at me. "If I'd known he was the one getting married, I would've picked up some champagne or something."

I returned his smile. "Thank you, but that's not necessary."

"Are you kidding?" Luis took the papers Dan had placed on the counter and continued as he scanned the documents, "Dan's the man. And that makes you the woman." As his eyes moved over the paper, his smile fell away. Luis blinked as though startled, his stare cutting to mine.

"Your name is Kathleen Caravel-Tyson?" The way he said my name, like he recognized it, sent a wave of foreboding goosebumps racing over my skin.

This was always the way. People didn't recognize me, as there were very few pictures of me anywhere, but they usually recognized my real name.

I swallowed, uncertain what to do, but ended up nodding.

He lowered his voice. "*The* Kathleen Caravel-Tyson?"

Tucking my hair behind my ears unnecessarily, I said nothing, attempting to clear my face of any expression. Who I was—or wasn't—was not his business.

His mouth formed an O, as though he were going to whistle, but he made no sound. Turning back to his computer, he went to work entering our information and sneaking curious glances at me every so often. My mind was working overtime. And I was sweating.

I didn't know this guy. Dan trusted this guy, so I had to trust him, too. But I hated—*hated*—trusting people I didn't know. I'd rather walk a tightrope between two skyscrapers than trust my well-being to a stranger.

Speaking of trusting people, the papers Dan had handed over were copies of my passport and birth certificate, my *real* passport and birth certificate. I had originals of both in my bag, so where the heck had he obtained his copies?

Equally confusing, and even more concerning? That meant Dan already knew my name.

Which led me to wonder, *what else does he know?*

The breadcrumb trail Eugene had helped Zachariah Tyson assemble pointed everyone seeking Kathleen Caravel-Tyson to a heavily guarded compound in Russia, owned by my father's good friend, Sergey Kroft. The board of directors had been led to believe I lived just outside of St. Petersburg, where I'd been receiving an education from private tutors for the last ten years.

When I ran away, my father couldn't bear the embarrassment of what I'd done, so he'd crafted a story and used a trusted web of people to make it look real. When I reemerged, I did my part by responding to inquiries about my absence with vague answers.

But my cousin had figured out the truth, obviously.

"Okay, all set." Luis stood from his stool, his gaze flickering to mine and then away.

It was exactly how people treated me whenever I went to Boston, even by a few members of the board. Like all that money in my bank account meant I could steal their soul and feed it to Cerberus, who I obviously kept chained at a compound in Russia.

Luis passed me the folded sheets of paper as well as a new one: the marriage certificate. "Just—uh—bring this back and you'll—uh —sign it when you—um—when the—when Lee does the ceremony."

"Thank you." I reached for the papers, intent on picking them up, but Dan appeared at my side and covered my hand with his.

I'm not going to lie, I liked it when he did that.

"Thanks for this, Luis." Dan removed the papers from the counter and I heard him unzip my backpack; he slid them into the main pocket. "Saves us a lot of trouble."

"No problem," Luis answered a little too loudly.

Dan seemed to hesitate at Luis's tone, his movements halting mid-zip of my backpack. Dan glanced at me, then to Luis, then me again. "Something wrong?"

Luis shook his head quickly.

I twisted the buttons at my sleeve, not knowing what to say and figuring, *I think it freaks your friend out that I'm worth seventeen billion dollars* wouldn't help the situation, especially if Dan only knew my real name but hadn't yet realized *who* I was.

"Oh, wait. She got you, didn't she?"

I looked to Dan and found him aiming a big smile at his friend, chuckling.

Luis's stare landed on me, suspicion and confusion written all over his features.

Draping an arm over my shoulders, Dan pulled me against him and leaned a little over the counter, whispering loud enough that I could hear, "Do you really think some billionaire heiress would be getting married to the likes of me?"

Oh . . . okay. So he does know. Well darn.

I was hot, and my heart thundered between my ears, and I was confused, too confused to speak. What else could I do? I followed Dan's lead.

Giving Luis a self-deprecating shrug, I hoped it was believable. Dan squeezed my shoulders, smoothing his hand down my back until his strong arm settled along my waist; everything about his touch felt possessive, like he was putting on a show for the benefit of a single audience member.

Luis looked to me and then at Dan, the stiffness easing from his features as he blew out an expansive breath. "She really had me going."

Dan chuckled some more, shaking his head at Luis as he backed away from the counter, bringing me with him. "See you next week. And hey, bub. If you see Brady and Giselle, tell them we say hi."

"Ha-ha." Luis rolled his eyes, but was also smiling. "Get out of here."

Keeping me tucked to his side, Dan maneuvered through the sparse collection of people waiting to be called to a window, past reception, glancing behind him as we exited through the front door.

Once outside, his smile fell suddenly and completely away, and he steered us down the steps to the sidewalk. "I should have anticipated that."

"What?" I kept my eyes forward, concentrating on putting one foot in front of the other. With all this thinking I was doing, I was surprised my brain had extra capacity for movement.

"That." He motioned with his head toward the building we'd just left. "Better he doesn't know until after it's all said and done. Luis owes me a favor, and he's a good guy, but—you know—the idea of money does funny things to people."

It certainly does.

His arm was still at my back, his hand at my waist. My hand had somehow moved to his waist as well, though I didn't remember that happening. Everything about the last twenty-four hours had been surreal, including this moment. I was tucked snugly against him, and it was strange walking with Dan. Like we knew each other well. Like we regularly spent time in each other's company.

I couldn't decide what to ask. I had so many questions, I couldn't settle on one. Obviously, I needed a moment to sort through my own frantic thoughts before I trusted myself to maintain my composure. So we walked in silence for several blocks while my mind went in circles.

Finally, after much internal debate, I decided to ask the most obvious and benign question first, "Where are we going?"

"To get lunch."

Lunch.

I'd planned to ask him out to lunch today so we could talk. But discovering Dan knew who I was—and had known for an indeterminate number of months—made me want to stress-eat all the cheese in Chicago. And the muffins. And not talk.

I was officially off-kilter. Again.

Given my history trying to form words around this guy while I was any shade of distressed, I knew avoidance was my best option. In my present state of mind, there was no way I could sit across a table from him for an unspecified period of time and *not* say something completely stupid. Like, I don't know, share unnecessary details about my sketchy past. For example, I might admit, while reviewing my list of misdeeds, that I'd never been intimate with a man while sober. Or something equally horrifying and embarrassing.

It wasn't just me being off-kilter that was a problem. And Dan being Dan wasn't a problem. It was me being off-kilter plus Dan being Dan that equaled the problem.

Allow me to provide an analogy in chemical poetry form:

Potassium is just fine.

And water is completely benign.

But introduce K to H2O, and shit explodes in real time.

We live in a serious world, and we should never mock other people for their struggles. But making jokes about your own struggles is a coping mechanism, and a damned good one. So, yes, every once in a while I like to poke fun at myself.

That said, maybe today wasn't the best day to have lunch with Dan. *But there is one more thing I need to know.*

I sucked in a deep breath, bracing myself. "How long have you known?"

Dan leaned away a little, looking down at me, his expression inscrutable. "For a while."

For a while.

For some reason, that answer made my stomach drop. Pressing my lips together, I dipped my chin to my chest and let my hair fall forward so I could think about the ramifications of Dan having known for a while.

Had he known in Vegas?

"Hey." He stopped us, pushing my hair out of the way and slipping a finger under my chin, forcing me to meet his eyes. They looked concerned. "It's no big deal."

"Oh? Really?" I laughed, knowing I sounded bitter. *Better bitter than hysterical.*

He didn't respond, opting to examine me instead. His gaze turned probing, intensely interested, yet also intensely warm and . . . kind.

The kindness made my lungs feel like they were burning. Kindness felt too close to pity. Unable to bear his scrutiny—or kindness—I took a half step back and gave him my profile.

"I need to get back to work. I can't have lunch today." I felt his eyes on me, which made it even more difficult to concentrate.

After a few seconds of this, I sensed Dan move, drawing my halting attention back to him. He'd taken his cell out, selected a contact, and was now holding the phone to his ear.

"Hey. It's me. Send a car for Kat. She,"—his eyes cut to mine, sharp yet aloof—"needs to get back to work."

CHAPTER FIVE

Trustee: An individual or corporation named by a person, who sets aside property to be used for the benefit of another person (e.g. children of person), to manage the property as provided by the terms of the document that created the arrangement.

WEX LEGAL DICTIONARY

Kat

I DIDN'T POWER on my phone for the rest of the day, which meant I didn't call Eugene back. I needed distance from chaos and demands, time and space to get back *on*-kilter. So I lost myself in spreadsheets, conference planning, travel booking, and updating meeting minutes.

I decided I would power on my phone—to check for messages from my therapist and to call Eugene—once I was home, in my pajamas, and under my covers. Sometimes, a girl needed the solace of her safe place to prepare for battle.

However, my plans were derailed when, just as I approached the front door to my building, I heard a car door open and close.

Then a voice from the direction of the street said, "Kathleen."

And I tensed.

He was here. He'd been waiting.

Darn.

"Do you always work this late?"

I turned to face Uncle Eugene and found him glancing up and down the street, taking the measure of my neighborhood.

"No. Not usually. But I had to take an extra-long lunch today. Do you want to come up?" I didn't fake a smile. Things weren't like that between us. I didn't feel the need to be polite.

"Yeah. Let's go up." Crossing to me, he motioned to my door. His blue eyes seemed to inspect the lock with critical focus as I released the latch, and his frown was severe as we walked down the hall to the stairs. "No second security door?"

I shook my head, climbing the stairs, knowing he would follow.

He grumbled something, but did follow, his footsteps echoing mine as we climbed the four flights to my floor. Once I was finished unlocking the three deadbolts, I preceded him into my apartment so I could switch on lights.

I only partially listened as he shut the door after us, securing all three deadbolts, before following me into my small studio. Once inside, he sighed.

"This is where you live."

I tried not to laugh at the dismay in his voice. "Yes. This is where I live."

He sighed again and I moved to the efficiency kitchen to make some tea.

"Earl Grey, coming up."

"Thank you," he responded in a way that sounded automatic, not moving from his place by the door.

Once the kettle was set, I turned back to him, inspecting him. He wasn't wearing his usual gray suit and power tie. Instead, Eugene donned khakis, a navy polo shirt, and brown loafers. He looked incredibly uncomfortable in the casual attire.

Or maybe it was my casual apartment.

"You're here about the prenup."

His gaze came to mine and he nodded. "You turned off your phone."

"You wouldn't stop calling."

"Are you married?"

"Come and sit." I gestured to my little kitchen table. He eyed it as though it might be a trap. Eventually, he took a seat, looking very out of place at my favorite thrift store find.

"Are you married?" he asked again, his tone infinitely patient.

I sat across from him and folded my hands on the table. "I am married."

He held very still. "And the prenup?"

"He didn't sign the prenup."

"Kathleen—"

"He couldn't. We were married a month ago."

Eugene flinched. "What?"

"Daniel O'Malley and I were married a month ago. Or so the marriage certificate says. And the security tapes will corroborate."

Eugene leaned back in his chair, his expression belying his astonishment. "Well."

"Well."

"Congratulations." His stare dropped to the table between us and he sighed again; this time it sounded full of wonder and relief rather than exasperation.

"Thank you."

After a long moment, during which I'm sure he accomplished a great deal of scheming, he lifted his gaze to mine. "I'll send a postnuptial agreement."

The water for the tea was ready, the kettle clicked off, and I glared at my father's oldest friend. "I don't want to do that."

"Kathleen."

"Stop saying my name like it's a magic word, like it'll force me to be *reasonable*. I won't ask Dan to sign anything. I trust him."

"It's not a matter of you trusting this man." Eugene's voice hardened and his blue eyes narrowed. "Lack of a pre- or postnuptial agreement brings your trustworthiness into question, not Mr. O'Malley's. Marriage without a contract isn't just inadvisable in your world—"

"My world?"

"—it's foolhardy. Caleb will use your foolishness against you; he'll point to it as proof that you're unfit."

"My mother didn't have my father sign a prenup."

"Yes. And look what happened!" Eugene slammed his hand on the surface of the table, leaning forward, his typically unassailable serenity alarmingly discomposed.

We stared at each other, fury crackling in his eyes, his teeth clenched. He was visibly upset, and that was enough to make me question my decision about the prenup (or, at this point, the postnup).

Resting an elbow on the table, Eugene shook his head, his eyes moving over me like I both infuriated him and worried him. "He has to sign it."

"Eugene."

"Don't say my name like it's a magic word, like it'll force me to be reasonable," he deadpanned, drawing a small smile from me.

"I'll think about it," I whispered.

"Good." He stood, staring down at me. "I have no desire to be visiting you ten years from now in an institution, because you were too selfless to do the right thing."

"That's an oxymoron. Selflessness is the same as doing the right thing."

Eugene shook his head, studying me intently, and answering with a cryptic, "Not always."

* * *

I NEVER DID MAKE Uncle Eugene his tea.

He left almost immediately after delivering his impassioned message about the postnuptial agreement. Then he emailed me a new draft of the document the next morning. I didn't have time to read it, nor did I particularly want to.

Skipping lunch, I opted for an impromptu touch-base meeting with my therapist Friday afternoon. Dr. Kasai's building wasn't too far from my work and, once I gave her a brief overview of the situation via phone, she fit me in for a session.

Sometimes I just needed her to tell me I was behaving within normal parameters, that my thoughts, feelings, and behaviors weren't too far off ordinary. These days, we usually met once a month—down from once a week—unless something major happened. Early on, I'd had difficulty trying to determine what was considered major. Now I was much better at making the distinction.

However, I left her office feeling both better and worse. Better because Dr. Kasai said my inner turmoil over present circumstances was completely normal and at the end of our session she'd assured me that she would happily testify—if the time came—that I was of sound mind, and seemed genuinely horrified that anyone would seek to prove the opposite.

I felt worse because . . . so many other reasons.

Whenever I found myself in the position of feeling dissonance with Dr. Kasai's advice, which wasn't often, I would call my friend Sandra, bribe her with yarn, and attempt to stealthily pick her brain.

Which is why I found myself in a yarn store on Friday night, perusing the aisle of chunky-weights, and reminding myself that I owned seven skeins of emerald green yarn in various fibers and weights. I definitely did not need another four hundred yards in a bulky weight cashmere blend.

"That's a pretty color." Sandra picked up the color I'd been eyeing. "Oh, silk and merino *and* cashmere!" She held it up to her face and stroked it over a cheek. "I love it. Are you going to buy it?"

Yes!

"No. You should get it." I forced a smile.

"Are you sure?" She held it out to me.

Mine!

"I'm sure." I pushed it back toward her, swallowing the childish urge to snatch it from her hand. I had a yarn addiction. It was a problem. *I will overcome.*

She gave me a quick once-over, her eyes narrowing with suspicion.

"How about this? I'll put it in my basket, and if you tell me what has you looking like an antelope in the middle of an enema, I'll buy it for you. For the record, if I had to guess, I'd say it has something to do with your family."

I breathed a short laugh; Sandra had an uncanny ability to read minds.

When I first met her and discovered she was a psychiatrist, I'd been resistant to her overtures of friendship. In the end, resistance had been futile.

"You don't need to buy it for me." I waved her offer away. "I don't need it, I already have a half dozen in this color."

"You're such an adult." She said this like being an adult was a bad thing.

Sandra was by far one of the funniest people I'd ever met. The things she said sometimes had us laughing the entire time at a knitting meetup. She once told me a story about a date of hers that had gone horribly wrong, and I laughed so hard I cried, my jaw hurt, and my stomach felt like I'd done a hundred crunches. Everyone needs a friend who can bring them tears and abdominal pain with funny stories.

She also happened to be the one who'd convinced me to give therapy another shot. Rather, she convinced me, but the ultimate catalyst had been my disastrous evening and morning with Dan in Vegas. I hated that I'd jumped to the absolute worst conclusion about myself with him, and I didn't want to do that to myself anymore.

"Yes," I nodded. "I do want your opinion on something. And yes, it has to do with my family. More specifically, it has to do with my session today at Dr. Kasai's and her advice about my family."

"You need a second opinion?" Her voice adopted the calm, soothing quality she used when she became therapist-Sandra instead of friend-Sandra.

"More like, I need a friend opinion."

Sandra already knew my real identity, who my parents were, their current health afflictions, and how evil my cousin had been to me in the past. She also knew about my time as a runaway, and that I'd been unable to reach *the end of the 'O' rainbow* without alcohol for several years. The reason she knew these things—ironically—was because she'd gotten me drunk one night and I'd spilled everything.

"Okay, spill. And while you spill, I shall stroke hairy fibers." Friend Sandra was back and she tucked the yarn into her basket, giving it another pet.

"I can't tell you everything, because things are still in flux." I didn't want to tell her about Dan or why we'd decided to get married. Dan was her friend as much as he was mine. As far as I was concerned, nothing was 100% decided between him and me. We hadn't reviewed my list of misdeeds; he could still back out. I didn't want Sandra to judge him harshly if he changed his mind.

"Okay, tell me what you can." She picked up bulky weight 100% merino yarn and stroked the back of her hand across it.

"So . . ." I cleared my throat, not knowing quite how to start. "There has been some upheaval at the company."

"And it has you stressed?"

"Yes."

She nodded. "And you're beating yourself up about . . . ?"

I huffed another laugh at her mind reading skills. *Or maybe she just knows me too well.*

"I guess, I could have it worse. Things could be worse."

"Things can always be *worse,* no matter who you are. You might never again wonder where your next meal is coming from, but life isn't the grief Olympics, it's not a competition for *who has it worse.*"

"Sandra." I stopped her with a hand on her elbow, whispering, "I'm worth seventeen billion dollars."

"So what? Allowing yourself to feel badly about the fact that you have so much, in terms of monetary assets, and others have so little in comparison will do nothing but cause you to be paralyzed by guilt. Money does not equal happiness or fulfillment. Some people will argue that you 'have it better' than ninety-nine point nine percent of the world, but those people can't comprehend the burden of what's facing you, or of the life you've lived so far."

I stared at my friend, absorbing her words. "I'm allowed to feel sad, disappointed, and frustrated."

"Bingo." She grinned, picking up another skein of yarn and brushing it against her neck. She immediately frowned, putting it back. "Ugh, scratchy. What is that? Acrylic?"

It had taken me a long time to accept that I had a right to sadness or anger. For so long I'd felt like, because of my birthright, I wasn't allowed to feel anything but gratitude and guilt. How could I feel sadness over the loss of my mother to her disorder when others in the world were suffering, starving, and couldn't afford basic necessities? How could I justify feeling disappointment about my father's disinterest in me when there were millions of children in the world without a home?

This emotional paralysis was the first issue I'd addressed with Dr. Kasai, but even now—especially when I felt overwhelmed—I experienced difficulty accepting my emotions, desires, and wishes as legitimate.

"I think you said to me once," Sandra turned to me, crossing her arms, "that you feel like your freewill is eclipsed by the responsibility you feel to the people employed by Caravel Pharmaceuticals. Also, responsibility to the people who might be helped by the products they develop, or might develop while you're the majority stakeholder."

"Yes." I gave her an accusatory smile. "I did tell you that. If memory serves, it was that one time you got me drunk and I spilled my guts."

She returned my grin with one of her own, not looking even a little bit guilty. "Out of curiosity, if you could give it all up, if you could sign it over to someone else and walk away, leave with nothing, would you?"

Stunned by the timeliness of her question, I blurted, "No. Of course not. It's my responsibility. I walked away once and that was childish and selfish. I would never do that again."

Sandra's gaze turned probing. "There's not even a wee, itty-bitty, little, teeny-tiny part of you that wants to walk away?"

I sighed, my chest tight with guilt, and felt my shoulders sag. "Perhaps a little part of me. A very little part of me."

Because then I'd be free from failure, wouldn't I? And right now—to that very small part of me—freedom from failure would be a relief.

Sandra nodded slowly. "Given the magnitude of what's facing you, I would be surprised if a part of you—a very little part—didn't entertain these thoughts. The urge to escape a trial by fire is normal. As long as you're not seriously entertaining escape as an option, then know that these thoughts are healthy. But!" She held up a finger. "I'm more interested in how the thoughts, this desire to escape, makes you feel."

I released a humorless laugh. "Guilt. Guilty."

"I suspected that might be the case." Sandra shook her head, giving me a sympathizing smile. "Dearest, Kat. You're an overachiever in every part of your life, including empathy and—yes—guilt."

"I'm an overachiever?"

Sandra gave me a *bitch, please* look and snorted. "You know you're an overachiever. You're living two lives, maybe two and a half. You go to school, you work full time, you fly back and forth to Boston and are learning the whole majority shareholder rigmarole, you visit and manage your parents and their illnesses. Dearest, you need to let go of the guilt."

I was . . . conflicted. And I'm sure it showed on my face.

I agreed with her, that I needed to let go of the guilt. But what about Dan? I worried for him. Caleb was going to do everything in his power to make Dan's life miserable, and that was entirely because of me.

"What's wrong?" Sandra tilted her head to the side as she inspected me. "What's holding you back from letting go?"

"I—" *Gah!* "I like someone."

Sandra's eyebrows shot up on her forehead and she straightened. "Oh."

"Yes. And, how can I ask him to become involved with me in any capacity when this is my life? When what's ahead of me is, as you say, a trial by fire."

She pushed her lips together, puckering them thoughtfully. "This man, does his name rhyme with *fan*?"

I laughed, rubbing my forehead. "I can't tell you."

"Will you tell me if it rhymes with *pan?*"

I laughed harder, but chided, "Sandra. I can't tell you."

"Hmm." She looked like she was trying not to smile, her green eyes bright and happy. "Okay, fine. You're not going to tell me. Fine. So, this man, let's call him *Dan*—"

"Sandra—"

"Hypothetically!"

I glared at her.

She giggled.

"Anyway, you like hypothetical Dan. I'm pretty sure non-hypothetical Dan likes you, too. So what's the problem?"

"Firstly, he doesn't like me."

"Oh, come on!" She rolled her eyes.

"Not in that way."

"Hmm." The *hmm* sounded more like a growl.

"And secondly, if I were going to enter into a relationship with *anyone*, shouldn't I tell that person about my past? Shouldn't I be completely honest?"

"Of course." Sandra appeared confused by my question.

"That's what I thought." I nodded, then to myself said, "Good."

"Wait a minute." She took a step closer and lowered her voice. "There's a difference between being honest with someone, and trying to drive someone away in the name of honesty. So tell me, specifically, how you intend to be completely honest with Dan the hypothetical frying pan."

I hesitated, hating how perceptive she was.

Sandra turned her head, giving me the side-eye. "Are you putting together a PowerPoint presentation about your past?"

"No!"

"Kat . . ."

I scoffed. "Not a *PowerPoint*."

"A handout? With charts?"

"No. A list of misdeeds on my phone."

"Ah-ha!" She lifted a finger between us again. "Why? Why does he need to know the details? Why not just provide a general idea, or list them in aggregate?"

"He has to know what kind of person he's agreeing to—" I stopped myself before I said *help.*

Sandra's eyes became slits. "Kat, you need to stop punishing yourself for mistakes you made when you were a teenager. This is self-flagellation."

"Owning my choices isn't self-flagellation."

"This is another case of overachieving. Confessing your 'list of misdeeds' as you call them to a man you have deep feelings for—"

"I don't have deep feelings for him." I had lots of feelings for Dan O'Malley, mostly about his body, and very few of them were deep.

And yet, despite his body, you do really like him as a person . . .

"—deep, deep, *deeeeeeeeeep* feelings for, *is* self-flagellation. Stop trying to reprimand yourself. You've already paid your debt to society, you've already served your time."

"He needs to know everything before he can make an informed decision. I'm attempting to be responsible."

Her whisper turned harsh. "You've said many times that you wish you'd never tried drugs, you hate that you stole from others, that you believe you were too young—mentally and emotionally too young—to be sexually active, and you regret that you were drunk or inebriated for all your early sexual experiences."

"Correct, with one clarification. I've been inebriated for *all* of my sexual experiences."

"Let me remind you that it is not uncommon for individuals—no matter the gender—who are sexually active at a young age, and who have not received appropriate education and guidance on the subject, to experience difficulty when they're older. Obviously, not all individuals experience difficulty, but many do."

"I'm a block of fromage that's been shredded when the recipe calls for sliced. You can't slice shredded cheese."

Sandra wrinkled her nose in obvious confusion. "What?"

"And before you ask, yes, I know the word for cheese in many languages. I can't be going about saying cheese all the time. With as much as I think about it, I need word replacement options. And fromage is among my favorites."

"You can call it whatever you like." Sandra picked up the same yarn she'd made a face at earlier, then quickly put it back. "You've used enough cheese analogies around me that I grasp it's forefront in your mind. What I need you to explain is the meaning of the *fromage* analogy."

"How can I ask anyone to sign on to a relationship with me, not knowing if I will bring shredded cheese to the table when the recipe calls for sliced? And keeping my past from hypothetical Dan would be like asking for cheddar on a hamburger and getting Limburger instead."

"Let's tackle one issue—and fromage analogy—at a time. First, do you want to be in a sexy-relationship with Dan? Yes or no?"

"No," I blurted. Forcefully. And I meant it.

"Really?" Her voice pitched high and disbelieving. "Then what are we talking about?"

"I just mean, if Dan had feelings for me—which he doesn't—I would only disappoint him."

"Please take a moment here to listen to yourself. No one expects you to be perfect."

I glanced at the yarn I'd inadvertently picked up; I was twisting it between my fingers. I stopped and put it back.

"I know no one expects me to be perfect. I'm pleased with the progress I've made in therapy. I have a place at work and I'm doing well. I love you and all the knitting ladies. I value and feel valued in our relationships. School is going well—"

"Better than *well*. Aren't you top of the class?"

I ignored her question. "I'm also resolved to taking my place at Caravel, and my sense is that I've been progressing towards that goal. Despite seeing my future laid out before me, with very little room for deviation, I feel steady and capable. I like who I am and the choices I've made, and I accept that my past is part of me, it has contributed to who I am today. Except . . ."

"Except?"

"Except . . ." I gave Sandra my gaze and, with my heart in my throat, admitted the truth to both her and myself, "I doubt I'll ever be able to fulfill the needs of a romantic partner."

She stared at me, and I got the sense she was trying to clear her face of any expression. At length, she nodded. "You know what I think?"

"What?" I couldn't help but be a little afraid, Sandra's thoughts were usually poignant and difficult to hear.

"I think you should do some research."

"Research?"

"Sexy research."

I lifted an eyebrow at my friend. "What are you talking about? Like, watch porn?"

"If porn dings your dong, go for it. But porn is rarely research because it's rarely realistic. My suggestion is to look up positions, approaches to intimacy. Try touching yourself without the goal being a one-way ticket to 'O' town. Enjoy the physical sensations. Figure out what you like and what you don't so you can communicate those likes and dislikes when the time comes."

"When the time comes? You're suggesting I should keep a list and give it to—to my partner?" My intention was for the question to be amusing, but Sandra didn't laugh.

Her gaze steady and serious, she nodded her head just once. "Yep. That's exactly what I mean." Sandra turned back to the yarn, reaching for a Madelinetosh worsted weight in bright red. "Delete your list of misdeeds, replace it with a list of sexy fantasies, and show *that* to your hypothetical Dan the ceiling fan."

CHAPTER SIX

Keynesian economics (/ˈkeɪnziən/ KAYN-zee-ən; or Keynesianism)
are the various theories about how in the short run – and especially
during recessions – economic output is strongly influenced by demand
(total spending in the economy).

International Monetary Fund

Kat

As it was the week before fall semester, I needed to read through
my class materials. Therefore, I spent the weekend studying,
trying to get ahead in my courses just in case I had a work emergency
during the semester.

Yet, I was distracted. Sandra's suggestion that I do *sexy research*
distracted me. Plus, I didn't know whether I should call Dan or text
him or what. My habit of avoiding him had become ingrained. We still
had a great deal to discuss. Yet, I couldn't bring myself to make
contact.

Instead, needing the diversion, I baked Janie a lemon loaf and took
it to her—and her husband Quinn—on Sunday night. He spent the first

half hour hovering, which wasn't a surprise. He'd been hovering since Janie had been placed on bed rest earlier in the summer.

I endeavored to distract them both, discussing various and sundry topics such as the rise of cryptocurrencies amid the volatility of global markets, and the applicability of Keynesian economics in the current political climate.

This worked. He was drawn out of his broody shell for an evening, and she seemed in better spirits when I left. Quinn insisted on calling a car for me, and I didn't turn him down. It was late and I'd loitered too long, enjoying their company.

While being chauffeured home, I received a call from Dan.

Except, it wasn't Dan.

I mean, it was.

But it wasn't.

I stared for a good four or five seconds at my phone before answering, as I was completely confounded by the word flashing on the screen. It read, *Husband.*

Bringing the cell to my ear, I asked tentatively, "Hello?"

"Hey," a masculine voice responded, like I should know who he was.

And I did. But my confusion lingered.

"Dan?"

"Yeah."

But how . . .

"My phone, it said—I mean—did you change your contact information in my phone?"

"No, I didn't." If I wasn't mistaken, his voice held a smile. "Why?"

I pulled the cell from my ear and, sure enough, instead of Dan O'Malley, he was listed in my phone as *Husband.*

"Kat?"

"Yes. I'm here."

"Why do you ask?"

"Because—" I stopped myself, nagging dread clawing at the back of my neck.

I must've changed it.

But I didn't remember changing it.

And for someone with my family history, this was a troubling realization.

"Hey? Are you still there?"

"Yes." I swallowed my trepidation, pushing it to the back of my mind. I would have to deal with it later. *Much* later. One emergency at a time. "You called?"

"Are you okay?" Now he sounded concerned.

"Yes. Fine," I answered tightly. "Are you okay?"

"Yeah," he said, then paused. I heard someone in the background call him Mr. O'Malley, and tell him they were almost ready to take off, and would he please buckle his seat belt. "Listen, I'm just about to leave London for New York, but I'll be back in town a day earlier than I thought, late Wednesday night."

"Oh." I held my breath for some reason. I didn't have a clue as to why.

Actually, I did know why. Part of me—a sliver of me—thought he might be about to ask me on a date. A real date. And that was weird, right?

. . . Right? Because, if he did ask me out, it wouldn't be a real date. It would be more like a work meeting than a date.

Yet, still, the sliver was excited.

It was times like these I wished I had a direct line to someone who could triage my perceptions, maybe even a committee, to tell me if my train of thought was on track or derailed.

"I called Luis," he continued. "He can't move the ceremony to Thursday because the officiant, Mr. Lee, is off. And he wants us to use that guy 'cause I guess he always wears the same suit. So we're still on for Friday."

"Oh. Okay." I glanced around the interior of the car, absorbing nothing of my surroundings. "I think that's fine—I mean—as long as that still works for you?"

"Yeah, yeah. That works for me. But I was thinking, since I'm back early, we should probably try to, you know, touch base."

"Yes. Absolutely." I was nodding, even as a spike of restlessness flared within me.

"Okay, yeah. Good. Thursday night?"

Preposterously, my sliver of self was happy with the non-date, because it would still be time spent over food and in each other's company. Apparently, my sliver was easy to please.

I couldn't decide whether the rest of me was excited for the non-date, or dreading it. I still needed to review my list of misdeeds with Dan and I knew it would be uncomfortably awkward.

Regardless, I was determined. It had to be done. I was just about to say yes when I remembered that the fall semester started next week.

"Oh shoot." I made a fist with my hand. "I have class on Thursday night."

"No biggie. Lunch?"

"I eat lunch!" I immediately scrunched my face at my overeager response.

Dan made a sound that sounded suspiciously like a laugh. "Oh, really? You do?"

"Yes. I do." My eyes still closed, I shook my head at myself.

"What a coincidence. I—also—eat lunch."

"That is a coincidence." I twisted my lips to the side, accepting his teasing.

"What are the chances?"

"I couldn't tell you." I smiled, though I was still distracted by Dan's name being changed to *Husband* in my phone. I honestly didn't remember doing it.

"Do you eat sandwiches?" he asked, as though the future of the world hung in the balance.

"I have been known to eat sandwiches on occasion, yes."

"Get out. Because—you're not going to believe this, but I swear it's true—I eat sandwiches."

Despite my attention being split, I smiled. He really was quite gifted at distracting me. "Unbelievable."

"We have so much in common, Kit-Kat. First lunch, now sandwiches." It might have been my imagination, but it sounded like his voice deepened when he called me by the nickname, his tone low and familiar. And then he applied that same tone to every subsequent word, including when he added, "We should probably just get married."

My heart did a little twisty thing. I tried to breathe normally. Tried and failed.

"Kat?"

"Yes, I'm—" I had to clear my throat so I wouldn't gulp air. "I'm here. Sorry. We just pulled up to my place."

"Oh? . . . We?"

"Nicolas is driving me home. I was visiting Janie and Quinn. I made them a lemon loaf." I rolled my lips between my teeth before I volunteered any of the additional information that was on the tip of my tongue, like what kind of lemons I'd used (Meyer) and when I'd bought the lemons (on Wednesday).

"That's nice. I'm sure Janie appreciated it. Quinn has been such a fucking—excuse my profanity—asshole recently."

"He's just worried."

Nicolas had pulled to a stop in front of my building and glanced at me in the rearview mirror. I covered the receiver with my hand and whispered, "Can I have a minute?"

He nodded. "Sure. Tell Dan I say hi."

I gave Nicolas a grateful smile.

"There's *worried*, and then there's *being-a-giant-pain-in-the-ass-and-making-everyone's-lives-miserable* worried." Dan sounded grouchy.

"Nicolas says hi by the way."

"He's good people."

We were quiet for a short moment, during which a deluge of apprehensions fought for dominance in my forebrain: How did I not remember reprogramming the name for Dan's number? Dan's life was already hectic and demanding enough, and now I was adding to it. Although I would do as Sandra recommended and allow Dan to help— if that's what he wanted to do—I still wanted to do something nice for him, to make it up to him, to show him how grateful I was.

This last thought had me asking, "Regarding Quinn, is there anything I can do? To help you? To make your life easier?"

He didn't answer right away, and for a minute I thought the call had been dropped. But then he said, "I have to go, the plane is taking off and you need to get to sleep. Make me a lemon loaf. And have lunch with me on Thursday. That'll help."

Oh jeez. My heart didn't just flip, it pined. A burst of something—a wish, desire, dread—sent zinging sensations outward from my chest to my limbs.

I wanted to respond with a loud, *I'll eat lunch with you every day of my life and make you eleventy hundred lemons loaves!*

But I didn't.

Because even I knew *that* wouldn't be normal.

* * *

MONDAY NIGHT I made three more lemon loaves: two for Dan, and one for my Tuesday night knitting group meetup. Tuesdays were always my favorite day of the week because of knit nights.

Several years ago, when I was new to the architecture firm and Janie worked in the accounting department, she'd noticed me knitting one day during lunch. She didn't knit, but she was part of a knitting group. This was mostly because her best friend from college was part of the knitting group and they'd made her an honorary member.

Because Janie was absolutely delightful and unlike anyone else I'd ever met, I took her up on her invitation to join the group one random Tuesday, and the rest was history.

This Tuesday was Sandra's turn to host; on my way to her apartment I had to walk past Dan's; this filled me with an assortment of indescribably odd feelings. I knew he wasn't there. I knew he was in New York. I knew I would see him on Thursday. And all of this knowledge was strange and clumsy. It was like we'd been on the sidelines of each other's lives for years, and now—quite suddenly—we were on the same field together, playing as teammates.

Shaking off the peculiar self-consciousness, I knocked on Sandra and Alex's door, pulling the lemon loaf from my bag. Alex answered.

I gave him a small smile and I held out the loaf. "Hi."

Instead of moving to the side and motioning me in wordlessly—which he'd done every single time I'd ever knocked on their door—he stepped forward, pulling the door behind him mostly closed, seemingly both startled by and keenly interested in my presence.

"Kat."

I backed up automatically to give him room, but I was so surprised by his abrupt movement into the hall, it took me a moment to react.

Alex was over six feet tall, so I retreated further backward rather than tilt my head to meet his gaze. "Is something wrong?"

"How are you?" he asked, sounding concerned, his attention disconcerting.

I'd known Alex for a year and a half, since he and Sandra had unexpectedly married. I knew he was a world-class hacker. I also knew he loved and was completely devoted to Sandra. And that was basically all I knew.

Like me, he didn't talk much. But he had this presence about him that made me wary, like he was dangerous. Or could be dangerous if he chose to be. As I usually did with people who made me nervous, I mostly avoided him.

"Okay. And how are you?" I clutched the lemon loaf to my chest.

He squinted. "What's going on? Do you need help? How can I help?"

That had me blinking furiously. "I—I—I'm not sure—"

"You and Dan getting married. That was sudden. I haven't told anyone. Not Sandra. Not Quinn."

I snapped my mouth shut, startled by his statements. His gaze was too intense, unsettling, but strangely not in a bad way. More like he was really, really concerned for my well-being.

Yet, still unsettling.

I released a breath, my eyes moving to the door behind him as I tried to pull my thoughts together. "Uh, Dan and I, it was sudden. How did you find out?"

"I'm tapped into government—uh—databases." He said databases slowly, giving me the impression it wasn't as benign as the word *databases* implied. "I have alerts set up for a few people."

"You have alerts set up for me?" I asked before I could consider my words.

Alex stared at me, his expression thoughtful. "Would it freak you out if I said I did?"

"A little, yes."

"Then, no."

I studied him for a beat. "You're lying."

"Correct."

I shook my head, closing my eyes, bringing my fingertips to my forehead, and freaking out a little.

"You're important," he said, as though those two simple words explained his actions.

Scoffing, I rubbed the space between my eyebrows. "I'm not sure how important I am."

I heard Alex gather a breath before saying, "You have the potential to make a real, lasting difference. You'll soon control over half the voting shares for the second largest pharmaceutical company in the world. You'll be able to influence drug development and health policy globally, maybe even cure a few diseases, control a vast number of lobbyists. So, yeah. I'd say you're important."

My eyes cut to his and I found him watching me with a peculiar kind of focus. I wasn't surprised he knew who I was. Dan had known; I imagined Quinn also knew.

And yet, none of them have ever brought it up until now, or made an issue out of it, or asked me about it, or asked for anything.

Alex continued, "Completely independently of all that, you're important. So let me help." He motioned toward the apartment behind him. "Why, if you've been married for a month, doesn't anyone else know?"

Frustrated that Alex knew as much as he did, I glared at him. It's not that I didn't trust him. But at the same time, I didn't trust him. I didn't know him. Making my problems other people's problems—especially people I didn't know very well—made me exceedingly uncomfortable.

Yet here we were. He knew Dan and I were married, and he hadn't shared the news, with anyone, not even his wife.

Choosing my words carefully, I allowed myself to admit this much. "I asked Dan to marry me on Thursday, and I haven't had an opportunity yet to fill him in on the whole story. This has all moved incredibly fast. Once I bring Dan up to speed, then we'll let everyone know."

"You asked him on Thursday?"

"That's right."

"The certificate says—"

"The date has been altered. But the marriage is," *or very soon will be,* "real."

His blue eyes were piercing, not precisely skeptical, more like curious. Eventually, he gave me a single nod. "You have to promise me that you'll ask for help if or when you need it."

I didn't understand his motivation and so I couldn't help but point out the obvious. "Alex, why do you want to help me? We don't even really know each other."

He balked, blinking once like my statement surprised him, and his hands came to his hips. I suspected for a moment he wanted to protest my claim. But then his features relaxed, as though he thought better of it, instead nodding as if to agree.

"I'd say it's more accurate that you don't know me."

A shiver of unease ran down my spine. "Well, that's cryptic."

"I'm mucking this up." He rolled his eyes toward the empty hallway. "This is why I don't speak."

Watching him, I realized he was irritated, but the irritation appeared to be directed inward. His statement about never speaking reminded me a little of myself. I often felt that way, like all my words were wrong, and I felt myself soften toward him. It was kind of . . . endearing. Dangerous and endearing? Was that possible?

"I know a lot about you," he said plainly, but also with a note of gentle earnestness I wouldn't have believed him capable of moments ago. "Not just from the work I do for Quinn, but also from Sandra. She talks about you. A lot. She tells me her worries and fears for you. She loves you, and that means I'm invested."

He pressed his lips together and they didn't exactly form a smile, more like a line that communicated amused surrender. "You don't trust me. Knowing what I do about you—and that's not meant to freak you out—I understand why you don't trust me. I wouldn't trust me either. Believe me, I get it. So trust Sandra instead. Just promise, if you need help, you'll come to me."

Thrown by his sincerity, I examined him closely for artifice and found none. "Okay. Fine. I promise to let you know if I—if we —need help."

"Good." Looking reassured, he reached for the doorknob and held the door open for me, lifting his chin toward the foil package in my hands. "Is that your lemon loaf?"

"Yes." I hesitated, then held it out to him.

He took it, his expression still intense. "I've been meaning to ask, can I have the recipe?"

I grinned as I walked past him and into the apartment. "Of course."

"Thanks. And—uh—Kat?"

"Yes?" I turned toward him, bemused by his sudden wordiness.

"This might not be the best time for me to admit this, but I hacked your phone. Sorry," he said, not looking sorry, but more like he felt like it was important that I know this information.

My mouth dropped open. "What?"

He lowered his voice to a whisper. "It was supposed to be a joke, but afterward, I wondered if you'd be upset."

"Upset? Of course I'm—wait, why did you hack my phone?"

"Dan and I are always pranking each other. When I saw you two were married, I changed Dan's contact name to *Husband* in your phone. And, on Dan's phone, I changed yours to *Wife*."

* * *

ALEX HACKING my phone and changing Dan's name to *Husband* was the second best news I'd had all week. The first best was—of course— Dan agreeing to marry me.

Giving into the urge to celebrate renewed confidence in my own sanity, I indulged in two lemon drops and didn't turn down the offer of a third.

So when Sandra suddenly declared, "I think we need to discuss the elephant in the room," I set my drink on the coffee table and turned a hazy smile in her direction. Knowing Sandra, this could mean literally anything, including an actual elephant.

But then Sandra said, "Anal."

And I laughed, recognizing that it might be the only time in my life I laughed after the word *anal.*

"Sandra." Fiona, sitting in the recliner on my left, made an exasperated face though her tone was even; she didn't glance up from her knitting.

Her reaction didn't surprise me. Fiona was difficult for me to describe because nothing ever flustered her. Due to this, she'd always been a bit of an enigma. Especially since I felt like I couldn't make it through twenty-four hours without being flustered.

She was older than me by more than a decade, had two well-adjusted, gorgeous children, and a brilliant husband who was madly in love with her. She always seemed to know exactly the right thing to say and had her shit together at all times, especially during impossible situations. Her husband, Greg, often teased that she was a robot. I could definitely see his point.

Take now for example.

Fiona was approximately the same number of weeks pregnant as Janie, but her belly was much, much smaller. Maybe this was because Fiona was just over five feet and Janie was almost six feet, but still. *Still!*

Her hair was done in a sleek bob, she wore a fashionable turquoise maternity dress and strappy black sandals, and her skin looked fantastic. She'd made the lemon drops everyone was drinking as well as canapés.

That's right. Canapés. Freaking canapés! Who does that while nine months pregnant? Ten days ago, she'd organized an impromptu dinner party at Janie's apartment—so Janie wouldn't be left out—and made everyone dinner.

I can't even.

Janie, however, my dear friend, was a hot mess. Her wild red hair was piled high on her head in a haphazard bun, curls and tendrils snaking out in every direction. She wore black horn-rimmed glasses, she'd confessed that this was to hide the bags under her eyes from lack of sleep, and she was wearing a tattered Wonder Woman bathrobe over Wonder Woman pajamas. Every so often, she'd stretch, her face contorting with discomfort, then close her eyes and sigh.

Fiona was too perfect. I couldn't relate.

Sandra wasn't finished. "Anal. Who has done it? Who is doing it? Who likes it? What is the deal with anal?"

Ashley, videoconferencing from her family's home in Tennessee, shook her head. Ashley had moved back to Tennessee about six months prior and had been joining us via computer ever since. Tonight, Sandra placed a laptop on a stool so our friend could see us and we could see her. The brunette sat on an old mustard-colored couch, a big family room behind her.

"Sandra, no one wants to talk about being impaled via the rectum." Ashley's Tennessee accent only emphasized her dry humor. "It's why I hated my emergency room rotation, folks coming in with lightbulbs and such stuck up their B-hole. That's not something they make a greeting card for. *Sorry you're a dummy who stuck a lightbulb up your ass, hope you get smarter soon.*"

Nico—aka Nicoletta, the only male member of our knitting group, and Elizabeth's husband—snorted and then laughed loudly. "Oh man, that's hilarious. You might see me steal that for the show."

I also smiled, but kept my eyes on my knitting. I still hadn't grown accustomed to Nico's presence, even though he'd been attending knit nights whenever he could for the last two years. He didn't *do* anything to make me uncomfortable. I was the problem.

The thing was, he was a famous comedian. He had a show on comedy central. He was down-to-earth, and funny, and insanely hand-some, and charismatic—so charismatic—and everything wonderful. He was basically a Disney prince come to life, who also spoke Italian and had blind devotion to his wife. I'd be lying if I said I didn't have the tiniest crush on him, but I felt like it was impossible not to.

"Use it for your show, Nicoletta." Ashley shrugged. "I aint' using it for anything profitable."

Not a second later, Ashley's youngest brother, Roscoe, poked his head in the frame. "Are y'all talking about anal?"

This drew smiles and chuckles from all gathered except Ashley.

Usually, I would've remained quiet for the rest of the evening. First of all, her brother Roscoe was seriously, *seriously* hot. And he was in veterinary school. As far as I was concerned, he embodied walking kryptonite for the virtuous-minded.

Secondly, I didn't know him. It wasn't like discussing this stuff with the rest of the ladies (and I included Nicoletta in that). I knew them. I trusted them. We'd been through *times* together.

However, since I was on my third lemon drop, my uneasiness was eclipsed by a general sense of ennui. And the realization that I wasn't uneasy had me pushing the rest of my lemon drop away. Alcohol made me braver; I knew this about myself. Which was why I only allowed myself alcohol when I was with my friends.

"Get out of here." Ashley shoved her little brother to the side, but he didn't leave, opting instead to join her on the couch.

"What do you think you're doing?" She scowled at him.

He shrugged. "I think I'll learn to knit."

Elizabeth and Nico shared an amused look.

Fiona heaved an aggrieved sigh, likely unaware of Ashley and Roscoe's spat. "Sandra—"

"Hear me out."

"For man on man, it makes sense." Janie rested her crochet on her stomach. She'd been treating her pregnant belly like a table for the past month. "Because men have the prostate and pressure on that area feels good."

This was a very Janie-like thing for her to say. She seemed to know a little—or a lot—about everything, and when topics were raised, controversial or otherwise, she always offered a deluge of random factoids on the subject.

I loved this about her, and it was likely one of the reasons I trusted her so quickly and easily. Rather than responding to something sensational with a knee-jerk reaction, she was always taking a step back to consider the facts first.

"No one wants to talk about this." Ashley covered her face.

"I kinda want to talk about it." Elizabeth shrugged, not trying to hide her devilish smirk, and her devilish smirk drew a smile from me.

I often wished I could be more like Elizabeth. Not only was she book-smart—she was an emergency room physician—but she was also unfailingly forthright and a consistent source of positivity and encouragement. I loved how generous she was with praise, always looking for ways to build others up.

She and Sandra were equally thoughtful in this way, and I may have had a little bit of hero-worship for them both.

"Oh? Really?" Nico sat up straighter.

"For man on woman, however, anatomically speaking, there's no reason it should feel good." Janie shook her head, wrinkling her nose. "So why do women do it?"

"It's been proven that women can orgasm without any physical contact at all. All that's needed is the right kind of mental stimulation." Elizabeth turned her knitting, lifting a suggestive eyebrow at her husband.

I averted my gaze, a tinge of embarrassed heat making my neck warm. This wasn't because Nico and Elizabeth were giving each other the sexy eyes—which they were, and did often—but because, even with three lemon drops lowering my inhibitions, her words had hit too close to home. I felt like I had a scarlet 'O' on my chest with a thick black circle around it and a line through it.

Luckily, no one was looking at me, and Marie—who'd been very quiet up to now—made a show of waving her index finger between Nico and Elizabeth, "Hey, hey, hey. Get a room."

Marie was a journalist and probably the best person I knew. I had a lot of moments when I'd ask myself, *What would Marie do?* and then I'd do that.

If any of us were in trouble or needed help, she was the first to volunteer. She babysat for Fiona and Greg all the time, and she'd dropped everything last spring to help them deal with an emergency in Africa. She also helped Elizabeth and Nico whenever their niece—who had cystic fibrosis—came to town and they needed an extra hand. She'd been the one to visit Janie and Quinn in the hospital when Janie had initially been placed on bed rest.

In addition to her incredible kindness, she was also funny, and smart, and freaking gorgeous. Basically, she was everyone's favorite because she was impossible not to love.

Embarrassingly, when I first met her, her unfailing generosity had confused me, made me suspicious of her intentions. I didn't like her, she felt too good to be true, and I was slow to trust her. I couldn't fathom that someone like her existed, someone so incredibly *good*. Using the Disney analogy again, she was like a fairy godmother.

Over the years, her abiding goodness had forced me to change my mind, and now I was just as much in love with her as everyone else was.

"So, most of y'all's orgasms is in the head." Roscoe turned to Ashley and nudged her with his elbow. "Get it? Get it? *In the head.*"

Ashley glared at her brother.

I swallowed a rush of bitterness at Roscoe's joke and decided to switch to water for the rest of the night.

"Moving on." Fiona didn't roll her eyes, but her tone spoke volumes.

"So some women like it because they think it's hot, therefore it is hot." Sandra took a sip of her drink, smacking her lips.

"On the other hand, anything that stretches out that hole can lead to an increase in sharts." Marie lifted her eyebrows at Sandra.

"Really, Marie? We've reached this level?" Ashley was making a disgusted face. "I grew up with six hillbilly brothers. You think I want to spend this precious time with my lady friends talking about sharts? I can do that here, anytime. In fact, I think it was the hot topic over dinner last night."

Marie giggled, not looking repentant.

"I don't know if that's true." Janie shook her head. "Increase in anal sex hasn't been shown to be a factor in loss of sphincter control. Not if it's done right."

"Done right?" I asked, my voice cracking before I could catch the question.

"I'm so afraid." Ashley covered her ears.

"Stop being a prude." Elizabeth rolled her eyes at Ashley.

"Just because I don't wish to discuss putting junk in my poop-shoot doesn't mean I'm a prude," Ashley volleyed back.

Sandra ignored them, answering my question. "Lots and lots of lube."

"Are you speaking from experience, Sandra?" Nicoletta sent her a flirty grin.

"No! God no. Have you seen Alex's yang? It's a monster."

Nico busted out laughing, and so did Marie and Elizabeth. "As a matter of fact, no. But I'll be sure to ask him about it the next time I see him."

"Can we please not talk about Alex's yang?" Marie's voice, though she was wiping tears of hilarity from her eyes, was pleading. "It's like talking about my little brother's yang."

"Your little brother is hot, though." Elizabeth pointed at Marie with her knitting needle. "And, for the record, feel free to discuss Alex's yang with me."

"Moral of the story: some women like it, some women not so much." Sandra seemed to be determined to push the conversation forward.

"I wouldn't like it." Ashley still had her ears covered.

"How do you know unless you try it?" Roscoe nudged his sister again.

Ashley batted his elbow away. "I don't want someone else to pick my nose, doesn't mean I need to try it first to know."

"Personally, I can't get behind it. See what I did there?" Sandra grinned at Roscoe. He grinned back.

"Then why are we talking about it?" Fiona asked, her tone dry and impatient.

Sandra didn't answer right away, instead glaring at Fiona, and the glare intensified the longer she looked.

Silence stretched and became uncomfortable; all of us, one by one, looked up from our knitting and glanced between Fiona and Sandra.

Visibly confused, Fiona lifted an eyebrow. "Sandra?"

"Because I can't talk about how sad I am," she blurted. "So I have to talk about something else."

Wait, what?

"Why are you sad?" I asked, examining my friend. She did look a little sad.

"I just—I feel like everything is changing." Sandra took a gulp of her drink and hid behind the glass.

Fiona and I shared a look before she asked, "Changing how?"

"Well, you're pregnant. Janie's pregnant." Sandra gestured to their bellies. "Soon someone else will be in the family way." Sandra glared at Elizabeth and Elizabeth gave her wide eyes of innocence in return. "And then—between sleep deprivation and hunting for deals on diapers, we'll drift apart. Pretty soon it'll be months between meetups, or years. And then once-in-a-blue-moon reunion specials. And then we'll only see each other at weddings and funerals."

Janie's eyebrows puckered. "Three of us live in this building—including you. It seems highly improbable for us to drift apart given our proximity."

"Are you seriously going to tell me that having a kid won't interfere with your social schedule? Because I remember how things were with Fiona when Grace was born. We didn't see her for months."

Fiona didn't look hurt, but she did look concerned. "Sandra—"

"By the way, you know I love Jack and Grace, so this isn't a complaint about your ridiculously stunning family. This is me trying to prepare myself for less frequent knit nights. Or poorly attended knit nights."

Another moment of silence settled upon us, and when Sandra spoke again, her voice was softer, her melancholy more obvious. "Things aren't going to be the same."

"Things are changing, it's true." Fiona's tone was gentle.

"And maybe we won't see each other as often." Marie's cadence was also soft, and maybe a little introspective. "But just because we won't see each other doesn't mean we won't know each other."

"*You* sound like a greeting card," Sandra grumbled, then sighed, and then shook her head. "I'm sorry, Marie. That wasn't—"

"Don't apologize to me." Marie held her hands up. "Knitting means never having to say you're sorry."

That drew a small smile from Sandra and another sigh. "I don't want things to change. I don't want things to end."

She sounded so sad, so desolate, that I couldn't help my heart's answering pang of despondency. Things were changing, and not just because Janie and Fiona were about to have their babies.

Abruptly, Marie stood, placing her knitting on the seat behind her, crossed to where Sandra was on the opposite sofa, and pulled her into a hug. Then I stood, as did Fiona, Elizabeth, and Nico. We all followed suit. Soon we were piled on top of, and next to, and behind Sandra, embracing her and each other.

And then we heard Janie's gruff, "Thor!"

Turning, we found the tall redhead struggling to rock forward, as though she wanted to also hug Sandra, but couldn't gain enough momentum to lift herself from her seat.

"It's like,"—Janie started to laugh, obviously with frustration —"I'm that cockroach in Kafka's *Metamorphosis*. I can't even get up."

Nico broke away and, giving Janie a huge grin, easily lifted her. Before allowing her to cross to the group, he pulled her into a hug first, smoothing his hand down her back. "You are not a cockroach, Janie. *Sei molto simpatica, incantevole, e bellissima.*"

Janie seemed to melt into his embrace, and she sighed. Or maybe that was me. Or maybe that was all of us.

"I don't even care what you said. You might've called me a dumpster fire and I would never know." Janie leaned away and grinned up at him with stars in her eyes.

He pushed her hair back from her face and returned her grin. "I said, 'You are sweet, charming, and very beautiful.'"

And then I was pretty sure we all sighed.

Even Roscoe.

CHAPTER SEVEN

Youth Detention Center: Also known as a juvenile detention center (JDC), A secure prison or jail for persons under the age of majority, to which they have been sentenced and committed for a period of time, or detained on a short-term basis while awaiting court hearings and/or placement in such a facility or in other long-term care facilities and programs. Juveniles go through a separate court system, the juvenile court, which sentences or commits juveniles to a certain program or facility.

SNYDER, H. & SICKMUND, M. (MARCH 2006). "JUVENILE OFFENDERS AND VICTIMS: 2006 NATIONAL REPORT"

Kat

WAITING FOR LUNCH Thursday afternoon was just as difficult as it had been last week. Like last week, I'd come into work early, just in case lunch took longer than anticipated. I watched the clock on my computer, glancing at it every three minutes or so. I tried to focus on work. I failed.

But I'd anticipated this and had worked late into the evening on

Wednesday, writing emails and saving them in my drafts folder, finishing projects, and preparing the final documents for the Friday staff meeting.

What did help keep me distracted was looking over my list of reckless choices on my phone. Reading the list was unexpectedly cathartic. It helped me refocus. It also helped dampen any silly shards of optimism I'd been carrying around that Dan might one day return my feelings.

Just keeping it real, I had a lot of what was often colloquially referred to as "baggage."

I had so much baggage, I could've opened a Samsonite outlet store.

Therefore, rather than fulfillment, happiness, and/or true love, I'd decided to settle for functioning member of society; *that* was my goal.

The first time I filed my taxes was the happiest day of my life up to that point. It felt like a victory. I threw myself a wine and cheese party, but without the wine, and spent the weekend binge-watching *Doctor Who*.

I was also a steadfast realist. No one with any sense—and especially not someone as amazing as Daniel O'Malley—would ever accept or deal with all my baggage. Who had that kind of room in their life? No house contained that many closets.

Moving on.

Finally, the time was nigh. Locking my computer and grabbing the bag with Dan's lemon loaves, I let Ms. Opal know I was leaving and made my way to the elevators, feeling remarkably calm.

My plan was to give Dan the list, allow him several minutes to read it, answer any questions he might have, and then—if he still wished to help me—I would explain the situation with my cousin and what Dan could expect from my vindictive family member.

I would be cool and collected. I would be marble.

But then, as the elevator doors opened on the lobby, the first thing I saw was him.

Dan.

Twenty feet away.

Leaning against one of the rectangular pillars, arms crossed, eyes aimed at me.

I hesitated.

He smirked. But not a jerky-smirk. It was an amused smirk. Even from this distance his eyes looked warm and teasing.

I reminded myself of the list, but it didn't help. In fact, it made me want to stay put, allow the doors to close and carry me back to my floor. His eyes narrowed, the smirk falling away, giving me the impression he suspected I was about to do just that.

And wouldn't that make *me* a selfish jerk? Here he was, helping me, and I was going to flee because I was too much of a scaredy-cat to own up to who I was? No. No, no, no.

No.

Gathering a bracing breath, I stepped out of the elevator and walked directly to him, my spine straight, my head held high. His smirk returned and his eyes swept over me as I approached.

Before I could decide whether to greet him with a handshake (would that be weird?) hand him the lemon loaves, or employ a succinct head nod, he leaned forward, slid an arm around my waist, and placed a soft kiss on my cheek.

Oh.

Well.

Okay.

Now I was completely disoriented.

Not quite letting me go, but drawing several inches away, he indicated to the bag. "Is that what I think it is?"

"Lemon loaves."

"Loaves?" His eyes grew wide. "As in more than one loaf?"

"Yes. Two loafs. I mean, loaves."

"You are my favorite person." His voice became low in that way it did, like he was telling me a naughty secret.

I swallowed, careful not to gulp air, and gave him a smile I was sure looked dazed. I was dazed. I was amazed and dazed and frazzled and bedazzled. And bewitched.

This was the worst. And the best.

He grinned, apparently finding something in my expression amusing as he reached for my wrist. "Come on." Smiling down at me and tilting his head toward the exit, Dan guided me forward as our fingers tangled so we were carrying the bag together. "I'm starving. I made the mistake of ordering pizza last night in New York. It tasted like kitty litter and cardboard. And that miserable cheese, silly putty."

My gaze was fastened to his profile. "You prefer Chicago pizza?"

He gave me the side-eye. "Do I prefer Chicago pizza? What kind of question is that? You look gorgeous by the way."

Oh jeez.

He was too much.

I glanced at my outfit, my stomach flip-flopping, an automatic thank you on the tip of my tongue, but then he said, "You wore that last Thursday, right? I like it, the purple. It brings out the color of your eyes."

My mouth opened and closed for a moment as I struggled to speak. Or think. I sucked in a large breath but stopped myself before I swallowed it. The last thing I needed was violent hiccups.

In the end, I hid my blush behind a curtain of hair and simply followed where he led, my heart in my throat.

It brings out the color of your eyes.

What was I supposed to do with that?

He was the master of flustering me. I was at a loss when what I needed to do was focus. I needed to forget that I liked this man—so, so much—because it was clouding my vision. Dan being Dan was making it difficult for me to think.

He opened the door for me, placing his hand on my lower back—unnecessarily—to guide me through, and then recaptured my fingers as soon as we were on the sidewalk.

"Have you ever been to Capriotti's?"

I shook my head, forcing myself to say, "No. But I've wanted to try it."

"They have this turkey sub with stuffing and cranberry sauce. It's like Thanksgiving in a sandwich, but without the additional seasoning of my drunk uncle Zip's politics, or my sister Cathy's failed attempts at pumpkin pie. The woman never met a recipe she didn't want to ruin by making it vegan. What the fuck is almond milk? They don't call it 'nut juice' but that's exactly what it is."

In any other circumstance, his mini-tirade would've made me laugh, or at least fight a smile. Many times over the years I'd overheard him ranting to Quinn, or Fiona's husband, Greg, about something completely prosaic made hilarious by his spin on it. Dan had that way about him. Even when he ranted he was adorable and charming, and whomever he ranted to always ended up laughing.

But not today. I was completely out of sorts, dangerously close to off-kilter. Like an idiot, all I could manage was a tight smile.

We walked the rest of the way in silence, and when we arrived he ushered me in, once again with an unnecessary hand on my lower back. Without pausing, he strolled into the restaurant and claimed a square table with four chairs, and the only one with no customers on either side of it.

I took the chair closest to the wall. I was hungry, but I was more nervous than hungry. Which meant if food were placed in front of me, there was a high chance I would shovel it into my mouth with alarming speed and maybe end up choking to death on a sandwich.

And wouldn't that make a great headline? *Heiress chokes to death on a sandwich, news at eleven.*

I placed my backpack and the bag containing the lemon loaves on the seat to my right. Almost immediately, he picked them up and claimed the seat they had occupied, putting both next to him, in the seat across from mine.

"Do you need a menu?" he asked, brazenly studying me.

"How about a grilled cheese?" A grilled cheese wouldn't present any size issues. I could take careful bites. It was the safe choice.

"That's it? Just a grilled cheese?"

"Yes."

Dan contemplated me for another half minute, then stood and motioned to the area where customers placed their orders. "Fine. I'll get you your grilled cheese."

"Oh, sorry. I can get it—"

"No, no. You stay there."

"But I can—"

"Seriously, I'll get it. The truth is, I'm getting two subs for myself. Because I can't ever choose between the thanksgiving one and the cheese steak. So, if you want a bite of either or both, fine. If not, whatever. No pressure."

Dan backed away from the table, holding my gaze, then turned and strolled toward the counter. I watched as he pulled out his phone, glanced at it for a short moment, and then stuffed it back in his pocket.

Rubbing my forehead, I closed my eyes and redoubled my efforts to focus. It was imperative that I separate myself from this moment, from Dan. For the hour, he would not be Dan the Security Man, who I couldn't stop ogling, or thinking about, or fretting about his opinion of me.

I needed to forget about that.

He would merely be the parts of himself relevant to the present situation: a good person; a person I needed to protect; a person I trusted to help.

Feeling steadier, I reached for my bag and withdrew my phone. Once on, I unlocked it and navigated to my list of misdeeds, intent on reviewing it when he returned to the table. Sandra's advice was in the back of my mind, encouraging me to be honest without putting myself down.

However, as soon as my cell had a signal, it buzzed, and then it buzzed again, and again. Eugene had called me three times and had left two messages, not counting texts. Tallying the notifications, I realized he'd sent twelve new text messages. The last one was three paragraphs long and seemed to detail a cautionary tale of someone named Harold Hamm who'd married without a prenup. The unfortunate billionaire— or ex-billionaire—was now in big trouble and on the precipice of losing his company.

More importantly, Eugene pointed out, Harold Hamm's employees were now at risk of losing *their* livelihood.

I gave my phone the side-eye. Uncle Eugene was a stinker. He knew I would be having lunch with Dan today and was clearly very adept at pushing my buttons.

"What's wrong?" Dan settled back in his seat, looking between my phone and me. "Bad news?"

"No. It's not bad. It's just . . ." I sighed again. I couldn't seem to stop sighing.

Dan tilted his head, his eyes on my cell phone screen. "Who's Eugene?"

"He's my lawyer—actually, my family's lawyer—and he's the executor of my father's will."

"Did your"—Dan covered my hand, his gaze impossibly soft and sympathetic—"dad die? Is that why you needed to get married?"

"No. He's still alive. But he has Alzheimer's and has for a while."

"Oh yeah. I knew that." Dan stripped his straw of paper with one hand, pushing it into his cup. "He and your mom are at the same care facility, right?"

I stared at him, no longer astonished or dismayed by his knowledge of my past, but rather suddenly irritated by it. Looking at Dan through a filter of suspicion—now that it was clear he'd had me investigated well before I'd asked him to marry me last Wednesday—gave my mind focus.

After a moment, he met my gaze. While we traded stares, his eyebrows lifted by millimeters, as though reading my thoughts and surprised by their direction.

"Your last name isn't Tanner," he said finally, his tone flat, and he released my hand.

"What else do you know about me?" I crossed my arms.

"You're the heiress to the Caravel Pharmaceuticals fortune. Your mother is Rebekah Caravel-Tyson, the famous painter and even more famous heiress, and your father is Zachariah Tyson, scientist and—with your mother's illness—now the majority stakeholder in Caravel Pharmaceuticals. Your cousin, Caleb Tyson, is the CEO."

"How do you know all of this?"

Dan shrugged. The movement was seasoned with the barest hint of embarrassment, but mostly pragmatism. "When Quinn started things up with Janie, the team prepared dossiers on all her friends."

"So you've known about me since Janie and Quinn started dating?"

"Yep."

I would not allow myself to think about the ramifications of this revelation until I was alone with my thoughts. And yes—you guessed it—cheese. Probably a sharp cheddar. Or maybe a brie.

But he wasn't finished. "I also know that Elizabeth's first boyfriend died of cancer, what kind of dog Sandra had growing up, that Ashley only entered those beauty contests in Tennessee in order to get a scholarship to college, that Fiona almost made it to the Olympics before she got that brain tumor, and that Marie's brother is a musician in New York."

This was information I knew as well, except the difference was he'd read about these experiences, whereas my friends had confided in me willingly.

Dan leaned back in his seat. "Listen, I can see this upsets you, and I don't blame you. But what's done is done. Cypher Systems was at a critical point when Janie and Quinn hooked up, and he wanted to make sure none of you were a liability."

"So you know all about me?"

"Not *all* about you."

"Really. What don't you know?"

"Let's see . . ." He twisted his mouth to the side and peered at me thoughtfully. "What'd you have for breakfast this morning?"

"Two hard-boiled eggs."

"So, the usual?"

My mouth dropped open, and I was sure dismay was painted all over my features, but Dan could only keep his face straight for approximately five seconds before he cracked a smile and started to laugh.

"Relax. I'm kidding. I have no idea what you eat for breakfast. It wasn't like that. We weren't spying. We just wanted to make sure none of you had any connections that might jeopardize or complicate Cypher Systems's migration to corporate security. So, no. I don't know everything about you." He added under his breath something that sounded like, "Far from it."

His clarification didn't make me feel much better, because the fact was he had—or Quinn and Alex and their team had—investigated us. Dan did know a lot about me. I was at a huge disadvantage; in comparison, I knew very little about him.

"You know I left home at fifteen?" I lifted my chin, bracing myself for his answer.

He didn't respond right away, instead he leaned forward and pushed his straw into his drink. "Yes."

"Do you know why?"

"No." He sighed, shaking his head, looking irritated. "But I can guess."

"Please." I gestured for him to continue, then re-crossed my arms.

His attention settled on my crossed arms and his frustration seemed to intensify. "Your mom. She has schizophrenia, right? The bad kind?"

I didn't flinch. I didn't show any emotion. "That's right."

"And your dad, he shipped you off to boarding school at five? He was a real workaholic type, right?"

"Yes."

"My guess is, you didn't like the school, and you never saw your dad, and your mom wasn't around, so . . ." His shoulders moved up and down once as he sipped his drink.

"So?"

"So you had nothing to stay for. No family to consider, or to guide you, or to protect you. As a kid, you needed to be protected. And if you didn't get on well at school, you had no reason to stay there either. You were young. You didn't like where you were, so you left."

I didn't confirm or deny his guess, mostly because his conclusion was definitely part of the reason I'd run away.

"I get it. I mean, I remember being a teenager and not understanding that I wasn't invincible. I was so eager to get out there and prove myself, how much of a big man I was, how much of an adult, that I made dumbass choices. I didn't understand that the big adult choices come with big adult consequences."

Big adult consequences.

This piqued my interest. "Specifically?"

"I joined my brother's gang when I was fourteen,"—he scratched his neck, not quite meeting my eyes—"and did some very, very bad stuff."

I considered him, what he'd said, what he didn't say. "Bad stuff?"

"Yeah."

Inexplicably, I found myself relaxing. "Like what?"

Dan gave me a close-lipped smile. His eyes seemed to dance with amusement while erecting a barricade at the same time. "You don't want to know."

"I think I do. We might get married tomorrow, right?"

"Not 'might.'" He gave his head a subtle shake, his eyes locked with mine. "We *are* getting married tomorrow. In fact, according to Cook County, we're already married."

"You know all about me—"

"I don't. I really don't."

"You know the nature of the *unwise* decisions I made, right? The drugs?"

His eyebrows ticked up, but I wasn't finished.

"How I lived on the streets? The stealing?"

"No, actually." Dan placed an elbow on the table, his hand rubbing his chin as he considered me. "I don't know about that."

Startled, I sat straighter in my seat. "You don't?"

"The files don't go into that much detail. If you weren't arrested for it, I don't know about it."

"But I was arrested."

"You've been arrested?" He made no attempt to hide his shock.

"Yes. For theft."

Dan sputtered, seemed to struggle to find words, and eventually asked, "What did you steal?"

"All sorts of things, always from a supermarket or a convenience store. Food mostly."

"This was when you were a runaway?"

"Yes."

"Huh." He was looking at me like I was something new and peculiar. "So they tracked you down?"

"No. A few months before my eighteenth birthday, I went to the police and turned myself in."

He reared back. "Get out."

"I did." I nodded firmly. "I made a list of all the stores and items I could remember stealing from and turned myself in."

"Fucking nerves of steel on you." He cracked a smile, now looking at me like I was something new and amazing, but still peculiar. "What happened?"

Remembering the first twenty-four hours after I'd turned myself in, the event that stood out the most was Eugene showing up, looking not just grim, but also furious. "Eugene was very angry."

"This is your dad's lawyer? I'll bet."

"Especially since I'd refused his help in favor of a public defender."

"No shit?"

"No shit," I repeated, smiling a little at my use of the cuss word. "But all I felt was relief. I served my time in the detention center. I completed my community service and was accepted to a work-release program. I paid restitution to the stores from my earnings. It took me three years, but I did it."

"You were in a detention center?" He scratched his chin, examining me. "Those places can be rough."

"It was scary,"—I shrugged—"but no more so than living on the streets."

"Was that story in the papers? I don't remember hearing about it."

"No, actually. By some miracle, the media never picked up on the story." I suspected that had been Eugene's doing, to spare my father any embarrassment.

Dan exhaled a disbelieving sigh, shaking his head. "This is unbelievable," he said. But I wasn't really listening to him.

I was lost to my recollections, and so I spoke without thinking, "Turning myself in was the best thing I've ever done. I was off the streets, off drugs, and my caseworker helped me figure out how to get my GED. Since I'd voluntarily confessed, and turned myself in prior to my eighteenth birthday, my records are sealed. It changed my life."

"You're unbelievable."

"It is unbelievable. I got lucky, so lucky, I know I did. Some kids don't get a second chance even if they want one. But the experience did teach me the importance of always doing the right thing—especially when it's scary—because the alternative is living in constant fear and shame."

I fingered my phone, knowing now was the right time to show him my list. And yet I hesitated. Once he knew, he would always know. There was no taking this back.

Dan reached over and moved my hair behind my shoulder, drawing my attention back to him. "You're different."

"Different? Than what?"

"Different than what I thought you were like."

My stomach wanted to drop, but this time I wouldn't let it. So what if who I was, what I'd done, disappointed him? There was nothing I could do about that now, and I certainly didn't have time to cry about it given my present circumstances.

I lifted my chin as ice entered my words. "Really? And how am I different?"

"You're tough."

I suppressed my wince, but just barely.

I wasn't sure if he meant *tough* as a compliment or as an insult. If you called a man tough, it was automatically considered a positive attribute. Guys were supposed to be tough. But if a woman was called tough—or hard, or experienced—it wasn't necessarily praise. My therapist and I had discussed this double standard at length, especially as it related to my own issues with self-worth.

We wanted guys to be tough, strong, capable, and decisive, hardened by experience.

We wanted women to be soft, vulnerable, retiring, and gentle, shielded from hardship.

I resisted the concept of being retiring, especially over the last two years as I worked to learn my place at Caravel. How was I supposed to assume the role of majority shareholder while also wearing a mantel of timidity? It was impossible to be both.

I couldn't afford gentleness, not with Caleb's scheming. And, other than Uncle Eugene, no one in my life had ever attempted to shield me from hardship. Except maybe my mother, and then only from her hallucinations.

My therapist had said these expectations, these ideals—for both men and women—were at odds with what was healthy and demanded by reality.

Yet still, I struggled. I didn't like being vulnerable. At all. I'd been vulnerable when I was a kid and clearly that had not worked out for me.

"You don't like being called tough?" he guessed, lifting an eyebrow at me.

I glanced over his head to the window behind him. "It depends on how you mean it."

"It wasn't an insult."

I looked to him, found his mouth curved with a whisper of a smile.

"You expected me to be weak?"

"No. I just didn't expect you to be *this* tough." He took another sip of his drink, watching me over the rim, then replacing it to the table. "But I guess maybe you've had to be tough."

"So then it's allowed?" I challenged, not quite understanding why his statement irritated me so much. "If a woman *has to* be tough, because of circumstances beyond her control, then it's allowed? Otherwise—"

"Whoa." He held his hands up, his eyes alert. "You can be anything you want or need to be. And don't assume this is me acting like I'm giving you permission, or like you need someone's permission to be what you are. I don't think you need my permission or anyone else's. No one does. But since you specifically asked, this is just me making some statements that are obvious—at least, they're obvious to me. Okay? You do you. You're tough, for whatever reason, and that's great."

I couldn't help it, his response—which I found surprising and wonderful—fractured my composure and made me smile.

And I was admitting before I could catch myself, "You're also different than I expected."

"Oh really? How so? And if you call me a mansplainer, I promise I won't say another word for the rest of our marriage."

That made me laugh. "No. You're not a mansplainer. And for the record, I hate that word."

He seemed surprised by this. "Why do you hate that word? I think it's hilarious."

"Hate might be too strong. I guess I don't like it."

"Why?"

"Because men aren't the only ones who do it." I was specifically thinking about two women on the board at Caravel who seemed to consider me an idiot because I was young, and I'd been born into my position rather than earning my seat at the table. Their hostility only made me want to prove myself more.

Dan gave me a look, like he didn't follow my logic.

"It should be dumbsplain, because women do it too."

"Yeah but—at the risk of being a mansplainer—may I suggest you think of it this way." He cleared his throat, sitting up straighter in his seat, his tone adopting an instructional air. "We use hu*man* and *man*kind all the time to mean everyone, right?"

"Right . . ."

"So, why can't *man*splain also apply to everyone? Also, for the record, most of the guys I know who get upset at the word 'mansplain' also call each other—and pardon my profanity—*pussies* all the time. So that's a dumb fucking double standard if you ask me."

I laughed, unable to stop myself, especially since he'd asked to be pardoned for using the word "pussies" but didn't seem to realize he'd just dropped an F-bomb.

He eyeballed me, looking a little confused by my laughter, like he wasn't sure if I was laughing at him. "So, how am I different than you expected? Am I taller?"

Still smiling, I allowed my gaze to examine his handsome face. "You're self-aware. In unexpected ways."

"I suppose you mean I have a sensitive side." Now he smirked, looking a little smug. He was really cute when he looked smug.

Once again, I was reminded of how exceptionally talented Dan was at distracting me and making me not care that I was distracted; or letting my guard down; or saying, doing, and feeling things I wouldn't typically allow myself to say or do or feel.

Like right now. I was staring at him and it wasn't through my filter of aloofness and control. He was also staring at me. My stomach colluded with my heart to switch places because—if my brain could be trusted—it looked like he was giving me the sexy eyes.

The sexy eyes.

The ones he'd been withholding since Vegas.

I melted. And I probably would have done something extraordinarily embarrassing—like tell him how much I liked him—except we were fortuitously interrupted by the arrival of sandwiches.

"Turkey, grilled cheese, and cheesesteak." The restaurant worker plopped the trays down in front of us, not caring whose sandwich was whose, and effectively broke the sexy-eyes spell.

Also, my phone chose that moment to buzz where I'd left it on the table. We both glanced at the screen and I snatched it up as soon as I read the message.

Eugene: *Did he sign the postnup?*

Dan peered at me, lifting his drink to bite on his straw. "Eugene again?"

I nodded, dismissing his text. It was exactly the reminder I needed, the bucket of ice water required to put this conversation back on track.

Navigating to my notes app, I offered my phone to Dan. "I need to show you something."

His gaze flickered between the phone and me, but he didn't take it. "What's that?"

"I made a list of all the things I've done, all the things you need to know about me. I didn't—I don't—want you marrying me before you understand the extent of my—"

"You mean it's like a list of bad stuff?"

"That's right."

His gaze morphed into a glower and he leaned away. "I don't want to see the list. I don't need to see a list of all the things you think you've done wrong in your life."

"But I want you to make an informed decision. Before you agree to marry me—"

"Like I said, it's too late. I've already agreed." He held his hands up, palms out. "No list is going to change my mind about that."

"But—"

"Do you want me to make a list of all the bad shit I've done?" He lowered his voice, looking suddenly angry and scowling at my phone like it had just attacked his dog. "Because I guarantee you, it's going to be longer than your list."

"No. I would never ask you for that." I brought the phone to my chest, hiding the screen that seemed to offend him so much. "You're the one helping me, not the other way around. I owe you everything, and you owe me nothing."

He shook his head, pushing his food away and crossing his arms. Inexplicably, my words seemed to have made him furious, and he appeared to be dangerously close to losing his temper.

"You have got to stop fucking thanking me." He pronounced each word slowly, meticulously.

"I don't know how to do that. You're saving my—"

"Listen," he ground out, closing his eyes, taking a deep breath before continuing. "The truth of the matter is, maybe we don't know each other all that well." He opened his eyes and his gaze hijacked mine with its intensity. "But we've known each other for several years. And in that time, I've never seen you do anything that would make me hesitate helping you now, okay? And obviously, there's nothing I've done over the last several years that had you hesitating asking me for help either."

I couldn't respond because my throat was clogged with an unidentified emotion. We held each other's stare for a long moment and I watched his anger dissipate, most of the tension releasing from his shoulders.

"Respect, right? Why can't that be the end of it?" He leaned forward, his gaze softer, but far from the sexy eyes he'd been giving me earlier. "And who we are now is pretty fucking awesome. So let's not try to color this mutual respect—or stain it, or whatever—with the things we've done in our past that we're maybe not so proud of, okay?"

I nodded, not convinced but knowing now was not the time to argue. Maybe, at some point, I'd try to reintroduce the issue. But now was clearly not the time.

"Good." He exhaled a breath that sounded enormously relieved. "So, let's get back to this guy, your dad's lawyer. Eugene? What's he keep calling about?"

CHAPTER EIGHT

Tried as an Adult: A situation in which a juvenile offender is tried as if he or she were an adult. Where specific protections exist for juvenile offenders (such as suppression of an offender's name or picture or a closed courtroom where the proceedings are not made public), these protections may be waived.

Young, M. C., & Gainsborough, J. (2000). Prosecuting juveniles in adult court: An assessment of trends and consequences.

Dan

She didn't want to answer my question.

I could tell by how she was messing with the buttons at her wrist. So I tried something different.

"He bothering you?"

"No. Not at all." She rubbed her forehead like she had a headache. "I mean, yes. He's currently bothering me because he won't stop calling and texting, but no. He doesn't bother me as a general rule.

He's great. In fact, he's the one who warned me about my cousin and advised me to get married as soon as possible."

She stared off into space, looking like the weight of the world was on her shoulders. That didn't sit right with me. No one should have the weight of the world on their shoulders, and Kat feeling this way made me agitated, restless. I wanted to do something.

I'd never put much thought into what her life was like, or what kind of stress she'd been dealing with, having the family she did. I'd figured, no use counting her particular grains of sand. In my experience, all families were stressful. It didn't matter if they were big or small, rich or poor, it's all the same struggle, right?

Looking at her now, I wondered if I'd been wrong.

"What's the rush? If you don't mind my asking." I took a bite of the turkey sandwich. It was good, but I was too preoccupied with important stuff to appreciate the nostalgia.

Her eyes came up, focused on some point over my shoulder. "My father isn't doing well, physically, and my cousin, Caleb—the CEO of Caravel—approached the family lawyers about obtaining guardianship over my person and property."

"What? Like adopting you?"

"No." She sighed. It might've been the hundredth time she'd sighed since meeting me for lunch. I'd stopped counting after thirteen. "Caleb is not a good person. If you marry me, he'll try to make your life difficult. He'll threaten everyone you care about, your family."

"*Pshaw*. He doesn't scare me. He's older than us, but he looks like the sort that still trips over his umbilical cord, you know? Needs everything spelled out with alphabet soup, doesn't get the picture unless it's finger-painted. I've known a lot of guys like that, fucktrumpet shitbags. Now if he were like Alex,"—I made a show of shivering—"then I might be worried. Too wicked smart for his own good, that kid isn't right."

She picked up her grilled cheese but didn't take a bite. Kat had this face when she was fighting a smile and I loved it. Her eyes were bright, like I'd said something hilarious but, for whatever reason, she didn't want to laugh. Just made me want to see her laugh even more.

Clearing her throat, she said, "To answer your original question, he wants to have me declared mentally incompetent and committed so he can control my shares in Caravel Pharmaceuticals once my father passes away."

"Committed?" I recoiled at that. "You mean put in a mental hospital?"

"That's right. Which is why I need to be married. If I'm married, then my spouse has priority of guardianship if I'm determined to be mentally incompetent." She took a small, careful bite of her sandwich, and then chewed super slowly.

I'd never seen anyone take so much care eating a sandwich. It was a little weird, but also cute.

"How can he do that? You're not crazy."

She winced a little at the word "crazy," placing her sandwich back on the tray and wiping her hands with a napkin. Her hair fell forward while she concentrated on wiping her hands. After a moment, she tucked the length of it behind her ears and lifted her chin, her chocolate eyes distant again. I swear, it was like this woman had an on/off switch for her emotions.

"One of the reasons I ran away from home was because my father planned on committing me when I was fifteen."

"Why?"

"I wanted his attention. I'd tried being the perfect daughter, getting straight A's, keeping my head down at school and avoiding all trouble —which was everywhere, and which basically made me a pariah—but each time I saw him, maybe once every other year, it was like . . ." Her eyes grew distant.

"Like what?"

She blinked, as though she was coming out of a trance. "Like he was waiting for me to show signs of schizophrenia. Like he was assessing my mental fitness. If I did anything at all suspect—an involuntary twitch, twisting my fingers, blinking too many times—he'd call in a specialist. Sometimes I wondered if he wanted me to be like her. So, eventually, I did what he expected. I was volatile, emotional. I did stupid things. One of those stupid things was fake a suicide attempt."

I nodded, completely understanding why a dumb kid of fifteen would do something so drastic to get the attention of someone like Zachariah Tyson.

I also didn't like seeing her eyes this way, like she needed to distance herself from me, from whatever freak-out she thought I would have, before she could talk about her past.

"Well." I picked up my sandwich, took a bite, chewed, swallowed, and then said, "This is some heavy shit."

Her lips hitched higher on one side, her gaze warming.

"Fucking angsty, emo, adolescent dumbass logic." I took another bite of my sandwich to hide my grin, because now she was grinning.

"Yep." Then she rained on her own good mood by adding, "That basically sums me up."

"Nah." I swallowed a gulp of soda, returning the turkey sandwich to the platter and reached for the cheese steak. "But if you want to take responsibility for your father being a suck-ass parent, ignoring you, and dealing with a cry for help by ignoring his kid some more,"—I shrugged—"then I guess that's your choice. Just like it's my choice to write your father off as a heartless prick."

She stared at me, looking a little confused and a lot irritated. "You don't know my father. He was—he is—a great man."

I shook my head, because *this fucking guy.*

I knew about this guy. I'd known a little about him before Kat had asked me to marry her and I'd researched him a lot over the last week. He'd developed a drug or cure for something, something big and profitable, though I'd forgotten what. And he'd donated a lot of money to a lot of charities. All the pictures of him cutting ribbons and holding other people's babies, he always looked so superior and *deserving.*

As far as I was concerned, he deserved jack-fucking-squat, and he certainly didn't deserve Kat's loyalty.

"No, he might've been a great scientist and philanthropist, but he was definitely a shitty man."

She looked like she wanted to argue, like it was important to her that I kiss the ass of this wankface's legacy. Fuck that.

Thankfully, her cell vibrated again in her hand, drawing her attention away from my words.

She sighed.

"Eugene?" I guessed.

"Yes," she growled.

I hid another smile behind my sandwich. Let the record show, Kit-Kat was wicked sexy when she growled. She was wicked sexy all the time. Maybe I should've had more respect for her struggle, for this difficult time she was going through, and shouldn't have been noticing how her bottom lip pushed out when she lifted her chin, or how her eyes—even when cold and detached—were the most gorgeous fucking eyes I'd ever seen.

Yeah. Good luck not noticing, Danny boy. Just pray to all the angels and saints that she doesn't bend over to pick something up.

I almost choked on my bite of sandwich just thinking about it. But then, as usual when I started thinking about her this way, Kat's declaration from that morning in Vegas echoed through my mind.

"I've never been good at monogamy," she'd said.

I'd decided a long time ago that, just like how my aunt Becks's choices wasn't my business, as long as nobody was getting hurt, other people doing what made them happy shouldn't concern me. It wasn't my place to judge, or even have an opinion. My aunt had found a lifestyle that made her happy. Why should I throw shit at her parade?

That said . . . I really fucking hated it that Kat was polyamorous.

You're such an asshole.

"He's not going to let this go," Kat muttered, rubbing her forehead again.

"Let what go?" I'd forgotten what we were talking about. I'd been too preoccupied lamenting Kat's lifestyle choices and what it meant for my dick.

Not for the first time since she'd asked me last week, I was having dumbass thoughts about maybe, possibly, this whole marriage thing working out for us. For example, let's say, hypothetically, if there were some way I could keep her all to myself while we were married, even if at first it remained platonic between us—

129

Wait a second, IF it remains platonic? Of course it's going to remain platonic. She asked you to marry her, Daniel. Not feed the kitty.

She needed help, not more complications. I knew this.

However—for example, let's say, hypothetically—if one day her kitty is hungry, I'll be there to feed it.

See? I'm an asshole.

But at least I'm an honest asshole.

"Don't worry about it." She glowered at her phone, leaning forward while she typed out a message.

My attention dropped to the screen and—if I squinted, which I did —I could make out the last few texts.

Eugene: *Did he sign the postnup?*

Eugene: *As a reminder, it's in your email inbox. An informal signature is fine. We can execute a more formal version with witnesses the next time you're in Boston.*

Kat: *I'm not asking him. Stop texting me.*

I snatched her phone before she could hit send on the last text.

"Hey!" She reached for her cell, but I held it out and to the side.

A postnup.

Again, another thing I should've anticipated. *Why the hell hadn't I thought about that?*

"You gotta be kidding me with this. Of course I'm signing a post-nup, Kat. Are you serious? You weren't going to ask me?"

"Dan—"

"You think anyone will believe you have all your marbles if you don't insist on some kind of marriage contract?" While I spoke I gave her my back and deleted the text she hadn't sent. Then I hammered out a response to this Eugene guy.

Kat: *Hey. This is Dan. Send me the thing. I'll sign it. Here's my email.*

I felt her eyes on me, the weight and heat of her displeasure, and fuck me, that was sexy too. When I turned back to her and held out her phone, she grabbed it. Then she read the message I'd just sent. Then her eyes turned into little swords of fury.

"You will not sign it."

I snorted, laughing a little. "Uh, yeah. Sure."

"Dan,"—she leaned forward and grabbed my wrist, looking stern and a little scary—"what if Caleb uses it as evidence that you're not fit to be my guardian? That I don't trust you?"

"You think your lawyer guy would have me sign something if it negated the marriage or exposed you to criticism? No. He's the expert. He wouldn't be calling you every five minutes if it weren't important. We both know the real reason you don't want to ask me to sign a postnup is the same reason you offered to pay me."

She was still uneasy, and though her hand remained on my wrist, her grip lessened. "It doesn't seem fair. I'm asking so much of you, and you get nothing out of this."

Oh Kit-Kat, if you only knew.

"Look,"—I covered her fingers with mine—"you don't seem to understand the situation here, so I'm going to mansplain it to you."

She huffed a surprised laugh, which grew as she tucked her lips between her teeth, her shoulders shaking with silent laughter. She stared at me, her eyes glassy with humor, but also desperation.

"You got something like, a gabillion dollars, right?"

She stared at me, her laughter tapering.

"I'll take that as a yes. Well, I don't have a gabillion dollars. So, to protect your ass . . . sets, it's a really fucking good idea to get a contract, a postnup." I could see she was still skeptical, so I added, "Plus, I need to protect my own ass . . . sets."

"From me?" Her gorgeous eyes grew thoughtful. "But I owe you everything—"

"I have Wally, don't I?" Of course Wally was the first thing I thought of, because he was rarely far from my mind. "You think I want you taking Wally if we divorce?"

The uncertainty behind her stare told me she wasn't convinced about the contract, and her words confirmed it. "It doesn't seem right. You won't let me give you anything in return. Please. Please let me pay you, or . . . or anything you want. Please."

She'd leaned forward, her stunning face just a few inches from mine—maybe six, or eight at the most—and I caught a whiff of something that smelled like coconut. Her perfume? Nah. More likely her shampoo or lotion. My sisters' perfume always smelled like flowers, but their lotions usually smelled like food.

Faced with Kat's pleading eyes, and her smelling like something I would eat, I had a selfish thought.

"There is one thing."

I wasn't a good person. But in this moment, I was really okay with that.

"What? What is it?"

"I do have one request."

"Anything."

"For however long we're married, however long you need me, I ask that . . ." I inhaled all the air that would fill my lungs, but—as usual—it didn't feel like enough; that shitty feeling in my chest was back in a big way. Don't worry, my selfishness allowed me to power through. "I ask that you don't have any relationships of an—uh—intimate nature with anyone else." Studying her closely, I didn't miss the blanket of frost sliding over her features. Or how she removed her hand from mine.

She swallowed. The face she made after swallowing had me wondering what tasted so bitter. "Yes. Fine. That's fine."

"Good. Then it's settled." I leaned back in my chair while we traded glares. She looked like she wanted to speak, like a protest was on the tip of her tongue, but she stayed quiet. Instead opting to look at something incredibly interesting in her lap, her hair falling forward to cover her face.

I heard her clear her throat from her hiding place—yes, I knew she hid behind her beautiful hair . . . often—but she said nothing.

Maybe I should've felt like an ass for asking, for making demands. I didn't.

I was getting hitched to a woman I was crazy about, so excuse me if I didn't want to watch her get all polyamorous in our marriage. Yeah, it was fake. Yeah, it wasn't going to last. But as long as it did last, why would I want to put myself through that masochistic bullshit?

No fucking way.

I might've been enlightened on some things, self-aware like she said, but not with this.

Never with this.

* * *

AFTER LUNCH I was in a bad fucking mood. Rather than meeting with Alex to go over security specs for the Caplan Banking job, I went home to see Wally.

I didn't like how Kat and I had left things. She'd grown cold as soon as I made my request, like it offended her, or I'd insulted her.

I wasn't trying to insult her, and it bothered me she'd taken it that way. But I wasn't going to bend on this, and that was fucking that.

So of course, while I was stomping around Grant Park, throwing a ball for Wally, broody as a grounded sixteen-year-old, my mother decided to finally return my phone calls.

"Daniel."

"Ma."

"Are you well?" She was angry. If the straight-to-voicemail treatment for the last week hadn't tipped me off, her tone now was a dead giveaway.

"I'm great," I lied. "And how are you?"

"Fine."

I laughed, silently. If she heard me laugh, she'd have my balls.

"Did you get my messages?"

"Yes. Thank you for calling."

I waited for a minute, for her to say more. She didn't.

"I leave you twenty-one messages, three calls a day, and that's all you got for me?"

"I'm not going to apologize for needing some time to cool off and

I'm not going to sugarcoat it. Who do you think I am? Willy Wonka? You missed my birthday." She sniffed. And these weren't crocodile tears either. I'd hurt her feelings.

Ahh, there it is. The acrid taste of guilt.

"Ma . . ."

"I don't ask for a lot. I love you. I love my children. I want you to call me on my birthday."

"I know." I was clutching my chest so my heart didn't fall out and bleed all over the grass.

"What could have been so important that you couldn't spare a few minutes for your mother? I was so worried."

"I did call you—"

"Don't shit on a plate and tell me it's fudge, Daniel. You called after midnight."

I hadn't come up with a plausible lie for why I hadn't called on her birthday, because I wasn't a liar. I hated lying. Premeditated lying, coming up with a story ahead of time, crafting it, was Seamus's game. If I absolutely had to lie, I subscribed to spur-of-the-moment lying; it made me less of a soulless maggot.

"That's true, Ma. But I swear I—"

"Don't you fucking swear, Daniel. Don't you fucking do that. I raised you kids better."

"Sorry, sorry."

"What was so important, huh?" She heaved a watery sigh. "I thought you were in a ditch, dying somewhere. I had Father Matthew on standby to give you your last rights. Was your phone broken?"

"No."

"Did you forget?" Her voice broke on the last word and it was like being stabbed. The worst.

"No, I sw—ah, I mean, I didn't forget." Lie. Lying lie. Lying liar.

"Then what?"

I grimaced, shutting my eyes, taking a deep breath and said, "I'm married."

Silence.

Complete fucking silence.

I thought maybe she wasn't even breathing.

Meanwhile, in my brain:

Oh.

Shit.

What.

The.

Fuck.

Have.

I.

Done.

. . . However.

However, on the other hand, I was married. *I am married.* Not a lie.

Yeah, we hadn't had the ceremony yet, but the paperwork was filed, and legally speaking, Kat and I were married.

I listened as my mom took a breath, said nothing, and then took another. "Are you pulling my leg with this?" On the plus side, she didn't sound sad anymore.

"No, no. I promise. I'm married. I—uh—was getting married."

"Wait a minute, you got married on my birthday?"

Uh . . .

"Uh . . ."

"Daniel?"

"No. We didn't get married on your birthday." *Shit. Fuck.* "We've been married for a month, and Kat had an emergency on Wednesday." Technically, not lies.

"That's her name? Cat?"

"Kathleen. Her name is Kathleen."

"Like your great aunt Kathleen?"

Kat wasn't a thing like my great aunt. "Yeah, the name is spelled the same."

"Last month? You got married last month?" She sounded bewildered, like she was having trouble keeping up. "Is she—is she Irish?"

"No."

"Oh. That's okay. Catholic?"

Oh jeez, I really hadn't thought this through. Maybe it was time for me to reconsider my spur-of-the-moment approach to lying and just surrender to being a soulless maggot.

"No. She's not Catholic."

"Oh." My mom didn't sound disappointed, just a little surprised and maybe a little worried. "Daniel, I—you were married last month and I'm only hearing about it now? How long have you known this woman?"

I winced. "Two and a half years."

"Two and a half years?" she screeched. "What else are you hiding, huh? You two have a couple of kids? You playing left wing for the Bruins next season? You and Tom Brady shoot the shit on the weekends?"

"Ma—"

"That's a long time, bub. You've been together over two years and you never wanted to introduce her to your mother?" The hurt edge in my mom's voice sliced me open. I needed to get this conversation back on track before I was dealing with full-out tears of acid.

"Listen, Ma. It was sudden. Really sudden. I've known her for over two years, yes. But we were friends. Then one thing led to another and we were married in a rush at the Cook County Clerk's office. It was nothing fancy."

"Is she pregnant?" She sounded hopeful.

"No."

"Oh." Frustration. "Let me get this straight. You were married in a County Clerk's office? What were you thinking? Were her parents there?" She sounded like she didn't know if she was hurt or irritated.

"No. Her parents are not—her dad has Alzheimer's. He doesn't know who she is."

"Oh no. That's terrible." She made a sad *tutting* sound. "And her mother? Was her mom there? Please tell me she had her mother there on her wedding day to my son."

"No, Ma. Her mother has—" I didn't want to finish that sentence. The word "schizophrenia" was loaded, conjured all sorts of scary assumptions. My ma was an ICU nurse, but still. As far as I knew, the closest my family had ever come to a diagnosed mental illness was

Uncle Zip's short-term memory loss. A construction crane falling on him during the Big Dig had caused that. He also got a metal plate in his head and would stick magnets to his face during parties, but that wasn't mental illness. That was just Uncle Zip.

"Her mother is unwell and is institutionalized," I finally finished.

She was quiet for a moment and, knowing my mom, I could almost see her expression as she stared into space, trying to sort through all I'd told her. "Who am I even talking to right now? I don't understand this. It's so unlike you. Didn't you want me there? Your sisters?"

"Yes. Of course I wanted—"

"What about your aunts and uncles? And cousins? I know you're not speaking to Seamus, but a wedding should be a celebration where you're surrounded by people who love you. Not an afterthought at the fucking courthouse during your lunch break. That's no way to welcome Kathleen into our family. What must she think of us?" Now she sounded disappointed. Really fucking disappointed. And angry.

So there was only one thing to do. Own it. "You're right."

"Of course I'm right." She sniffed. "And now it's time for *you* to make this right."

"What if we throw a big party in Boston? Invite the whole family. It'll be like a wedding reception, with cake, a bouquet toss, the whole thing."

"Really?" She perked up, but then she huffed. "No. That's no good. I don't want the future mother of my grandchildren throwing a party for my family *and me*. I should be throwing a party for *her*. Did she get a bridal shower? Anything to celebrate the occasion? And what do I tell people who want to send gifts?" My mom made a strangled sound of frustration. "And what do I tell Father Matthew? Goddamn Father Matthew. He's gonna be pissed."

"Ma . . ."

"Don't *ma* me. This isn't right, and you know it. Do you love this girl?"

"Yes." I didn't hesitate. Easiest lie I'd ever told.

"You love your family?"

"Of course."

137

"Then bring her home. I've been waiting to meet her my whole life."

"You just found out about her ten minutes ago!"

"Don't be a smartass. You know what I meant. Introduce her to your mother, your family. Show her you respect her, that you're proud of her. Don't be a fucking sneak. Loving a person isn't something to be ashamed of."

"It's not like that—"

"Good. You'll bring her home. You'll stay here in your old room."

When I hesitated, she said, "Daniel, you forget my birthday and now you're keeping my daughter-in-law from me?"

"I'm not keeping her from you."

"So help me God, if you don't bring that girl home, I'll take out an ad on Craigslist for season tickets to the Sox and list your cell phone number. There's no problem, is there? I expect you both over Labor Day. I'll call Kathrine, she'll tell Quinn to give you the day off."

Kathrine was Quinn's mother, and one of my mother's best friends.

"Don't call Mrs. Sullivan. If I want to take the day off, then I'll take the day off."

"Great. Love you. See you both soon."

"Ma, wait—shit."

She hung up.

Fuck.

Fuck that fucking duck.

CHAPTER NINE

Fashion Police: Authorities that will arrest you for wearing the wrong thing.

URBAN DICTIONARY.COM

Kat

WHILE PULLING ON my Friday sweater—which coordinated with the rest of my Friday outfit—I remembered that I needed a wedding dress.

I knew it didn't really need to be a *wedding dress*. It just needed to be something different than my Thursday outfit.

It could be what you're wearing now, for example.

Biting my thumbnail, I stared at the sparse contents of my closet. I didn't want to wear my Friday outfit to get married. And my Wednesday outfit was dirty. My eyes slid to my Monday outfit—gray pants and a white shirt—and I frowned. There was nothing wrong with Monday's outfit, but I couldn't bring myself to wear it.

The truth was, I didn't want to wear any of my weekday attire for the ceremony. Perhaps I was being ridiculous, but the thought of getting married in khaki pants and an Oxford shirt made me feel an indefinable kind of unhappy.

My eyes moved to the far left side of my closet without me explicitly telling them to do so, likely because the left side of my closet was where I stored all the clothes I bought but rarely had a chance to wear: high heeled shoes, funky shirts and sweaters, and pretty dresses that I'd found on sale.

I ignored a new kind of indefinably unhappy and thumbed through the hangers. Seven items deep, I stopped, my heart jumping to my throat with longing as I rubbed the thin satin material between my thumb and forefinger of a pale pink halter maxi dress. The waist was shirred and pleated leading to an ankle-length trumpet hem. The back was open and would expose my skin from neck to waist, which was why I'd never worn it outside of the store. I didn't have a halter bra.

But it was just so darn pretty, and I felt so darn pretty wearing it, and—darn it—I wanted to feel pretty on my wedding day.

Fake wedding day.

Fake.

But still.

I didn't know how long I stood there, staring at it, debating. But when I glanced at the alarm clock next to my bed, I yanked the dress out of the closet on a rush. My dawdling was in danger of making me late. Since I was leaving work early—hopefully my last modified schedule for the foreseeable future—I needed to get to work by 5:30 AM.

Hurriedly, I tucked it into my simple canvas garment bag, the one I used to carry dry-cleaning home, stuffed my pair of nude heels into my backpack, and was out the door. I didn't allow myself to think about the dress. Short of skipping work and buying something else, I was stuck with my choice and that was that.

Luckily, despite my closet contemplations, I arrived at my desk with a few minutes to spare. Unlike the last two times I knew I'd be spending time in Dan's company, I was able to concentrate just fine.

I suspected this was because his request at the end of lunch yesterday had left me annoyed.

Annoyance flavored with righteous indignation.

It was as though he thought I was incapable of controlling myself, or having respect for another person's feelings. This was especially aggravating because my problem was the exact opposite. I couldn't *not* control myself. Control was what I lived and breathed and consumed. The only treatment I'd identified for my crippling control was drugs and/or alcohol, and I refused to self-medicate anymore.

Coming from him, someone I liked and admired as much as I liked and admired Dan, it stung. More than a paper cut , more than a bee sting, the hurt lingered after lunch and for the rest of the day—during my Thursday night class, walking home from the university, while I tossed and turned in bed—until I'd fallen asleep and dreamt of Dan being revealed as a Dalek in disguise. And then I had to exterminate him.

Which was why, when Steven called after lunch on Friday, pulling me out of the work-zone, I was surprised it was already 4:14 PM.

"How is it already past three?" I scratched my jaw, clicking over to my emails to ensure there weren't any emergencies that needed to be addressed. Seeing none, I enabled my out-of-office responder.

"What time are we meeting your man, Dan, at the Clerk's office? Five? BTW, aren't you impressed I haven't been calling you all day?"

I was impressed. It was very un-Steven-like.

"He's not my man. He's helping me because he is a nice person." *Though, maybe a tad uncharitable. And judgmental.* "Dan and I are leaving here at four thirty. You're supposed to meet us at the County Clerk's office between five and five fifteen. We'll be the last ceremony of the day."

"Oh, that's right. I remember now. I can't wait. I will be the best witness. The best. I will put all other witnesses to shame. I will give witness harder than—"

"Yes. I know." I laughed at my friend. "Just be there before five fifteen, earlier if you can manage it. Do you have any plans after?"

"No. Not really. Why? Do you want me to come out with you and Dan?"

"Uh, no. I won't be going out with Dan afterward. I'm sure he has other things to do. But maybe you and I could go see a movie?"

Steven was quiet for a second. He found this surprising? We often saw a movie on a Friday night.

"Let me see if I have this right." Steven paused again, and then said, "You and Dan are getting married this afternoon, and then you propose that you and I head out to catch a movie afterward? Is that right?"

"Only if you have time."

"What would you do if I didn't have time?"

I shrugged. "I guess go home and study."

He sighed. Loudly. "This is so wrong. This just feels so wrong. Kat, you're getting married to Dan the Security Man, the guy of your dreams, and you sound like we're discussing having a mole removed."

"He's not the man of my dreams." I checked the time, ignoring the burst of aggravation in my chest.

"Since when?"

"Since Vegas," I snapped, but then pressed my lips together, shaking my head at myself.

"Kat?"

"I'm sorry, but you were right, I should have stopped obsessing about him when he left me in that hotel room. I'm so tired of this."

"Of what?"

"Of . . . hiding. Of letting other people drive the conversation. Of letting what other people think about me *matter.* Of being quiet and well-behaved. You know what? I should've believed him when he showed me who he was."

"And who is that?"

"Someone who might be enlightened and open-minded about some things, but who jumps to condemnatory conclusions." The words arrived harsher than I'd intended, and I winced at how acrimonious I sounded. "No, that's not true. He's . . . he's a good guy. Obviously, he's an amazing guy. And he's helping me, and I'm so grateful. I owe him so much, and I'm not being fair. He's a great guy. So great."

He seemed to be waiting for me to continue; when I didn't, he prompted, "But . . . ?"

"But the man of my dreams wouldn't hold my past against me, not if I've learned from it. I guess I'm grateful that I put him on a pedestal, because doing so taught me not to put people on pedestals. And it taught me that no one will ever be happy with me—no matter how polite I am, or quiet, no matter how accommodating—so maybe I just need to be happy with myself. Dan will make someone *else* very happy, and that someone else will be very lucky." *Someone with less baggage.*

"Okay." Steven didn't sound convinced. "Whatever you say."

"Listen, I have to go." I rubbed my forehead, feeling suddenly tired. "Are you at Dan's place? Because the Clerk's office is super close to his apartment."

"No. I'm in the building."

"Did you want to ride over with us? I'm changing there."

"No. I can't. I have a few things to finish up before the weekend. Don't worry, I'll be on time."

"For once," I teased.

"Ha-ha. And yes to the movie as long as I get to pick. And you let me smuggle contraband York Peppermint Patties in your purse."

"Deal. Oh, hey, you could bring the guy you've been seeing. What was his name?"

"I haven't told you his name," he deadpanned, shutting me down. "See you soon."

"See you."

Ending the call, I reflected on Steven's unwillingness to disclose his love interest's identity. *Who could it be?*

I mulled over the potential suspects on my way to the lobby and came up empty. Steven had always been more than willing to discuss his disastrous love life. Sometimes he had Janie and me in stitches recounting his hilarious, but unfortunate, escapades. But he'd never mentioned anyone in particular who'd caught his eye.

When the elevator doors opened, I found Dan standing in the same spot he'd been in yesterday. Like yesterday, he wore all black—pants, shirt, jacket, no tie. Unlike yesterday, I didn't feel the need to hesitate, to mentally prepare.

Stepping off the lift, I walked to him, contented in my numbness.

"Hi," I said, giving him a little wave as I approached. I pushed one hand in my pocket, and the other held my garment bag. Careful to stop a good five feet away, I didn't want a cheek kiss or embrace repeat from the day before. "Should we go?"

His gaze flickered over me, his expression inscrutable. "Sure."

"Please. Lead the way." I gave him a tight smile.

Dan didn't move. Instead, he lifted his chin toward my garment bag. "Are you planning to change?"

Looking him over, the dark suit that was basically his uniform, I felt a renewed burst of embarrassment and silliness about my desire to look my best. But then I chloroformed that burst of embarrassment.

I wanted to look nice for *me,* and there was absolutely nothing wrong with that. I desired it. End of story.

Dan could wear a Speedo for all I cared—*gah! Dangerous imagery! Alert! Divert thoughts! Fury, determination, indignation . . . much better*—but I would wear this pretty dress and I refused to feel silly about it.

Lifting my chin and feeling defiant, I responded, "Yes. I was planning on it. But I can change at the Clerk's office."

"Do you mind if we stop by my place to change? Wally could use a quick walk and I was planning on changing too."

Hey! Maybe he's planning to switch into a Speedo.

I chloroformed that thought too and shrugged, nodding once. "Sounds good."

Dan's gaze lingered on my garment bag, his features still inscrutable. He then turned, his shoulders rising and falling as though taking a deep breath, and strolled to the lobby doors.

Perhaps he was no longer my dream man. But the simple truth was, *not* ogling Dan the Security Man was impossible.

I walked a few feet behind him, possibly thinking about how nice his butt would look in a Speedo.

CHAPTER TEN

Marital Privilege (aka spousal privilege): There are two types of
marital privilege recognized by US law:
1. Testimonial Privilege: In criminal cases, one spouse may refuse to
testify against his/her defendant spouse as a witness.
2. Communications Privilege: In both criminal and civil cases, communications between spouses during the marriage are privileged. This
applies to both words and acts intended to be a private communication.

WEX LEGAL DICTIONARY

Dan

STAN PICKED US up in one of the company cars. We were close
enough to the East Randolph Street property that it made sense to
change there, check on Wally, and then head to the clerk's office for the
ceremony.

I glanced at the back of Kat's head. She was sitting in the back seat
with me, but had herself pressed against the door on her side, keeping
as much distance as possible between us.

Her posture had me antsy. I felt like I needed to apologize. I ignored that feeling. Mild discomfort now would likely save me some seriously nasty discomfort later.

But still, I was antsy.

So I tried, "What are you doing tonight? Got any plans?"

She stiffened, then held perfectly still. Eventually she responded, "I need to study."

"No class on Fridays?"

"No. Monday and Thursday nights." Her voice was quiet. Controlled. Distant.

"Oh," I said, rubbing my chest with the fingers of one hand, because that shitty feeling was back and it felt a lot like heartburn.

Having nothing more to say to the back of her head, I turned my phone back on to check messages. I'd turned my phone off while waiting for her in the lobby. I'd wanted the next hour to myself. Really, I'd wanted Kat to myself.

But now that she was giving me the silent treatment, there was no reason for me to dodge work. As soon as my phone connected to the cell network, all my notifications went off. One in particular caught my attention. It was from Alex.

Alex: *We took Wally for the night. You're welcome.*

I lifted an eyebrow. Typical Alex. I'd given up trying to keep him out of my apartment. My dog liked the kid too much, and I wasn't going to complain if it meant Wally got more exercise and company.

But last week, Alex had changed Kat's contact information in my phone to *Wife*. He hadn't owned up to it, but I knew it had been him. Who else could it be? He knew everything, was like some sort of fucking mind reader. Or a genius. One or the other.

Probably the latter . . . probably.

Stan parked in front of the apartment building and opened Kat's door while I climbed out my side.

We entered the building, took the elevator to my floor, and walked down the hall and into my place, all the while I answered text messages.

"So, Alex just messaged. He has Wally. We can get changed and go."

"Okay."

Holding my cell to my ear, I listened to Betty list off all the changes to my schedule next week, and I gestured toward the second bedroom. "You can use that room. I'll be right back."

She tugged her backpack higher and clutched her garment bag to her chest. Still not looking at me, she disappeared into the bedroom.

I put Betty on speaker while I changed in my room, pulling on my newest suit. Quinn and I used a guy in Chicago for our suits and shirts, all handmade, all custom-cut. Once you went custom-cut, you never went back. There was no comparison between a bespoke suit of clothes and something off the rack.

It was the difference between watching a Sox game on TV versus Fenway Park. You knew something was lacking, but you couldn't comprehend the disparity until you took your seat behind home base and "Sweet Caroline" played over the loudspeaker. No comparison.

But enough about suits and baseball.

I glanced at myself in the mirror, my attention snagging on the Celtic ink at the side of my neck. I frowned at the tattoos, or what was visible of them, and turned from the mirror to the bureau. Opening the top drawer, my attention settled on the velvet box in the front right corner. I'd bought it in London, from the same guy—or, I guess *bloke* —Quinn had used for Janie's engagement ring.

Maybe I was an idiot, but I wanted Kat to wear a ring I'd bought for her. Yeah, it was a fake marriage. Yeah, it didn't mean anything. I knew it was all a ruse, we both did. So what was the harm?

If she didn't like it, then she didn't have to wear it. No harm. No biggie.

I stuffed the box in my front pocket and grabbed my keys and wallet.

Taking Betty off speaker, I held my phone to my ear as I strolled out of the master bedroom, making a mental note to double-check the figures for our clients in the London financial district before next Monday.

And then Betty's voice faded away, and all thoughts of work and clients and next Monday completely fled my mind. Because I was staring. At Kat.

She was . . . there were no words.

But I could tell you she was standing next to the couch, reading something on her cell, and wearing a dress.

It was long, almost to the floor. The material looked soft and thin, and would've been see-through except there were layers of it. It was the same color as her lips: rose pink. Her gorgeous shoulders and arms were bare. From the looks of it, so was her back, except the tie at her neck—hidden by her hair—trailed between her shoulder blades, along bare skin of her spine to her waist.

The woman was a fucking vision.

And I was so fucked.

I hadn't quite recovered when she looked up and caught me staring. And like the dumb fuck I was, I just kept staring, particularly when I realized there was no way she could show all that skin *and* wear a bra. Unless there was some bra made of witchcraft and the invisible wings of fairies that I didn't know about.

Miraculously, she didn't seem to notice my staring. Her eyes were too busy moving over my suit.

So, there we were. Me looking at her with lust in my heart, her looking at me with . . . I don't know, maybe appreciation? Hard to tell. I couldn't see past the lust.

Thou shalt not covet thy neighbor's cow, Daniel, came a stern voice in the back of my mind. It sounded a lot like Sister Mary Roseanne, my first grade teacher. I mentally made a rude gesture at the voice. First, because Kat wasn't a cow. Second, because my neighbor was Steven, and everybody knew he liked dick.

"Should we go?" Kat turned away from me, her hair falling forward over her shoulder and hiding her face. But it also revealed the tie at the base of her neck and the olive-toned expanse of her back. I suspected that one pull of the string would cause a wonderful cascade of events.

Then I couldn't stop thinking about those events.

I didn't answer, because the words I wanted to say were the wrong ones. Instead, I ripped my eyes from her and walked to the door, holding it open. She walked past, this time fiddling with bracelets at her wrist.

The walk down the hall, the ride in the elevator, the stroll in the lobby—all of it was spent in tense silence. Tense and agitated. I was combatting a serious case of blood loss to my brain. No matter how I sat in the back of the SUV on the trip to the Clerk's office, I couldn't get comfortable.

Neither of us said a word as we exited the car, and we both kept our own company when we reentered the building we'd visited last week. We walked through the security line and metal detector. Not bothering to give our name to the receptionist, I led the way to Luis's cubicle and knocked on the counter to gain his attention.

Much like before, my friend glanced up from his computer monitor and gave both Kat and me a smile. Luis hustled out from behind his station to greet us. In his hand was a bottle of champagne.

"Your friend is already with Mr. Lee. You two clean up well." His eyes were on Kat as he handed her the bottle.

"Thank you. So much." For the first time since we'd left the restaurant yesterday, I saw her face brighten and she grinned, moving forward to give Luis a brief hug and a kiss on the cheek. "This really wasn't necessary."

I noticed he hadn't let her go. His hand had settled on the bare skin of her upper back. And . . . I was jealous.

Fuck.

I'd never been jealous *in my life.*

My sisters had dated jealous guys. I never wanted to be one of those guys. But here I was, one of those guys, and Kat and I weren't even really together.

So fucked, Daniel. You are so incredibly fucked.

I suppressed the urge to break all the bones in Luis's hand— because I was a motherfucking adult, *thankyouverymuch*—and instead cleared my throat. With meaning.

Luis glanced to me, a happy smile on his happy face. But then his smile dropped and so did his hands.

"Uh, Mr. Lee is expecting you. You're the last ones he's seeing today." Luis took a step away from Kat, his eyes big and uneasy.

If my expression was anything like my mood, I understood why he was wearing his *please don't murder me* face. Even so, and not allowing myself to think too much about the impulse, I stepped next to Kat and wrapped an arm around her, my hand settling on her waist.

"We'll follow you." I lifted my chin, indicating that Luis should lead the way, which he promptly did.

Kat and I followed, her stiffly walking by my side, while I cursed myself for being such a fucking idiot.

Over the course of our knowing each other, I figured we'd spent less than five hours total talking—including quick hellos and goodbyes —and maybe seventy-two hours in each other's company, counting last week, yesterday, and today. Seventy-two hours. Mostly consisting of me watching her while she knitted and laughed with her friends. That's it. Maybe less. Our conversation during lunch yesterday was the longest discussion we'd ever had, if you didn't count what happened in Vegas.

For the record, I didn't count what happened in Vegas. She'd been drunk for most of it.

How was it possible, then, that I'd be this worked up? That she'd been all I could think about over the last week? It didn't make any sense. I needed to get this thing—this shitty feeling—under control, because not only was I making myself crazy, I was making her uncomfortable.

And that was bullshit.

Using a mental crowbar, I removed my hand from her back and scratched my neck, glancing at her profile as we walked and wracking my brain for something—anything—that might put her at ease.

Retracing our conversation yesterday, I knew the trouble between us had started when I'd made my request at the end of lunch—that she remain relationship-free during our marriage.

Maybe she thinks you're judging her lifestyle?

That was a definite possibility, and I could see why that would piss Kat off, make her go all stiff and distant. After my big speech over sandwiches about how I didn't want to look at the list on her phone, she probably thought I was a hypocrite.

We paused outside a set of double doors and Luis turned to us. "Just through here."

"Thank you for your help," she said, holding the champagne bottle to her chest. "I really appreciate everything."

"No problem. Happy to do it. Oh, let me hold that for you, just until you're finished." Luis gave Kat one more quick grin, taking the bottle back.

She entered the room ahead of me and I turned to Luis.

"Thanks." I gave him a conciliatory smile, reaching my hand out to shake his.

He accepted. We stared at each other for a second or two, working through my stupid moment from earlier. When he released the shake, I knew we were cool again, and I followed Kat.

The room wasn't big. It wasn't small. But medium didn't seem to be the right word either. Whatever it was, the space resembled a small chapel, just without any religious affiliation.

Steven—who was there as our witness—and Kat stood just inside the door, next to a little circle table with a vase of fake flowers. A stained-glass window of geometric shapes was behind an older man hovering next to a small podium at the far side of the room.

The little old man, who I assumed was Mr. Lee, waved his hand, motioning us forward. "Come on in. I don't bite."

I nodded to Steven and then looked at Kat. She looked at me. She was nervous. Wanting to give her comfort, I smiled and offered my hand. She took it—thank fuck—and I exhaled a quiet sigh of relief as we walked forward together.

"Where do I stand?" Steven asked. I glanced over my shoulder and saw he was trailing behind us.

"Anywhere is fine." Mr. Lee motioned to the left of the podium. "How about here? Good spot for pictures."

Steven walked around us, taking the place Mr. Lee had indicated, and clasped his hands in front of him like he didn't know where to put them. He also looked nervous.

Why the fuck was he nervous? All he had to do was stand there.

We hadn't quite made it to the podium when Kat said, "You know . . ." and then stopped. She pressed her lips together, shaking her head.

"What?"

"I wasn't—" Kat took a deep breath. She whispered very, very softly and in a hurry, "I wasn't coming on to your friend."

I glanced at her, surprise slowing my steps. We were still a good ten feet from where Mr. Lee and Steven were waiting. Kat was blushing, her cheeks and neck were tinted pink, but her jaw was set, and a stubborn light in her eyes.

"Despite what you think, I wouldn't do that," she continued, still whispering, a frown between her eyebrows. "You don't have to worry about me coming on to every random person."

Whoa.

"Kat,"—I stepped closer to her, dipping my head toward hers and also whispering—"I didn't—I don't think you were—or are—or—"

We'd made it to the podium. Frustrated, I reached into my breast pocket and yanked out the marriage certificate, handing it to Mr. Lee. Meanwhile, I knew she was pissed. At me. And I needed to fix it.

So in the short time it took our officiant to look over our marriage certificate, I decided it was a good idea to inform her, "My aunt is polyamorous."

She blinked. Then she turned her face to mine and blinked some more, like what I'd said was a riddle. "Pardon?"

"I mean, I get it." My attention flickered to Steven—who was watching us with rapt interest—then back to her. "No judgment."

She gave her head a subtle shake. "What are you talking about?"

"You know."

"No. I don't."

"Your lifestyle," I said on a rushed whisper.

"Lifestyle?"

"Polyamory."

"Mr. O'Malley, Ms. Caravel-Tyson." Mr. Lee nodded to us, one at a time. "Before we begin, do you have any questions?"

"Did you just say *polyamory*?" This question was not whispered. Kat pulled her hand from mine and shot me an intensely confused glare.

"Excuse me?" The old timer inclined his head forward, as though he couldn't hear us, or hoped he'd heard her wrong.

"Just a minute." I held a finger up to our officiant, and then faced Kat. "It's cool. Consensual, ethical, and responsible non-monogamy. I dig it. I'm just not into it."

She glared at me for several seconds and I lifted my eyebrows, tilting my head meaningfully toward Mr. Lee.

But Kat either didn't catch the hint or didn't care. "Dan, I have no idea what you're talking about."

"Listen, we'll talk about this later."

"No. We won't. We'll talk about this now." Kat's tone was demanding, and she didn't seem to be bothered that our officiant was glancing between us like we were fruitcakes.

"All right," I ground out, then offered Mr. Lee a flat smile. "We need another minute. Be right back."

I looked to Steven and found him looking at us with engrossed, wide eyes, his mouth open. I wouldn't have been surprised if he'd pulled out a bag of popcorn and started munching on it. Sparing a single glower for my coworker, I gently wrapped my hand around Kat's elbow and guided her to the door at the other side of the room.

Once there, I began with—I swear—the patience of Job. "You said, in Vegas, that you didn't believe in monogamy."

Her eyes darted to the officiant, who—God love this guy—looked like he was taking our drama in stride. "I didn't say that. I said, and I quote, 'I've never been good at monogamy.'"

"Exactly."

"That doesn't mean I'm polyamorous." A wrinkle appeared between her eyebrows and she sounded equal parts confused and annoyed.

My eyes narrowed, moving between hers. Now I was confused.

"Then what the fuck does it mean?"

"It means,"—she stepped closer and lowered her voice—"I was a kid who slept with a bunch of guys while I was drunk and strung out. I thought what I was doing was living life to the fullest before I lost the ability to do so." Then, she muttered like she was arguing with herself, "And maybe I was. It was fun at the time. Or maybe it wasn't. Because it wasn't fun after. I don't know. Does it matter? I just don't want to feel like crap about this anymore."

I blinked at her. "Then why'd you say you weren't monogamous?"

"Uh, Ms. Caravel-Tyson—"

"A minute." I held up my finger again to Mr. Lee, never taking my eyes from Kat. "You were saying?"

"I've only had one-night stands. I've never been with the same person twice."

"What? Never?" I found that shocking as hell, because if I'd been one of those guys, I would've moved heaven and earth to make sure there was a second time. And a third, and a fourth, and a—*you get the picture.*

"No." She shook her head. "Never. But that doesn't mean I'm against monogamy."

"You're not against monogamy?"

"Shh!" She glanced over her shoulder, giving Mr. Lee and Steven an apologetic smile. She stepped even closer to me, again whispering, "It just hasn't come up with anyone."

"It hasn't come up with *anyone*, she says." I threw my hands in the air, giving my eyes to the ceiling and turning away. "I guess I don't count," I muttered, shrugging to myself.

"Can we just—" She followed me, tugging on my sleeve, but didn't seem to know how to finish her sentence.

This was unbelievable.

Unbelievable.

Un*FUCKING*believable.

Not polyamorous.

"If you want to change your mind about this, because of my past, I completely understand—"

I turned to face her. "No. I don't give a flying fuck about your past. I thought—in Vegas, when you said—because my aunt Becks, she's—I thought you meant you weren't—you didn't want—" Shit. I couldn't even speak. Nothing made sense.

She started, frustration evaporating from her features, replaced with dawning surprise. Meanwhile, here I was, caught in the startled, unblinking depths of her eyes.

"I don't understand . . ." The words tumbled from her lips, like she'd spoken without thinking. Her breathing had ticked up, her mouth was open, and her stare was unfocused.

Approaching movement caught my attention. Steven was strolling toward us, a huge smile on his face. "Hey kids. How ya doing? Turns out Mr. Lee needs to go pick up his grandkids so his daughter and her husband can go out to dinner. It's their sixteenth wedding anniversary. They've had some hard times, but things are good now between them —his daughter and son-in-law—so he doesn't want to be late. You understand."

Steven reached for Kat's hand and pulled her back to the front of the room. I watched them for a stunned second. She glanced back at me, her gaze a mess of confusion and something else, something that had my feet moving to catch up.

"Thank you." Mr. Lee turned a grateful smile on Steven.

My coworker winked at him, reclaiming his spot to the left of the podium and pulled out his phone. "Okay. Wedding time," he said, lifting his cell. "Smile for the camera."

I didn't smile.

This changed everything.

Right?

No.

No, you asshole. For you it changes everything. But for her? Big question mark.

In a disconnected stupor, I stood next to her while Mr. Lee talked at us. Steven filmed the whole thing. At one point, we faced each other. Kat looked completely bewildered. She also looked goddamn gorgeous. Her beauty struck out at me, and it felt like an assault. Also an assault, the openness and vulnerability in her eyes. Looking like this, her eyes were hooks, digging deep, made breathing and thinking at the same time impossible.

When my moment came, I repeated the words I was supposed to repeat and put a ring on her finger. She did the same with me. Then the words stopped and we were staring at each other.

Someone said, "You two should kiss."

It sounded like Steven.

I wasn't sure.

But I didn't care who it was, and I definitely didn't need to be told twice.

Her brown eyes dropped to my mouth, growing hazy. She swayed forward. I didn't sway. I advanced on her, moving into her space and putting a finger underneath her chin, Not because I needed to—she was already offering me her mouth—but I did it because I wanted to touch her and that seemed like the safest place.

The truth was, if I touched her anywhere else, this was not going to be a Clerk's-office-appropriate kiss for very long.

Lifting her straining mouth to mine, I brushed my lips against hers, and—*oh man*—I wanted this moment to last. I wanted it to last forever.

Mostly forgetting that we had an old guy on the sidelines, I pressed our mouths together, telling myself to memorize the feel of her. She was so warm, and soft, and sweet. She reached for me. I felt her fingers twist and grab the front of my suit jacket. It was probably going to wrinkle. I couldn't fucking care less.

She tugged me forward. I covered her mouth more fully with mine, licking my tongue against her lips. Immediately—no hesitation—she opened up and her tongue came out to taste mine. I groaned, or she did, it didn't matter. I felt her tremble and I wanted to hold her.

Completely forgetting all my earlier levelheaded ideas about limiting my touch to her face, my arms moved around her waist and my fingers immediately massaged and caressed the bare skin of her back. *God, she was so fucking soft. Like silk.* I brought her flush against me. She released the front of my jacket and slipped her hands beneath, holding me with equal force.

And what started as a very appropriate kiss quickly escalated into basically me trying to eat her face off, because she tasted so fucking good. I was in very real danger of doing something that was illegal in fourteen of the forty-eight contiguous states. Everything was legal in Alaska. In all fairness, she was biting and sucking on my lips like they were made of Kat-nip.

This woman, the taste of her was something I would never recover from. Heaven. I couldn't think.

That wasn't true, I could think, but it was all urges and need. I *needed* more of her.

Before I knew what I was doing, I walked her backward. Why I did this or where I thought we were going, I had no clue. Eventually Kat's back connected with a wall and—because it was there—I used it as leverage.

Her hands grabbed fistfuls of my shirt and yanked it from my pants, she made a lithe rocking motion against me. I returned it, grinding against her, letting her feel how hard I was and growled into her mouth. Maybe I'd feel like an asshole later, but my thoughts were completely consumed with how beautiful, magnificent, and gorgeous she was like this, and how beautiful, magnificent, and gorgeous she was going to feel when we fucked.

Either she sensed the direction of my thoughts and liked it, or her mind was moving on a similar track, because her hands reached into my pants and she grabbed my ass, kneading it with greedy fingers. She gasped as I bent my head to taste her throat, one leg hooking around mine.

It was at this moment that I thought I heard someone clear his throat.

It sounded far away.

I ignored it.

Sliding my hand from her back, needing more of her, more softness and heat, I cupped her breast over her dress and groaned again, because she wasn't wearing a bra. She felt perfect, her nipple hard against my palm. Kat covered my hand with hers, her tongue and mouth ambitious as hell, devouring me with each suck and bite. And then I felt her tug my fingers, encouraging me to slip my hand inside her dress, to touch her without any barriers.

I almost did. I almost fucking did.

But then I felt a goddamn tap on my shoulder.

A. Tap.

On. My. Fucking. Shoulder.

Who the fuck would be tapping me on the shoulder and how the hell did they get in here?

Ready to unleash a world of hurt on this asshole, I tore my mouth from her body, and then I . . .

I blinked.

Steven Thompson, from Cypher Systems, accounting department.

He was glancing between us.

"Time's up. Mr. Lee has to go," he said, grinning like an idiot. "But don't worry, I got the whole thing on video."

CHAPTER ELEVEN

Ledipasvir/sofosbuvir: sold under the trade name **Harvoni**™ among others, is a medication used to treat (and has been shown to cure certain types of) hepatitis C. In the US, Harvoni™ costs $94,500, in Europe less than 50,000 €, and in India (where most international drug patents are not recognized) ~$1,000.

HEPATITIS C SOCIETY

Kat

STAN GLANCED AT us, squinting at our reflections in the rearview mirror, and then away. He appeared equal parts nervous and confused. His discombobulation didn't surprise me given our behavior since leaving the Cook County Clerk's office and entering the car.

Wait a minute. I'm getting ahead of myself. Let me back up.

Dan and I kissed.

That happened.

Excuse me while I take a moment for an internal squeal of exhilaration.

EEEEEEEEEEEEEEEEEEEEEEEEEEEEEEEEEEEEEEEEEEEEEEEEEEEEE!

By the time Steven interrupted, it would be inaccurate to label what we were doing as *a kiss*. We were full-on making out. Therefore, Steven's interruption had been completely appropriate. Not appropriate, however, making out in the officiant's office at the Downtown Clerk's office.

No.

Not. Appropriate.

Not responsible behavior.

My only defense was that I had truly lost control of myself, starting with the moment Dan revealed his assumption that I was polyamorous —and that was why he'd put on the brakes after Vegas—and ending with Steven's interruption. Even in this moment, I was still a little high on his touch, a little loose and uninhibited, and a lot avaricious for it to happen again.

Dan seemed able to pull himself together much faster than I could. Wrapping his arm around my waist, he steered us both to Mr. Lee. A profusion of apologies were on the tip of my tongue, but before I could give voice to them, Dan pulled out a wad of cash, handed it over, thanked the officiant for his time, said nothing to Steven, and led the two of us out of the room.

Keeping me tucked to his side, he retrieved his phone, unlocked it, typed something, then shoved it back in his pocket as we walked past the waiting area, the receptionist, metal detector and bag check, the line of people waiting to get in, and through the front door.

He paused on the steps, craning his neck as though searching for something, or someone. Presumably finding what he sought, Dan guided me down the steps and toward a waiting SUV.

The squeal of exhilaration repeated in my head. I hadn't caught up with, or reconciled, or otherwise successfully moved beyond the kiss.

What did it mean?

That's easy. He's into you.

But, what did it mean for the future? And the past?

That left me to sort through all my previous ideas and potential misconceptions about Daniel O'Malley, which had me blurting, "Polyamory?"

160

He glanced at me as he opened the door to the SUV, giving me his enigmatic smile. "I have an aunt."

"An aunt?"

He placed his hand on my lower back, precariously close to my bottom as I slid into the back seat. "She's in the lifestyle. Seems happy."

Dazed, I scooted to the other side of the bench, allowing Dan plenty of room as he followed me in. Once he closed the door, he looked at me.

I looked at him.

His eyes dropped to my mouth, darkened, and smoldered. That's right, they freaking *smoldered*. I'd never had someone smolder in my general direction, or if I had, I hadn't realized it. But a Dan smolder was impossible to miss and it made my insides feel hot and heavy. It also made me want to climb on his lap and kiss his face off. Based on his smolder, I doubted he'd stop me.

And all of this was very confusing.

How did we get here?

"Where to?" Stan asked from the driver's seat, breaking my trance and reminding me that we weren't alone.

"My place." Dan's eyes were still on my lips.

My heart twisted—a pang, stretching and flexing—and then began to race.

"Your place?" I glanced between Dan and the back of Stan's head. "Wait. No. Wait."

Stan, who'd just flipped on his blinker, flipped it off. "Wait?"

Dan lifted an eyebrow at me. "Wait?"

"Yes. Wait. I need to—I need to think."

"Okay." Dan turned to the control console and pressed the button to lift the privacy window.

"No, wait." I reached over him, knocking his hand out of the way to halt the window's upward progress.

My position, reaching over his lap, my body pressed to his, our mouths inches apart, registered gradually. Heat spread up my neck. His eyes darkened to almost black.

Smolder.

"Kat." My name sounded like a purr. "What are you doing?"

"I need a minute."

"Let me raise the window." His voice was low again, like he was telling me a dirty secret, and shaded with something else that felt hazardous, but also full of promise. Hazardous promise. Dirty secret.

"No." I shook my head quickly, my mouth watering for some reason. "I need to think."

"That's why I'm going to raise the window." He titled his head toward the front of the car and in doing so he brought our mouths closer.

You should kiss him, my heart advocated, and soon the recommendation became a chant, *Kiss him, kiss him, kiss him.*

Holding my gaze, Dan slid his hand atop mine and pressed the button, my heart accelerating further, so the chant sounded more like *kiss, kiss, kiss, kiss!*

I turned my fingers and caught his, stopping the window once again. "I mean," I whispered, "I meant, I need a minute where we—you and I—aren't alone."

His face did this strange and completely adorable thing. First, his eyebrows pulled together as though to frown, but then his mouth hitched as though to smile, and his eyelids drooped as though to increase the smolder. He licked his lips, drawing the bottom one into his mouth, sucking it. Biting it.

That wasn't adorable. That was indecent. I loved it.

I held my breath while engaging in an internal brawl between myself and myself.

Perhaps I should just let him close the window. What was the worst that could happen? Likely, I'd end up in his lap, straddling him, and maybe we'd have sex in the back seat. That sounded freaking amazing.

Yes. Yes. Do that.

Except.

Except.

Except, what if I couldn't? What if we started and I froze?

What if I can't?

I tensed. He must've seen something in my features he didn't like because in the next moment, his smile fell away and he lowered the privacy window.

"Okay," he said, removing my hand from the control panel and entwining our fingers. "We can drive around, if you want."

I nodded.

Dan gave me one more long look, like he was trying to read my thoughts.

He turned to Stan. "Drive around."

"Drive around? Here?"

"Yeah. Here."

"But it's rush hour," Stan grumbled, flipping on his blinker again.

"What? You got someplace to be? Your landlady waiting for you to round out a pinochle foursome?"

Stan's eyes flickered to me, then back to the road, saying nothing.

"Dan," I chided, shaking my head at him.

"Yes?" He looked at me, his tone infinitely gentle.

I leaned close, whispering, "Don't get mad at Stan. It's not his fault I need a minute. He's right. It is rush hour. And I guess he should probably just take us to your place so we can talk and he can get home." I turned to Stan, lifting my voice so he could hear. "I'm sorry, Stan. Please take us to the East Randolph Street property."

Which brings us back to now and Stan looking at us, squinting at our reflections in the rearview mirror, and then away, equal parts nervous and confused.

I'd attributed this to how we'd been behaving since we left the Clerk's office. But then Dan leaned to the side, drawing my attention back to him.

"Kit-Kat, I'm not mad." His tone was both soothing and teasing, and he lifted his chin toward Stan. "He really does play pinochle with his landlady on Fridays." Dan rubbed his thumb back and forth over the back of my hand and gave me a lop-sided smile.

"Stan plays pinochle?"

"It's true," Stan confirmed, meeting my gaze briefly in the rearview mirror. "I dig it."

"Oh." I sat back, unsure what to say, so I went with my default. "I'm so sorry."

"No need to apologize." I felt Dan's eyes on me, watchful. He bent to my ear, whispering, "What's wrong?"

I swallowed once, fighting a tingling shiver caused by his hot breath falling over the sensitive skin of my neck.

I lifted my eyes to his as he drew away. "It's just, clearly I have trouble reading you. I'm sorry. I thought you were—"

"Giving him a hard time?"

"I'm sorry."

"No need to apologize. It's no big deal."

He considered me for a few seconds. Actually, we considered each other. And as we did this, I was left with the impression that Dan the Security Man really, really liked looking at me. And that made my blush increase by tenfold, my neck and cheeks hot with both pleasure and self-consciousness.

His voice low, just above a whisper, his eyes smoldering anew, Dan said, "Maybe it's about time you and I get to know each other better."

I nodded, trying to smile. "I have a bad habit of assuming the worst, I think."

His gaze moved to my hair and he threaded his fingers into the strands at my temple, pushing it away from my face. Dan released a soft breath, almost like a contented sigh.

"Come here." His fingers now on my neck tugged me forward and he pressed my cheek against his chest, wrapping his arm around my shoulders and holding me close to his side. "You think. I'll be quiet."

I tried to look at him. Due to the angle at which he held me, I could only see his chin, but I was unwilling to move or readjust myself. Instead, I grabbed his lapel and leaned against him.

It was nice.

It was better than nice.

It was *amazing*.

He—his body, his warmth, his strength—felt amazing. Plus, he smelled great.

And I couldn't believe I was leaning against him voluntarily. More precisely, I couldn't believe I was allowing myself to be held.

Searching my brain, I sought to recall the last time I'd been embraced, the last time I'd allowed it to happen without overthinking and forcing myself to relax. Or, the last time I hadn't automatically stiffened and felt suffocated.

When he'd greeted me prior to lunch the day before.

And knit night.

The ladies always hugged each other. I'd hugged Sandra last week as part of a group embrace. A few weeks before that, Sandra and I had cuddled under a blanket on Elizabeth's couch. Sandra loved to cuddle and her enjoyment of it had rubbed off on me over the years, but only with them.

I only enjoyed cuddling with my friends.

My boss had initiated a hug last winter break. After giving me an effusive speech about how valuable I was and handing over my bonus check, she'd hugged me and I'd turned into a statue. When she'd backed off and apologized, I made some excuse about having menstrual cramps, heartburn, gas, and diarrhea. That's right, all four.

One of the architects at work had tried to give me a hug. I'd made him and his wife soup and a loaf of bread while they were sick with the flu, and I'd watched their two kids so they could sleep on a Saturday afternoon. He was overwhelmed with gratitude upon returning to work. I stuck out my hand hurriedly as he opened his arms for an embrace, leading to a full minute of the awkward do-we-shake-or-do-we-hug tango, a close relative of the which-side-of-the-sidewalk-are-you-walk-ing-on polka.

Dan wasn't holding me tight, and his hand rested on my shoulder. His other hand fiddled with my fingers where they lay on my leg in a way that felt absentminded and therefore natural.

Embracing wasn't something I did lightly. Hugs required a level of trust, and it placed a person in a physical position of weakness. Yet here we were, cuddling, and for some magical reason, I let it happen.

"We're here, and it looks like—" Dan shifted beneath me and I felt his muscles tense. "What the—"

I lifted my head to look at him. He was staring out the window, frowning. The hand that had been fiddling with my fingers was on the door handle, like he was ready to jump out of the SUV as soon as it came to a complete stop.

Following his gaze, I tilted my head to the side to see out the glass. Janie and Quinn were standing just outside the front door of the building along with Lawrence, the concierge, and Charles, the doorman. Quinn had his arm around her, like he was helping support her weight, and she was holding her belly. Even from this distance, I could see her forehead was knotted, as though she were uncomfortable or in pain. Charles and Lawrence appeared agitated, looking at her and then away toward the underground parking garage exit. Quinn's eyes were trained on our car as we pulled up.

As soon as we stopped, Dan gave my knee a quick squeeze and then was out the door, jogging to our friends. I jumped out after him, having to settle for a power walk instead of a jog due to the height of my heels.

"What's wrong? Are you okay?" Dan stepped next to Janie, his arm coming around her like he planned to pick her up.

"No. Don't. She wants to stand." Quinn's tone was even, but I knew the calm was deceptive. His eyes were wide and rimmed with worry, his gaze sweeping over Dan, moving to me, narrowing. "She's in labor. Her water broke."

"Okay. Okay. What can we do?" Now Dan's face contorted, like he was also in pain. "Should we call an ambulance?"

I inserted myself between Dan and Janie, but I didn't touch her. She'd complained early in her second trimester about people feeling entitled to touch her just because she was pregnant.

"What can I do?" I asked, a pang of worry slicing through me.

She reached for my hand, her grip tight, her forehead clearing as her eyes met mine. "Sorry. Contraction. Call Elizabeth. Let her know we're on our way. And can you get my bag? And the baby's? Quinn didn't want to wait for me to finish packing."

"Now is not the time to pack." His voice was cold, remote. But I knew him well enough by now to recognize this was how he handled fear.

"He's just upset I didn't tell him when my water broke," she explained, giving me a little smile. "Only about fifteen percent of women have their water break before they go into labor, and the number is even less for first pregnancies."

Quinn slid a glare to his wife, but spoke to Dan. "Nicolas is bringing a car."

"When did your water break?" Feeling helpless, I held her hand in both of mine, wanting to transfer all my love and good vibes to her through the contact.

"An hour ago. Most doctors agree that, after your water breaks, both the baby and the mother are at an increased risk of infection due to organisms that can enter the amniotic sac. Of course, this doesn't necessarily mean it's automatically unsafe to labor longer than twenty-four hours after one's water breaks, though most medical professionals will recommend antibiotics to prevent infection if a woman labors longer than twenty-four hours, which makes sense to me. I was packing the baby's bag when it happened, so I stopped and made a sandwich."

"Your water broke so you made yourself a sandwich?"

"Yes. And some lemonade. I've been told they won't let me eat at the hospital during labor." Her grin widened and she started to laugh. "You should have seen Quinn's face when he figured it out. I tried to cover the wet spot in the baby's room with a towel but I couldn't bend down to pick it up."

Ignoring Janie, Quinn lifted his chin toward the SUV we'd just evacuated, to where Stan looked on anxiously, hovering just outside of the driver's side door. "We'll have Stan drive us since your car is already here. Kat will bring the bags and follow with Nicolas."

"Yeah, makes sense. Okay." Dan moved around me, forcing me to release Janie's hand, and slipped his arm behind her back once again. He then helped Quinn walk her to the car.

"I can walk, you know." I couldn't see her expression, but her voice sounded amused. "It only hurts when I have a contraction, and not even that bad."

Quinn said nothing, stubbornly keeping his arm in place.

When they reached the car and Quinn moved to help her in, she said, "I can also get in the—"

He cut her off, grabbing her face and fastening his mouth to hers. And then he kissed her like they were alone, like maybe this was their last time kissing, like she was the love of his life and he hungered for her more than life itself.

I glanced at Dan. He glanced at me. We shared a wide-eyed look.

Janie groaned, breaking the kiss to suck in a breath, her hands coming to his wrists.

Quinn leaned away and touched his nose to hers. "Please stop fighting me and let me help." It was the first time a note of something other than calm entered his voice.

"Fine." The wrinkles reappeared on her forehead and she spoke as though words were difficult. "But if you hover and boss me around in the delivery room, I will send you on a snipe hunt."

CHAPTER TWELVE

Trade Secret: A formula, practice, process, design, instrument, pattern, commercial method, or compilation of information not generally known or reasonably ascertainable by others by which a business can obtain an economic advantage over competitors or customers.

WEX LEGAL DICTIONARY

Kat

S TAN DROVE JANIE, Quinn, and Dan. I was relieved Stan was driving. Both Quinn and Dan looked like they were incapable of steering a remote control car.

Charles escorted me to Janie and Quinn's penthouse while I texted Elizabeth to give her a heads-up. The baby's bag sat on top of the changing table, open and half packed. I checked it, filling it with all the necessary items, plus a few unnecessary items—three changes of clothes, blankets, diapers, wipes, pacifier, burp cloth, hat, mittens, socks, etcetera. Once satisfied, I went to the master bedroom and easily found Janie's bag in the closet, all packed and ready to go.

Catching my reflection in the bedroom mirror, I realized I was still wearing my pretty dress, which reminded me that Dan was still wearing his gorgeous suit.

His suit brought to mind our wedding at the Clerk's office and everything after, especially how natural it had felt to be held by him. This, of course, had me wondering if everything between us would be just as natural and easy. I hoped so.

God, I hope so.

Perhaps Dan would be my lucky charm, my get-out-of-jail-free card. Maybe he would be the answer to my inability-to-enjoy-physical-intimacy-without-alcohol problem, and all this fretting and therapy was just to prepare me for this moment and—

Wait. Wait a minute. Don't get ahead of yourself.

Blowing out a breath, I pushed those thoughts away. Daydreaming about Dan and his magical talent to distract me and make me feel comfortable even while turning me on would have to wait until later. Janie was in labor. I needed to change, get to the hospital, and support my friends.

"Hey Charles." I wheeled Janie's bag to the living room, searching for the doorman.

"Yeah?" Charles already had the baby's bag over his shoulder and reached for Janie's rolling suitcase as soon as I drew near.

"Will you let me into Dan's apartment? I want to take him a change of clothes."

"Sure thing." His gaze flickered over me, landing on my left hand before he turned and crossed to the door. "You don't have a key?"

Caught off guard, I covered my ring finger. "No. Not yet."

"It's okay. I have one."

I followed him out and down the hall, feeling a tad puerile for some reason. "Thank you."

"It's all good." Charles called over his shoulder, arriving at the elevator and pressing the down arrow. "Nice people should marry nice people, that's what my mom says."

I gave him a grateful smile and was about to thank him as we boarded the lift, but he wasn't finished.

"Does his mom know? About you two getting married?"

The elevator doors closed and I didn't know what to say. I couldn't say, *I don't know*. The admission felt like revealing too much: Dan and I hadn't yet discussed his family, we'd married in a hurry, so many things were unresolved and confusing between us.

Charles reached into his pocket and withdrew a key, handing it out to me. "Don't lose this, it'll get you into all the doors on this floor. I'll meet you downstairs when you're done."

"Thank you." Accepting the key, I moved to depart.

But then Charles stepped forward and inserted his foot into the opening, preventing the doors from sliding closed. "She's a nice lady."

"Pardon me?"

"Mr. O'Malley's mom. She's a little scary, but nice. She's going to be protective." He removed his foot, adding just as the doors slid shut, "Don't take it personally."

I stared at the reflective surface of the closed panels for a half minute, my mind tripping over the ramifications I'd neglected to fully consider and plan for prior to marrying Dan.

He had a mother, a family. I knew this.

But what I didn't know? What would he tell them about me? Would I meet them? What would we say?

Will they like me?

Preoccupied, I made my way to Dan's apartment and changed into my Friday outfit. I then selected a set of clothes for him—something comfortable, that he could sleep in if needed—while endeavoring not to ogle his underwear drawer.

For the record, he wore boxer briefs.

Also, for the record, I felt oddly guilty that I'd ogled his boxer briefs, but not so guilty as to deter me from purposely grabbing a red pair for him. However, the guilt did extend to the fact that should he change into them, I would know he was wearing red boxer briefs.

But enough about Dan's underwear.

I also grabbed a few toiletries and placed everything in my backpack.

More guilt because, I'm not going to lie, I sniffed his cologne. I closed my eyes, lifted it to my nose, and took a deep breath, sighing dreamily.

Obviously, it smelled like him—not exactly like him, but pretty darn close—and it gave me squishy feelings in my middle. Seconds turned to minutes as I debated whether or not to snap a picture of the label. In the end, I succumbed to temptation, justifying the action by telling myself I'd buy him more for his birthday.

Buying one's husband cologne for a birthday is completely normal, therefore I am completely normal. I'm the normalest in all the land!

But I wasn't normal. I was creeping on Dan's underwear drawer and cologne. How would I feel if he'd done the same to me?

Excited.

And flattered.

I had no idea if those thoughts were normal. I hoped they were, but I suspected they were not.

Shortly after indulging myself, and after a brief moment of searching for Wally, I remembered Dan had mentioned Wally was with Alex. I sent Alex a quick text as I made my way to the lobby.

Kat: *Janie is in labor, Dan is at the hospital, and I'm meeting them there and have their bags. Can you keep Wally tonight?*

Alex: *Yes. I'll let Sandra know and track down the others. She'll be there as soon as she gets off work.*

Kat: *Thank you.*

Alex: *No problem. Keep us updated.*

I read and re-read Alex's texts, an odd pang in my chest. With very few words, he'd communicated so much about how he and Sandra valued Janie and Quinn. It warmed my heart, this community we'd built. I wondered if it was rare, or if these little pockets of love and support existed elsewhere.

I hoped they did.

* * *

THE FIRST WORDS Quinn said to me upon my walking into the private waiting room were, "She sent me on a snipe hunt."

"Pardon me?"

His elbows were on his knees, his head in his hands. He spoke to the floor, "She kicked me out."

I didn't laugh. He looked so stressed.

Instead, bolstered by my hug success with Dan earlier in the day, I walked to him, sat next to him, and wrapped my arms around his shoulders. Granted, he was so big my hands barely touched, but I held him anyway.

"I'm not going to say everything will be okay,"—I rested my chin on one bulky shoulder while his big hands came to my arm and held on —"but, Quinn, thousands of babies are born every day. We're in one of the best hospitals in the world. Elizabeth will be there every step of the way. Janie is a force. So . . ."

He lifted his head, looking at me.

I held him tighter. "Everything is going to be okay."

Quinn nodded, drawing in a deep breath, and twisted in his seat to return my embrace.

My heart stuttered, and the instinct to stiffen was almost overwhelming, but I fought it. I told myself to relax and snuggled closer, determined to provide support for my good friend's husband in his time of need.

He's your friend too, a little voice whispered.

I couldn't figure out if it was a reminder or a revelation, but whatever it was, it helped me relax. Quinn was my friend. He might've been six foot forever and felt like he was made of granite, owned a global security firm and barely spoke six words at a time, had unsettling blue eyes and had always struck me as a little frightening, but he was still my friend.

He released me and sighed, glancing at the door to the delivery room and sitting back in his chair. Silence surrounded us, more or less. We could hear people speaking on the other side of the door, but the words sounded muffled. Hospital noises—like beeping machines, rolling carts, footsteps—approached and faded from the hallway.

I fretted. I didn't know what to say. I wasn't wise like Marie or Fiona. They would know what to say. Nor was I Elizabeth, who would be able to distract Quinn from his fears by annoying him. And I wasn't Sandra or Ashley, who would be able to make him laugh.

I was Kat. The quiet one. Why was I the quiet one?

In non-business situations, I never know if what I'm going to say will make everything worse.

And so I fretted.

After a time, Quinn cleared his throat and crossed his arms, glancing in my direction. "You and Dan are married."

I stiffened.

His mouth curved in the barest of smiles. "Is it a secret?"

I inspected him for a few seconds. Apparently, Quinn found this development amusing.

"No. It's not a secret."

"I have a lot of questions." His piercing blue eyes studied me, and if it weren't for his mouth's subtle curve, his probing gaze would have made me nervous.

"Why don't you ask Dan?"

His smile fell away and was replaced with a look of slight confusion. "We don't talk about that kind of thing."

"What kind of thing?"

"Feelings."

"You were going to ask me about my feelings?"

"Yes."

I felt my eyebrows jump. "Really?"

"What are your intentions toward Dan?"

I couldn't help it. I smiled. And then I laughed. I laughed partially because the moment was so surreal, but also partially because Quinn's worry for Dan—because, make no mistake, he *was* worried—was adorable.

These two guys . . . Friendship goals.

Once more, his mouth arched into a hint of a smile, but he continued staring at me like he was waiting for my answer.

Returning his almost grin, I shrugged. "Honestly?"

"Honesty is my preference."

I don't know what spurred me to do it—perhaps it was a mixture of the bizarreness of the moment and my own lack of clarity on what was going on with Dan and me, or maybe bravery caused by elation caused by kissing Dan—but I told the absolute truth.

"He married me so my cousin Caleb wouldn't commit me to a mental hospital. Everything was rushed, but I think he likes me. No, I'm sure he likes me. Or he wants to kiss me at least. And I like him —*a lot*—and want to be with him, hopefully for more than just kissing. We just discovered that maybe the reason we haven't acted on our feelings is because of some stupid misunderstanding from over two years ago, and that's tough to swallow. But at the same time, it might've been a blessing in disguise, because it forced me to take a good look at myself and decide to make some changes for the better. If we'd gotten together two years ago, then I wouldn't have made those changes, and who knows if we would have lasted. I don't know."

I brought my gaze back to Quinn. He was looking at me. Just . . . looking. No expression.

Squirming in my seat, I blurted, "My intentions are to deserve him."

Quinn blinked, his features visibly relaxing, his eyes moving between mine. He took a deep breath as though to speak, but we were interrupted.

"Sorry it took me so long." Dan shouldered through the door leading to the hall, holding two paper cups. "This better be the best fucking cup of coffee you've ever had, because—"

He stopped short when our eyes met and my stomach became a hot mess of lovely knots.

"Kat."

"Hi."

"Hi."

We stared at each other until Quinn cleared his throat and stood, drawing Dan's attention to him.

"Where's the bathroom?"

"Make a right, it's at the end of the hall." Dan gestured with his chin.

Quinn nodded once and left.

I also stood, crossing to Dan and taking the coffee out of his hands; I placed both cups on a small side table next to the chairs where Quinn and I had been sitting moments prior and grabbed my backpack.

"I brought you a change of clothes." I held the bag between us. "So you'd be more comfortable."

"Thanks." He accepted the bag, examining me for a moment, then placed it on one of the chairs closest to him. "We need to talk."

"Okay." More lovely knots. A few tangles of uncertainty as well.

"We should talk about what happened at the Clerk's office, about the thing."

"You mean when we—uh—after we were married and the ki—"

"No, no. Not *that* thing." He lifted an eyebrow, his mischievous little smile making an appearance. "I'm pretty clear on that thing."

I pressed my lips together, twisting them to the side so I wouldn't grin.

He did grin. But then it fell away, and a more thoughtful expression took its place. "I have an aunt—Becks, on my dad's side—she has lots of relationships, with lots of people. It's all consensual, out in the open. Told me when I was old enough to ask about it that she's never been good at monogamy."

"Ah. I see." His assumption about me being polyamorous now made a lot more sense. "I've never been in a relationship, let alone several at the same time."

Dan scratched his chin, his eyes narrowing just a hint. "You're in one now."

"It was supposed to be a fake one."

Dan bit his lip, staring at me, but said nothing.

So I asked, "All this time, you thought I was polyamorous? In Vegas?"

"Yes."

"And that's why you left? That morning? Is that why you left the room so suddenly?"

"Yes."

"Because—"

"I wanted monogamy." He shrugged, not looking repentant. "And the woman I was way into *heavily implied* she wasn't into that."

"You were 'way into' me?" My voice was squeaky and my heart beat excitedly. Now I was smiling and I didn't care, nor could I help it.

"Yep." He seemed to be amused by the size of my grin, or maybe it was the squeak in my voice.

"You were?" I didn't know why, but I needed to hear him confirm it again.

"Yes."

"In Vegas?"

"In Las fucking Vegas. And before that, too." He grinned, shaking his head.

"So you didn't leave because I—"

"Because you what?"

"Because you were disappointed?"

"Fuck yeah, I was disappointed. I didn't want to share. Maybe more importantly, I don't want someone who's willing to share me."

"But you weren't disappointed in—in—"

"In what?"

I became aware that I was twisting my fingers, so I curled them into fists. "That I'd . . . I had . . . I was—" *Darn it!* I just needed to spit it out.

Abruptly, Dan's expression cleared, his eyes suddenly wide, dawning comprehension. "You thought I left because you'd slept with other guys?"

"A lot of other guys."

He recoiled an inch. "Why would I have an opinion about that? As long as you're cool with it, why is it my business? That would make me a judgmental assclown."

My gaze fell to the ground.

"Kat?"

I swallowed, unable to meet his eye.

"Holy shit, Kat. That's what you thought?"

I nodded, still not able to lift my gaze.

This was exactly the reason why I'd gone into therapy. I'd assumed the worst—about myself and therefore about him—and now two years later, here we were. If I'd just given myself a little credit, if I'd been kinder, if I'd had more self-confidence, maybe today, instead of a fake wedding, it would have been a real one.

Okay, that's one heck of a jump. Slow down there, Miss Havisham.

"This is unbelievable." Dan turned from me, throwing his hands in the air, rubbing his face as he turned back. He leaned against the door, shaking his head, his gaze distracted.

I huffed a laugh.

"That's a lot of time wasted because of a stupid misunderstanding. If you'd just asked me—"

"Me? I'm not the one who thought you were polyamorous. Why didn't you ask me about *that*?"

He glared, continuing to shake his head. "Two fucking years. No wonder you avoided me. I would have avoided me, too. This is the dumbest fucking thing I've ever heard."

I agreed with him on this point. It was dumb. Jumping to conclusions, misunderstandings, pride and avoidance—it all felt incredibly trite in retrospect. Trite and idiotic.

And yet, a part of me was glad for it. As I'd confessed to Quinn, I'd needed the time. Not only had I made assumptions about Dan, I'd made assumptions about myself.

Dan's features showcased a mixture of intense confusion and frustration, and a small little voice in my head wondered if it was too late. If our chance had passed.

I glared at that voice and shut a door in its face. *What a stupid voice. You can't sit here, voice. NEVER COME BACK!*

While I was berating my doubt, the cloud of confusion hovering over Dan's features abruptly cleared and his stare cut to mine. It startled me because—lo and behold—the sexy eyes were back.

Boy oh boy, were they back.

Dan was *legit* bringing sexy back.

Whoa.

In the next moment, his mouth hooked upward and he pushed away from the wall, sauntering toward me. Instinctively, I took two steps back.

"Kit-Kat." He wagged a finger at me, like I'd been naughty. "You liked me."

"You liked me, you just said so," I volleyed back, the words sounding like an accusation.

"I did." His grin grew and his voice deepened. "And I do."

Oh.

Okay.

Here we go.

He was using his naughty-secret voice.

Am I ready for this?

"We can't do this right now."

What? What is wrong with you? Do it now! Do it right now!

"Why not?"

"Because—"

"I know you're not seeing anyone else."

"Because—because I smelled your underwear and touched your cologne!"

Dan stopped, his eyes widening with what looked like alarm. "You what?"

"Ah!" Heat surged to my face, hot and mortifying. "No. Sorry. No, I mixed that up. Not what I did. I mean, I touched your underwear and smelled your cologne."

"O-o-o-o-kay. That's . . . interesting. And strangely arousing."

"I want to deserve you." Like before, this was blurted. But I stopped myself before I could also confess, *I want to be stable, rational, healthy, and sensible for you.*

"Deserve me?" He grinned at that, my words apparently confusing him because his grin seemed shaded with both amusement and concern.

"I owe you so much and—"

Dan made a face, flinching, all traces of sexy-humor dissolved in a single instant. "Uh, no. You don't owe me."

"I do. I really do. I'm so, so grateful."

"You do this every time we're together. Like I told you before, you gotta stop thanking me." He pulled his hands through his hair, turning away. "Shit."

I didn't know how, but I seemed to be making things worse. Rushing forward, I placed a hand on his arm and stepped in front of him, anxious to get this right. "Sorry. I'm doing this wrong. Let me start over. You are so kind, and generous, and I—"

"Stop making me out to be some Mother Theresa. You think I married you out of the kindness of my heart? Think again."

I couldn't help my smile. "Dan."

"Kat."

"Come on."

His hands were back on his hips. "Where're we going?"

I chuckled, my smile beaming. "Why do you want me to believe you're not a good guy?"

"I didn't say I'm not a good guy. I didn't say I am a good guy. I said I didn't marry you out of *kindness*."

Squinting at him, I gave him a rueful grin. "I don't believe that."

"You should."

"Okay, well,"—I rolled my eyes to the ceiling—"fine. Whatever your reason, I'm allowed to be grateful for your help."

"I don't want your gratitude." He stepped back, shaking his head adamantly as he folded his arms. He wasn't smiling. In fact, he looked frustrated. Or angry. Or both.

I didn't understand him. "I'm not allowed to be grateful?"

"No." He lifted his chin. "Being grateful is like giving me a participation ribbon when I'm after the goddamn gold medal."

I winced at his voice's volume and sharpness, but before I was able to ascertain Dan's meaning, Quinn opened the door.

The big man stopped short, glancing between us for several seconds with his trademark lack of expression. Eventually, he strolled into the room and to the coffee. Selecting a cup, he claimed the seat he'd been sitting in earlier and pulled out his phone.

"Don't mind me."

"I—" I started, paused, looked to Quinn and then back to Dan. Dan hadn't even looked at his friend. His eyes remained on me the whole time, his usually luscious lips an angry slash on his handsome face, his jaw rigid.

I worried for his dental work.

But at the same time, I wanted to shout at him. His unwillingness to accept my appreciation was infuriating.

Worried I would yell, I turned for the door, murmuring as I went, "I'll go get more coffee," and hurried out of the room.

I needed a minute to think about what he'd said and review our conversation. I needed to examine each of our words, but especially his last comment about gratitude.

What am I doing wrong? How am I messing this up so badly?

I'd made it three steps to the door when I felt a hand close over my arm, bringing me to a stop, and effectively turning me around.

I was given just a single second to recognize that the hand belonged to Dan before he tugged me forward, slid his arms around my waist, and captured my mouth.

I twined my arms around his neck, lifting to my toes and pressing my body to his as I sought his tongue with mine. He obliged, and though his kiss was hot and sweet and savoring, his fingers dug into my back and he held me tighter than necessary.

Melted and reformed, my new shape soft and pliable, heat seeking and greedy for him, I poured myself into the kiss, hoping it would succeed where my words had not.

Sliding his hands along my sides to my arms, he broke away. I opened my eyes, eager for his. But Dan released me and took a step back. His gaze was on the floor between us and he reached into his pocket, his large hands concealed the object he withdrew.

Dan reached for me, opened my fingers, placed the object there, and let me go.

I stared, not quite able to breathe, because a ring so beautiful that it defied comprehension lay in the center of my palm.

An exquisite colorless diamond cut into a shape that wasn't quite a square and wasn't quite a circle surrounded by a halo of smaller diamonds in a filigree art deco platinum setting—maybe white gold?— sparkled back at me.

"I don't want your gratitude," he said, his voice rough but firm.

I lifted my gaze and blinked at him, at his chin's determined tilt and the figurative barricade he'd erected between us with his stubbornness.

The last thing he wanted to hear was another *thank you*.

Okay. Fine. I understood, loud and clear.

Which meant I didn't know what to say. So I said nothing.

CHAPTER THIRTEEN

A Private Company: (Or privately held company) A business company owned either by non-governmental organizations or by a relatively small number of shareholders or company members which does not offer or trade its company stock (shares) to the general public on the stock market exchanges.

INVESTOPEDIA

Kat

THE NEXT SEVERAL hours passed in a hectic blur.

Dan was absent when I returned with more coffee, two large thermoses full. I'd purchased them at the gift shop and filled the containers from the cafeteria machines. Quinn explained that Dan was off someplace taking calls, sending emails, and working with Quinn's executive assistant to rearrange meetings and schedules for the following week.

We received a text from Fiona's husband, Greg, not to tell us they were on their way, but rather to inform us they were already at the hospital. Fiona had gone into labor.

Sandra arrived just after 7:30 PM, bringing dinner from the cafeteria and possessing the forethought to order enough extra food in case more people showed up.

Quinn paced the room like caged animal and deflected any and all attempts at conversation. Eventually, I gave up and stewed in my own anxious contemplations, glaring at the gorgeous rock on my finger, and endeavoring to untangle the lump of nerves in my stomach. However, Sandra had managed to pull a laugh out of Quinn with a few of her dirtiest jokes. Nico also would have made him laugh, but the comedian was stuck in New York filming his show.

Elizabeth poked her head out at intervals to give us the thumbs up, tease Quinn, and ask if we'd heard from Marie. No one could reach Marie, not even Alex with his super sneaky computery skills. Alex didn't come to the hospital. He stayed behind at Cypher Systems to cover things there.

Ashley and Drew were on high alert in Tennessee, debating whether or not to drive up now or wait a week and visit once everyone was home.

Close to 9:00 PM, I left Quinn with Sandra to see if I could check on Fiona. I didn't want to text Greg while he was obviously concentrating on more important things; instead, I found the nurses' station and asked about her progress. Unsurprisingly, since I wasn't an immediate family member, I was unable to discover any information.

I was just typing a text to the group, asking if I could bring anything back, when I heard Dan's voice from behind me call, "Kat, wait up."

Automatically, I glanced over my shoulder, my heart giving a leap. The first thing I noticed, gone was his sexy suit from the wedding. Which of course made me wonder if he was wearing the red boxer briefs I'd brought him. Which of course sent a delightful spike of alertness through me because I was picturing him in nothing but the red briefs. Which of course made my cheeks and neck red hot.

Right on cue, I felt a little ashamed of my objectifying thoughts.

"Hi." I waved, sticking the phone in my back pocket. Forgetting about the half-written text, I turned to meet him while trying to swallow past the tension in my throat.

The way we'd left things earlier weighed heavy between us. He didn't want my thanks, and I didn't know how to get my point across without voicing my gratitude.

"Hey." He drew closer, and though his momentum led me to believe he planned to greet me with a kiss, he stopped abruptly a few feet away. "Where you going?"

"Back to the waiting room." I indicated with my thumb over my shoulder, my stomach now mildly unsettled for no reason. "Sandra brought food. Are you hungry?"

"Yeah . . ." He scratched his neck, contemplating me. Giving me the impression he'd just decided something, Dan took two steps forward. But then the buzzing of our cell phones interrupted us.

Anxiously, I leaned close to Dan to read the message on his screen.

Sandra: *Where are you? I'm running out of jokes.*

He sighed, tapping out a response.

Dan: *I just found Kat. We'll be right there.*

Dan gave me a regretful smile and held out his hand. "Shall we?"

I slipped mine in his, my heart skipping, and stepped much closer to him than strictly necessary. His gaze moved over my face for a few short seconds, and then he sighed again, turning back toward the waiting room.

When we arrived, Dan and I sat next to each other, still holding hands. And that was very, very nice.

He distracted Quinn with talk of work while Sandra and I looked up jokes on her phone, adding the best ones to her notes app for later.

After another hour or so, I received a text from Greg.

Greg: *Don't tell Quinn, as I'm sure the poor bloke doesn't need or want to think about anything else right now, but baby Archer entered*

the world a few minutes ago. She's atrociously loud and has already
asserted her dominance by pissing all over the doctor. We're so proud.

I tried not to laugh, but I did show the text to Dan, who rolled his
eyes and stifled a laugh.

The next few hours consisted of endless waiting. At one point, Dan
left to use the bathroom. I made an excuse so I could intercept him in
the hall again, hopefully to steal a few minutes to clear the air between
us. But Sandra texted us again, foiling my efforts.

Sandra—who had to work the next day—left just before midnight
with promises to return early. Quinn's parents landed from Boston and
met us in the waiting room around 1:00 AM. Elizabeth opened the door
to the delivery room shortly thereafter, looking ridiculously chipper
and inviting Quinn's mom to join her, the nurse, and Janie, earning a
scowl from Quinn.

I dozed off around two or three o'clock and awoke near four
o'clock to find Dan gone again. I snuck out of the room, hoping to
catch him on his way back. Again, I was thwarted, this time by a text
from Elizabeth.

But when I fell asleep around five, I woke up to find Dan had
carried me to a set of chairs with no armrest between them. His arm
was around my shoulder and I was leaning heavily on his body,
sleeping on his chest.

"Shh. Go back to sleep." He smoothed my hair away from my face,
kissing my forehead.

Bleary eyed, I glanced around the room and found Quinn and his
father sitting across from each other, arms folded. It took me a minute
to realize Quinn's father wasn't an actual mirror image of Quinn; they
looked so much alike.

Neither were asleep and they were both still as statues, except
Quinn's knee was bouncing. Mr. Sullivan displayed no outward sign of
anxiousness.

"Is Janie okay?" I snuggled closer to Dan, placing my hand on his
stomach and enjoying his body beneath my fingers. Clearly, my sleepy
brain was an opportunist and it high-fived itself all over the place.

"She's fine. Her labor slowed down, but everything is fine. If she doesn't progress, they're going to give her some drugs to speed things up."

"Oh." I nodded, stroking my hand back and forth over his stomach. He felt fantastic.

He caught my fingers mid-stroke and brought them to his heart, whispering tightly, "Go back to sleep."

"What about you? Don't you need to sleep?" I yawned, stretching against him.

Dan groaned quietly, threading his fingers into my hair and massaged my scalp. "Please go back to sleep."

"Feel free to use me, too. You can sleep on me if you want."

The groan became a deeper sound in the back of his throat. "I will give you a million dollars if you go back to sleep right now."

I wrinkled my nose, my sleepy brain not understanding why in the world Dan would offer me a million dollars when he knew I had billions.

Closing my eyes again, I inhaled the scent of him. "You smell good."

Another kiss on my forehead. "I'll wake you up if anything changes."

"Thank you," I said, smelling him again. He really did smell good. So good. Dreamy.

I felt him hesitate, like he was searching for words, but then finally settled on a strained, "You're welcome," and his other arm came around me and hugged me close.

As I drifted back to sleep, I wondered how long people in relationships waited until they slept in the same bed together.

I hoped the answer was immediately.

* * *

I NEEDED CAFFEINE.

I'd consumed three cups of coffee earlier in the day, but I was still exhausted from the paltry four hours of sleep from the night before.

Paltry and magnificent, as they were spent curled up next to and on top of Dan.

Yet, four hours was still four hours. I could've gone home and slept, but I was unwilling to leave the hospital. My unwillingness stemmed from a number of factors:

Janie had her baby earlier in the morning, just after Marie finally arrived at the hospital. A healthy baby boy, and they named him Desmond, after Quinn's father and oldest brother. My hope was to see her and baby Desmond before I left, but I wasn't holding my breath. She'd labored all night, so sleep took priority.

Presently, most of our group were assembled in Fiona's room. It was larger than most—one of the two VIP suites—and provided ample space for us to sit and visit. Reluctance to end the impromptu gathering kept me from being the first to depart.

Dan and I hadn't had a moment to talk. I didn't want to leave until he was ready to go. Even if all we discussed was making plans to talk later when we weren't so tired, at least we would have a plan.

I needed caffeine.

"Is anyone thirsty?" Stretching as I stood, I grabbed my empty soda can. "I'm going to go get another drink."

Dan, who'd been sitting next to me on a little sofa, came to his feet. "I'll help."

I was relieved he'd offered to come along and I was about to thank him when Marie said, "No," drawing both of our gazes to her.

She crossed to me, placed her arm through mine, and tugged me to the exit. "I'll help."

I glanced at Marie, lifting an eyebrow at her abrupt intervention, but she said nothing until we'd left the room and the door shut behind us.

Then, she spun on me. "Kat."

"Yes?" I steadied myself, because Marie was wearing her take-no-prisoners journalist face, her blue eyes sharp and focused.

"Why are you wearing a wedding ring?"

Damn.

I tried to smile, but I knew it looked weird, so I gave up and sighed. "I had to."

"You had to?" Marie glanced between the ring on my finger and me.

"I had to."

Now she looked worried. "Did your family make you marry someone?"

"Yes. But it's not like you think." I was so tired, I was sure some of my words were slurred.

She gripped me by the shoulders, presumably to keep me from crumpling into a ball and falling immediately asleep on the floor. "What's it like, then? And why didn't you come to me for help? Or if not me, then Fiona? Or Sandra and Alex? Or—"

"I went to Dan for help." I closed my eyes, force of habit making me pick my words carefully. "Dan helped me."

Dan helped me.

But it had been more than that.

Help was letting someone borrow a ladder or a cup of sugar. What he'd done was save my life.

And now things between us were a mess. But also not a mess. They were wonderful and precarious. My current mental state consisted of being perplexed and elated and fearful. Each emotion was segmented into different yet related emotions, and all this emotion plus exhaustion added up to a Niagara Falls level of uncertainty and hope.

I needed to think. I needed to concentrate. And, for the life of me, I didn't understand why I was being so circumspect with Marie.

Because your problems aren't her problems.

"Dan?" She sounded worried and confused. "Helped you how?"

I opened my eyes, stalling any longer was pointless. "He married me."

She blinked, her mouth falling open. It was several seconds before she managed to speak. "You and Dan are married? You're married? To Dan?"

"Yes."

"Okay." She dropped her hands from my shoulders and nodded, clearly thinking a million thoughts. "Will you tell me what happened?"

I hesitated.

"Let me rephrase that." She gave me a hopeful smile, her stare softening, her expression beseeching. "Will you please, please, please allow me to help you?"

Sighing tiredly, I held up my empty soda can. "I will tell you everything on the way to the vending machine. And then you can decide if you want to help me."

"Deal." She looped her arm through mine again and we set off at a snail's pace.

I told her a truncated version of the story, starting with Vegas and my avoidance of Dan and ending with our weird argument last night about gratitude.

Going back over everything with Marie felt cathartic in a way it hadn't with my therapist. Dr. Kasai's focus was my mental well-being, that's why I paid her. She was an expert. I trusted her to give me solid advice.

Whereas Marie was my friend. I trusted her. Unlike Sandra, she was no mental health expert and she didn't know all the sordid details of my past (she only knew *some* of the sordid details). She wasn't looking at me through the lens of my upbringing. She was looking at me and listening to me as a friend. Unburdening myself without any expectation that actionable advice was forthcoming, just an open heart and support, felt great.

"Caleb Tyson is a bottom feeder," she spat, making an angry face and glaring off into the distance. "Man, I'd love to take him down."

Of course Marie knew who Caleb was. As a reporter, she was up-to-date on all the latest domestic, political, and business news. Caleb was always in the news for something, usually having to do with lobbying efforts in Washington D.C., or hiking drug prices, or buying another huge yacht.

"Well, he's my closest relative and my only family not institutionalized. How do you think I feel?" I huffed a humorless laugh.

Her gaze cut to mine. "That man is *not* your family."

"Every time I leave the Boston office, I feel like he's hiding something from the board, from me. Something isn't right."

"What do you mean?"

Again I hesitated, studying her. "I want to tell you, but you're a reporter."

Her eyes grew wide. "Oh. Yes. I mean, I wish I could tell you I won't report or share anything you don't give me permission to share or report, but I can't really do that and maintain my ethics as a journalist. If you feel like your cousin is hiding something from the board, maybe talk to Alex?"

"You think so?"

"Yes." She grinned. "What he lacks in professional ethics he makes up for in morals and loyalty. I want to help—and if you think I can help, please let me know—but obviously you don't want me to dismantle your grandfather's company in the process. I mean, I understand your concern for the people who work there. If having a journalist involved will hurt the stability of the company, best to keep me in the dark."

I nodded, appreciating her honesty, but wishing I could discuss the situation with her. I could've used her level head, inquisitive mind, and uncanny abilities to quickly comprehend new concepts and adapt to new situations.

We'd almost made it back to Fiona's room when Marie stopped me with a hand on my elbow. "What are you going to do about Dan?"

I glanced to the ceiling and exhaled. "I don't know."

"What do you want to do?"

"Kiss him."

She gave me a gleeful grin and folded her hands under her chin. "Yay!"

I laughed and rubbed my forehead. "But, Marie, I've spent so long thinking of him as off-limits, not even a possibility. I know him, but I don't. And he doesn't know me, but he does."

"Yes. So what? That's the nature of friendship. You know a person as a friend, but not intimately, and that's fine. Your relationship will now be built upon a foundation of years. Years of mutual respect and—as Dan would say—wicked attraction."

"Don't get me wrong, I'm excited—no, elated—ecstatic. But I'm also concerned for him."

"About what? Give me some specifics."

"Other than the obvious Caleb-lurking-in-the-shadows concerns?"

She nodded. "Forget your sinister cousin for a moment. He doesn't exist. What worries do you have about Dan?"

"His family. I don't want to cause difficulty between him and his family. We're married and—"

She waved my words away. "That's normal stuff. Everyone worries about their significant other's family and related opinions. I think they'll love you, but either way it always works out. Or it doesn't. All you can do is be yourself—which is wonderful—and give them every chance to be equally wonderful."

"Okay, second fear, what if he loses interest in me? What if things don't work out between us?"

She blinked once and then laughed. She laughed and laughed, eventually wiping the tears of hilarity from her eyes. "I'm not—I don't have an answer for you. You're just going to have to have faith in Dan that he'll realize how amazing you are and never want to let you go."

"But what if I don't have faith in myself?"

"What do you mean?"

"What if there are things about me that make me not amazing?"

"Kat." Her eyes narrowed and she shook her head. "I'm not going to stand here and try to convince you that you're—"

I gripped her arm, tugged her forward, and whispered on a rush, "I've never been able to relax enough to have sex without alcohol."

I felt her stiffen. She drew away, but remained close enough to whisper very, very quietly in return. "When is the last time you tried?"

"Over six years ago." I couldn't believe I was being so candid.

"Holy cow!" Marie flinched, shook her head, and then winced. "Sorry."

"No need to apologize. It's been a long time and it definitely deserves a sacred bovine exclamation of surprise."

"Sacred bovine—? What about when you're alone?"

I shook my head, glancing to the side to make absolutely sure no one could hear us, the heat of mortification slithering up my neck and down my spine. "Sometimes it works, most of the time it doesn't."

She covered my hand on her arm, her eyes wide with compassion. "You're seeing someone, right? A therapist?"

"Yes."

"What does she say?"

"It's been a long time since we discussed it. But I spoke to Sandra, and she told me to do research, on my likes and dislikes, come up with a list of things that, you know, turn me on."

"That makes sense. What did Sandra say about Dan and you?"

"I didn't confirm or deny Sandra's suspicions about me and Dan."

"Well then, what did your therapist say?"

"I haven't talked to Dr. Kasai since last Friday, and at that time the marriage was supposed to be a fake one. Which, I guess, is fake. But the relationship might be real. Which means the marriage might eventually become real." *What a mess.*

"You should talk to her. Maybe,"—her wide blue eyes moved between mine as she considered her next words— "maybe Dan can help?"

I removed my hand from her grip as a surge of guilt made it difficult to speak. "All he does is help me. And what do I do for him? He won't even let me thank him."

"He cares for you."

"And I care for him."

"Good. Then let him help."

Spiky, hot sensations prickled in my chest and I rubbed the spot under my breast, over my heart, where the pain was worse. "If he would let me do something for him in return—"

"That's not how relationships work. And if you would talk to us— not just to me, but to Janie and Fiona, Sandra and Elizabeth, to Ashley —we could all tell you this together."

"I don't want to be—"

"I swear, if you say 'I don't want to be a burden' I will do an exposé in the *Chicago Tribune* and I'll entitle it, 'Heiress in Hiding.'"

Her threat worked even though I knew she'd never follow through. This was Marie's version of tough love. I snapped my mouth shut.

But she wasn't finished. "Do you think Janie was a burden when she was going through that mess with her sister? When she was planning her wedding? Or was Elizabeth a burden when her dad remarried and Nico showed up and we all danced in our underwear on that stage? How about Sandra? When she asked us to help save Alex and pull together a wedding at the last minute? What about when Ashley's mother died? Or when we helped her move last year? Or Fiona when she needed our help with Greg in Nigeria? No." She stared at me, then added firmly, "No. This is what we do."

I nodded, my eyes stinging for some inexplicable reason.

"You are not a burden." Her gaze turned softer, once again beseeching. "*This* is what a family looks like. Not that serpent you call cousin. This is what a family does."

* * *

THE IMPROMPTU GATHERING only lasted a short while longer before Greg kicked everyone out, saying, "You don't have to go home, but you can't stay here."

Hugs were handed out liberally, but Dan and I—through some unspoken agreement—loitered together in the hall until everyone else departed.

As soon as the last of our friends were out of sight, he turned to me. "Hey, I know you gotta be tired. But can we go someplace? Just you and me?"

I was nodding before he finished speaking. "Yes. That would be so great."

Dan offered me a smile and held out his hand. I took it, loving that holding his hand was quickly becoming the norm. We walked together through the hall and onto the elevator. Since we were surrounded by people, neither of us spoke. Instead, I enjoyed how our fingers tangled, how our shoulders touched, how he glanced at me a few times and gave me an irresistible smile.

We disembarked on the parking garage level and Dan steered us to a waiting black SUV. While I marveled at how the car seemed to magically appear, Dan opened the door for me. I skootched in and buckled my seat belt. He climbed in after, taking the middle spot, and did the same.

"Hey, Stan. Take us to Kat's place, okay?"

"Okay." Stan nodded. "Have you seen the baby?"

"Yeah." Dan glanced at me, then lifted his chin to the privacy window controls.

"Is it cute?" Stan pulled out of the garage and onto the street.

"What do you mean, 'Is it cute?' Of course he is cute. He's a baby."

I placed my finger on the button to close the window, but waited, not wanting to be rude and interrupt their conversation.

"Not all babies are cute. I've seen some ugly babies in my time, let me tell you." Stan turned onto the highway ramp.

"Will you listen to this guy?" Dan appealed to me, rolling his eyes. "How many babies could you have seen? What? You hanging out in nurseries in your spare time? Judging baby beauty contests on the weekend?"

"I know people with babies." Stan shrugged.

"What people do you know with babies?"

Without me pressing the button, the window started sliding shut.

"Let me close that for you." Stan's gaze met mine briefly in the rearview mirror. "Give you and Mr. I've Never Seen An Ugly Baby a little privacy."

I had to roll my lips between my teeth because Dan was mumbling, "He knows people with babies."

I wrapped my arm through his and turned my face into his shoulder, laughing silently. Dan also huffed a laugh, his hand coming to my face and encouraging me to tilt my head back.

I did, and our gazes met. His eyes were tired. But they were also happy.

"Hi," he said, and I allowed his voice's soft, seductive cadence to pour over me, warming me, filling my insides with delicious restlessness.

"Hi."

He conducted a sweep of my features in a way that felt cherishing. "We need to talk."

I nodded, suppressing dread and hope, focusing instead on resolve. "We do. I have—I mean—there's a lot I need to tell you."

Dan's mouth curved into a regretful frown. "It'll have to wait. I have to leave. I have a business trip to Australia. I won't be home until next Monday at the earliest."

Oh. Darn.

"When do you leave?"

He glanced at his watch. "In three hours."

I swallowed my disappointment, my gaze falling away.

"Okay." I would miss him. As bizarre as that sounded—since nothing between us was settled—it was true.

"Hey." He slipped a finger under my chin, bringing my eyes back to his. After gazing at me for a long moment, he brushed a light kiss against my lips. I gripped his wrist, seeking more of his mouth, more of him, but he retreated.

Dan peered down at me, his handsome brown eyes earnest. "I'm going to miss you."

My heart suffered a minor explosion of happiness and without thinking, I responded, "I'll miss you, too."

"And we'll talk."

"I'll call you. All the time."

He laughed lightly, looking at me like I was funny. I winced at the eager tone of my voice, trying to amend, "I mean, not all the time. I'll call you when you want to be called, or we could set up a call. You know what I mean."

"No." He shook his head, still smiling. "You said all the time, I expect calls all the time."

I tried to glare at him but failed.

"Just don't call me from the bathroom." He made a face. "My sister Colleen does that and it's fucking gross. Called me from a new French restaurant to tell me it gave her diarrhea *while* she was having diarrhea in the ladies' room. Who does that? It's why I won't ever touch her cell phone."

"Is this the one who is vegan?"

"What? No way. Colleen wouldn't touch a carrot even if it'd give her magical powers. I've never seen her eat a vegetable unless you count potatoes. You're thinking of Aileen. She's the health nut."

"How many sisters do you have?"

"Four." Dan glanced at his watch and cut me off before I could react to the fact that he had four sisters or ask him anything further about his family. "I have a favor to ask."

"What? Anything," I offered immediately.

His eyebrows pulled together and he studied me, giving me the sense my eager response troubled him. Eventually, pulling a key from his pocket, he said, "I'd like you to move into my place."

I blinked at him, the key he held out to me, and his request. "You want—"

"I've been thinking about it since last week. Your uncle said this thing needs to look real, right? How real is it going to look with you still in your apartment and me still in mine? And another thing, what if Caleb shows up while I'm gone? That building of yours only has one door to the outside, easy enough to get through. Our place on Randolph has a doorman, touch sensors on the door, and a concierge with a security lock on the elevator—and that's just the lobby level."

I nodded, trying to separate my instinctive and gleeful first impulse from logic. I needed to think this through rationally, carefully. What were the long-term implications of sharing a space with Dan? I needed to consider not just right now, but also the future.

As though reading my mind, he reminded me, "I have a guest room. You can have the master or the—"

"No. I'm not taking your room. The points you make are good ones. It's just, it would be one thing if this marriage—if things were completely fake between us. I mean, I know the marriage is fake. But we're, we—"

"We dig each other."

"Right." I couldn't stop my grin.

"And you're worried about what happens if things don't work out between us."

"I guess so." But that wasn't quite right.

His expression turned thoughtful, but it looked carefully thoughtful, giving me the sense he was working to keep his features blank.

Dan reached for my hand and placed the key in my palm, encouraging my fingers to close around it. "There is one more thing."

"What's that?"

"Wally."

"Wally?"

"Yeah. I could really use your help with Wally. I've been traveling a lot, and I know it's hard on him." Dan scratched his neck. "And, you know, he likes you, so . . ."

Was he . . . ?

No.

Did he . . . ?

No way.

Is he trying to guilt me into moving?

I stared at Dan, at his handsome face's practiced innocence, and my mind gasped.

He is!

I couldn't believe him. He was using his dog to manipulate me!

On principle, I knew I should be upset.

But in reality, I was completely charmed.

Try to make sense of that, I dare you.

Subduing my smile, I endeavored to wipe my features of anything that might me give away. Instead, I said, "Yes. I'll do it. I'll move in."

Dan nodded, his expression still meticulously thoughtful. "Good," he said, covering my hand with his. "You should start boxing things up tonight. Stan will help, and Nicolas is already on his way."

CHAPTER FOURTEEN

A Public Company: A business company that has issued securities through an initial public offering (IPO) and is traded on at least one stock exchange or the over-the-counter market.

INVESTOPEDIA

Dan

I WAS A bastard.

And I couldn't even claim to be an honest bastard. Not this time.

Fiona had her baby Friday night, Ava Evans Archer.

Janie had her baby Saturday morning, Desmond Daniel Sullivan, if you can believe it.

Now it was Monday, over a week later, and I was on my way back to the States after meeting with our clients in Sydney, Melbourne, Brisbane, and Perth. A freaking Australian tour.

And I was a bastard.

I knew what I'd done. I wasn't one of those cumcakes who had illusions about the ends justifying the means, or any of that wishy-washy bullshit. I was a jerk bastard and I'd manipulated her into moving in with me.

Note, the placement of *man* in the word *man*ipulate. Coincidence? Nope.

I wanted Kat safe while I was gone. I didn't want her cousin sneaking in and carting her off while I was halfway across the world. So I'd laid a guilt trap and she'd tripped into it beautifully.

I hadn't even felt bad.

Okay, I kinda felt bad.

All right, I'd felt really bad.

And I would tell her the truth when I got back from the future in the land of Oz. Telling her over the phone wasn't an option, as I didn't want her changing her mind. Plus, the time difference had been a killer. When I was waking up, Kat was going to sleep and vice versa. My early morning meetings and late night dinners made it worse.

Texting proved to be sporadic, but more successful than trying to arrange a call. We replied to each other when we could, adding random thoughts and carrying on an unconventional conversation, with a ton of gaps in response times.

I was so damn tired, and the only thing keeping me awake was the anticipation of seeing Kat within the hour. As I buckled in for the landing, I scrolled through our messages from the past week for maybe the hundredth time.

Dan: *Just landed in Sydney. What day is it there?*

Kat: *It was the middle of the night on Sunday when I received your message, now it's Monday morning. How are you? How was your day? I hope you are well and you were able to sleep on the plane.*

Kat: *Steven says hi. He is forcing me to type this. He told me to tell you he has video of us kissing at the Clerk's office and he's using it to blackmail you into giving him a raise.*

Dan: *Tell him to put it up on YouTube so I can watch it. How are you? How was your day? Are you up yet?*

Dan: *I shit you not, I just saw a fucking kangaroo hopping down the fucking street! Holy shit.*

Dan: *Goodnight.*

Kat: *Good morning. I can't believe you saw a kangaroo hopping down the street!! :-O That's crazy. I did a little research last night and Australia is supposed to have all the poisonous and dangerous animals, and spiders the size of dinner plates. I WANT TO GO SO BAD!!!*

Kat: *My boss just got back from her business trip and is so jet-lagged. I went into her office to bring her some reports and she was passed out, forehead on her desk. I didn't have the heart to wake her up, so I cancelled all her meetings this afternoon and rescheduled them for next week and I finished her financial report for the division heads meeting for tomorrow morning. I thought about covering her with a blanket, but it felt like crossing a line.*

Kat: *Good night. Thinking of you.*

Dan: *Thinking of me? Were you in bed as you typed that? What were you wearing?*

Dan: *Just read your text about your boss sleeping on her desk. You're a good person. If it had been Quinn, I would've woken him up with a police siren.*

Dan: *Here's an Australian joke for you: Why did the manager hire the marsupial? Because he was koala-fied.*

Dan: *Flying to Brisbane. Miss you.*

Kat: *Good morning. I miss you, too.*

Kat: *When you come home I'd like to take you out on a date.*

Kat: *That joke was very punny.*

Kat: *Please send me a picture of yourself.*

Kat: *I know you're asleep, but I am feeling like my last few text messages aren't coming across as I'd intended. I'm sorry if I make everything weirder than it needs to be.*

Kat: *Goodnight. I'm thinking of you, in my bed, wearing my TARDIS pajamas.*

Dan: *I love waking up to your messages. You make everything both weird and better.*

Dan: *You want me to pick the place? Sandra has me hooked on that Indian restaurant. I can't get enough of the butter chicken. Glad she moved out of that building. The neighborhood is nice, but her building was shit. Your old building wasn't great either. It only had that one security door and your apartment door wasn't reinforced.*

Dan: *Here is a picture of me next to their snake terrarium. This guy behind me is a tiger snake and is one of the deadliest in the world. Send a picture of you.*

Dan: *Goodnight. Thinking of you in your bed, wearing your TARDIS pajamas.*

Kat: *Good morning. Thank you for the picture. I'm missing you today.*

Kat: *This is a picture of me in front of The Bean on my way to work. I'm supposed to see Janie and Desmond today, so I'll send another one later.*

I paused a moment here, as I'd been doing since she sent the photo. I liked how wide her smile was, how her eyes were big and happy. I couldn't wait to see her again, the real her. She was probably in my apartment right now. Maybe she wasn't waiting for me, but she'd be there when I got home.

My stubbornness refused to admit her being there and her waiting for me weren't the same thing.

Kat: *Here I am with Desmond. Stan took the picture. P.S. Stan thinks Desmond is cute, so he must be cute. As we know, Stan is the baby expert.*

I paused here, too. Chuckling at her text, but also liking the way she looked holding a baby. The shitty feeling in my chest had become something else as soon as she'd sent this picture. Something good. Something I would miss, probably mourn, if I never saw her again.

Kat: *Time for bed. I hope you have a good day. <3*

Dan: *Thanks for the pictures. Sweet dreams.*

Kat: *How was your day?*

Dan: *Hey, I'm just finishing with a meeting, and I was thinking about you. Have you heard from Eugene? Anything new going on with your cousin? We should call that guy by the code name Tiny Satan.*

Dan: *I'm on my way to a dinner thing. Day was good but long. These people make fun of the way I talk, one guy asked if the letter "R" was against my religion. Cheeky fuck.*

Dan: *These people can hold their liquor. I switched to water an hour ago and these guys are still going, and one lady is drinking them all under the table. She doesn't appear to be affected yet, liver of steel on this one.*

I wasn't yet finished going through our messages—I still had four days' worth—when a new message flashed on my screen. The number wasn't one I recognized, but that didn't matter because the sender announced himself right off the bat.

#: *This is Eugene Marks. Please call me ASAP. Use this number.*

There was only one reason Eugene would use ASAP, and that one reason was Tiny Satan.

The plane landed, just touched down. Certain in the knowledge that I'd be stuck on the runway for a few minutes as we taxied to the hanger, I leaned forward and returned his call, a spike of adrenaline waking me up.

He answered on the second ring. "Mr. O'Malley."

"Eugene."

The old guy hesitated, like he hadn't expected me to use his first name even though I'd used it every time we'd talked.

He recovered. "Where are you? Where is Kathleen? She has her phone off."

I saw no reason to evade his questions. "It's the middle of the night, so I assume she's asleep at home. I'm on a plane at O'Hare. Why?"

"You're leaving?"

"No. I'm arriving. What's going on?"

"Kathleen isn't at her apartment."

"No. Like I said, she's home. She's at our place."

Again, he hesitated, but this time he hadn't quite recovered when he spoke. "Your place? She moved in?"

"Yeah."

I picked a piece of lint from my pant leg while I listened to him sigh a big sigh of relief.

"That's great."

"What's going on, Eugene? Talk to me."

"Caleb flew out to Chicago this afternoon, with reinforcements."

Motherfucker.

I gritted my teeth, feeling a lot less bad that I'd tricked Kat into moving to my place. "Private security?"

"Yes. But he may involve the local authorities at this point. He has a temporary emergency order for guardianship, which is of course invalid since the two of you are married. But he doesn't know that, not yet. I've been attempting to reach Kathleen. I discovered this information an hour ago when Caleb called me, asking me to confirm her address."

"That fucktrumpet was waiting for her? At her old place?" Adrenaline took a back seat to fury, fury took the wheel, and fury was a terrible driver.

"He doesn't know she's married, but it might make strategic sense for me to tell him." No hesitation this time, but I also got the impression he was talking to himself.

"Why would you tell that cumbucket anything?" I was yelling. When I'm pissed, I yell, and Tiny Satan made me want to yodel from a damn mountain. Like I said, fury was a terrible driver.

"As long as he trusts me, I'm privy to information that might prove advantageous." Meanwhile, Eugene didn't sound even a little bit ruffled.

"Okay, yeah. That makes sense." Resolve took over from fury, but fury stuck close by, just in case some skulls needed cracking. "So why haven't you told Caleb that Kat is hitched?"

"Mr. O'Malley—Daniel—you haven't sent the postnup. Did you receive the new copy? With the changes you requested?"

"Oh, yeah. I signed it, but data has been spotty since we took off. Kat still needs to sign."

"Yes. Good, good. Have her sign and then have your lawyer send it to my work email. I'll text you the address. If your lawyer adds language suggesting their firm drafted the document, I would not object."

"Gotcha."

"Then, I will notify the judge and Caleb that Kathleen is married. The order will have to be rescinded." The way he said this had me fighting off a smirk.

"Sounds like breaking the news to Caleb is going to be a real hardship, huh?"

I didn't know Eugene very well. Before now, we'd only spoken on the phone twice to review changes I wanted to the postnup. But sometimes—like now—he reminded me of Mr. Burns from *The Simpsons*, whenever the greedy geezer would say, "Excellent" with his fingers tented.

"At times, it is necessary to willingly undertake an unpleasant task, or make a personal sacrifice, for the collective benefit of one's friends or colleagues." I thought I detected a smile in his voice, but I couldn't be sure.

"Taking one for the team, Eugene?"

"Precisely. Send the postnup. Have a pleasant evening, Daniel."

"You can call me Dan."

"Then have a pleasant evening, Dan."

"You too, Eugene."

Cracking up, I ended the call. Splitting my attention between adding Eugene's new number to my contacts and checking our progress on the runway, I decided I really liked this guy. No wonder Kat felt comfortable calling him Uncle.

* * *

YOU KNOW how you have fantasies about everyday shit? Like someone doing a good job on your quarterly tax returns, baking you a cake for no reason, or sweeping up all the dog hair in the corners of your apartment?

Guess what? My apartment smelled like cake.

The scent of vanilla was the first thing I noticed as I entered. Leaving my bag by the door, shutting it, locking it, and then tossing my suit jacket to the chair in the hall, I inhaled deeply. Fucking heaven, that smell.

The second, there were no traces that Kat lived here. No shoes by the front door, no coat in the closet, nothing.

Third, Wally was nowhere to be seen.

"Wally?" I whispered, not wanting to wake up Kat. Even though I didn't see any of her stuff, I assumed she was in her room asleep.

Toeing off my shoes, I unfastened my cuffs, loosened my tie, and undid the first few buttons of my shirt while I strained for the sound of my dog.

Silence.

"Hmm." I frowned into the darkness. He was probably all cozied up next to Kat, unwilling to move.

Next to my wife.

Now there was a thought made to erase a frown. Not going to lie, the fact that Kat was my wife—and that was a fact—also did things to me.

Using light steps, I strolled into the great room, intent on the bureau where I stashed my mail. I almost didn't see the figure on the couch—almost—but she moved at the last minute, stopping me in my tracks.

Pushing back the blanket covering her and lifting herself to a sitting position, Kat's sleepy voice said, "Dan?"

I held my breath for a second, maybe four, as I took in the sight of her. Her hair was in a ponytail, or a braid—yeah, a braid—over her shoulder, and she was rubbing her eyes. She wore a tank top of undistinguishable color. The room was dark, but city lights from the windows illuminated enough.

She was gorgeous.

"Hey," I said into the grayish darkness, stuffing my hands in my pockets and keeping my tone soft. "What are you doing out here?"

At the sound of my voice, a furry head lifted and a tail tapped out a slow beat against the leather couch. Wally sneezed, and leaped down from where he'd been sleeping. Taking a moment to stretch and shake, he walked over to me as best he could given the fact his tail was wagging so hard now it almost knocked him over.

"I wanted to see you." Kat yawned, placing her feet on the ground like she was planning to stand, but paused to fold the blanket she'd been using and draped it neatly over the back of the couch.

I squatted to accept Wally's affection, scratching him behind the ears and patting his back. "You take good care of my lady while I was gone?" Wally snuffed, and I had to dodge a lick straight to the kisser. "Whoa. Settle down, boy. Buy me a drink first."

The light, musical sound of Kat's laughter filled the air, and something in me that had been on high alert since learning Caleb was in town shifted.

It eased.

It settled.

Now for the tenth time since hanging up with Eugene, I thought, *Thank God she moved in.* I knew she'd be safe here. I'd been counting on it. But hearing her laugh made me think maybe she was happy, too.

I stood and so did she, her arms crossed over her middle. Wally continued to dance around my legs as I looked at her. I was tired, but not too tired to notice all she had on was that tank top and the smallest shorts I'd ever seen. The effect on my pulse was instantaneous.

"Come here," I said, speaking a wish.

Kat stepped around the coffee table and shuffled over to me, her eyes on mine, clearly in a wish-granting mood.

"I missed you," she said, her words slurred with what I assumed was sleep. Standing in front of me, she made no move to close the final few inches, so I lifted her arms to my neck. Her chin lifted to keep looking in my eyes, like we did this. Like every day I came home and she was waiting for me on the couch, baking me cakes, wearing (almost) my favorite outfit.

I fucking loved it.

Even as I touched her, my hands coming to her body, the heat of her skin beneath my fingertips, my greediness for this woman arrested my lungs. That new aching sense of rightness, the one that had replaced the shitty feeling in my chest, took hold, sinking hooks and anchor into me.

"Kiss me," I said, another wish.

She did. Her arms twisted tighter and her sweet lips brushed against mine. Unable and unwilling to prolong the moment, I crushed her to me and invaded her, the stroke of my tongue an echo of what I really wanted.

Kat tasted like mint and heat and something else. Something distinctively her that made me want to taste every inch of her body. I wanted more, of course I wanted more, and the more I wanted oscillated between the fucking hearts and flowers and happily ever after variety, and the just plain fucking variety.

Images of me pulling down her top and worshiping her bare breasts flashed behind my eyes. Maybe she'd like it when I sucked her into my mouth; maybe she'd squirm when I stroked her over those tiny shorts; maybe she'd let me peel them down her legs as I knelt and opened her, spread her, and tasted her hot, wet—

"Dan," Kat pulled her mouth from mine, her breath ragged. "We need—"

I chased her mouth for one more kiss.

Just one more.

Because as tempting—so fucking tempting—as the promise of my overheated imagination was, the hearts and flowers part reminded me that there was too much unresolved. We needed to talk before we had a repeat of our kiss-turned-soft-core-porno at the Clerk's office.

Plus, I was tired. If or when things escalated, I didn't want sloppy one-hour jet-lag shagging. I wanted sports drinks and carbohydrates at the ready for a fuckathon of twelve to seventeen hours, with a warm up and cool down period. And a hot tub.

I softened the kiss, reluctantly loosening my hold so I could lean away.

"Hey, Kit-Kat." I struggled to keep my voice steady, keep my eyes on hers, and keep the raging hard on in my pants from unduly influencing my next two or three decisions.

Her chin still tilted upward, her eyes still closed, she said, "Hey,

Dan the Security Man." The words were still slightly slurred, and this time I heard how sleepy she was in the sloppy way she said *security*, too many syllables.

I lifted an eyebrow at her. "You okay?"

Her eyelashes fluttered open and she stared at me, her lips parted. "Uh . . . just a little tired."

"Hmm." Unable to help myself, I pressed my lips to hers one more time before separating our bodies, sliding my hands down her arms and raising her knuckles to my mouth for more kisses.

"Thanks for waiting up." I kissed her right hand. "Did you bake me a cake?" I kissed her left hand.

"Yes. Cake." She sounded and looked dazed, watching me trail my lips along her fingers.

"Can I have some?"

She nodded, her eyes trained on her wrist where I kissed the soft skin of the inside and then licked it. Kat shivered, releasing an unsteady breath.

I grinned, liking her reaction. I liked how she clearly needed time to gather her wits after waking up. I liked her being here. *I'd like it better if I hadn't tricked her into moving in.*

The thought was a wet blanket to the face and the nuts. I sighed, lowering her hand and tugging her to the guest room. "Come on."

"Where are we going?"

"You're going back to sleep."

Three more steps and then she stopped suddenly, bringing us both to a halt. "What? But you just got home."

"Yeah. I'm going to sleep, too. After I eat some cake."

Kat turned, now she was tugging us toward the kitchen and she said through a yawn, "We'll have some together. You tell me about your trip, we'll catch up. Then we'll sleep."

She sounded better, her words more solid, so I gave in. Allowing her to push me into a dining room chair, she placed a quick kiss on my cheek and then left me, turning to the cupboard. She stood there for a minute, frowning.

"What was I doing?"

"Cake?"

"Yes." She nodded once, then shook her head. "Yes. Cake. Sorry. Still sleepy."

Kat pulled plates out of the cupboard, setting them very, very carefully on the counter like she was afraid they would break. The kitchen was illuminated by a single light from above the stove, but it was bright enough that I could see the counters were absolutely spotless. If she'd baked the cake in this kitchen, there was no sign of dirty dishes or pots and pans.

Also, her tank top was blue and so were her itty bitty shorts.

"How was the flight? Did you get any sleep?" She yawned again.

My stare lifted from her backside and I leaned my elbows on the table, rubbing my eyes. "It was—uh—fine. Got work done. I slept when we left, but not much after that. How was work?"

"Good. The reports I finished last week for my boss—I texted you about them—she wants to share with a potential investor." Kat set the plates, forks, and a big, round Tupperware container on the table. She turned away again, grabbing two glasses and moving to the water dispenser in the door of the fridge.

"Oh. That's great. Right?"

Kat grinned at me, like she thought I was cute. "Yes. That's great. It's exciting. Well, it's as exciting as my work gets. It means she was impressed with my work."

I returned her smile automatically, because there was no way I could see her smile and not return it.

But then, as she finished filling the last glass, she said, "Oh, I'm almost completely moved in. Anything we have in duplicate, like dishes and such, Stan said I could put mine in the basement storage."

My neck itched (to the surprise of absolutely no one), and holding a smile became impossible after that.

Tell her. Confess.

If I told her now, she might not give me cake.

Daniel, confess.

But . . . cake.

No cake until you confess.

Shit.

"So, uh." I itched my neck. "I have to tell you something."

"What is it?" Kat brought the waters to the table, sitting across from me.

I gathered a deep breath, prepared to spill my guts, but then she opened the Tupperware to reveal a cake.

But not just any cake.

This cake looked like something out of a magazine. The frosting was smooth and burnished, varying shades of dark blue, like the night sky complete with little gleaming dots for stars. In the center of the cake were the words "Welcome Home Dan" in bright green, yellow, and blue surrounded by what looked like fireworks. It wasn't huge, but it was definitely the most impressive cake I'd ever seen.

I frowned even as my mouth watered, because—intricate or not—it smelled like cake. "You made this?"

"Yes." The hint of uncertainty in her tone drew my attention to her face. She looked regretful as she sat across from me and I couldn't figure out why.

This woman is magical. Why would she regret her own magic?

"I . . ." I huffed a laugh. "You decorate cakes on the side or something?"

"No." She shook her head, not smiling, her eyes watchful and wide. Even in the dim light I could see she was blushing.

"This is—I mean, this is the most amazing cake I've ever seen. It's unbelievable. I feel like I need to take a picture. Are we allowed to eat it?"

"I'm sorry, it's too much." She twisted her fingers, two wrinkles appearing between her eyebrows. "I thought I'd try—I'm sorry."

"Hey. No. No way. Never apologize for being amazing, otherwise I suspect you'd be apologizing all the time. Although, if it tastes as good as it looks—even one tenth as good as it looks—I might die. You might murder me with happiness."

A tentative smile brightened her face. "Murder you with happiness?"

"Cake is my favorite. I'd eat it for every meal if I could and not get the diabetes."

"*The* diabetes?" Her mouth kicked up.

I reached for the cake and the knife she'd brought over; it might be the world's most impressive looking cake, but it was still cake. What good was a cake if you didn't eat it?

"My Uncle Kip has the diabetes, almost lost his leg a year ago."

"Kip? I thought his name was Zip."

"No. Zip is a different uncle." I sliced into the cake, dishing her out a piece first. "Zip has the metal plate in his head and his cellar smells suspicious."

"Suspicious?"

"Vinegar and chili or something." Passing her the slice, I admired her cake's intricate interior. The bottom half was chocolate and had the consistency of a brownie; the top half looked to be vanilla; and she'd put raspberry jam—or something that looked, smelled, and tasted like raspberry jam—between the two layers. "He was in the hospital for over a month. And you know what my aunt did when he was discharged?"

"Zip?"

"Kip. With the diabetes."

"Got it. What did she do?"

"She baked him a cake." I glanced to the ceiling, appealing to heaven for patience. "My Aunt Sheila means well, but she's dumb as paint."

Kat chuckled a little, but when I looked back to her she was shaking her head at me. "That's not nice."

"Sometimes the truth isn't nice, but that doesn't make it any less of a truth. If people stop telling the truth just because it might hurt someone's feelings, what good does that do? I'd rather have a painful truth than a cushy bed inflated by lies. Besides, Aunt Sheila made her husband a cake after he'd been hospitalized for eating too many cakes. She's either working a long game, trying to murder him with vanilla frosting, or she's two sandwiches short of a picnic."

Careful to get the brownie layer, raspberry jam, vanilla cake, and blue frosting all at the same time, I shoveled a piece of the cake into my mouth while she laughed.

And then I moaned.

"This is the best fucking cake in the history of cakes," I spoke around the bite, wanting her to know as soon as possible. I motioned with a wave of my hand to the piece on my plate, the Tupperware, to her. "Magical."

She laughed again, more like a giggle this time, shaking her head as she watched me. I watched her right back, because she was licking frosting off her fork, her tongue a shade of blue from the confectionary night sky.

"I'm glad you like it."

Swallowing, I lifted an eyebrow at her. "Like it? I love it. I'd marry it, but I'm already married to you."

That made her laugh anew and she took a sip of water, watching me eat over her glass's rim.

I was almost finished inhaling my first slice when she asked, "What were you going to say?"

"Uh, more cake please?"

Grinning at me, she shook her head and served me another slice anyway. "No. Before that. You said you had something to tell me. What did you need to tell me?"

"Oh. Right. That." Damn.

Rip the Band-Aid off, Daniel. Rip it off.

I set my fork back on the table next to the new piece of cake and I cleared my throat. "When we were driving to your place, before I left for Australia, while what I said about Wally was true—that I could use your help—I said it hoping it would push—or rather, guilt—you into accepting my offer to move in. It worked, and I'm glad it did, but I wanted to be honest about my intentions. So. There you go." I crossed my arms over my chest, bracing for her reaction.

She grinned at me like I was something adorable. "I know."

I felt my eyebrows jump on my forehead. "You know?"

"Correct."

"Really?" I turned my head slightly, peering at her. "And you moved in anyway?"

"Our marriage wouldn't look real if we didn't live together, and I need it to look real. Knowing my cousin as I do, I wouldn't put it past him to hire goons to take me to Boston, to lock me up while he pursued his case for guardianship."

"Oh yeah, about that." I heaved another sigh, shaking my head. "I have news. Eugene was trying to call you earlier—a few hours ago—and couldn't reach you on your cell. So he called me right after I landed. Turns out, you're right, Caleb did hire some guys to pick you up."

Kat sat straighter like I'd startled her, her lips parting. "What?"

"He—they—flew in this afternoon and were waiting for you at your old place. Eugene wants you to sign the postnup ASAP." I reached into my pocket and withdrew my phone, navigating to the DocuSign screen. "All you need to do is sign, then we're done. I'll email it to him. He wants me to make some broad statement about my lawyers preparing the document, I've already drafted the email. Let me see . . . here, sign here."

I handed her my phone and pointed to the spot where she needed to sign with her finger.

She stared at the screen for a moment, her eyebrows knitted in plain confusion, then signed and handed me back my phone. "Why do you need to make it look like your lawyers drafted it?"

"My guess is he wants to make it look like he didn't know anything about our marriage until after the fact. Lisa—you know, Nico's sister?—she's my lawyer, now *our* lawyer. She's supposed to attach the postnup to the email,"—which I was sending to Lisa as we spoke—"tell him you're married, your address has changed, and then it looks like he wasn't involved. If he wasn't involved, then it keeps him off Caleb's radar and he can still feed us information." I hit send and the email to Lisa was off.

All done.

She stabbed at her cake, still looking disgruntled. "I can't believe Caleb."

"You can't?"

"No. I mean, I can. It's just, I'm . . ." She stabbed at her cake again, and she was grinding her teeth.

"Pissed?"

"Yes." She smiled like she surrendered. "Moving in here was a good idea. It was the best course of action given the constraints of time and resources. I saw through your ploy at the time, but it didn't really matter. I was going to say yes anyway. And now, I'm gratef—I mean, I'm glad you thought of it."

By the time she was finished, I was squinting at her, trying to keep the pleased grin from my face. "You 'saw through my ploy'? You think you're pretty smart, don't you?"

"I am smart." Kat took a bite of cake, licking the excess icing from her fork. My attention dropped to her mouth. I would just have to accept that every time she took a bite of cake she was going to lick her fork afterward. But I swear, it was the best kind of torture.

"What are you thinking about?" She sounded honestly curious. "Are you concerned about Caleb?"

"That shitbird?" I snorted. "No. Eugene said his guardianship order was rushed, temporary, and something about it not being valid if you're married."

"That's a relief."

She licked her lips. Hypnotic.

"Yeah."

"Dan?"

I bet she tastes like cake.

"Yeah?"

Only one way to find out.

"What are you thinking about?"

"Cake."

"My cake?" She smiled, her voice soft and expectant. She had a beautiful voice, and a beautiful smile.

"You could say that." I lifted my eyes back to hers, wishing I wasn't jet-lagged. Wishing this was months from now, and things were settled, and she was naked.

"Any requests for next time?"

"Next time?" I was still distracted by thoughts of her naked.

"Yeah, next time. What's your favorite kind of cake?"

I cleared my throat, scratched my jaw, figuring I probably shouldn't say, *Kat flavored.* So I opted for, "I like big bundts and I cannot lie."

A surprised laugh erupted like a choking sound, and then she covered her mouth when a new wave of laughter overtook her. Her laugh was beautiful.

Meanwhile, I lopped off a large piece of my second slice, again careful to grab some of the top and middle layers of frosting. And then I groaned all over again. Kat, Wally, and cake—could life get any better?

Still smiling and chuckling a little, she set her fork down and rested her elbows on the table, staring at her plate thoughtfully. "Can I tell you, I like that you ordered two sandwiches at Capriotti's. I've been thinking about it a lot and I think I need to be more like that. I need to order two sandwiches when I can't decide which one I want. I can always take leftovers home, so it's not like it'll go to waste. There's no reason I shouldn't order two sandwiches."

Her little tirade had me grinning.

Then she asked, "Can I try yours next time?"

"Of course." I shrugged, my voice lowering in the way I knew would make her blush. "You can have anything you want."

At the suggestiveness in my tone, her eyes cut to mine. She did blush. She also leaned back in her chair to study me.

"Dan."

"Yeah?"

"Talk to me about gratitude."

"Gratitude?" I blinked.

"Why do you hate it when I thank you for helping me?"

Grimacing, I moved my attention to some random point over her shoulder. "So, here's the thing . . ."

I didn't know how to start, and that was the God's honest truth. Things were good up 'til now, even with the talk of Tiny Satan. But this shit? I hated talking about my dad. I hated thinking about him.

217

But she'd asked. And she deserved an answer.

"I don't know if you have any experience with something like this, but I don't like the idea of making the same mistakes as my parents."

"I might have some experience with that, yes." She smiled warmly, giving me the impression she didn't mind the absurdity of my statement, and nodded for me to continue.

I placed my fork next to my plate, wiped my hands on my napkin, crossed my arms, and stared at a crumb of vanilla cake on the table. Tired to my bones all of a sudden, I was too exhausted to explain the whole sordid history of my family.

"Look, gratefulness isn't a reason for two people to be together. It always ends, and it always ends badly. One person feels worthless, the other person feels bitter and trapped. I need to know the reason you're giving us a shot doesn't have anything to do with gratitude."

She studied me, the movement of her hands snagging my attention. She was twisting the ring on her left finger, the ring I'd given her at the hospital. Seeing her wearing it, realizing that she'd been wearing it all week, improved my mood like not much else could've in that moment.

"You don't want me to be grateful because you don't want us to start—for things between us to start—with gratitude as a foundation?"

I gave her a small smile, wanting to convey that I wasn't upset with her. It was the memory of what my father had done that pissed me off.

"Yeah. That's part of it. But I also don't want you to be grateful for something I did thinking only of myself."

"You're telling me, you married me because you wanted to? You want to be *married*? To me?"

I tilted my head back and forth, considering how best to answer. "More like, anything that paves the way for you to give me a shot—as long as you weren't doing it out of gratitude—and anything that kept you from marrying someone else, I'd sign up for."

"I still don't understand why this is such a big deal to you. But, Dan, I am grateful. I can't help that."

A familiar coldness, frustration snuffed out all my good humor.

Kat reached across the table, her palm up in invitation. "But gratitude has nothing to do with the way I kissed you at the Clerk's office.

218

When I think about you, when I've thought about you over the last two plus years, gratitude was never the first—or the second, or the third—thought in my mind."

Oh.

Well.

If she's going to put it like that.

"What was the first thought?"

She huffed a self-conscious laugh, moving to withdraw her hand but I caught it before she could.

"You tell me yours and I'll tell you mine." I dropped my voice again, hoping to see her pink cheeks while I held her hand and gaze captive.

Her stare grew a little hazy. "Lust."

I grinned, because it was the right answer, and I leaned forward. "And what's the second?"

She didn't hesitate. "I didn't deserve you."

What the—?

If one of us didn't deserve the other, I was definitely the undeserving asshole in this scenario. "Why would you think that?"

"Because—"

"Because of the guys you've been with? Because, I have to tell you, being with other people doesn't make you any more or less deserving of happiness. It's like owning a couch. Why should anyone care if you own a couch?"

"I know that. Or rather, I know that now. But my thoughts about deserving good things? It's so many things." She rubbed her forehead with her free hand. "Until Janie and Sandra, Ashley, Elizabeth, and Fiona, my closest friend—if you can even call him that—was my family's lawyer. It's difficult—no, it's impossible—as a child to see yourself as worthy or worth knowing if no one else does."

I felt my frown intensify at her confession, but before I could offer my opinion on the subject, she spoke over me. "I've been going to therapy, and I'm so much better. It's not magic, and it's not a cure-all, and it's been work to get to this point, but I like myself, who I am now, the choices I'm making now—which is a big step. Even though it might sound trite to like oneself, it's a big deal for me. And so, I have these scripts—that's what my therapist calls them—in my head, of certain things, and they make having normal, healthy relationships—they make intimacy, being intimate—very difficult. Not just for me, but for—for—"

I waited, watching her as she struggled. Make no mistake about it, she was struggling. Whatever she couldn't bring herself to say bumped up my heart rate.

"Okay. Back up. What do you mean by script? What does that mean?"

"A script is like, when the first time you do something, or the first few times you do something—like have—like be physically intimate—you do it a certain way, or in a certain state."

"A state? What? Like Florida?"

She closed her eyes, clearly trying not to laugh. She also covered her face, mumbling, "This is so embarrassing."

No.

No way.

I didn't want to embarrass her. Nor did I want her to feel like anything she said to me was embarrassing. Didn't she understand by now? Nothing she said or did was going to send me running.

"You got kink? I can work with kink. As long as it isn't illegal. Or painful." I thought for a moment, and then added, "Or polyamory."

A laugh burst from her lips, but she still couldn't bring herself to open her eyes. "I want to tell you, because you should know before you decide whether you want to—to—"

"Okay, stop right there." I let her hand go and her eyes flew open at the sound of my chair scraping against the wooden floor. I walked around the table, took the seat next to hers, and recaptured her fingers. "Look. We got time. Just because we're married doesn't mean you owe me anything. We take things slow, no biggie." I shrugged. "You don't have to tell me anything you don't want to tell me, or you're not ready to tell me. But—this thing, with us?—it's already happening."

Whatever it was, if she wasn't ready to say it, then I didn't want to hear it.

Needing the feel of her, I lifted my hand to her beautiful face, her skin unbelievably soft, and something in me relaxed when she immediately covered it with hers, leaning into my touch.

"It's already started. There is no more *before I decide*," I added, softening my tone, tugging her forward and whispering just before taking her mouth, "I've decided."

CHAPTER FIFTEEN

Shareholder: Any person, company or other institution that owns at least one share of a company's stock.

INVESTOPEDIA

Kat

THE SUN WASN'T up, but I was, sorta.

In a sleepy yet not quite asleep haze, I reached for Dan, finding a warm patch of bed instead.

We'd fallen asleep together in my bed. I'd lured him into the guest bedroom, asking him to show me where the light switch was for the closet—I already knew where it was, but it was the only way I could think to get him into my room—and then I suggested he try out my comforter as it was the world's most comfortable blanket. Dan hadn't required much convincing.

At first I tried to get comfortable, giving him space. But then he'd reached for me, pulled me to him, and it was heavenly. I'd fallen asleep curled around his body, my cheek on his chest while he lay next to me, his arm around my shoulders and back, his big hand on my hip.

Sleeping with Dan as my pillow had been a blissfully relaxing and thrilling experience, and I'd dreamed sweet, soft dreams of contentment.

Presently, as I lifted myself on an elbow and blinked at the surrounding darkness, I couldn't remember a time I'd ever slept so peacefully. "Dan?"

"Hey," he whispered, and I spotted movement from the far side of the room, his form a vague silhouette against the city lights beyond the window. "I'm here."

"Can't sleep?" I yawned, glancing at the clock on the nightstand. It wasn't yet 5:00 AM.

"Did I wake you?" Dan crossed the room and sat on the edge of the bed, releasing a laugh that sounded frustrated. "My sleep is all fucked up. It feels like moon o'clock and I'm on the south pole of Mars."

I could just decipher his outline. He still wore the pants and T-shirt he'd been in earlier. "Maybe you're wearing too many clothes, those pants can't be comfortable." I snuggled under the covers even as I flipped the blanket open on his side, hoping he'd climb in again. "What do you usually wear to sleep?"

He hesitated, then said, "Usually nothing. Or just my boxers."

Quite abruptly, I was awake.

I was more than awake.

I was officially alert.

"Oh." My heart beat double time, images of a birthday-suit-wearing Dan danced in my vision. I mean, he wasn't dancing, but the images of him were.

Dan seemed to consider me before finally asking, "Do you mind if I—"

"No I don't mind!" I blurted, and then cringed as soon as the words erupted. Grateful for the scant illumination provided by the city and moonlight through the window, I cursed myself silently for the overly eager response,

It wasn't that I was afraid he'd change his mind about us, or want to back out if I let my puerile flag fly. More like, I didn't want to subject him—or anyone—to the puerile flag. I wanted to be someone thoughtful, who didn't blurt, who didn't react without careful consideration. I wanted to be sophisticated and mature.

And, mostly, I felt I was firmly on the road to becoming that thoughtful, considerate, even-tempered person. Except, apparently, when asked my opinion about spending time with Dan, or Dan being naked. Then I morphed into an immature dork.

To his credit, he didn't seem to mind my outburst. His luscious lips curved into an irresistible smile and he stood, holding my gaze, his eyes glinting in the grayish light. Reaching for his shirt's hem, he pulled it off, and my hands fisted in the covers.

Now I was cursing the inadequacy of the scant moonlight, and my heart was beating triple time.

Shadows of ink swirled over the bulk of his shoulders and strong arms. Unable to see the details clearly, I could tell the designs at his neck were the tip of the tattoo iceberg. Smoky lines hinted at intricate patterns, all of which ended at his chest, his toned stomach and sides had been left untouched.

I'd been so distracted by his torso, I didn't realize he'd already removed his pants—but kept on his boxer briefs—until he was climbing into bed next to me.

My heart gave a little jump as one muscular leg slid against mine, the fine hairs an exhilarating texture, the weight of him substantial, his chest a formidable wall. He pulled me against his body, placing a light kiss on my lips, and then leaned slightly away.

"Hey," his voice rumbled. I felt the vibration of his words, and everything about him felt so solid and intense and electrifying.

I told myself to calm down. I told myself not to be a puerile dork. I told myself to be sophisticated.

"Hi," I responded, my tone steady, firm, not dorky. "Are you tired?"

He shook his head, his eyes moving to my lips. "Are you?"

His knee bent then, his upper leg brushing lightly against the apex of my thighs, causing my breath to hitch as a spark ignited at my center. I told myself to breathe in, and then breathe out, each inhale and exhale precise, least I do or say or blurt something embarrassing and ruin the moment.

Don't be a ruiner.

But the resultant spark of heat became a multifaceted thing, curling and twisting, a knot low in my belly. Tendrils of hot, raw sensation expanded with each of my measured breaths, his leg's firm press, making thought difficult and speaking impossible.

Therefore, I shook my head, answering his last question wordlessly and braced myself for the impact of his smile. What I didn't prepare for was the smolder and intent in his eyes. The obscuring darkness made everything feel closer, weightier, louder, like a whispered secret.

Dan's hand slid down my arm to my hip, gripping me; his head bent, his tongue and teeth loving my neck. I closed my eyes, taking another careful breath, and felt . . . okay.

Worry, mostly absent until now, tightened my throat, and ballooned slowly in my chest, because I wanted to feel more than just okay. I wanted to feel *great*. Anxiety was a different kind of burn, like frostbite, and it unfolded itself. A silent monster, standing and stomping out the spark in my abdomen and the feelings of *okayness,* replacing everything with nothing.

No chill, no warmth, just a sudden void of agitation.

No. No, no, no!

Tears pricked my eyes and I blinked them away, my hands moving over his stomach, his sides, my legs shifting against his as I chased the earlier spark. But though I felt a tad frantic, I continued regulating my breaths. I didn't want him to know.

He hadn't done anything wrong. He was Dan, funny and sexy, sweet and stubborn. His body was amazing, the way he moved the fulfillment of all my dirty dreams and desires.

He was perfect.

I was the problem.

He touched me, his palm caressing my backside over my sleep shorts, his fingers trailing around to the front of my stomach, his touch light against the hem of my pajamas. I held my breath, waiting for... something. For my body to, I don't know, kick in. Work correctly.

Dan's mouth lowered to my shirt, suckling my breast over the fabric as his finger dipped into me. I concentrated on that, on him, on the light massaging movements, on how much I wanted him, needing so very, very desperately to feel one tenth the amount of hot and bothered I'd felt just moments ago.

But I didn't.

I clenched my teeth, battling against the tide of disappointment.

Dan paused at my breast, his movements stilling. Lifting his head, his narrowed eyes found mine. "Hey, are you okay?"

"Yeah. Great." I tried to sound convincing, giving a little moan.

His hand at my pelvis ceased stroking me. "Are you . . . Kat—"

I lifted my chin and kissed him, pressing my body against his, trying my best to recreate the heat between us as I flattened my palm against the bulge at the front of his boxers. But I couldn't.

He felt amazing.

And I felt numb.

Why isn't this working? What is wrong with you? Why don't you work?

Renewed tears of frustration stung my eyes and I swallowed, telling myself to calm down. Maybe if I relaxed and retraced my steps. *Maybe if I—*

Dan caught my wrist and moved it away from where I touched him, flipping me onto my back and rising above me.

I saw he was frowning, his eyes searching. "Hey. What's going on?"

"What do you mean?" I tried to kiss him again and he dodged it, tilting his head to one side.

"You're not into this, I can tell."

"Don't be silly."

"Kat." His voice grew firmer and now he held himself completely away. "You don't have to do anything you don't want to do."

"I know."

He looked confused, but not irritated. "If you don't want this, just say so."

"But I *want* to." I reached for him and he evaded me, sitting up on his heels.

"You don't."

"I want you," I cried, hearing the edge of desperation in my voice and cringing again at the new outburst.

He stared at me for a beat, his gaze probing. "Maybe you do, but your body sure as hell doesn't. Excuse my crassness, but you're as dry as a fucking desert, and I can tell when your moans are fake and when they're real."

I closed my eyes at his brutal honesty, biting my bottom lip to keep my chin from wobbling. I covered my face with my hands and turned away. Melancholy crushed me, breathing felt impossible let alone any attempt at measuring my inhales.

I'd been so certain this time would be different because this time I was with Dan. He was magical, and I could hug and snuggle him without having to force myself to relax, and I loved holding his hand, and we'd kissed before with passion and heat and fire.

And I trusted him. I trusted him completely.

"I'm so sorry," I whispered, pressing my lips together so they wouldn't tremble.

"Kit-Kat, don't be sorry," his tenderness struck me like a blow even as he reached for my shoulder with gentle fingers. "I'm not going anywhere. You're going through a lot, with everything. I'm being an asshole—"

"You're not." I shook my head vehemently.

"—and I don't want you to regret anything that happens between us. We'll wait." He kissed my temple, tucking me against him, holding me close. "We'll wait to fool around until things are better, calmer."

"It won't make any difference," I said bitterly, shaking my head and rolling my eyes at myself.

"What do you mean?"

"I can't." *Ugh.* I hated how I sounded, so small, weak. And I hated how I felt, exposed, like a failure.

"You . . . can't?"

"It's not the stress. I want to, I want you, but I don't know how to . . ." I huffed, irritated with myself for how I was basically hiding against his chest. He needed to know, and I should have told him before now, before I'd let him down.

Pushing away, I forced my eyes to his and blurted the truth of it, "I can't do this unless I'm drunk."

He reared back, his body now tense, as though he'd been shocked by an electric current. Dan's gorgeous eyes moved between mine and he seemed to be struggling to find words.

Eventually, he said, "Are you serious?"

"I've never—I'm sorry." I covered my face with my hands again. A stabbing pain cut through the numbness, almost unbearable, and I choked on a ridiculous sob as I tried to move away.

"What? No. Don't apologize." He encircled me in his arms, not letting me leave.

I didn't struggle against him, and I didn't cry. I held my breath and forced myself to get a grip, to focus, to step away from all the swirling wishes and hopes and desires I'd been carrying around, and surrender to the fact that maybe I was just built this way.

I wasn't a sexual person.

I didn't like sex.

And that was that.

The cold certainty eclipsed the stabbing pain, morphing it into a dull, tight ache. I slowly exhaled through my mouth, relaxing against him, letting go, and swallowed bubbling resentment.

Yeah, it sucked.

But what could I do?

Even the mere idea of trying and failing again with Dan made me want to lock myself in a room made of cheese for all eternity.

His hand stroked the back of my head and he tugged my braid, bringing my gaze back to his. "Why do you think you need to be drunk?"

He sounded curious, not concerned, not upset, and some of the bitterness I'd been choking on subsided, making it easier to breathe.

"It's just how I am, it's how I've always been. I can't—I can't relax. I'm too much in my own head. Even when I . . ."

"When you?"

"When I touch myself," I said on a rush, wincing, my cheeks heating with mortification.

Why are we even discussing this? Why do I insist on asphyxiating on my own failure?

"You drink before you touch yourself?"

"Yes. I used to." I cleared my throat, forcing calm into my voice. "I have to drink if I want to, you know, get to the end. I used to drink a lot, before I did *it*. So I don't drink anymore if there's a chance I could. . . if I might . . . be physical," I said this last part quickly and cleared my throat again. "Anyway, my therapist said the drinking was unhealthy, self-medicating. And she said there's nothing wrong with me physically, I've been tested and screened for everything. I even stopped taking birth control just in case it was a hormonal thing."

"You're not on birth control?"

I shook my head. "No."

A soft sound rumbled from his chest, then he said, "Now that we're on the topic, I'm STD free. Just had my summer physical in June."

The ferocity of my blush increased; despite my past, I wasn't used to having these kinds of conversations. "I'm STD free, too," I said, but had to clear my throat again before speaking. "But, it doesn't matter anyway because I can't and it's all *psychological* and—oh, dammit! Never mind." I didn't want to talk about this, about all the ways I was messed up.

He made a distracted, thoughtful noise, like *huh*.

"I'm sorry, I'm so sorry—"

"Please stop apologizing." Dan held me tighter. "I'm thinking here. Give me a minute to think."

We lay like that for several minutes, during which his hold loosened, but his hands began moving in absentminded circles on my hip. His touch felt good, the friction and heat on my bare skin and over the thin fabric of my pajamas. Intermittently, I told myself to relax while also cursing myself for being this way.

"So, it's like you can't stop thinking? Or what?" His voice was infinitely gentle and still laced with curiosity, giving me the impression he really wanted to understand.

"That's right. Or something like that." I sniffed, now more in control and no longer in danger of breaking down. "My therapist suspects it's because I don't feel like I'm, uh . . ."

"What?"

"Desirable."

His eyes came to mine and held, a look of complete disbelief claimed his features. "Are you fucking with me?"

"No." I shook my head.

"You don't think you're beautiful?"

"It's not really about that." My voice was much smaller than I would have liked, so I lifted my chin. "I don't know what it's about. If I knew what the problem was, I would fix it. But I don't. I don't know how to fix myself. And I'm so, so sorry I'm this way. But, I want you to know, I still want to be with you."

Dan was full-on scowling now. "You want to be with me even when it doesn't feel good for you?"

I nodded, laying a tentative hand on his stomach. "I'd like to make you feel good."

He breathed out, like he couldn't believe what I'd just said, and two severe lines of discontent appeared between his eyebrows. "No. No way. I can't do that."

I removed my hand from him, balling it into a fist, and shifting away. "Okay. I understand."

"No, I don't think you do." His gaze dropped to my mouth, and as though unable to resist, he placed a light, teasing kiss on my lips, licking the bottom one to taste me before pulling away, his eyes conducting a cherishing sweep of my face. "Thank you for telling me."

Some combination of emotions made the use of my voice impossible, so I nodded.

"Tell me one more thing." He brushed several strands of hair that had come loose from my braid away from my face, tucking them tenderly behind my ear.

"Okay."

"What do you want?" Once again, he sounded merely curious.

I frowned at him, seeking to unravel the question's meaning.

What did I want? Wasn't it obvious? I wanted to be normal.

Certain I didn't understand what he was after, I asked, "What do you mean?"

"You said you want to be with me."

"I do."

"Even if it doesn't feel good for you."

My eyes dropped, I couldn't look at the patient warmth in his eyes and have this conversation. "Yes."

"That's not what I want," he said firmly.

I nodded, feeling heartsick.

"So, since that's off the table, what do you want?"

"To not be this way."

I felt his eyes move over me. "You said you're in therapy and this has been brought up."

"Yes."

"Do you think, if we talked to her together, she could help?"

I wouldn't cry over this, I refused. So I swallowed and nodded.

"Would you be willing to try again? Not—I mean, we don't have to go all the way, and I didn't plan to tonight, I just wanted to fool around a little—it's just, I'd like to—not that it's about *me*, but I'd like to try to help you—" he made a low sound of frustration. "That's not right, not *help*, but—"

I cut him off with a kiss, each word more painful than the last—not because he was hurting me, but because I could hear the self-doubt in his voice, and I hated that I'd put it there.

So I kissed him. I pushed him onto his back and kissed him with all the tangled emotions in my mind and in my heart. His hands framed my face and didn't move, didn't wander, giving me the sense he wasn't sure what he was allowed to do, or where he was allowed to touch me, making my heart splinter all over again.

I broke the kiss, lying on top of him and squeezing his big chest as tightly as I could.

Bending to his ear, I whispered, "Please, please, please don't ever think you are less than perfect. My issues aren't a reflection of you, they're a reflection of me, and it was wrong of me to not tell you."

"I'm not perfect, Kit-Kat. Far from it." Dan's hands hovered on my shoulders and I felt him take a deep breath before saying plainly, "Let me help."

"Dan—"

"I'm not going to take it personally if I can't get your engine running—you're right, that's on you—but not trying again seems like a waste of an opportunity." His hands slid down to my bottom, stroking and then squeezing me shamelessly. Then moaning, "Holy fuck, you've got a great ass."

I huffed a small laugh, something in me relaxing, and I allowed him to roll me away. He settled next to me, grabbing my hand and bringing it to his lips while he continued conversationally, "Let me be clear, I consider this an opportunity *for me*. Sure, I hope you get something out of it. But think about this from my perspective."

"Your perspective?"

His gaze swept over my body and he licked his lips. "I'm guessing we'll be spending a lot of time naked?" Dan drew his bottom lip into his mouth as his eyes met mine again, held, and smoldered.

Try as I might, faced with his smolder, I was having difficulty holding on to my worry for him. I was also having trouble remembering why I'd been determined to give up and accept defeat just moments ago.

So, in an attempt to refocus myself and the conversation, I asked, "What if I'm never able to enjoy sex? What if I can't? What if I try, we try, and I always fail?"

His mouth tugged upward. "I think you're asking the wrong questions."

"Really?" A note of desperation bled into my voice, and I didn't even try to hide it. "What questions should I be asking?"

Dan trailed a barely there touch down my arm, along the bare skin of my stomach where my shirt had lifted, leaving a veil of goosebumps in its wake.

I shivered.

"The only question, as far as I'm concerned, isn't whether you'll fail, that doesn't matter. It's whether you'll enjoy the *trying*."

CHAPTER SIXTEEN

USA **Median Value** of Annual CEO Compensation, n= 300 sample, large U.S.-traded public companies
2016: $13 million

THE ASSOCIATED PRESS (AP)

USA **Average Value** of Annual CEO Compensation, n= 248,760 comprehensive, all US companies (small, medium, and large), some private, some publically traded.
2016: $178,400

US BUREAU OF LABOR STATISTICS

Dan

I MADE KAT breakfast—pancakes, bacon, eggs—the whole nine yards. She'd made me cake to welcome me home, the least I could do was make her the breakfast of champions after what happened last night.

Plus, I couldn't sleep. I kept thinking about her "problem."

She had a problem.

She thought it was a big problem.

However, as I thought about it, sipping my coffee as the sun rose over Lake Michigan, it didn't seem like much of a problem to me.

Some couples go hiking.

Some cook together.

We'd be making out and giving each other sexy massages all in the name of mental health.

For the life of me, I couldn't see a problem.

Granted, I wouldn't tell *her* that. Early in my life, my four sisters had taught me the last thing I ever wanted to do was trivialize a lady's emotions. Kat was tied up in knots about the whole thing. Okay, I could see that. Kat might've been tough, but I would validate the shit out of her feelings insomuch as she needed me to.

Meanwhile, I would look forward to untying those knots, then tying her in different knots.

What I was tripping over was as follows: did this mean I was exploiting her problems for my personal gain?

. . . I had no idea.

Maybe.

Probably.

In order to cauterize potential guilt, I reminded myself it would be a symbiotic relationship. And like all symbiotic relationships, this would be to the advantage for each person involved.

See? Everybody wins!

You just win the most.

When Kat emerged from her room, she was already dressed and ready for work. Her hair was meticulous, her makeup like something out of a magazine. Her pants even had those creases down the front. Her shirt was ironed and starched to such an extreme degree, her collar looked dangerous, so stiff the points could be used as a knife or a weapon.

"How'd you sleep?" I asked, moving to intercept her for a light kiss, and fighting the urge to mess her up a little, smudge her lipstick, run my fingers through her hair, and wrinkle her starchy shirt.

I didn't. But I wanted to.

She gave me a stiff smile as we separated and held out a slip of paper, her eyes distant in a way that had me frowning. "It's Dr. Kasai's number, my therapist. I've emailed her your phone number and asked about setting up a time for us to talk."

I took the slip from her, noticing it was folded so precisely none of the edges overlapped. "Thanks." I glanced between her and the paper. "Do you want me to call her this morning?"

"Yes," she blurted, then sighed wretchedly, her façade of calm cracking as her face crumpled. "I'm so so—"

"Nope. None of that." I swept her into my arms, crushing her to me and kissing her again.

This time I did smudge her lipstick, and I pushed my fingers into her hair, grabbing a fistful to angle and open her mouth like I wanted as I backed her against the kitchen counter. And I grabbed her ass, because I wanted to.

She moaned into my mouth, scrambling to get closer, her nails digging into my back through my suit shirt as I teased her tongue, ending the kiss with a frisky bite of her lip. I leaned away, admiring my handiwork.

Her mouth was pink, devoid of paint, and a little swollen; her hair was disheveled; her eyes dazed.

Her shirt wasn't wrinkled.

But mine was, and that was even better.

* * *

WE DROVE INTO WORK TOGETHER, and made plans to meet up after. She reminded me that the gang was scheduled to go to Fiona and Greg's to clean the place, do laundry, and watch the kiddos so Fiona and Greg could catch a nap.

The day went as planned. I printed out a copy of the postnup to review with Kat when we had a chance. I'd made some changes, nothing huge, but I still wanted her to see them just in case she wanted something different. I thought about calling Kat's Dr. Kasai, but decided to wait until she was around, so we could do it together.

Work was work, but to Betty's astonishment, I was mostly caught up, having managed a good deal of backlog while on the flight back from down under. So, around 11:00 AM, I took a nap on the couch in my office, unbearable exhaustion hitting me like a bat upside the head.

Refreshed, I stopped by Kat's floor around 4:30 PM and we left the Fairbank's building together, making small talk about our days while I tried to get over the fact that this—being with her, talking over her day, telling her about mine, holding her hand and stealing kisses when no one was looking—was my life.

We were taking things slow, but still. I felt like the luckiest fucking bastard in the world, and a part of me thought about sending Tiny Satan a thank you note for being such a dickweasel. Not to worry, most of me still wanted to kick him in the nuts.

Later—much later—as we left Greg and Fiona's, it finally sunk in: we would be going home together. It seemed to hit her at approximately the same time because the interior of the car grew quiet, and I could almost hear her thinking.

I was debating whether or not to raise the privacy window when I heard Stan say, "Uh oh." His eyes met mine in the rearview mirror. They looked alert and concerned. "I think we got trouble, boss."

I craned my neck, peering out the window. Three police cars were parked in the circle outside the East Randolph Street property and a cop was waving us down as we pulled closer to the building.

Stan glanced at me, I gave him a short nod, and he continued forward slowly.

"You want to do the talking?" I asked Kat, "Or should I?"

She didn't answer. Instead, her hand squeezed mine and I felt her tense, like she was preparing to flee, or she was fighting the instinct.

Pulling to a stop, Stan rolled down his window. "Can I help you officer?"

The cop examined Stan, then glanced at us. "I need to see some identification from everyone in the car."

"Sure." I squeezed her hand back, hoping to reassure her. "Sure thing." I reached in my back pocket, lifting my chin towards Kat's purse, encouraging her to take out her ID.

She did, but I could see her hands were shaking. I didn't blame her. I had uncles and aunts who were cops. My grandpa on my mom's side was a cop. Even so, even now, after being in jail, police offers who weren't my family made me jumpy.

The officer came to my window and I rolled it down, passing over our driver's licenses. He barely glanced at mine, instead peering at Kat's like it held this week's Powerball numbers. His stare shot to hers, held, and then he opened the door.

"Miss, I'm going to need you to come with me."

She didn't move. And she still hadn't answered me. So I took the lead.

"Excuse me, sir." I shifted in front of her, instinctively protecting her body with mine. "What do you want with my wife?"

The officer blinked, flinching and frowning. Clearly, the question had taken him by surprise.

"Your wife?"

"Yes, officer. Wife."

He gave me a look, like he thought I was lying, and lifted his chin. "You have proof of marriage?"

"I just so happen to have our marriage certificate in my pocket." I made no move to reach for it, I knew better than that. Waiting a beat, I asked, "Do you mind if I reach for it? Or you can remove it. It's in my left breast interior pocket."

He opened my jacket, his attention snagging on the ink at my neck for a half second, bouncing to my eyes, then back to my coat. He withdrew the folded copy of the postnup I'd printed at work, which happened to have—thank God—the marriage certificate at the back.

"It's the last page." I kept my hands on my legs where he could see them.

Frowning at me, he flipped to the end of the document, peered at it in the same way he'd peered at Kat's ID. His expression clearing, he lifted his eyes back to mine and gave me a little smile.

"Mrs. O'Malley, huh?"

"That's right."

Reaching for the radio on his shoulder, and not taking his eyes from mine, he clicked the call button. "This is Officer Denver, from location BETA. I have eyes on the target, over."

Not two seconds later, an answering call sounded from the radio. "Secure target and hold position. We'll be right out, over."

"There's a bit of a problem with that. Seems Miss Caravel-Tyson is married. I don't think that guardianship order is still valid if she's married, over."

A bit of static, then a voice I thought I recognized sounded over the radio, "She's not married, she's crazy. You can't believe a word she says."

I glanced over my shoulder at Kat, witnessing her sudden mood shift. She'd been startled and scared one second, and furious the next. But she kept her mouth clamped shut, giving Officer Denver's radio a look that might kill a small mammal.

"Target doesn't look crazy to me, sir. Nor does her husband, who is sitting here with her and just handed me a legal marriage certificate dated over a month ago." He paused, his smile widening, then added, "Over."

I smirked at Officer Denver, lifting an eyebrow at his strange behavior.

He must've detected my confusion because he leaned closer and said, "You folks can relax. And—sorry ma'am, no offense—but your cousin is a real dick."

Kat huffed a surprised-sounding laugh. I leaned back in my seat, no longer shielding her body with mine. She and I shared a look while we waited for his radio to respond. We waited for a while. We waited so long, some of Officer Denver's good mood began to deteriorate. He was just about to press the call button when the voice screeched over the radio.

"Now you listen to me, dipshit. You will not allow them to leave. I still have a court order and as an officer of the law you are bound to carry it out!"

Officer Denver leaned his head away from the radio, wincing and turning down the sound. To us he said, "If I were you, I'd tell him to get lost."

"Thank you, officer." Kat's steady voice cut in. "If you could give us a moment to call our legal team, I'm sure we can get this settled."

"Take all the time you need." He pulled out his cell phone, stepping back from our car. "I'll call this in and see what the captain says."

I exited first, extending my hand for Kat. She took it, grasping her phone in her other hand and bringing it to her ear just as I shut the door after her.

"Hey. It's me. Caleb is here and he has the police with him." Her eyes found mine, and I was relieved, and maybe a little surprised, to discover she looked as cool as the other side of the pillow.

I motioned to Stan and she nodded, moving with me as I stepped to the driver's window.

"You want me to drive you two out of here?" His eyes were huge as they glanced between me, Kat, and the officer.

"No need for that. Yet. I'll let you know." I wasn't ruling anything out. If Caleb somehow managed to convince the police that his guardianship order was valid, no way was I allowing them to take Kat. "Call for backup, everyone in the area. Empty the building. Have them meet us down here."

Stan nodded, grabbing his phone. "You got it."

"And keep the motor running."

He nodded again, already typing out a text to our nearby teams.

Kat, meanwhile, was pacing some three feet away and then back again, listening to the other side of the call.

She said, "Email it to Dan," her gaze coming to mine. "He'll do most of the talking."

I mouthed, *Is that Eugene?*

She nodded, coming to stand next to me, leaning close, and tilting the phone so we both could listen.

". . . that's wise. He'll try to get a rise out of you and he'll have an audience, you know how he gets with an audience. I'll send over the motion, but a document they've already seen will be more convincing than one they haven't yet verified on a phone screen. Worst-case scenario, the Chicago PD will take you into custody until tomorrow when it can be sorted. At that point, you'll be released."

Kat nodded again, still looking calm and unruffled. Meanwhile, I was thinking, *Over my dead body.*

Which is why I spoke without thinking, "No fucking way they're taking her into custody."

"Ah, Daniel. You're on the line."

"I'm right here. They're not taking her, do you hear me?"

"Mr. O'Malley—"

"It's fine. We'll be fine." Kat pulled the phone from me, giving me a hard glare. "Thanks for everything, Uncle Eugene. We'll be in touch."

I scowled at her and sent a sideways look to Stan. He gave me a subtle nod. He was ready to go, just needed one of us to give the word.

She hung up, slipping her phone into her purse while leaning close and whispering harshly, "If the Chicago PD needs time to work this out, we're giving it to them. I can stay overnight at a facility."

"What if they put you in lockup?" I crossed my arms. "You been training with Fiona? She teach you how to be a ninja? You have moves I don't know about?"

"They won't put me in lockup." She huffed an exasperated-sounding sigh, but her features softened. Inexplicably, a little smile tugged at her mouth. "And no, I'm not a ninja." And then under her breath while holding my stare she added, "And yes, I have moves you don't know about."

Before I could react to that, the weaselly voice from the police radio called out to us, "Thank God you're all right, Kathleen. I've been worried sick."

Kat and I turned toward the voice at the building's entrance, finding her cousin flanked by ten private security guys, all dressed in black suits, ties, and shirts. Once more without thinking, I stepped in front of Kat. Also without thinking, I sized them up, the lot of them. They arranged themselves in standard formation, but didn't seem to be on high alert. That was good.

Also good, not five seconds after Caleb and his black suit gang left the building, I spotted Alex, Quinn, and another dozen of our team emerge right behind them. And then I had to do a double take, because among them were Sandra, Steven, Nico—Elizabeth's husband and world famous comedian—Ashley Winston, and her guy, Drew Runous.

Ashley and Drew were in town to visit the new babies; we'd just spent the evening with them at Greg and Fiona's. I'd forgotten they were staying with Elizabeth and Nico for a few days.

Caleb opened his arms as he opened his mouth, like the little fucker was planning on giving Kat a hug, but then his steps slowed until he eventually stopped, still a good distance away. He and his crew halted, glancing behind them.

I almost laughed when the little shit's shoulders stiffened, probably when he caught sight of freaking Nico Moretti. Or maybe he caught sight of Drew, who—I kid you not—was the size of a mountain, looked like a Viking, and wore a murderous expression to match; I wouldn't have been surprised to see him carrying an axe. Or maybe it was the death glares coming from Quinn and Alex.

Whatever it was, Caleb and company didn't take another step in our direction. But bad news, now his guys were on high alert.

Quinn made it to us first, quickly assessing the situation. "We have more on the way."

"We have fifteen, I think this is enough." I lifted my chin to the Chicago PD. "Things won't get ugly, but this makes for a good show of strength."

He and I traded a brief nod as Nico, Alex, and Drew flanked me and Kat. Sandra and Ashley greeted Kat and then assumed positions just behind her, their arms crossed, eyes narrowed, looking like they were hoping someone would give them a reason to kick ass. As was my habit, I checked their hands for knitting needles and tequila bottles, which seemed to be their weapons of choice when faced with goons.

Caleb was shooting his cousin a confused, slightly maniacal smile, his fingers coming to his suit jacket. He unbuttoned then re-buttoned his coat.

"Uh, what is this?" His tone was light and condescending as he motioned to all of us. "Are you in some sort of gang? Again?"

Kat stared at her cousin, her features clear of expression. She didn't respond.

I took that as my cue to—as she'd told Eugene earlier—do most of the talking.

Clearing my throat, I stepped forward, Alex, Quinn, and Nico close behind me. Sticking out my hand, I gave him my most shit-eating grin. "You must be Colin. You can call me Mr. O'Malley. I'm Kathleen's husband."

His smile diminished by degrees and his pale blue eyes narrowed into slits. He looked down at my hand like I was offering him shit and his nose twitched. He didn't take it.

Yeesh, this guy looks even more like a weasel in person.

Really, it wasn't the way he looked. It was who he was. He was a weasel, and so he looked like a weasel.

Lifting his chin, he gave me a spasmodic smile. "Kathleen's *husband?*" He laughed, definitely forced, and glanced around at his security team. They didn't laugh, likely because they weren't in on the joke, nor were they paid to play the role of sycophants to a psychopath. "I find that extre-e-e-mly unlikely. How much did she pay you?" He took a step closer, lowered his voice but not enough to keep from being overheard, "Or what did she promise you? Hmm?"

I let my hand drop and glanced to the officers who were standing off to one side, like referees on a football field. They seemed to be engaged in deep conversation, probably trying to figure out what to do.

I pulled out my phone. "Listen, Colin—"

"Caleb."

"What's that?" I glanced up from where I'd navigated to my emails.

"My name." His eyes were hard and flat, soulless weasel eyes. "It's Caleb."

"Okay, sure. That's nice for you. Whatever. The thing is," I tapped open the document Eugene had sent, scanning it quickly and lifting my voice so the officers would hear, "I just received this from my legal team. This is a motion to dismiss your petition for guardianship, and your judge just signed off on it since, you know,"—I shrugged

—"Kathleen and I are married. And that means, correct me if I'm wrong here, but guardianship over her person and property, if needed, passes directly to her spouse. Which is me."

Officer Denver was the first to approach, holding out his hand. "May I?"

"Certainly." I passed him my phone and he took it back to his colleagues.

Caleb gave me a smarmy little smile. "I see. You're clearly concerned for her. When did you start suspecting her instability? Is she still hearing voices?"

I shook my head, seeing through his pathetic attempt at a trick question. "I'm concerned about you, Conner."

A laugh erupted from his lungs. "You can call me Mr. Tyson, and why would you be concerned about me? I'm not the one with a history of severe mental illness, or living on the streets, or thievery, or prostituting myself for drugs."

Because I'm going to rip your eyeballs from their sockets and shove them so far up your dickhole they're going to call you Jimmy-Four-Balls when I'm finished, you sheisty motherfucker.

Quinn shifted restlessly at my side, so did Alex. I didn't have to look at them to know they were having similar thoughts.

Making my tone carefully light, I returned Caleb's grin. "You lied to the judge who signed the initial order, and you've been lying to the Chicago PD."

His eye twitched. "I've done no such thing. Obviously you're as paranoid as she is."

"We've been married for over a month." I tutted at him, shaking my finger like I thought his behavior shameful. "Obviously, your petition for guardianship is a reaction to our marriage. But lying to the police is a criminal offense, Carl."

"I did no such thing—"

"While I don't understand this troubling obsession with your own cousin, I do strongly encourage you to seek help from a licensed professional."

Tiny Satan bit his bottom lip, his eyes big, a little wild, reminding me of a rat backed into a corner. "You refuse to admit she is sick and needs help? Then I'm not satisfied. I have a court order here which gives me emergency guardianship and you have, what? A document on your cell phone? How do we even know that's real? No. No, no, no." He turned to his security team, waving them forward. "Kathleen, for her own safety, will be coming with us. Let's go."

He darted to the side, as though to walk past me, motioning again with his hand for his guys to follow, so I side-stepped him, forcing him to back up or walk into me. Meanwhile, my guys took a step forward, preventing the black suits from making a move.

"Whoa. Okay, Cody. Settle down." I held my hands up between us, like he was the crazy one, all the while I fought the urge to grab him around the throat and throw him across the courtyard. "I get it, I do. You have your hired guys here, and so you think you can do whatever you want. You think . . ." I leaned a little closer, dropping my voice to a whisper, "When you're a jet, you're a jet all the way. From your first cigarette, to your last dying day. Right? That's your little fantasy?"

His face pinched, he reared back, eyes flashing. Who knew show tunes would piss him off so much? Or maybe it was the mocking way I'd said them.

Raising the volume of my voice, I continued, "But that's not how this works, Carter. This might come as a shock to you, but the law supersedes your wet dreams."

Before Caleb could respond, Officer Denver stepped forward. "We can't get ahold of the captain, and so we're going to have to make a judgment call here." He handed me back my phone, his mouth set in a grim line as his attention moved over the guys flanking me. "We're going to need time to figure out . . ." Officer Denver blinked. "Hey, wait a minute. Are you . . . ? You're Nico Moretti!"

I followed his line of sight and found he was looking at Nico. For that matter, now everyone else was as well.

Nico huffed a practiced, self-deprecating laugh and held out his hand. "Yes. Do you watch the show?"

"Holy shit, I can't believe it's you." Officer Denver, as well as his two colleagues, came forward to shake Nico's hand.

But not only that, they started patting themselves down, presumably searching for paper and pen.

But not only that, Nico had moved on to Caleb's team, now stepping closer as he introduced himself to each of them, one at a time among whispers of *That's Nico Moretti*, and prompt requests for pictures and autographs.

But not only that, everyone seemed to have forgotten about Caleb.

"Hey! Wait a minute." Caleb glanced around at his security detail as though mystified, and more than a little pissed, but no one was paying attention to Tiny Satan.

Nope.

"Thank you for all that you do, officer." Nico had turned back to Officer Denver while he signed a receipt for one of Caleb's crew. "My wife works in the ER near downtown. You boys in blue make all the difference."

"I appreciate that. Thank you, Mr. Moretti."

"Please. Call me Nico." His perfect teeth flashed in a moonlight, little fucking stars in his eyes.

Ah Nico, so smooth. He was butter and cream all wrapped up in a sparkly, pretty Italian package.

"Okay, Nico." Officer Denver was looking at our friend with stars in his eyes and I made the mistake of glancing at Quinn, then at Alex, then finally at Drew.

Quinn, arms crossed, rolled his eyes.

Alex, his hands stuffed in his pockets, watched the scene unfold with a whisper of a sardonic smile.

Whereas Drew and I shared a furtive smirk.

I admit, the first time I'd met Nico, I was a little starstruck, too. On TV he was so funny. And in person he was just so friggin' nice.

I'd moved past the starstruck stage after a year or so. Now he was just Nico, funny guy, good guy, great cook. Mostly, I was glad to know him.

But right now? Right this minute?

Thank God for freaking Nico.

"What are you doing here? Do you live here?" One of the other police officers asked while the security guards pressed forward, each handing him something to sign while they took turns snapping pictures.

Caleb glanced at his Rolex, gritting his teeth, then crossed his arms. His eyes darted beyond my shoulder, presumably to Kat, and narrowed into threatening slits. So I stepped in his line of sight, sending him a few eyeball threats of my own.

"Actually," Nico addressed this to Officer Denver, "Kathleen—Kat —is a friend of mine."

"She is?"

Caleb sighed, loudly.

"Yep. We've known each other for a long time, one of my best friends. And how about this?" Nico glanced at Caleb meaningfully, then back to Officer Denver. "I'll vouch for her, give you some time to figure things out with the judge. In fact, I'll give you my phone number and you can reach out if you need anything."

All the officers were nodding before Nico had finished, with Officer Denver giving Nico a grateful smile. "Yeah. Yes. That's fine."

Caleb continued watching us all with his weasel eyes while Nico gave the officers his number, then turned a big grin to the nearest of the black suit gang, offering a handshake and a joke. The joke had everyone nearby laughing, including Quinn.

Or maybe Quinn was laughing at Caleb, like I was.

A few minutes later, the officers were gone, leaving Caleb's private security to fanboy over Nico. I was struck by the sudden urge to dust off my shoulders with the back of my fingers, disaster averted, problem solved.

I was about to turn back to Kat, suggest we head inside, maybe take Wally for a walk, when Caleb abruptly darted forward, making a reckless beeline for his cousin. I moved to intercept, but Drew got there before I did, interrupting the man's trajectory and staring him down with a glare of Viking-level frost and ice.

"Back off," Drew rumbled, taking a threatening step forward.

Caleb ignored him, leaning to the side to snipe at Kat, "You're staying here?"

"I have nothing to say to you." Her voice was devoid of emotion.

"Are you sure about that? While you were off getting married to Sinn Féin over here," he gestured to me as I came to her side, "your *father* had a stroke, and was admitted to the hospital."

Kat stiffened. "What are you talking about?"

"Zachariah is in the ICU," he spat, giving Kat a mocking glare. "He was admitted three weeks ago."

"ICU? Three weeks . . . ?" Kat's gaze dropped and I could see she was trying to process this news.

"Marks didn't tell you?" Caleb's mouth twisted into a smug smirk and he took a step away, looking satisfied by her bewilderment and his point scored.

Her gaze cut back to his, but she said nothing.

"He didn't tell you . . ." He seemed surprised. "Of course. Don't you see? He's been making all the decisions, keeping the old man on life support for three weeks, so he won't die, so *you* won't inherit. Marks has been pulling your strings for years, he's pulling everyone's strings. You're his puppet. You think he's going to like your new thug of a husband? Hmm?"

Ashley came to stand in front of Kat, blocking Caleb from view and slipping her arm around Kat's waist. "Come on, baby. Come with me. We'll call, check on your daddy."

Meanwhile, Sandra placed a staying hand on my arm, giving me a little headshake and mouthed, *He's not worth it.*

She then inserted herself between me and Kat, wrapping her arm around her from the other side. "Yes. Let's make tea and check on your father. Now that you've crushed this little man's evil hopes and dreams, I imagine he has a hairless cat to stroke and a monologue to prepare."

The three of them strolled slowly into the building, Drew in front, Alex between Sandra and Caleb, with Nico bringing up the rear as he waved and smiled to his adoring fans.

I watched her go, made sure she was safely inside and the door was shut, before turning my attention back to her cousin, ready to administer any and all nature of threats to ensure he backed the fuck off, including but not limited to raining down an ungodly firestorm of—

"Dan." Quinn stepped into my line of sight, his arms crossed, his voice low. "You need to go."

"I need to cut his tongue out and shove it up his ass."

"Yeah, maybe later." He shrugged. "But right now, you need to take the plane and go to Boston with Kat."

That pulled me out of my violent reflections, my eyes refocusing on Quinn. "What?"

"Take Kat." His expression was patient, but concerned. "Take her home to Boston. Her dad's in the ICU. She needs to see him. You can get there tonight, three hours from now she could be sitting at his side."

I was nodding before he was finished. "Yeah. You're right."

"Take the plane." He gave me a pat on my shoulder. "I'll call ahead. Everything will be ready. Just take her and go."

I started around him, but then stopped. "Wait, what about Wally?"

Quinn blinked at me once, giving me a look like, *come on man.* "Alex," was all he said.

Right. Alex. *Wally loves Alex.*

My friend lifted his chin toward the building. "Go. And don't worry about this dipshit." Quinn's eyes turned cold as we both glanced at Caleb, now several feet away and ranting to someone on his cell phone while intermittently screaming at his security detail that they were all fired.

"He won't be bothering you for a few days." Quinn's mouth curved into a subtle smile. "Maybe even longer."

PART II

WHAT HAPPENS IN BOSTON, BECOMES HEADLINES ALL AROUND THE WORLD

CHAPTER SEVENTEEN

Medical Power of Attorney: "A legal instrument that allows you to select the person that you want to make healthcare decisions for you if and when you become unable to make them for yourself."

WEX LEGAL DICTIONARY

Kat

I MESSAGED MY professors and informed them my father was in the hospital and I didn't know when or if I'd be returning to class. I also promised to keep them in the loop as much as possible. Then I sent an email to my boss and Ms. Opal communicating a similar message.

I then sent a text to Steven, letting him know I'd be out of town. Dan messaged Quinn and asked Janie to spread the word.

I didn't feel like talking during the flight. Mostly, this was because I didn't know what I was feeling apart from angry with Eugene and stunned by the news about my father.

Dan, apparently sensing this, didn't try to speak to me. But he did hold me the entire time we were in the air. He held my hand as we walked through Logan Airport, in the car on the drive to the hospital, and once we arrived.

He held my hand as I approached the reception desk, when the hospital administrator—who'd been expecting us because Ashley had called ahead—guided us to the ICU. As we boarded the elevator and as we walked the halls, I noticed he seemed to be looking around, perhaps expecting another ambush from Caleb, or for someone to stop us.

No one did.

When we finally arrived at my father's room, Dan pulled me close, bringing me against his chest and holding me there.

We didn't go inside. Instead, we stood outside the glass room and looked in. I could barely see him. He was hooked up to some kind of breathing apparatus that covered the bottom half of his face. Plastic tubing traveled from him to various machines, which beeped or buzzed, but held no significance to me.

Dan was the first to speak. "What can I do?" He punctuated this with a kiss on my temple.

"I don't know." I shook my head. "I expected to feel something different than what I'm feeling."

"What are you feeling?"

"Ms. Caravel-Tyson?"

Dan and I both turned toward the sound of my name, finding a doctor hovering some feet away. Next to her was the hospital administrator who'd led us through the labyrinth of elevators and hallways to the ICU.

"I'm Dr. Merkel, your father's attending."

Shaking myself, I extended a hand. "Oh. Hi. Nice to meet you. This is my husband, Daniel O'Malley."

She took my hand, then Dan's, giving us both a perfunctory smile; I was grateful for her professionalism. "I understand that you haven't been informed about the full extent of your father's condition?"

"Please assume I know nothing."

Her smile fell completely away, and the grim set of her mouth reminded me a little of Eugene's when he was about to deliver bad news.

"Your father is on life support. He had a stroke three weeks ago, a very severe stroke, and had no heartbeat for over seven minutes as they attempted to revive him."

The hospital administrator stepped forward, butting in eagerly, "Please know, Ms. Caravel, we've done everything we possibly can. No hospital in the world could do more. We understand your father is a very important person—as are you—and his support to our institution has meant—"

"Yeah, she gets it. This place is the best." Dan held out a hand, effectively cutting the man off. "Now isn't the time. Okay?"

"Yes. Of course. I'm so sorry." The administrator glanced between us, nodding, then took a step back, clearing his throat and looking a little embarrassed.

Dr. Merkel shot the man an impatient look, crossed her arms, and continued, "Mr. Tyson's brain shows no frontal lobe activity. He is effectively brain-dead." She paused here, as though waiting for me to cry, or gasp, or demonstrate some emotion.

I didn't.

She continued, "He is only alive because of the measures taken, but —in our team's opinion—he will not recover from his present state. He cannot breathe on his own. This means you should prepare yourself for when the life support measures are removed. He will not survive beyond a few minutes."

I nodded, absorbing this information, and feeling very detached from it. "I understand."

Dr. Merkel studied me, then asked, "Do you have any questions?"

"No. I don't think so."

"Do you want to go inside?" She lifted her chin to the glass box behind me, her tone gentle. "Do you want to say goodbye?"

"Goodbye?" I felt Dan stiffen at my side. "You just said he'd live as long as he's hooked up to the machines."

"Yes. That's right. But, the order came down earlier today, your father is to be removed from life support tomorrow."

"Tomorrow?" Dan and I shared a look. "You're taking him off life support tomorrow?"

"I thought that was why you were here." Her gaze moved between the two of us. "To say goodbye."

I shook my head, looking to Dan. This was all happening too fast, I couldn't keep up.

"Thank you, Dr. Merkel. We're going to need a minute." He held me to him and I was grateful, because he felt like the only solid thing in the world at that moment. It wouldn't have surprised me if the floor beneath my feet shifted into quicksand.

"Of course." Her gaze lingered on Dan for a protracted moment, her eyes narrowing slightly. "Mr. *O'Malley*, was it?"

"That's right."

She seemed to consider him before asking, "Are you related to Eleanor?"

Dan drew in a quick breath, standing up straighter. "Uh, yeah. She's my mom."

The administrator perked up at this, a small smile brightening his face. "Nurse O'Malley is one of our best, we're very proud to have her on our team."

Dan gave the man a look that told me he was uncomfortable, but he only nodded, muttering, "Thanks."

Dr. Merkel lifted her chin, looking at us like we were something new, her voice losing some of its formality. "Does she know you're here?"

Dan shook his head. "No. Is she working tonight?"

"Your mom?" I looked at him, not following the conversation.

He gave me a contrite shrug paired with an apologetic smile, whispering close to my ear so only I could hear, "She's an ICU nurse here."

I started and my mouth fell open.

"I saw her earlier." Dr. Merkel checked her watch. "I'm not sure, but I think her shift may have just ended." Then she looked at me. "Do you want me to call her? You should lean on your family, let them take care of you."

"I—I don't—" I struggled to respond. Did I want Dr. Merkel to call Dan's mom? A woman I'd never met? So I could lean on her?

I didn't think so.

But I couldn't quite think. And before I'd managed to pull my wits together, I felt Dan tense again, this time his fingers dug into my upper arm.

"Oh no," he said quietly.

I looked at him. He was staring with wide eyes beyond Dr. Merkel, his posture rigid. I followed his gaze, and found the object—or rather, the person—of his focus.

A woman about my height, with auburn hair pinned in a bun, wearing scrubs with little puppies on them, was walking toward us. Eyes, big and brown and almost identical to his, swung from Dan to me.

I could only stare as the woman approached, as she greeted Dr. Merkel, as she sent her son a hard look, and finally, as she stepped forward, standing directly in front of me, her eyes impossibly warm and compassionate.

"Oh Kathleen, my darling. I'm so very, very sorry," she whispered, reaching for my hands and holding them in hers, her eyes misting as they moved over my face in a look that could only be described as compassionate. "Take a few moments, gather your thoughts, and decide what you want to do. If you want to spend the night here, just say the word. We can set you up in a room nearby, or you can sit with your father. It's entirely up to you."

I nodded, and—inexplicably—I felt my chin wobble.

She tutted, her hand coming to my face and cupping my cheek lovingly, making me feel like she'd done this to me a hundred times.

Maybe she had, but not to me. Maybe she'd comforted a hundred daughters, perhaps over a thousand.

"But if you want to leave and come back tomorrow, you should. That's completely understandable. You have some difficult days ahead of you and you'll need your strength."

I nodded, blinking against my blurring vision.

"Oh, my dear. My poor dear." The next thing I knew, she was pulling me into a hug and I was clinging to her. I was also crying.

* * *

I DIDN'T WANT to stay.

I sat with my father for fifteen minutes. The sound of the machines, watching his chest's artificial rise and fall, but otherwise his body's complete stillness, it felt like he was already gone.

So I left the glass room and rejoined Dan and his mom, Eleanor, in the hall and we all left together. She wrapped her arm around me as we walked, encouraging me to lean on her shoulder and promising me tea and cookies when we arrived home.

Home.

I didn't think about it. I just let the tide take me. The three of us got in a car, minutes passed, Dan held my hand. Eleanor's pleasant voice filled the silence with news about various family members; the way she spoke reminded me of Dan, and her stories probably would've made me laugh in normal circumstances.

After a short time, we arrived at our destination, a three-story house on a tidy street in Jamaica Plain. Dan and the driver brought in the bags while Eleanor escorted me into the house.

The first thing I noticed was the giant crucifix hanging over the entryway table where some people might've placed a mirror. Around the crucifix were several beaded necklaces with more, smaller, crucifixes attached to the end of them. On one side of the big cross was a picture of Jesus and a picture of the current pope. On the other side was a picture of John F. Kennedy and a picture of Martin Luther King Jr.

I huffed a little laugh, not because I thought anything about the display was funny, but because it caught me by surprise.

"I have cookies, but I know it's late, and I know you just got off a plane." She led me out of the entryway, an arm looped in mine. "Let me show you where you'll be sleeping, and you decide what you want to do."

Belatedly, as she guided me up the stairs, I realized the first floor of the house smelled like fresh baked bread and cookies. As we climbed the wooden steps, the aroma of orange oil and caraway seed greeted me. I glanced at the gleaming wooden banister, deciding she must polish it often for the wood to look so fine.

We skipped the first door in the second floor hall, and stopped in front of the second.

"This was Dan's room growing up." She gave me a little smile paired with a slight shrug as she revealed the room and encouraged me to walk in.

It was medium-sized, with a sturdy if not beat up dresser, a queen-size bed, and a nightstand. The walls were wallpapered with posters, some were of bands, some were of women in very little clothing, but most were of hockey players.

"He liked the Bruins," she gestured to a team poster. "Takes after his mom that way."

"He's great," I blurted, nodding for no reason. "He's so great. He's the best. I don't deserve him."

Her smile was immediate, but subdued. She opened her mouth, like she was going to respond, but we were interrupted by the sound of heavy footsteps coming up the staircase. Dan appeared a moment later in the doorway, holding our bags.

He stopped short, looking between the two of us. "Can I come in?"

"Of course you can. It's your room. Bring in the bags." She wrinkled her nose at him like she thought he was funny, slipping out to presumably give him more space.

He didn't move. "You're gonna let us sleep in the same room?"

Her smile widened and she chuckled at her son. "Married couples don't sleep together in Chicago? Is this a new custom? What's wrong with you? You've been spending too much time with the puritans." She patted his shoulder, motioning him forward, "Now get in here. She's got nice teeth but I don't think she bites."

Dan's eyebrows lifted high over his forehead as he walked slowly into his room, as though he was reluctant, or didn't trust her to mean what she said.

"Daniel, show Kathleen where the bathroom is, and where to find the towels." She fussed at the doorway, glancing up and down the hall like she was looking for something. "I'll start the tea—but no pressure to come down for a cup. You must be tired, do as you please."

Eleanor strolled into the room and gripped me by the shoulders, placing a kiss on my cheek. "If I don't see you before you go to bed, sleep tight." Then she turned to Dan and did the same, reaching for the doorknob as she left, and pulled the door shut behind her.

I stared at the closed door for a moment, then looked to Dan. "I like your mom."

"Yeah. I like her, too." He smiled, then frowned, his gaze moving over me. "I want to ask if you're okay, but I don't want to keep asking if you're okay. So I'm gonna limit myself to asking once every six hours."

Huffing a laugh at that, I walked to the bed and sat, placing my elbows on my knees and my head in my hands. "I don't know what I am."

I felt the bed depress as he sat next to me, his hand coming to my back and moving in slow, massaging circles. "You be whatever you want to be. Good cop, bad cop, I'll be here to roleplay whichever part you need."

That made me laugh and I turned, tucking myself under his neck, and wrapped my arms around his chest while he encircled me and held tight.

"I'm sad," I said.

He sighed. "That seems normal."

"Is it? Because I don't have one good memory of my father."

"Now that is sad. My dad wasn't around much, and he might be a sonofabitch, but I got a handful of good memories with the guy."

"I don't know why I cried, at the hospital."

"My mother has that effect on people. She's like a Hallmark commercial that way."

I shook my head at him, adding, "Mostly, all I feel is acceptance."

"Acceptance?"

I nodded, not really understanding it myself. "This was inevitable. He's been sick for years. He hasn't recognized me for years. And, even before that, he never really knew me. And maybe I didn't know him. So I *am* sad, but mostly about that . . . I think." I shook my head, blinking away the image of my father hooked up to all those machines

—or the shell of him—and rubbed my forehead. "I'm not making any sense."

"You don't have to make sense." Dan guided me to his chest as he lay us back on the bed. "Your father is dying. If there were ever a time in your life to make no sense, now is the time."

I stared at the ceiling of Dan's room, also covered in posters, looking but not seeing. "It's so strange."

"What's that?"

"My mother doesn't speak. When I visit her, she stares at nothing. But I've always felt—" my voice broke, so I swallowed and cleared my throat before continuing. "I've always felt she knows I'm there. That's she's locked inside herself, but she knows when I come to visit. She can't speak to me, but she can hear me. But my father, he never heard me. Even when he was well, he could see me, but he never looked."

Dan was quiet for a moment, then asked, "How often do you visit your mom?"

"Every time I'm in town, so usually twice a month."

We were quiet for a moment, Dan stroking his hand up and down my arm. "Can I come with you?"

"Yes. Absolutely." I lifted to my elbow, gazing down at him, feeling a rush of warmth that he'd want to come with me. "We'll— we'll go next week." Or maybe the week after.

Tomorrow they take him off life support. He'll be gone next week.

I didn't look forward to telling my mother about my dad, and I'd have to talk to her doctor's first. I'd need their input before sharing the news of his death. I knew that in a way, in the way that mattered, he was already gone. He'd been slipping away even before that.

Dan nodded, his fingers moving into my hair to push it away from my face while his stare turned introspective. "Things are going to be tough for the next few weeks."

"That's okay. I can handle it."

His mouth curved subtly while his gaze moved over me, his eyes warm. "I know. You're tough. It's one of the things I like and admire most about you. But know I'm here for you. I want to handle some of it."

I studied him, unable to stop myself from wondering how much more it would take—how much more drama, how much more of my dysfunction and baggage—before he threw his hands up in the air and walked away.

All I did with him was take. And take. And take. And disappoint. And I couldn't give him anything in return, not even myself, not even my gratitude.

Before I could make up my mind how best to respond, or manage to swallow the lump in my throat, he said, "Otherwise I'll just get up to no good." His fingers fiddled with the ends of my hair.

Giving him a small, albeit sad, smile, I shook my head. "I'm not sure what to say."

"You don't have to say anything. Just nod your head, and when Tiny Satan shows up, send him my way. He's not worth your time."

"But he's worth your time?"

"No. He's not worth anybody's time. But I gotta admit," a devilish glint sparked behind his eyes, "I did enjoy pissing him off."

CHAPTER EIGHTEEN

Lobbyist Spending in US
In 2016, the total spending on lobbyists and lobbying in Washington,
DC amounted to 3.15 billion U.S. dollars. The top five lobbying
groups were:
Pharmaceuticals/Health Products: $246,663,814
Insurance: $153,010,996
Business Associations: $143,241,396
Electronics Mfg & Equip: $121,237,108
Oil & Gas: $119,229,657

OPEN SECRETS.ORG

Dan

K AT WAS PISSED. Luckily, she wasn't pissed at me.
We'd arrived at the hospital at 9:00 AM. My ma came with
us. She was great. She was supportive but didn't hover. She fetched
stuff, like the good coffee from the employee breakroom, and thought
ahead about bringing a shawl for Kat, 'cause the ICU was so cold. She
also snuck in cookies and tissues in her purse.

Eugene arrived around 10:00 AM and that's when Kat went from making easy small talk with my ma about Boston traffic to—I swear—turning into a freaking icicle. The way she looked at him had me shivering. I hoped she never looked at me that way, like I'd betrayed her, and she was going to impale me, squash me, and then maybe set me on fire.

This was my first time meeting him in person, so I was a little surprised by how young he looked—maybe 60, tops. He was also fit, tall, and dressed like he had someplace fancy to go. To be honest, I'd expected a sinister looking miser, pushing 102 and refusing the use of a wheelchair in favor of a cane, a bad attitude, and sheer grit.

Eugene didn't look particularly surprised to see us, and endured Kat's silent treatment with admirable patience. What else could he do? He'd kept the fact that her father was dying from her. For three weeks. He was lucky she let him keep all his teeth.

I introduced my mother to Eugene, they exchanged a few words, no big deal. Kat left us to sit with her father for another ten minutes, saying she wanted to be alone to say goodbye. That didn't sit right with me, made me antsy to take action, but it was her decision. Nothing I could do.

Meanwhile, Eugene signed some papers. The attending doctor reviewed what to expect once more. Eugene indicated that he understood.

They took Mr. Tyson off life support at around 10:30 AM.

The doctor was right, he didn't last long after everything was removed. Kat stared at her dad's face until he stopped breathing, and then she continued staring as the line on his heart monitor flattened. The nurse switched off the machines, giving her a minute on her own.

I didn't know the guy, didn't particularly like what I did know, but it was sad. My ma held my hand as we looked on from behind the glass. Eugene was on my other side, the old guy looked somber.

"Your cousin Debora says hi, by the way," my mom said, her voice sounding faraway. "She's riding her bike to work every day after the DUI, lost fifty pounds."

"What?" This was a shocker. "All the way down to Logan?"

"That's right."

I frowned at that. Actually, I was frowning at Kat, wishing I could go into the glass box, wrap her in my arms, and take her home to Chicago, get her away from all this depressing shit.

"Wait, how'd Debbie know I was in town?"

"She saw you at the airport and called me."

My attention flickered to my mother. "When was this?"

"Last night. I was packing my things, leaving after my shift, and she calls me. She tells me you just landed at Logan with your wife," her gaze came to mine, and the look she gave me wasn't exactly accusatory, but it was on the spectrum, as she added, "Kathleen Caravel-Tyson."

"Oh jeez."

"Imagine my surprise, especially since I was Mr. Tyson's nurse for the last three weeks, off and on." She lifted her chin toward the glass box.

"Small world," Eugene murmured.

"Yeah. It is," she agreed, sighing, sounding sad.

"So Debbie called you."

"And Margaret. She saw you, too."

"Margaret?" Margaret was my Aunt Sheila and Uncle Kip's kid. "When'd she see me?"

"Walking by the gift shop downstairs. I got her a job here earlier in the summer."

"Huh."

"Your spy network is impressive, Mrs. O'Malley," Eugene said, his tone matter-of-fact. At first I thought maybe he was making a joke. But after I studied him, I realized his admiration was serious.

"Yeah, well, it helps that I'm related to half of Boston, and most of the police force, and all of the first responders."

And half of the gangs, thieves, and drug dealers.

I was still studying Eugene, so I didn't miss his microscopic smile at her response, nor did I miss how quickly his expression sobered, his eyes clouding with something like misery, his gaze still on Kat.

"Does Mrs. Zucker know you're in town?" my mom asked. I could tell she was making chit-chat to fill the silence.

"Uh, no. Not yet." I made a mental note to call the lady.

"When is the last time you talked to her?"

"Last week. But, I didn't talk to her, I spoke to her plumber. She's having problems with the upstairs bathroom."

My mother gave me a sideways look. "You just had that fixed last winter."

"Yeah, but now it's a problem again."

She grunted. "Maybe go over there this week and take a look yourself."

I nodded at the wisdom of this, distracted by the image of Kat standing from her chair and covering her father's hand with hers.

"How long did you know Zachariah Tyson?" I asked Eugene without thinking, suddenly curious.

"His whole life," he responded flatly.

"What can we do?" My ma's eyes remained on Kat while she addressed Eugene, sounding melancholy. "When is the funeral? Will it be in Boston?"

Eugene glanced at my mother. "It'll take place late this afternoon, at the family cemetery. I've already arranged for a rabbi and wooden coffin."

My mother moved her gaze to his, held it, and I recognized the look. She disapproved.

"So fast?"

"According to our custom, funerals typically take place within twenty-four hours after death, and burial immediately after."

"He won't be embalmed?" My mother looked confused. "What about a viewing?"

"No. He'll be washed—again, according to custom—but not embalmed. And there will be no viewing."

She sputtered for a minute, shaking her head. "What about people who need to travel? The rest of his family? They won't get here in time."

Eugene's glare seemed to soften as he looked at her, the faint smile returning to his eyes. "Usually, after the funeral, there is a gathering at the home for additional mourners, which marks the beginning of shiva."

"Shiva?"

"In Conservative Judaism—actually, in all Judaism—the week following the funeral is known as shiva. The family stays at home and receives visitors, who provide support and help them pray after their loss. But in this case, there is no one else. Just Kathleen, her husband, and me. There will be no gathering, and there will be no visitors."

"No one? No mourners? No one wants to pay their last respects? Friends? Relatives? Coworkers? What about people from the synagogue?"

The older man contemplated her for a moment. "Zachariah removed himself from the Jewish community well before the Alzheimer's took hold. Therefore, if there were people who wished to call on Kat this week, it wouldn't be friends from the synagogue, there to provide to support, bring food, or to pray with her and reflect on her father's life. His world ceased to function that way a long time ago, Mrs. O'Malley."

"His world?" She wrinkled her nose. "I'm sorry, did we get transported to Mars without my knowledge? Is this an alien spaceship?"

His eyes seemed to twinkle, but his tone was subdued as he said, "Upon his death, Zachariah Tyson was the thirtieth richest man in the world, with a fortune totaling over seventeen billion dollars." The twinkle dimmed. His eyes lost focus, and then he moved his stare back to Kat where she stood next to her father's bed, her arms wrapped around her middle. "When you have that much money, only your child mourns you."

* * *

MY MOTHER, to the very best of her ability and with the help of Google, observed shiva for the next seven days. And everything was kosher. Everything. When we'd arrived home from the funeral, she was carrying bags of meat and cheese from the kosher grocer on Harvard St. as well as a Jewish-American cookbook.

My ma's special trip turned out to be unnecessary. Eugene arranged for three meals a day to be delivered to the house for me, Kat, and my mother—all of them kosher. Apparently, Kat wasn't supposed to do any cooking or housework, according to the rules of the shiva thing.

I wasn't 100% certain what made something kosher, but as far as I could tell it involved special preparation and absolutely no bacon.

During these seven days, whenever Ma was home, Kat was babied within an inch of her life. My mother insisted she relax, read a book, sleep, watch a movie, knit, nap some more. Kat didn't check in at work; again, she wasn't allowed.

My mother also gave Kat sneak attack hugs and kisses every time they passed in the hall, or on the stairs, or in the kitchen. At first, I thought about pulling Ma to the side and asking her to back off, give Kat some space. After the second day, I dismissed this idea when I spotted Kat's face as my mom placed a kiss on her the cheek and held her in a long embrace.

Kat looked peaceful.

During the day, she seemed relaxed in a way that reignited that familiar tightness in my chest. It ached, and I wished—hoped—one day she'd look that peaceful all the time. Or at least most of the time.

After that, I let my ma do her thing. Clearly, she was the expert.

On the third day, after Kat had gone to bed, I found my ma in the kitchen. She'd just come home from her shift at the hospital and I asked after my sisters. And, for that matter, whether my aunts and uncles, or any of my cousins were going to stop by. The house was eerily quiet, and this house had never been quiet. Growing up, and whenever I'd visited since moving to Chicago, someone was always stopping in, coming or going or staying for dinner. Or hiding from the rest of the family, usually down the cellar where she kept the beer.

"I told them we're having a Jewish shiva, someone's staying here who was in deep mourning, and to stay away. I don't want to overwhelm Kathleen."

Ah. That made sense. I was just impressed everyone had actually listened. *Especially Seamus the shitbag.*

"We'll have a family dinner once the seven days are over," she replied tartly, giving me a pointed stare. "So don't you go asking any of those dumbasses up the corner to come over."

I tilted my head to the side, glaring at my mother. "Ma. Come on. I'm not Seamus. I'm not like that anymore. And I wouldn't do that to Kat."

"You better not." Her tone was so salty, it made me thirsty. "I want her to feel comfortable here, I want her to think of this home as her home." My mom sighed, glancing at the ceiling. "I just wish there were something more I could do. Maybe I could take a few days off next week."

I reached across the kitchen counter and covered her hand with mine. "You've done a lot. I know she wasn't expecting it, but I'm sure she appreciates it."

She huffed a little laugh. "Yeah, I know. She thanks me every time she sees me, like I forgot she just said thank you five minutes ago." Looking at me, her eyes narrowed, turned sharp. "You did good, Daniel. Your wife is an angel."

"Yeah. I did."

"And she loves you."

Startled, I blinked at my mother, the comment hitting me like a punch to the gut. But I was careful to clear my face of expression. Instead, taking a drink of my beer and changing the subject to one I knew would distract her.

"Please tell me you're not inviting Seamus over for the dinner."

She pulled her hand from mine and glowered. "He's your brother, Daniel."

And so we argued—as we did—about my good-for-nothing older brother and all the reasons I needed to forgive him, and all the reasons she needed to write his dumbass off.

Shortly after, I placed a kiss on her cheek and went to bed, the shitty feeling still in my chest, persistent and painful.

She loves you.

No.

It was too early.

Kat wasn't ready.

She needed time.

First, we needed to wait for the stench of gratitude to wear off.

Second, I still needed to prove myself.

One day I would earn a place in her heart.

One day.

But not yet.

For now, I'd just be the asshole sleeping next to her and waking up before she opened her eyes, because every night since we'd arrived had been agony.

I'd been a witness to Kat falling asleep three times—at the hospital in Chicago, once in my apartment when I'd come back from Australia, and once here, the first night we'd arrived in Boston.

The night in my apartment and the first night here had started out similarly. She'd lain on her side, her legs slightly bent. She'd toss and turn a little, flip from one side to the other. Both times it had been torture, having to feel her toss and turn next to me as she tried to fall asleep, the incidental touches and brushes or her skin against mine.

In Chicago, I'd eventually pulled her body to mine and she'd fallen asleep against me.

But here, I'd backed off. I made sure she was sleeping before I turned in. Given what happened at my apartment and what she was going through with her father's death, I figured a wide berth was best, give her space to set the pace when she was good and ready. That was the plan.

However, by the time she'd fallen asleep, she'd curled herself into a tight ball next to me. I'd found her this way every night since.

Every. Single. Night.

Her knees to her chest; her chin tucked in; and she slept silently, didn't move again once she was asleep. A few times I'd woken up in the middle of the night and looked over at her. I didn't like how she slept, like she was cold, or protecting herself, or hugging herself all night. I'd wanted to reach a hand over and pull her against me like I'd done in Chicago, warm her up, loosen her limbs.

But that wouldn't have been right either. She didn't need me taking over, telling her what was best. If she wanted me, she knew where I was.

Plus, just being honest, Kat might've been an angel, but I wasn't.

You'd think I'd be able to channel my inner gentleman, keep my mind out of the gutter, especially given all she was dealing with.

Nope. Not me. Not good old Daniel O'Malley.

It's a freaking shiva, for Christ's sake! Let the woman mourn. Give her some space. And stop thinking about her naked.

Not think about her naked? *Fucking impossible.*

So I continued giving her space, *a lot* of space, both day and night.

I worked long hours remotely, using my laptop in the study, taking care of business. I also stopped over at Mrs. Zucker's a few times to meet with the old lady's plumber. I took her car into the shop and did her grocery shopping, visiting for two of the afternoons.

Meanwhile, Kat knit, read books, and had quiet conversations with my mother over tea and kosher cookies. And slept.

My ma did her thing, Kat had a respite, I was a horny scumbag, and the days passed in quiet calm. But that didn't mean I didn't notice stuff about her, like how she took her coffee—two scoops of sugar, two tablespoons of cream—or how she bit her lip when she read a knitting pattern. Sometimes her mouth moved when she knit, like she was counting. She seemed to prefer sitting on the floor rather than a chair or a sofa.

She never wore socks, her feet always bare, and seemed to favor dresses over pants. Her hair was always down except right before bed when she'd braid it. Her nighttime lotion smelled like vanilla, like cake. Her daytime lotion smelled like coconuts and made me think of a tropical vacation, which made me think of Kat in a bikini, which had me taking a cold shower.

The only time she was messy—and this struck me as very important —was when she knit. Her yarn, papers, needles, and hooks spread out everywhere like she needed to see everything or have it within arm's reach. All other times, everything was picked up, cleaned up, buttoned up, and put away. She put away her toothbrush and toiletries, back into her suitcase, after every use. Kat even folded and stored her pajamas.

Who folds their pajamas?

Just like my apartment back in Chicago, she was here, but she didn't want to be seen. She hid behind orderliness and routine, making as little noise as possible. She held herself back, like she didn't want to be a bother, like she didn't trust us to see who she was and want her here anyway.

It pissed me off, but what could I say about it? Nothing. At least, not yet. Her father had just died, and she needed to grieve on her tidy terms.

And another thing, despite Eugene's prediction, mourners did come to visit.

Katherine and Desmond Sullivan, Quinn's parents, came by on Friday, bringing dinner and pictures of baby Desmond.

Eugene himself stopped over on Sunday for a short visit, during which Kat gave him the look of stone cold betrayal and left the room.

His eyes followed her as she climbed the stairs and disappeared around the corner. "He didn't deserve her worry when he was alive."

I studied the man for a moment, his sharp tie, the solid gold tie clip. "Is that why you didn't tell her?"

His stare cut back to mine. "I needed her focused on more important things."

"More important than her father dying?"

"Her future was more important. She didn't need the distraction." He sighed, looking tired. "She'll come around."

I didn't know if he was speaking to me or himself, but I scoffed. "Yeah, I don't think so."

Eugene's eyes cut back to mine, his eyebrows lifting in question.

"If you want her to talk to you again any time before your deathbed, or acknowledge your existence, you're going to have to apologize in a big way. And I don't know how you're going to do that, since she won't even look at you."

"Fine. I'll apologize on Wednesday," he grumbled.

"What's on Wednesday?"

"Reading the will, estate business. The appointment is for eight thirty, but the transfer process will take all day. It might be good for you to also attend. You need to get a sense of her properties, assets, investments, and material worth."

"Yeah, all right." I scratched my jaw. "I'll move things around on my schedule, clear the day, and we'll drive over together."

"Good. Our estate management group will be arriving at noon, and I've arranged for the New York office vice president of estate finance at Brooks and Quail to join us at three."

"Brooks and Quail?" Holy shit. Quinn and I had been trying to get a meeting with the elusive finance giant for years, and she had the VP of estate finance flying to Boston to meet with just her.

Eugene nodded, his shrewd gaze drifted back to the stairs where Kat had disappeared.

I tugged on my ear, continued inspecting him, trying to figure out this guy's motivation. Cutting to the chase, I stated the obvious, "You love her. Like she was your kid."

"Yes." He didn't hesitate, or seemed surprised by what I'd said. But then he added, his eyes turning shrewd, "But loving her doesn't mean she owes you anything."

We traded glares, because I got the sense he wasn't just talking about himself. His words were a warning shot, a reminder not to get my hopes up or expect too much.

Or want too much.

He was right.

I'd had a front-row ticket to the implosion of my parents' marriage, he didn't need to remind me what tragic, one-sided love and unequal affection looked like.

And so, I continued to keep my distance.

But on Monday . . .

On Monday, she ambushed me.

I'd just finished a phone call with our main resource in Australia, a follow-up from my trip, when Kat knocked on the study door and poked her head in.

"Hey," she said, like she wanted to say more, or had a speech prepared.

I also noticed she was wearing a dress, a little black dress, with long sleeves and a short skirt. Not ass-cheeks hanging out short, but— you know—short. Her feet were bare, which meant her legs were also bare.

"Hey." I swallowed and I stood. It felt like the right thing to do at the time, but then I was stuck standing for no reason, like an idiot asshole. "Uh, how you doing?"

"Okay." Kat walked into the study and I saw she was clutching her phone to her chest. Her hair was down. "Are you busy?"

I shook my head, walking slowly around to the other side of the desk. "Nope. What's up? Are you hungry?"

"No. What time does your mom get off work?" She closed the study door behind her.

"I think seven." My attention dropped to her legs, then I crow-barred my eyes back to her face. "Or maybe eight."

She licked her lips, nodding, still clutching her phone. "So, I know this is short notice, and maybe it's not appropriate—not that we have to take any action—but I just spoke to my therapist on the phone."

"Oh?" I scratched my neck. I didn't know why I was scratching my neck.

Because you're picturing her naked, shitbird. Oh. That's right. My bad.

"Yes." She stood before me, shifting her weight from one foot to the other, staring at me like she hoped I would read her mind.

So I said, "That's good."

"It is. We've been talking for the last hour. I just talked to her about everything with my dad. We also talked about . . . *other things.*"

"Other things?"

She nodded, took a breath, and waited.

Her meaning dawned on me all at once, and I stepped away from the desk. She meant sex stuff.

"Oh. Did you want—I mean, is she—does she want to talk now?" I couldn't get the words out fast enough.

"Dr. Kasai can't, she has another client, but she did give me some direction, um, suggestions that I thought I'd go over with you." Kat seemed to study me intently. "Do you think this is okay? I mean, while I'm in mourning? Does this seem disrespectful?"

"I don't know the rules of shiva, but I think it's fine," said the horny scumbag. "I mean, we're just talking here, right? And talking to your therapist about anything right now seems like a good idea." Clearly, I had no shame.

She nodded, taking a deep breath. "Okay. Good. That's what I was thinking."

"Is she—?" I gestured to Kat's cell.

"No. I already hung up. Can we sit in here? To talk?"

Why am I nervous?

Don't be a dummy.

"Yeah, over here." I guided Kat over to the leather sofa parked against the wall. It was the same couch I used to sit on while we waited for my ma to pass judgment on us when we were kids; we'd called it "The Discipline Couch." My mother didn't spank us, but my dad did during the rare times he was home.

So, it was probably weird that my first thought was that I'd like to pull her over my knee, lift her skirt, and give Kat some sexy spanks, right?

Definitely weird.

Kat set her phone on the coffee table, sat at one end of the couch, and faced me. She tucked a leg under her, her hands in her lap, her fingers twisting.

Just as I took my seat at the other end, my phone buzzed. I pulled it out, glancing at the screen. Alex's name flashed on my screen. I sent the call to voicemail and set it on the coffee table next to Kat's. He was probably calling me about Caleb.

On a hunch, I'd asked Alex to look into the fitness of Caleb Tyson's financials. Unlike most CEO's in the USA, Caleb Tyson's salary was capped. Bylaws prevented the Caravel CEO from earning more than a certain amount, which included stock options. In my cursory research, I'd discovered Caleb had cashed in all his stocks a few months ago. This raised a big fat red flag for a few reasons:

Firstly, that meant he was going to have a hell of a tax bill this year, unless he also had losses to report.

Secondly, Caravel was a solid venture. Selling now was just bad investment strategy.

Thirdly, what did he need with all that cash?

Alex had probably discovered something, but I'd call them back later. I didn't know why I'd checked my phone at all. No matter who it was, I would have sent it to voicemail. I was busy with Kat. Everything else could wait.

"Did you need to get that?" Kat motioned to my phone.

"This is more important."

Her eyes flickered over me. "Who was it?"

"Alex."

"It might be work."

"Yeah."

"It could be about Wally."

"I'll call back later. So, what'd Dr. Kasai say?" I faced her, my arm along the back of the sofa, and *did not* look at her legs again.

"Uh." Kat blinked at me, looking a little dazed, or maybe startled. "Um, so . . . Dr. Kasai. Yes. She suggested we find someone local, a— a—a sex therapist, if our early attempts are unsuccessful." She was stumbling all over her words.

"That makes sense." I nodded, trying to sound calm and objective, even though I really liked the sound of *early attempts.*

Kat was looking everywhere but at me, and her cheeks were the color of the *Boston* on the Red Sox game jerseys. "But that we should take it slow, really slow, and give it plenty of time. We should focus on the process and not the finish line. We should try to enjoy each other and not . . . orgasm."

Um . . . what?

"Excuse me?" I was with her until the very last word.

"She said she thought it would be best if we—neither of us—

orgasmed until I talked to her in two weeks," Kat said on a rush. "She said it would take the pressure off, if we just focused on the enjoying part and not the finishing part."

I sat back, my eyes moving over Kat, snagging on her fingers where they twisted the hem of her short skirt. She looked really anxious, like she thought I'd be upset by this news or something.

For the record, I wasn't upset.

I was confused, not upset.

Because, wasn't the whole point of this trying to get Kat to orgasm without alcohol? How could we do that if she wasn't allowed? I didn't ask this question, because she already looked stressed out enough.

Instead, I said, "Okay. Sounds good."

Kat exhaled like she'd been holding her breath. Then she rubbed her forehead. Then she sighed again and her hair fell forward, hiding her face. Clearly, she was tense. Good thing I had some idea on a few ways to help her relax.

I slid closer to her, until our legs touched. Then I pushed my fingers into her thick, dark, glossy hair, rubbing her scalp, tracing the line of her neck to her back.

She leaned into my touch, angling her head toward me, like she wanted me to do it again.

She liked to be petted.

She liked to be stroked.

She liked affection.

So did I. Maybe once all this was over and things settled down, she'd trust me enough to let me pet her, stroke her, and hold her.

Or maybe she wouldn't, not yet. Maybe never. The thought was depressing, but I couldn't dismiss the possibility. Like Eugene had said, she didn't owe me anything.

She sighed, sounding more relaxed, her fingers no longer folding and rolling her skirt.

What we did and when we did it, she had to initiate it. Or she had to give me a sign that I was supposed to take the lead. I wasn't a mind reader, particularly where she was concerned.

It was just the two of us, the length of her leg pressing against mine, her soft hair brushing my shoulder, and I figured now was as good a time as any to let her know I was ready whenever she was.

"Kat."

"Yes?" She studied her fingers for a sec, then lifted her eyes to mine.

Fuck me, but I could drown in her eyes. It wasn't just that they were gorgeous, it was everything behind them—the smarts, the goodness, the toughness, the compassion—and they made me stupid when we were this close.

So I spelled it out. "Let me know if you want to take the lead, or if you want me to."

Nice finesse, dumbass.

I would've rolled my eyes at myself, but I didn't want to look away from her.

Her lips parted, and she blinked, like I'd surprised her. I'd been blunt, so perhaps I did. I watched her swallow, her stare dropping to my mouth, her eyes swirling with a shitload of emotion.

I thought she was going to kiss me.

Instead, she nodded, gave me a forced smile—making me suspect she didn't trust her voice, or didn't trust herself around me—and said, "Okay. I'll, uh, let you get back to work."

With that, she stood like she was in a hurry, grabbed her phone, and on bare feet silently walked to the door.

She opened it. She left. She closed it.

Meanwhile, I sat there, staring at the far wall and wondering why I was now alone rather than making out with my wicked amazing, wicked smart, wicked hot wife on the discipline couch.

Fuck my life.

Picking up my cell, I returned Alex's call. I figured if I couldn't be helping her feel good, I could do something to help her in general.

Three rings later, he hadn't picked up. I was just about to end the call when Sandra's voice said, "Hello?"

"Hey. It's me. Alex there?"

"He stepped out."

"Oh." I sighed, real loud. *Because I'm frustrated, OKAY?* "I'll call back later."

"What's wrong?" The sound of plates being stacked sounded from her side of the call. "Is Kat okay?"

"She's . . . fine."

Sandra didn't say anything for a second, and it sounded like she'd stopped stacking the plates. "How is she dealing with the loss of her father?"

"Actually, she seems okay about it. After the first day, she was fine." I scratched at a little mark on the couch that looked like it had been made with a Sharpie.

"And your mom? Are she and Kat getting along?"

"Yeah." I laughed, knowing I sounded a little bitter. "*They're* getting along *great.*"

"Hmm . . ." Sandra paused again, and I thought she was about to say goodbye.

So I said, "Tell Alex to ca—"

"Has she orgasmed yet?"

And I choked. "What?"

"Please tell me you've been helping her with the orgasm thing."

"Fuck, Sandra!"

"No. Not Sandra. Fuck Kat, Dan. She needs you more than me." She sounded so calm.

I choked again.

And then I laughed.

And then I choked.

"I'm not talking to you about this."

"Don't hang up!" she shouted, but then lowered her voice to say, "You should talk to me about this because I can help you. I can help you both. I can give you help-able facts that will be so helpful."

I sat forward on the edge of my seat, gripping my forehead with my fingers. "Seriously, I can't talk to you about this. This is her deal. If she wants to discuss it with you, then she will. It's not up to me."

"Then will you listen? And for the record, she has talked to me about it."

"Oh? Really?" I didn't try to disguise my disbelief.

"Yes. Really. How else would I know it's an issue?"

She had me there.

"Dan. Please. Let me give you some perspective and advice. Please. You don't have to say anything, you don't even have to answer any questions. Just. Listen."

I glanced at the wall clock behind the desk and shook my head. "Fine. You have ten minutes."

"Yay! Thank you. Okay. *Ahem*." I heard a chair scrape against the floor, like she was taking a seat to get comfortable. "Have you ever experienced any sexual performance or anxiety issues?"

I stared at the wall clock.

And then I blinked.

And then I frowned.

"I'm sorry, but what the fuck did you just ask me?"

"Let me back up a bit." She sounded like she was trying not to laugh. "We've all seen those commercials on TV, advertising medication to help with male sexual performance issues, right?"

I nodded, my frown persisting. "Yeah. So?"

What the fuck is this?

"As a society, we talk about the fact that men sometimes have performance issues. In a way, these commercials normalize performance anxiety for men, they tell us, 'Hey, it's okay. You're not alone. This is nothing to be ashamed of. Many men have the same problem, and we have a way to help you.' But have you ever seen a similar commercial for women?"

My eyes lowered to the carpet. "No," I finally answered. "I guess I haven't."

"So, you see what she's dealing with here. For better or worse, normalizing an issue—like Viagra commercials do for men—has a halo effect for those impacted. It provides support, even in a subtle way. But for women who struggle, there are no commercials. There is no normalizing of the problem, and so, even from the start, many women do not seek treatment. They believe they have an issue that affects them in isolation. If a woman does not enjoy herself during sex, they believe that they are alone, or broken, or 'just made that way.'"

"That's beat."

Sandra chuckled. "It is. But the good news is that there is treatment. I'm sure Kat has told you that her particular issue does not have a physical cause. It can't be treated with medication or surgery."

"Except as a Band-Aid." I scratched my jaw.

"What?" I heard Sandra shift in her seat, like she was passing the phone from one ear to the other. "What did you say?"

"Except alcohol, right? In Kat's case. But that would be a Band-Aid, not really solving the problem, just covering it up."

"Exactly." Sandra sounded like she was smiling again. "That's exactly right. In fact, it wouldn't just cover it up, it would make things worse in the long run. But, anyway, what I wanted to say is that sexual health is impossible if fear is present. That includes fear of disappointing another person, fear of not meeting society's expectations, fear of missing out on a full life, fear of losing a person, fear of being alone, fear of being judged for one's desires, likes, or dislikes. That means, from now on, absolutely none of Kat's—or your—motivation in the bedroom can come from fear."

I was nodding vehemently before Sandra had finished speaking, and when she did finish, I said, "Preach it." With feeling.

Sandra laughed again, but then cleared her throat, taking on an instructional tone. "When sexual acts result in feelings of stress or anxiety, the body releases stress hormones, specifically epinephrine and norepinephrine. The entire point of these hormones is to prepare a person to hide from or confront a threat. In this instance, the threat to a person's security or welfare is the fear of displeasing her partner." I heard Sandra gather a deep breath. "A few weeks ago, I advised Kat to do some research and think about what she liked, what aroused her, want turned her on, what she *wants*. She should share that list with you. I'll send her an email and encourage her to do so."

"Sounds good." I was impressed with how *not* like a horndog I sounded, given the fact that I was a total horndog for this woman.

"But, I will also tell her—and I hope her therapist told her—that she needs to trust you when you offer to help. She has to stop feeling guilty or being worried that she's taking advantage of you."

"She feels that way?" That had me sitting up. "She shouldn't feel that way."

"Then you should tell her, too. Ask her to trust you. But, and this might be the most important part, if, at any time, what Kat is asking of you *is* a burden, you are to tell the truth. You must not be afraid. Kat cannot trust you, she won't believe you, unless you are honest about your boundaries and desires. Just as she must not be afraid that she is a burden, you must not be afraid to 'make things worse' as it were, by being honest. Do you understand?"

I scratched my jaw as I thought about her words. "Yeah. Makes sense. If I'm not honest and don't tell it like it is, then she'll doubt my honesty, and then we're right back where we started."

"Exactly. That's exactly right. Good." Sandra sounded relieved.

"I have a question." I couldn't believe I was going to ask Sandra this question, but I wanted to get a good ballpark figure. "How long does this usually take?"

"Take?"

"Yeah. How long until she feels relaxed? Good about things?"

"Don't worry about how long this will take. I'm sure Dr. Kasai told Kat that there would be setbacks—three steps forward, two steps back. That's fine. That's all perfectly normal. But to answer your question, sometimes it takes months, sometimes it takes weeks, sometimes it takes days."

"Days?"

"When I work on this issue with my patients, I tell them they're not allowed to orgasm. I tell them that they can kiss, make out, approach—but do not cross—third base. What you both must prioritize is enjoying the process. Roleplay, for example, can be a great way to step outside of anxieties."

Roleplay?

Fuck a duck, my mind exploded with the possibilities.

Please say naked sexy massages. Please say hot tub sex. Please say sexy spanking on the discipline couch. Please say boss/secretary inap-

propriate performance review time. Please, please, please tell me you want to dress up like a librarian and—

I was going to hell. That was definitely going to happen.

"Dan, listen. I don't think I'm breaking the BFF code when I tell you that Kat thinks you're gorgeous. And sexy. And an all-around wonderful person."

I smirked, and was about to say something self-deprecating, but then Sandra added, "She cares about you. Deeply."

More than anything suggested or stated so far, this statement got me hot. It made my heart take off like a rocket. Spanking, massages, hot tub sex, and orgasms were great, don't get me wrong.

But, *fuck.*

I just wanted to hold Kat.

I didn't want her to curl into a ball at night.

I wanted her arms around *me.*

Naked hugging, that's what I wanted.

I wanted to touch her.

That's it. *That's all.*

Suddenly, Sandra's voice turned fierce, "And you better feel the same way about her or I will castrate you, Texas style."

"I do," I confirmed softly, my heart in my fucking throat.

"Good." Sandra sounded appeased. "But she needs to know that her self-worth and sexuality isn't based on your desire for her. She is a strong, capable, intelligent, talented, beautiful woman. She needs to learn how to bring that confidence in herself to the table—and to the bed—and demand enjoyment from herself and her partner, whoever that may be."

"*Whoever that may be?*" I growled, not liking the sound of that.

Let me clarify, I didn't have a problem with the first part of what she'd said—I agreed wholeheartedly with all of that—but the second part, the "whoever that may be" part, that was bullshit.

Sandra laughed again. "Don't worry, Dan the Security Man. I would never suggest or encourage Kat to look elsewhere for satisfaction. I'm just pointing out that her satisfaction and enjoyment must be something she prioritizes, and it must be something her partner prioritizes."

"Yeah, okay. I get you."

Still, though. I didn't like the thought of Kat looking elsewhere.

Well, dipshit, if you don't want her seeking satisfaction elsewhere, then you better deliver.

At that thought, I nodded and shrugged. Once again, I didn't see a problem.

"Dan, you know I love you both. I hope I've helped."

"You have helped. Thanks for . . ." I looked at the clock. We'd been talking for longer than ten minutes. "Thanks for explaining things. It makes more sense now. I wish I'd been on the call with her therapist when they talked about this."

Sandra made a soft sound, like she felt a little sad. "Oh Dan, trust will come in time."

I blinked at that.

And then I flinched.

And I didn't know what to say because for the first time it hit me. I finally understood.

Kat was hiding.

She was willing to let me help as long as she didn't have to be too exposed, too vulnerable.

She didn't trust me.

That was a problem.

CHAPTER NINETEEN

The **Uniform Trade Secrets Act** (UTSA), published by the Uniform Law Commission (ULC) in 1979 and amended in 1985, was a uniform act of the United States disseminated in an effort to provide legal framework to better protect trade secrets for U.S. companies operating in multiple states.

Wex Legal Dictionary

Kat

MARITAL RELATIONS WERE prohibited during shiva. Even I, who'd lapsed almost entirely in the practice of my faith for more than ten years, knew that.

As I sat at the kitchen table Tuesday night after Skyping with my knitting group, presently waiting for Eleanor to come home, I decided that Dan must also have known. I assumed the mourning period was why he'd been coming to bed after he thought I'd fallen asleep, and left in the morning before he thought I was awake.

He'd been trying to give me space. To mourn. To respect traditions I didn't really know how to navigate. Certain I was making all kinds of mistakes, I did my best to follow the rules faithfully. Even so, I couldn't bring myself to feel the level of distraught I should have.

During shiva, the mourner must refrain from doing those things which have even the possibility of evoking joy, such as unnecessarily playing with children, or even engaging in heated discussions with visitors.

My lack of melancholy was why I'd ended the video call with my knitting group early. They'd conferenced me in—both Ashley in Tennessee and me in Boston—and I'd been having a good time. But then I felt badly about having a good time. So after finalizing the details for the group's upcoming visit to Boston, we'd ended the call.

Hearing the front door open then close, I jumped to my feet. First, I stopped by the fridge to pull out the dinner for Dan's mom. I then placed it in the microwave and set it to reheat. Checking once more that everything was in order, I left the kitchen to meet her.

She looked tired, but seemed to perk up as soon as she saw me. "Kat. You didn't need to wait up."

Eleanor opened her arms; I stepped forward to accept a hug and a kiss on the cheek. "Did you eat? There's dinner."

"You're not supposed to make dinner." Eleanor made a face, but mostly smiled. She'd said the same thing the last three times I'd waited up and had dinner ready for her. She was right, I wasn't supposed to be cooking or cleaning, but being waited on and doing nothing made me feel useless. Also, so far, she seemed to enjoy both the food and the company.

Also, technically, I hadn't made it.

"It's the delivery that Uncle Eugene arranged. I promise, I wasn't cooking."

"Okay, good. Sit with me and tell me about your day." She left her stuff on the console table by the front door and we walked to the kitchen together. "Did you finish your shawl?"

"Almost. I just need to weave in the ends. I'll show it to you." I'd left my knitting bag on the kitchen table so I could show her the finished piece as soon as she got home. She didn't knit, but appeared to admire my works in progress. "How was work?"

Eleanor sat at the place I'd set for her and told me about her day while I retrieved her food and grabbed new ice for her water. I settled in across from her, hiding away most of my mess in my knitting bag and picking up the shawl I'd just finished. Using my darning needle, I wove the ends of the yarn along the sides.

As I listened to her, it was clear she was especially tired. I stood, crossed to the counter, turned on the electric kettle as she neared the end of her meal; I knew she liked tea before bedtime.

I pulled down teacups, located the chamomile tea bags, and placed the bags in her old blue willow teapot. She'd told me earlier in the week that it was her grandmother's. The antique had a small chip at the spout and the handle for the lid had been glued on repeatedly, but Eleanor believed it was important to use heirlooms, even fine china, as much as possible.

"A thing has no value except through use and the accumulation of memories from its use," she'd said. "What good would it do to leave such a thing in the china cabinet collecting dust? What value would it have? I remember my grandmother and my mother every time I use this teapot, and I use it with my children, so they'll remember me."

At present, she was silent, sipping the last of her water and watching me as I moved around the kitchen. I sent her a small smile, which she returned with genuine warmth, but then her features turned thoughtful.

"How—" she started, stopped, sighed, and then started again. "Let me first say, I can't tell you how much I've enjoyed having you and Dan this past week, despite the sad circumstances that brought you here."

"Thank you. I can't thank you enough for opening your home to me."

She waved away my gratitude. "This is your home now, too. I know you're going through a tough time." She stopped again, openly examining me. "Tell me, how are you doing? With the loss of your father?"

"I didn't know my father very well," I hedged, an acute spike of shame flaring within me.

Still examining me, she leaned forward, her elbows on the table. "Forgive me, but I'm not so good at dancing around things, being polite for the sake of politeness, especially when things need saying. So, Kathleen," she waited until I met her eyes before continuing, "I'm just guessing here, but it seems like you're experiencing some guilt about not feeling grief—or, a lot of grief—that he's gone."

I gathered a deep breath and passed her a teacup, exhaling an excess of pent up self-recrimination. "Yes. I should be devastated. I should be inconsolable. Right?"

"Not necessarily. Your father has been sick for a long time, slipping away little by little. Sometimes you mourn a person before they die, so that when they pass, you've already made your peace with it. I see that kind of thing all the time with families in the ICU."

"But it's not that. I mean, it is that. He has been sick, he hasn't recognized me in years, but it's also . . ." I shook my head, feeling frustrated.

"Can I ask, and tell me to back off here if I'm overstepping. I never seem to know when I'm overstepping. But from the outside, and from our conversations this last week. the way you've avoided talking about your childhood, it seems like maybe your dad wasn't very nice to you. Is that right?"

I met her gaze, saying nothing.

It didn't feel right to pass judgment on the dead, or speak ill of my father. He was my father, and I wanted to honor him. I wanted to think he'd done the best he could given difficult circumstances.

On the other hand, I also wanted to believe, even if I were faced with similar circumstances, that I would make different, better choices. That no matter how busy I was, I'd never treat my children with indifference.

She gave me an understanding smile. "Now I'm going to give you unsolicited advice, which—if you're anything like my kids—you'll ignore. And that's fine. But I like giving it anyway."

"Okay." I returned her smile, seriously doubting her kids ignored her advice.

"You can't make yourself feel something for a person if it's not there. Trust me, I have firsthand experience with this." She gave a little laugh, it sounded self-deprecating.

"You felt that way? About someone?"

"Uh, no. Not quite." She glanced at her plate, a sudden sadness claiming her features. She buried the feelings quickly, sighing. "What I'm saying is, whether they're alive and well, or dead, or dying, trying to force a connection with someone is like trying to light rain on fire. And feeling badly about your lack of emotion, filling that void with guilt, is a waste of time and destructive, not only to you, but to those who care about you. So, if you can't bring yourself to mourn his passing, maybe, instead, mourn the relationship you wished you'd had with your father, so you can let him go."

We sat in silence for a minute, her words of wisdom ringing in my ears. I latched on to the idea that I could mourn the relationship I wished we'd had. Then at least I'd be mourning *something.* I'd spent the week trying to locate my grief, whereas my thoughts had gravitated anywhere and everywhere else:

What was Caleb up to? Where was he? What sinister plan was next on his agenda?

What would happen at the reading of the will? Would there be any surprises? Would the transition be seamless? Or would the company suffer? And what could I do to minimize potential instability?

And, of course, there was Dan.

Sigh.

"Well." Eleanor stood, the movement startling me and yanking me from my thoughts. I watched as she moved to the sink with her dishes, her steps shuffling, like she was out of energy.

"No." I stood, inserting myself in front of the sink. "Let me do those. You relax."

"Maybe it makes me terrible, but I'm not going to turn you down." She yawned, giving me another hug before she backed away.

"Why don't you go change? I'll finish making the tea."

She nodded tiredly, her hand covering her mouth as she yawned again. "Yeah. Okay. I'll be right back."

I washed and dried the remaining dishes, putting them away and busied myself straightening up the rest of the kitchen while my thoughts invariably returned to Dan.

Yesterday, just after my impromptu therapy session with Dr. Kasai had ended and I'd gone to the study so we could talk, Dan received a call from Alex. I watched as he'd sent it to voicemail, placing his phone on the table so we could finish our discussion.

I couldn't even explain it to myself, but something about him sending the call to voicemail had sent a thrill from the base of my spine up my neck, around my heart, to my forehead, and behind my eyes.

Like nothing else, Dan sending the call to voicemail had made me feel like I was important. To him.

And that was probably nuts, because he'd already done so much for me, so many big things. He'd married me. He'd opened his home to me. He'd rearranged his life. He'd made me part of his family. Huge, sweeping, selfless deeds I could never hope to repay.

Sending the call to voicemail wasn't a grand gesture. It was an everyday, likely unthinking, demonstration of his priorities.

It took my breath away.

See? Nuts.

And then, Dan had looked at me and said, "Let me know if you want to take the lead, or if you want me to."

Another grand gesture.

No pressure, no thought for himself.

And in that moment, I was arrested by a single thought.

I'm falling in love with him.

My feelings exploded. An atomic bomb of emotions, laying waste to every feeble wall I'd tried to erect, to keep us both safe, to maintain an arm's length between us for his benefit as well as mine. I'd felt like crying, bursting into tears and covering his lips and hands and body in kisses.

Instead, red in the face, I gave him a quick smile and excused myself.

But I'd thought of little else since. And today was the last day of mourning.

The sound of the front door opening then closing pulled me from my thoughts. I straightened from where I'd been cleaning the sink, grabbing a towel and walking slowly toward the foyer. I hadn't heard Dan come downstairs and, as far as I knew, he was still in the study. We hadn't spoken since I left him yesterday. I was anxious to see him, spend time with him, be intimate without worrying about reaching the finish line, but I'd also needed time to plan my attack.

Rounding the corner to the entryway, I spotted a man.

The sight of him astonished me for many reasons; not the least of which, he was going through Eleanor's purse.

"Hey!" I stepped forward, obviously startling him, and grabbed her purse off the console table. "Who are you?"

The man, his hand over his chest—further evidence I'd caught him by surprise—stared at me with wide, stunned eyes. "Who am I? Who the fuck are you?"

He wore black pants, maybe jeans, a Bruins T-shirt, and black boots. A silver chain hung at his side, a wallet chain, and the letters F U C K were tattooed on the back of one set of fingers; on the other set were Y O U S.

The man looked a lot like Dan, just with gray-blue eyes, and older. It was difficult to determine how much older because—even filled with surprise—his eyes looked hard, weary in a way Dan's weren't. But his hair held some gray, salt and pepper at the temples. I deduced the age difference must've been at least ten years.

"You're Seamus." Now that I really inspected him, I recognized the face from pictures around the house.

"Yeah. I am." His gaze slithered over me uncertainly. "And you are?"

Regardless of familial relationship, I didn't like the fact that he'd been digging in Eleanor's bag. I held fast to my righteous indignation and advanced on him.

He took a step back.

"I'll ask the questions." I lifted my chin, glaring. "What do you think you're doing with Eleanor's purse?"

He raised an eyebrow, his head sliding back on his neck. Seamus peered at me like I was something strange, or maybe like I was something crazy. "None of your goddamn business."

I shook my head, looking him over. "You should be ashamed of yourself."

He blinked at me, like I'd again surprised him. "You don't even know what I was doing. Maybe I was leaving her a birthday card."

"Her birthday was last month."

"That's right. It's a belated birthday card." His gaze traveled over me again and his tongue swept along his bottom lip, obvious admiration behind his eyes as they settled on my breasts.

Ugh. *Gross.*

I turned from him and walked back to the kitchen, bringing Eleanor's purse with me and putting it in the cupboard where she kept the plates. As soon as I shut the cabinet, I heard shuffling footsteps enter the kitchen. He was watching me. I felt his eyes on my back as I continued scrubbing the sink.

"Who are you?" he asked, his voice quieter.

Without turning around, I said, "I'm Dan's wife."

A few seconds passed, during which I rinsed out the sink. His footsteps came closer.

"Dan has a wife?"

"Yes."

"Since when?"

"A few weeks ago." I glanced at him. He'd come to stand next to the sink, five-ish feet away, and he wore a confused frown.

"Was there a wedding?"

Turning off the water, I faced him, a little surprised by the subtle hint of vulnerability in the question, like he was hurt—but was trying to hide it—that he hadn't been invited.

"No. Not really." I watched him closely. "We were married at the Cook County Clerk's office with one witness."

His eyes dropped to my stomach. "You're pregnant."

Despite myself, I laughed. "Not that I know of."

Seamus scratched his jaw thoughtfully, a movement that was eerily similar to one I'd seen Dan do several times, and my heart warmed a little—just a very little—towards this scoundrel.

Maybe I'd jumped to the wrong conclusion. I had a bad history of jumping to the wrong conclusion, so it was a definite possibility.

Maybe there was a perfectly reasonable explanation for his earlier behavior. I doubted he was leaving his mother a birthday card, but I wondered if perhaps his reasons for digging in her purse were not as sinister as I'd originally suspected.

I opened my mouth to ask him again why he was going through his mother's purse when we were unceremoniously interrupted.

By Dan.

"Get the fuck away from her."

In unison, we both turned our heads to find Dan, fuming, standing by the entrance to the kitchen. His usually warm brown eyes now almost black, and most definitely cold.

"Baby brother."

"Fuck off."

Seamus slid an inch closer to me and grinned. "You're married. That's so great. Your lady and I are becoming fast friends. Would you like to join us for a cup of tea? Share the story of how you two love-birds met?" His voice was ridiculously cheerful.

Dan was not amused. He strolled into the space, placing himself between us.

"I said, you fuckfaced shitstain,"—his words were low, slow, measured— "get the fuck away from her, or I will fucking fuckily fuck you the fuck up."

I stared at Dan, my lips parting in wonder. He'd just used some variation of the F-word as a noun, verb, adverb, and adjective all in one sentence. I didn't know whether to be mortified or impressed.

Seamus's forced cheer dissolved, his eyes narrowing and turning just as cold as his brother's. After another two beats of my heart, Seamus backed away, his hands coming up like he surrendered, but the twist of his mouth was bitter.

"Nice to see you, too," he muttered.

For the first time since entering the kitchen, Dan turned to me, his gaze on mine. "Are you okay?"

I blinked at him and the question, perplexed. Dan was serious. He appeared to be truly concerned that his brother might hurt me.

I nodded, struggling for words for a half second. "I'm—I'm fine. We were just talking."

Seamus snorted from behind Dan, sounding insulted. "Come off it. What do you think? I'm going to come in here and assault your *wife*?"

Dan slow blinked, not looking at his brother, and I saw that he was gritting his teeth. "Yeah. That's what I think. Given the fact that you're not opposed to roughing up women."

"Jem Morris isn't *women*, and you know that crazy bitch gives as good as she gets. Didn't Jem put a cigarette out on Quinn's chest?"

Now Dan turned back to Seamus. "You sent your boys to Chicago to kidnap Quinn's *wife*. They held her friends at gunpoint. I don't think I'm overreacting."

What the frickedy frick?

I peered around Dan's bulky shoulder at Seamus. "That was *you*?"

"You're still not over that, Danny boy?"

"Oh hey," Dan's tone was dripping with sarcasm. "I finally got the last knife of the set you've been stabbing in my back all these years. Heads up: I re-gift."

Seamus snorted. "What did my guys get for their trouble? A fucking knitting needle to the chest, knocked out by a tequila bottle, and two years stateside, that's what. *You* should be apologizing to *me*."

"You know what you and our nephew's diaper have in common, Seamus? You're both self-absorbed and full of shit."

Seamus rolled his eyes and pulled out a pack of cigarettes. "And you're like a plunger, you keep bringing up old shit."

"Acting like a dick won't make yours any bigger." Dan took a threatening step forward. "You can't smoke in here."

"Yeah, okay dad." Another eye-roll. "If I was meant to be controlled I'd come with a remote."

"Why don't you make like a tree and die in a forest fire," Dan mumbled gruffly and moved like he was going to grab the pack from his brother, but stopped short when Eleanor entered the room.

"Don't smoke in here," she said evenly but firmly. She walked directly over to Seamus—like she wasn't at all surprised by the scene in the kitchen—and pulled him into a hug. "And stop trying to piss off your brother."

"Jesus Christ, I haven't done anything, Ma. I swear."

"Watch your fucking mouth. You don't take the Lord's name in vain, and you don't swear. Not in this house." She pointed a finger at him, lifting her eyebrows meaningfully, daring him to contradict her.

He gave Eleanor a small, conciliatory nod, stuffing his cigarettes back in his pocket.

Seemingly satisfied, she turned to Dan and patted him on the shoulder, "You. Be nice to your brother. I mean it."

Dan made a low sound in the back of his throat and crossed his arms, saying nothing. His mother placed a kiss on his cheek.

She moved to me and pulled me in for a hug, her voice adopting a sweeter tone. "I'm taking my tea and going to bed. I don't know why, but I'm exhausted. Thanks for dinner." As she pulled away, her hand came to my cheek and she smiled at me. "And thanks for being such an angel."

I nodded. "Thank you for the conversation."

"Anytime, sweetheart. I mean it."

No one spoke as Eleanor poured hot water into her cup, reached into the teapot I'd prepared, and took a tea bag. Glancing around the counters as she left, she called over her shoulder. "Turn the lights off when you go to bed. And if you find the clicker, put it above the TV. It's been missing since Saturday."

Then she was gone.

No one moved for half a minute, maybe more. I studied Dan's back, the rigidity of his shoulders, the stiffness in his spine. Seamus's posture was more relaxed, but he looked equally surly.

I decided I wanted tea.

"Anyone want tea?"

Dan shook his head. "He was just leaving."

"Tea sounds lovely." Seamus, his eyes on Dan, pushed away from the counter and sauntered to the kitchen table, taking the seat Eleanor had sat in earlier.

I poured hot water from the kettle into the teapot, thinking to myself that I would look at this old blue willow teapot and always remember this moment. I moved around Dan to the table, setting down the steeping tea and three teacups.

"Dan?" I asked, turning, finding his eyes on me.

He gave his head a subtle shake, the muscle at his jaw jumping.

I walked to him and placed a hand on his arm while he watched me. Gazing into his eyes and not liking his stony, aloof expression, I lifted on my toes and placed a light kiss on his mouth. His arms immediately unfolded and his hands came to my waist. It felt good to kiss him, to feel his hands on me—so, so good—and my body reacted in an instinctual way, relaxing, pressing closer.

Leaning just my torso away, I gave him a smile, whispering. "Chamomile or Earl Grey?"

He was frowning, but some of the ice in his eyes melted. "I fucking hate that guy."

"I can tell." I gave him another quick kiss, I was addicted to his mouth. "Your mom said to be nice."

"He's still breathing, isn't he? This is me being nice."

I leaned closer again. "Dan."

He tilted his head to the side, saying, "Kit-Kat," and a tiny shiver raced down my spine. He'd lowered his voice to the naughty-secret level.

Warmth, like a hot hand on cool skin, blossomed in my stomach. "One cup of tea."

"I'll have tea with you," he lifted his chin toward the table, "after he fucks off."

"I can hear you," Seamus sing-songed from behind me.

"Then fuck off," Dan sing-songed in response.

"You know," Seamus started conversationally, "I would tell you to go fuck yourself but I'm pretty sure you'd be disappointed."

"Since you know it all, you should know when to shut the fuck up."

I watched Dan's luscious lips form the insult, his eyes never leaving mine.

He's so beautiful. I sighed.

It was a strange thought to have at the moment, but he was beautiful, distractingly so. His eyes, the line of his jaw, the color of his skin, his nose, his stubbornness, his protectiveness, his naughty mouth, his goodness. I could have looked at him all day.

"Please." I let my gaze roam over his face.

"Why is this so important to you?" he mumbled, sounding curious. "I swear Seamus was conceived by anal sex. There's no other explanation for him being such an asshole."

"Because I really, really like your mom. And I know it would make her happy if you made nice with your brother." His frown deepened, and even frowning he was beautiful. Little starbursts of acute sensation erupted in my chest and behind my eyes, the warmth in my stomach spreading lower as I stared at him and he stared back.

He studied me for a beat, his eyes narrowing. "Why are you looking at me like that?"

Because I love looking at you.

. . . Because I'm growing addicted to you.

"One cup," I whispered, swallowing my emotions and the troubling thought, "and then bedtime."

His eyes flared, and I realized too late how that had sounded.

But oh well. So what? Maybe it was our bedtime. Maybe it was past our bedtime. My heart rate increased, precariously close to racing, as his eyes moved between mine, and then dropped to my mouth.

"Irish breakfast," he said, no longer frowning. "And I'll get it. You sit. You're not supposed to be cooking."

He kissed me again, just a light brush of lips, and then his hands slid away. I mourned the loss of him, his heat and closeness, immediately. I wanted to chase after him, stay by his side on his quest for tea, but that was a ridiculous urge. A nutty, neurotic, loco urge.

So, on slightly wobbly legs, I stumbled back to the table and sat/fell into my chair, attempting to get myself under control. Seamus cleared his throat and I blinked him into focus. He was smirking at me, one eyebrow raised.

I straightened in my seat, returning his gaze evenly and pulling the veil down on my feelings; being a besotted fool for Dan was one thing when I was by myself, being a besotted fool for Dan in front of his brother was quite another.

Seamus's eyes flickered to where Dan was hunting for his tea at the far end of the kitchen and then back to me. "How'd you two meet?"

"None of your fucking business how we met," came Dan's grouchy response, shutting a cabinet louder than necessary.

"I used to work with Janie, the woman you tried to abduct." I poured him a cup of tea and handed it over.

"I wasn't trying to abduct Janie, I was trying to get my money back from her crazy bitch of a sister, Jem. You work at Quinn's company?" Seamus's tone during all of this was light, like we were discussing the best way to skin a fish, and when he picked up his teacup I couldn't help but notice he kept his pinky finger straight.

"None of your fucking business where she works." Dan shut another cabinet.

"I work at an architecture firm."

Seamus leaned back in his chair. "You an architect?"

"None of your fu—"

"Yeah, yeah. I get it. Nothing is my business." Seamus rolled his eyes again, and I had to roll my lips between my teeth to keep from laughing.

Dan finally joined us, his movements jerky as he pulled out the seat next to mine and poured himself a cup of tea straight from the teapot. "There's no Irish breakfast."

Seamus, his posture once again lazy and relaxed, looked between us. "Who's watching your dog? You still got that dog?"

"Wally?" Dan glared at Seamus over his tea. Dan also kept his pinky finger straight when he sipped his tea, muttering, "Fuck, that's hot," as he set it down.

"What's his full name again?" Seamus was rubbing his chin.

Dan hesitated, glancing at me and then away. "Bark Wahlberg," he grumbled.

My eyes bulged and I suppressed a laugh. And then I frowned, my mood shifting suddenly because, who would name their dog Bark Wahlberg?

Only the funniest, cleverest, most amazing man in the world, that's who.

Dan being Dan was making this impossible.

Every time he opened his mouth he tugged on a string wrapped around my heart, bringing me—and him—closer and closer to calamity. Soon, I wouldn't be able to help myself. I'd be completely and utterly in love with him, I was already teetering on the edge of disaster.

And this was a disaster because I had no outlet for these feelings. He wouldn't let me do a single thing for him in return; he didn't want my gratitude; he wouldn't accept money. So I was left with a mountain of feelings and frustration.

Marie's words from weeks ago echoed in my mind, *"That's not how relationships work."*

I released a silent sigh, wishing I had her here with me now.

"That's right. Funny name. I love that name." Seamus grinned at his brother, showcasing a mishmash of intense dental work and one missing canine. "What'd you used to say? About him not being allowed here?"

"It's just a stupid joke," Dan responded flatly.

"Yeah. And it's fuckin' hilarious. What was it? Why isn't he allowed someplace?"

"It's nothing." Dan lifted his teacup and blew some steam away from the tea. I had to blink several times to keep from becoming mesmerized by the movements of his lips.

"Come on. Do the bit. Do the thing." Seamus leaned forward and motioned to me. "Come on. She'll love it."

"Fine." Dan set his cup down and crossed his arms over his chest, clearly irritated by Seamus's pushing. Then, to me, he said, "Ask me why Wally isn't allowed in Boston."

"Why isn't Wally allowed in Boston?" I asked, loving his eyes on mine, feeling like a junkie waiting for my next hit.

"Unpaid barking tickets." Dan rolled his eyes even as he grinned, like he thought the joke was dumb, but also hilarious.

I couldn't help it, I laughed. His grin widened, which made me laugh more. "That is funny."

Seamus, however, was laughing his butt off, clutching his stomach, tears leaking from his eyes. "Unpaid *barking* tickets! Funniest fucking joke I've ever heard."

"Yeah, well, you need to get out more." Dan scowled at his brother over his teacup. But this time, I could tell he was forcing it.

CHAPTER TWENTY

Executor: "The individual appointed to administer the estate of a person who has died, leaving a will which nominates that individual." *(Not to be confused with "Trustee")*

WEX LEGAL DICTIONARY

Kat

SEAMUS DIDN'T STAY long.

Based on the way Dan continued to look at his brother, I made no attempt to shake Seamus's hand, let alone embrace him when he left. Dan escorted him to the door, glared at him while he waved goodbye to me, and turned every single deadbolt after he left.

Mumbling something about changing the locks under his breath, Dan gave me a distracted half-smile, placed a kiss on my cheek, and removed himself to the study. He didn't close the door, leaving a sliver of light spilling into the family room. Leaning against the entryway wall, I stared at that sliver of light for an indeterminate period of time —longer than ten minutes, shorter than a half hour—debating my next move.

It was bedtime. He was waiting for me to go to sleep first. I didn't want to go to sleep without him. I wanted to be with him. But I didn't know if that was a good idea.

You're falling in love with him.

I swallowed past a tightness in my throat, breathing through a painful flare, immobilized by . . . *fear.*

You're afraid.

I straightened from the wall, because I refused to be afraid. I was going to march in there and spend time with him. We were going to kiss, somehow I'd make that happen, and I would not allow fear to make my decisions.

Solid plan.

But then the light switched off and Dan strolled out again, pushing his fingers through his hair as he walked to the stairs. I watched him go, taking them slowly, tiredly, his chest rising and falling with a big sigh.

For the first time since we'd fooled around last week in Chicago and my anxieties had taken over—and I'd failed miserably—I wanted to try again. I wanted his hands on me. The mere thought filled me with renewed anticipatory restlessness.

Where Dan was concerned, anticipatory restlessness had become a chronic condition.

As soon as he made it to the landing and turned towards our room, I tiptoed to the base of the stairs and climbed them, my heart beating in my throat.

No need to freak out. You're not even allowed to orgasm.

No. Orgasming.

Just. Touching.

And enjoying.

I nodded, figuring I could do that. I could enjoy myself. I enjoyed knitting, didn't I? And cheese. I knew how to enjoy things, how to savor. All I had to do was apply the same principles to being with Dan.

Dan is cheese.

I made a face at that, because as much as I loved cheese, Dan definitely wasn't cheese. Maybe a fine wine? He was intoxicating, so it was an apt analogy. Of note, wine goes with cheese. Maybe *I* was the cheese.

As I rounded the corner to the hall, thinking about wine and cheese pairings, I collided with a fine wine—er, Dan.

But we didn't just collide, we crashed into each other with enough force that, for a second, I thought I was going to tumble backward down the steps. The impact jarred me, scattering my wits.

I flailed, reaching out and grabbing on to him. Dan sucked in a startled breath and he caught me by the shoulders, saving me from the tumble.

"Holy shit. You scared me." He pulled me forward, taking several steps away from the stairs.

"I scared me too," I admitted, huffing a laugh. It might have been slightly hysterical.

Shaking his head, he removed his hands from me, carefully setting me away, and pushed his fingers through his hair. "I didn't hear you come up the stairs, you're so quiet."

"Your mom is asleep," I whispered, twisting my fingers, stepping around him hurriedly, my heart galloping. "We shouldn't wake her up."

I marched into his room, my stomach a bundle of nerves made worse by the hallway collision. Straining my ears for sounds of him following, I turned. To my relief, he'd followed, but he hovered outside the door, his hands in his pockets.

Dan watched me with a wary expression. "Are you okay?"

"Yes. Sorry. I'm fine. How are you?"

He looked at me like the question confused him. "Fine."

"Sorry," I repeated, then clamped my mouth shut. There was no need for me to apologize.

"Don't worry about it. I'll give you some time to get settled." He took a step back.

"No. Don't leave." Unthinkingly, I rushed forward and caught him by the hands, pulling him forward into the room, releasing him, and shutting the door. I placed myself between him and the exit.

He stared at me, the confusion plaguing his features intensifying.

I stared back at him, nervous. But also determined.

"Are you tired?" I asked, advancing on him.

"Not really." He didn't move, just let me come, invade his space, his eyes watchful.

I didn't touch him, and I realized—abruptly frustrated—I didn't know how to initiate what I wanted. All that time, standing downstairs like a weirdo, staring at the sliver of light from the study, and my plan hadn't extended beyond being both awake and alone with him.

It had been shortsighted of me.

From now on, all plans would have numbered steps. Perhaps I'd make a flowchart with if/then/else statements, to prepare for the most likely eventualities.

But I didn't have time to make a flowchart now.

Staring at his chin, because I couldn't quite lift my eyes any higher, I cleared my throat. "Should we get ready for bed?"

"Sure," he said, his voice a rumble. Dan's eyes were on me, I felt the weight of them.

My hands came to the hem of my skirt and I hesitated, feeling winded for some reason. Sneaking a glance at him, I immediately wished I hadn't. His gaze was watchful, but it was also unmistakably hot in a way that seemed at once both avaricious and accusatory. The vice tightened around my lungs.

Kiss him! Just freaking kiss him! You want numbered steps? Fine. You kiss him- check. He kisses you back- check. Then you make out-check. Check the boxes.

I licked my lips, balling my hands into fists at my sides again, preparing to follow my hasty list.

But then he said, "Undress me."

My breath caught. On instinct, my eyes lifted and collided with his in much the same way our bodies had collided at the top of the stairs just moments ago. Jarring. Startling. Thrilling. This time I couldn't look away because this time I was falling. He made no move to catch me.

"What? What did you say?"

His eyes narrowed, which served only to increase the intensity of his gaze from smolder to inferno. "Take my clothes off."

I stared at him, licking my lips again, and shaking my head. That wasn't one of my steps.

Lifting my chin, I moved to kiss him. He leaned to the side, evading me even as his eyes dropped to my mouth.

"Take off my shirt and I'll give you a kiss." He'd used his naughty-secret voice.

An explosion of heat erupted in my belly, and now I was hot all over. I couldn't figure out if the heat was embarrassment or arousal or both.

He didn't give me a chance to figure it out. His hands lifted and he undid his cuffs; then they moved to the top button of his shirt.

"You better take over," he said darkly, "or else you're not getting that kiss."

I didn't let myself think about it. Acting on the urge, my fingers lifted to the next button and I unfastened it, then the next, and the next, and the next, until the two sides hung open and a sliver of skin—like that sliver of light in the study downstairs—was bared to me. Entranced, I didn't hesitate. I slid my hands inside, parting the shirt, pushing it open like I should have opened that door.

His skin was taught over muscle, smooth, hot, and he felt divine. I stroked a path down the ridges of his stomach, caressed the sharp angles of his obliquus, and around to his muscled back. Even though I knew he had the tattoos, unwrapping him now, seeing the ink up close in the light, felt like uncovering a secret.

"Take it off."

My heart jumped at the command and my eyes darted to his. A new spreading warmth moved outward from my chest to my limbs. The way he looked at me, the cadence of his voice, was inebriating.

But not like the dulling daze of alcohol, or the superficial saccharine dream-state of MDMA. This was something better, because it was real. He was real.

I pushed his shirt from his strong shoulders, my hands stalling briefly over the deliciousness of his arms, and then completely off. It dropped to the floor at his feet, soundless in its descent.

His lids had dropped over his eyes; his gaze no less intense, but now with a languid quality, giving me the impression his thoughts had taken a wicked turn.

Slowly, so slowly, he bent. He placed an achingly soft kiss over my mouth. And then . . . he retreated.

I moaned mournfully, not meaning to, but—*damn it*—that was barely a kiss. The anticipatory restlessness became something else, a beast, and it demanded . . . something!

Again, I moved to kiss him. Again, he evaded me, his hands dropping to his pants, settling on the waistband.

"Do you want something?" he asked.

His question made me feel like my lungs were on fire. I grinned despite myself, feeling something like resentment—but not quite—set up camp by the fire.

"You know what I want."

Now he grinned, just a little one, and glanced down at his pants. "Then you know what to do."

My mouth fell open and his gaze drifted to my lips, his smile spreading, his eyes still at half-mast. More wicked thoughts danced there, intoxicating me.

"Fine," I said, the resentment becoming renewed determination.

In a way, he was trying to torture me. In a way, it was working. It also gave me an idea.

I moved my hands to the front of his pants, but instead of unbuttoning his fly, I brushed the back of my hand over his groin, stroking down and then up, pressing firmly against the growing stiffness.

He moaned, eyelashes flickering, like I'd blown dust in his eyes. But his jaw was tight, his teeth on edge.

"Kat."

"Yes Dan?" I answered sweetly.

I couldn't remember ever being so raw and desperate and turned on. He still had most of his clothes on and not a single article had been removed from my body. And yet, I felt wild, mindless, drunk on his reaction to my touch.

"What are you doing?"

"Nothing." I angled my chin closer to his mouth so we shared a breath and continued to stroke him over his clothes.

He felt impossibly hard, and I had a fleeting thought, wondering if it were painful for him and sadistically hoping that it was. I hoped it hurt. I hoped he wanted me so much he couldn't think straight.

But the thought was driven away by a rising ache within me, frantic and agonizing.

"Touch me," I heard my voice say. I watched one of my hands move to and tangle with his. On autopilot, I brought his fingers to my thigh, encouraging him to lift my skirt, guiding him to the tormenting throb at my center.

He groaned, his forehead dropping to mine. Dan touched me over my underwear, stroking me covetously, his breathing labored.

"You're so wet." His voice dropped, deeper than the naughty-secret level, to something infinitely baser.

I nodded, not sure why I was nodding.

"Touch me." The words were inane, because he was already touching me. I wanted more, so I said, "More."

"Kat."

"Please," I begged.

"Fuck."

Dan charged forward, backing me against the wall, his mouth crashing to mine, his kiss mercenary, incendiary. Fingers wrapped in my hair and he pulled, forcing my chin upward as his other hand slid into the waistband of my panties and parted me. Though his kiss was rough, his strokes were slow, lightly rubbing circles. This, too, was torture. Wicked, wonderful torture.

I gasped, struggling for air, my nails scratching down his sides on the way to his fly. Touching him, holding him in my hands and stroking his hot skin was the only option. I had no choice. I needed to feel him. I *needed* it.

But as soon as I had his zipper undone, he pulled his hands from my body and caught my wrist, wrenching it away. Then he turned and stalked to the other side of the room. His hands coming to the back of his neck, he threaded his fingers together.

"Fuck, fuck, fuck." He was shaking his head, facing the opposite wall, still breathing hard. "Fuck."

I hadn't recovered, was nowhere close to recovering, so I stumbled after him as though pulled, following him across the room like an infatuated puppy, hungry for his attention.

I reached for him. "Dan—"

He flinched away from my touch, placing new distance between us. "Just give me a minute, okay?"

My stomach dropped, sobering me, and I nodded. I stepped back, trying to find a place in the small space where I wouldn't be crowding him, at a loss as to what to do or where to look.

This is why you need a flowchart.

I returned to the far wall, placing my back against the corner and waited, my gaze settling on a team poster of the Bruins from 1997 as I tried my best to not jump to the worst conclusion. I wouldn't think the worst, I wouldn't. Not with Dan. He'd never given me a reason to think anything but the best. I would be reasonable, not neurotic.

I stood there, regulating my breathing, thinking back over the last few minutes, immersing myself in the memory of how it had felt to be touched by him, teased, kissed. I'd lost control. I hadn't been thinking. I wanted him and the wanting had seemed like the only thing that mattered.

"No orgasms."

I looked to him, blinking through the haze of my recollections. "What?"

"Your lady," he still stood on the other side of the room, his hands on his narrow hips, his gaze moving over me, "she said no . . . orgasms." He said *orgasms* like the saying of it was painful.

"So?"

"So. We're doing this right." His tone was firm.

"Dan—"

"Don't look at me like that."

"Like what?"

"Like you want me to fuck you."

An image of that, of what that would look like, flashed behind my eyes and made my knees weak. I leaned completely against the wall behind me, my gaze dropping of its own accord to his torso.

"I do want. So, I'm not sure how to *not* look like that."

"Cross your eyes, make a face or something."

I stared at him for several seconds, and then covered my over-heated cheeks, laughing—not because I found this funny—because I was frustrated.

Meanwhile, Dan paced the room. I peeked at him from between my fingers. He was a restless wolf, prowling a cage.

So beautiful.

My hands dropped, and I took a step forward. "Dan—"

He held out a palm. "Nope."

"I want you—"

"Yeah, well, I want a lot of things." His glare pivoted down and then up my body, and he sounded almost angry.

I'd been close, so close, and there'd been no numbness, only desire and sensation. Didn't he understand how monumental that was? And then he'd pulled away.

"Couldn't we—"

"No!" He stopped pacing, his eyes a little wild. "We're taking this slow."

"Because Dr. Kasai told us to? Or because you want to? Or because you don't think I can?" I couldn't disguise my bitterness.

His eyes were a jumble of emotions. "Because . . ."

"Because?"

"Because it means something!"

He'd shouted the words and the ensuing silence was deafening.

An answering swelling in my heart reached out to him, and before I knew it, my feet had taken me across the room again. He watched me come, his gaze wary, bracing, as though he expected me to strike or otherwise hurt him. But when I was close, he pulled me into his arms, holding me tight and releasing his favorite expletive under his breath.

I clung to him.

"I have to be honest here," he said on a rough rush next to my ear, his voice was much quieter, yet doubly impassioned. "I have to tell you my limits, because you have to trust me. So you have to know . . . you mean something to me. It's never going to be a finish line with you, or something to cross off a list. It's—I want—I *need*—it to be everything."

I stiffened a little at his words, recognition giving way to guilt. Before he'd thrown me for a loop by trading kisses for items of clothing, I'd been contemplating flow charts and check boxes. Touching him, being in the moment with him, *enjoying* the tension between us had been infinitely more substantial.

And dangerous.

A difference I hadn't comprehended until right now. Dan was not a box to be checked. He was not a task, a risk to be measured against potential benefit.

He wants surrender.

"I can't control this," I said, my eyes and nose stinging—not sure if I was referring to what had happened moments ago, or how I was falling in love with him, how I was probably already in love with him —and I pressed myself more firmly into his embrace. "It's overwhelming."

"It's supposed to be." His hold shifted to my shoulders and he held me away, just a few inches so our eyes could meet. "Trust me," he said, and it sounded like a plea.

"I do."

He shook his head, telling me he disagreed. "Trust me that I want every part of you."

I stared at him, panic ballooning within me. "What if parts of me are messy? Or ugly?"

He smirked. "Parts of you are ugly and messy. I still want you. I want the ugly and the beautiful and everything in between. You don't pick and choose the parts of a person you want. Shit, I'm the ugliest fucker I know, and I want to give it all to you."

I laughed even as my chin wobbled and, damn it, I was already crying.

His smile was soft, his gaze focusing on the tear that had spilled over my cheek. He didn't try to wipe it away.

"I want it all, Kit-Kat. I want all of you."

I nodded, sniffing. "I want all of you, too."

He placed a gentle kiss over my mouth, and then brushed his lips over the tears on my cheeks before resting his forehead against mine and closing his eyes.

"And I want it to last." It was a rough whisper.

The words sounded like a wish.

CHAPTER TWENTY-ONE

Generic (drug): A pharmaceutical drug (typically the chemical name of a drug) that is equivalent to a brand-name product in dosage, strength, route of administration, quality, performance and intended use, but does not carry the brand name.

FDA.GOV

Dan

I WOKE UP in a great fucking mood.

We'd kissed. A lot. And then we'd fallen asleep tangled in each other. Kat hadn't been naked—if she'd been naked, I wouldn't have been able to sleep—but she was wearing those little pajamas I liked. One of her legs between mine, her arm draped over my stomach, her head on my chest. She smelled like cake.

The best. We should have been doing this all week. A missed opportunity.

But we overslept. We had an appointment with Eugene to go over the will at 8:30 AM; it was now 7:45 AM. I showered first, dressing in the study while she used the facilities, and we left in a hurry. Not even rush hour traffic and wreckers on the Pike could make a dent—no pun intended—in my mood.

She was wearing one of her starched white shirts, buttoned all the way to her neck, and a slim dark blue skirt to just beneath her knees. Her hair fell around her shoulders, meticulously arranged, straight and sleek.

Kat was prim, impeccably ironed, all buttoned up. Seeing her like this made me feel like one of those bad kids who go around knocking down other kids' towers made out of blocks, just to watch them fall. My first instinct was always to reach my hand up her skirt and watch her blush, sweat, and moan. The urge to undo all her careful work, wrinkle her clothes, mess her hair, and leave a hickey on her neck—or on the inside of her thigh—was always there, like a song on repeat in the back of my mind.

Hmm . . . Maybe later.

Adding sunshine to roses, next to the offices of Sharpe and Marks, lawyers extraordinaire, was a Dunks— Dunkin' Donuts for all the plebeian Starbucks drinkers out there. She finished her makeup in the car while I grabbed my usual, hot coffee with one sugar, and ordered Kat's the way I knew she liked it.

She took a sip as I held the lobby door open for her, and I grinned when she glanced at me in surprise over her shoulder.

"This is perfect."

I shrugged, scanning the lobby. "I know." *Three visible exits, one security guard.*

She shook her head. "How did you know how I take my coffee?"

"I have my ways." I shrugged again as we approached the receptionist.

Her eyes narrowed while she tried to frown and failed. "How do you take your coffee?"

I scoffed. "You can't just ask a person how he takes his coffee, Kit-Kat. That's a very personal question."

"I'll find out."

"Oh yeah? How're you going to manage that?"

"I have my ways." She grinned.

Her grin made me dumb for a minute. All I could do was blink at her and wonder about these *ways* of hers.

Meanwhile, Kat turned her attention to the guy at the desk. "Hi, Aiken."

The guy was concentrating on his computer screen. He looked up distractedly and then did a double take. "Ms. Caravel-Tyson," he said, sounding pleasantly surprised.

Then he stood, smoothing his hand down his tie, and smiled at her in a way that sobered me up real fast. Because it wasn't just a smile. It was an *invitation*.

"Can I get you anything? Coffee? We can send someone out to pick something up, anything at all," he offered as he navigated the big semicircular desk, walking straight for her, still wearing that smile.

The guy tried to get closer to her, like he was planning on pulling her into a hug. He couldn't. I'd angled my body in front of hers and Kat slipped her hand through my arm.

I didn't know this guy.

Sure, he didn't look like a threat—tall, younger than me, from the looks of it he worked out a lot, probably played cricket, or rowed a boat, or something else stupid—but you never can tell just by looking at people.

All I'm saying is, maybe he was a serial killer. Who knows? Just to be safe, I made sure he couldn't get too close.

After a long, awkward minute of him trying to get at her and me shifting from one side to the other, staying between them, he shot me a furtive look of exasperation.

"No, thank you." Kat sounded like she was fighting a laugh. "We already have coffee. But if you could take us to Eugene's office, that would be great."

"Of course," he said, his voice going all deep, his eyes dropping to the front of the shirt she was wearing, then coming to me. "Is this person accompanying you, or will we need to find a place for him else-where?" There was no invitation in the smile he was sending me.

I blinked at the guy. Not going to lie, his question and tone irritated me, like I was last Thursday's leftovers from an all-you-can-eat fish and sauerkraut buffet.

I heard Kat take a deep breath before saying, "Darling, this is Aiken. He's an intern here at the firm. Aiken, this is Mr. O'Malley, my husband."

Darling. . . Yeah.

I liked that.

Mr. Harvard's smile slipped, and he blinked like Kat had just thrown a drink in his face.

That plus *darling* had me smiling, but I didn't extend my hand. "You wanna lead the way, barney?"

"Of—of course." His eyes moved between us; it took him a few seconds to find his composure. Eventually he did, pasting on a new grin. "Right this way."

Smoothing his hand down his tie again, he turned and walked toward the elevators. We followed at a distance since I still wasn't clear on his serial killer status. He used a key card, then pressed the call button. The doors slid open right away and he gestured for us to enter. We did, Kat standing in the corner, me next to her, him walking in and taking the spot by the buttons.

He glanced over his shoulder, giving my wife another of his inviting smiles. "Did you have a nice summer?"

Apparently, he'd recovered from the near-heart attack inducing shock of our marriage.

"Yes. Thank you."

The tightness in her voice had me checking on her. She looked at me, her eyes big and solemn, like she was frustrated. Arranging my eyebrows into the universal expression for, *Are you okay?* Kat nodded quickly in response, squeezing my bicep, and placing her head on my shoulder.

Hmm . . .

I shifted my coffee to my other hand, covered her fingers with mine, and placed a kiss on her temple. She sighed, sounding content.

Good.

Turning back to the doors, I spotted the guy watching us, his forehead's wrinkles and his lips' slight sneer communicating loud and clear that he found the idea of us confusing.

Narrowing my eyes, I asked, "And how was your summer?" *Get a chance to visit the club with mummy and daddy? Take the yacht for a spin down the Cape?*

"Great," he replied, giving too much emphasis to the "T."

Thank Christ, the doors finally opened. Our tour guide stepped out first, and we followed. I spotted the stairway immediately and made a quick mental map of the layout as we walked. It must've been the executive level because everything was quality, from the art on the wall to the plasterwork on the ceiling.

But there was too much glass for my liking—glass doors, glass walls—something I hated about Cypher Systems's offices as well. Seemed like a safety hazard.

He led us to a big set of wooden double doors, knocked twice, and then entered without waiting for a response. He held the door open.

The barney stopped in his tracks as the sound of arguing voices—wicked pissed voices—greeted us. Frowning, I peered around our escort's shoulder and found Eugene yelling at another guy, and I caught the tail end of the rant.

". . . unacceptable, Sharpe. You can't make these decisions, and you can't just show up here, minutes before a scheduled meeting, and drop this on me. The Caravel-Tysons are *my* clients."

"You're retiring, Eugene. You need to let us handle it."

"You're not handling it, you're fucking it all up."

"It's time for you to—"

Kat cleared her throat loudly, cutting off whatever Sharpe was going to say. She stepped around me and the barney, strolling into the office like she was the Queen of Sheba. "I have an eight-thirty appointment, Mr. Marks. It's eight thirty."

I followed her in, coming to stand at her shoulder. Her back was straight and her voice dripped with disdain. I couldn't see her eyes, but I could only imagine the ice she was sending their way.

The guy named Sharpe seemed to sigh, his attention moving

between us. I didn't miss the disapproval forcing his eyebrows lower as he inspected me.

Eugene was pissed. He didn't look at us. He continued glaring at Sharpe.

Belatedly and unnecessarily, the barney said, "Mr. Marks, Ms. Caravel-Tyson is here."

While being scowled at, I surveyed the layout of Eugene's office. Right away, I spotted the closed door to the left of his desk. My money was on private bathroom. The first thing rich people wanted to do when they achieved any success was stop shitting on the same toilet as poor people. Or other rich people for that matter. They wanted their own damn toilet.

Fucking weirdos. Regardless of how much money I had in the bank, I was never going to be one of these people.

"Thank you." Eugene, standing by his desk and still shooting daggers at Sharpe, dismissed Aiken with a lift of his chin. He then walked around his partner to us, his eyes on me, and then moving his attention to Kat.

"Ms. Caravel-Tyson." He nodded his head, not reaching out to shake her hand. "You know Mr. Sharpe, my partner."

His use of her last names hit an off note with me, but she didn't seem to care.

Sharpe stepped forward, making no effort to shake her hand either. "You've made the trip for no reason. According to the wishes of the inheritor designate, we are unable to—"

"Inheritor designate? What are you talking about?" Stepping away from me and walking past the two men, she took a seat at a medium-sized conference table, setting her coffee on the surface. "I'm the sole beneficiary."

Eugene was grinding his teeth, the corners of his mouth at an unhappy angle. He looked tense and I got the impression he wanted to say something.

Sharpe opened his mouth to respond, but just then the door on the left side of the room opened, revealing Tiny Satan. I heard the telltale sounds of a toilet recently flushed. Of course the shitbag didn't wash his hands. Disgusting.

My stare turned into a glare and my sigh was automatic. I shook my head, strolling to the conference table, inserting myself between Kat and her cousin. *This fucking guy.*

Quinn and Alex had been able to thwart and delay Caleb's attempts to return to Boston for the last week. They'd also sent me plenty of valuable info about Caleb's finances, which I'd planned to tell Kat about. But, honestly, with everything else and all the good stuff between Kat and me last night, it had slipped my mind.

Long story short, he was no longer a threat. So I wasn't worried seeing him here now. That said, this Sharpe guy was an unknown threat.

"Oh good, you're here," Caleb said, wiping his nose with the back of his hand and grinning at both of us, all teeth and no lips.

Poor Eugene.

Firstly, Kat had been giving the old guy the iceberg treatment for days.

Secondly, his partner seemed like a tightass.

Thirdly, what was the point of having his own rich-person bathroom if this sheisty fuckstick comes in and pisses all over it? Not even washing his hands after.

"Mr. Tyson," Sharpe sounded relieved. "I was just explaining to your cousin that there was no need for her to make the trip, and that we'd be in contact with next steps for her."

"Why is he here?" Kat addressed this question to Eugene, her tone impressively dispassionate. "He's not mentioned in the will."

"And how do *you* know that?" Caleb swaggered further into the room, shoving his hands into his pockets. Based on the continuing movements of his hands, I'd bet my collection of bird skeletons—if I had a collection of bird skeletons—that Caleb was playing with his dick.

"I don't have time for this." Kat sounded bored. "Mr. Marks, please call my lawyers to arrange an alternate time to read the will."

"Your lawyers?" Caleb sounded gleeful. The sheisty fuckstick was up to something. "But, how will you pay them?" he asked dramatically.

Kat's glare slid to her cousin and she gave him the meanest fucking look I'd ever seen, like he was maggot pus at the bottom of a garbage can. She didn't respond, instead picking up her coffee like she was prepared to leave.

"Are you going to tell her, Marks? Or should I?" Caleb shifted back and forth on his feet, like he had to take a piss. But we all knew that wasn't the case, he'd just taken one and not washed his hands.

Sharpe took a step forward, looking displeased with his client. "Ms. Caravel-Tyson, if you would please just leave. We will be in contact—"

"Never mind, I'll tell her." Caleb spoke over Sharpe. "I've frozen all your assets. Surprise!"

My eyes widened. I was surprised. I glanced at Eugene for confirmation.

He nodded subtly. "Caleb has been working with Sharpe to freeze the Caravel-Tyson assets since last week." Eugene looked like he was ready to explode with contempt, which was why the coolness of his tone was so remarkable. "He's had some . . . communications and transportation issues on his return trip from Chicago. But Sharpe's team received approval for the motion yesterday."

"On what grounds?" Kat continued addressing her questions to Eugene, as though neither her cousin nor Mr. Sharpe were present.

"We're not able to disclose that." Sharpe took a half step toward the door, like if he moved to the door then Kat and I would follow.

"Your marriage." Eugene's stare moved from Kat to me. "Caleb is working to have it invalidated on the grounds of mental incompetence and Mr. O'Malley's questionable character. He plans to invalidate your marriage and then proceed with his guardianship petition."

"Eugene!" Sharpe was clearly shocked by his partner's willingness to openly share information with us.

I looked over at Eugene—the sneer of his lip, the cold rage behind his eyes—and realized the old guy had finally decided to not give a single fuck what his partner thought.

But Caleb plainly reveled in Eugene's announcements. "If you don't want people to think you're crazy, maybe don't marry a felon whose brother is a notorious Boston gang leader," Caleb piped in cheerfully.

Man, he was super cheerful. Yeah. He was definitely playing with his dick . . . *assuming he can find it.*

I chuckled and then laughed at the thought, drawing everyone's attention to me.

Tiny Satan's eyes narrowed. "Something funny?"

I scratched my jaw. "Actually, yeah."

"Oh yeah? What's that?" His hands came out of his pockets and he crossed his arms, arrogant weasel eyes pointed at me.

"Where are you gonna get the money to pursue this kind of legal action?" I asked, making sure I sounded super curious.

Caleb blinked. And then he blinked some more. "Where am *I* going to get the money? You fucking moron, do you know who I am?"

Fucking moron? Pathetic. His insult game was weak.

"The retainer for Sharpe and Marks is paid through the end of the quarter, so you got three months. That's it. After that, the Caravel-Tyson assets are frozen, right? That was your doing. Which means there's no one to pay the bills. Which means . . ." I shrugged.

His eye twitched. "This won't take three months."

"That's right. It'll take three years. At least," I promised.

He scoffed. "Didn't you hear Marks? She has no access to anything. She can't even write a check from the family accounts. That means no access to bank accounts, stocks, investments, all properties, even the compound in Duxbury." To Kat he said, "You have nowhere to go, no place to live. You have no choice but to—"

"Of course she has somewhere to live. With me."

"Not for long."

"And why would we need Caravel-Tyson assets?" I shrugged, glancing at Sharpe and happy to see he was paying attention.

Caleb's confidence slipped. "You don't have the kind of capital required to fight us. You'll go bankrupt." He didn't sound so sure, which was good, because that meant he obviously had no idea.

I chuckled again, shaking my head. "Oh, Cameron. You ratfaced cumcuke. If you'd done your homework properly, you'd know—in addition to being a felon—I'm also a multi-millionaire. Millions and millions and millions, and I don't waste my money on dumb shit like yachts and gold-plated toilet seats—no offense, Eugene."

Caleb straightened, sharing a hurried glance with Sharpe. "I've—I've had you investigated. You—you're not—"

"I'll keep this thing going for decades, just for fun." I grinned, first at Caleb, then at Sharpe. "Fuck, I think I'll even sue you for defamation of character, and I'll file an ethics complaint against this firm for the conflict of interest, representing your case against their own client, Ms. Caravel-Tyson. Why not? I got the money, making shitbags suffer is a hobby of mine."

"You can't do that." The color drained from Caleb's face.

I ignored him. "Whereas, I *know* you can't afford a countersuit, you can't even afford that suit you're wearing. Your salary is capped. You cashed in your stocks, that money is gone. You don't get another distribution until January, assuming you're still at Caravel when January rolls around. Your bank account is empty. Maybe you could sell one of your yachts, but the boating season is almost over. So good luck finding someone to buy it. You'll never make back your investment, and with this firm's billable rate—" I sucked in a breath through my teeth, "that'll only buy you another three months. Tops."

"How do you—?" He began to blurt but then stopped himself, presumably from asking, *How could you know that?* Now the look he sent Sharpe was nervous. Caleb swallowed and lifted his chin. "You're bluffing."

"No. *You're* bluffing. And I got you in a corner. You can't afford to pay Sharpe. You're sending his people on bullshit fool's errands, trying to get my wife committed? Good fucking luck, because that is *never* going to happen."

His cheerfulness had completely evaporated. In its place, his beady eyes darted around the room but focused inward. The rat was scrambling.

Caleb Tyson might've been a skidmark shitstain on humanity, and he might've been an egotistical Masshole, and he'd definitely overestimated his abilities and underestimated mine, but he wasn't stupid.

He knew I was right.

Even so, I couldn't help myself, "If I use alphabet soup to spell this out for you, will you get the fucking picture? Or do you need it finger-painted?"

His glare came back to me. "I will destroy you."

"Oh jeez, by golly. What'll I do?" I clutched my chest, giving the fucker a little show.

I doubted he heard me, because his next words were shouted in a rage. "I will fucking ruin you, do you hear me? You are nothing! Nothing!

I sighed, tired of his irrelevant presence. "Yeah, yeah. I'll be sure to file that info right between *fuck this* and *fuck that*."

He made a choking sound as I turned from him, looking to Kat. Her gaze was on me, one hand on her hip, the other lifting her coffee cup to her lips and taking a sip, like she didn't have one fucking care in the world.

"You want more coffee, Kit-Kat?" I asked, giving her a wink.

She shook her head, her eyes were laughing. "No thanks. This one is perfect, darling."

CHAPTER TWENTY-TWO

Pyrimethamine (trade name **Daraprim™**) is a medication used to treat toxoplasmosis and cystoisosporiasis and has been "out of patent" since the 1970s.

In the United States, as of 2015, Turing Pharmaceuticals acquired the US marketing rights for Daraprim™ tablets and increased the price. The cost of a monthly course for a person on a 75 mg dose rose to about $75,000/month, or $750 per tablet (up from $13.50 a tablet prior to Turing's acquisition). Outpatients can no longer obtain Daraprim™ from their community pharmacy, but only through a single dispensing pharmacy, Walgreens Specialty Pharmacy, and institutions can no longer order from their general wholesaler, but have to set up an account with the Daraprim™ Direct program.

In 2016, a group of high school students in Australia created 3.7 grams of Daraprim's™ active ingredient in their chemistry lab for just $20 - an amount that would sell in the US for between $35,000 and $110,000 at the current rate.

As of the writing of this book, there are no generic versions available for Daraprim™.

THE NEW YORK TIMES (PARAPHRASED FROM)

Dan

I'LL SPARE THE ugly details, but after a few more empty threats, Caleb stormed out.

Then Sharpe, looking like he'd just had a near-death experience, rushed forward to Kat and tried to apologize. I got between them, forcing him to back off. But I mean, the guy tripped all over himself trying to kiss her ass, telling her they'd withdraw the petition to freeze the Caravel-Tyson assets as soon as possible, which meant later today. Which meant she'd have full access again by tomorrow.

She gave him the same look she'd given Caleb earlier, the maggot-pus look, and said nothing. This was her M.O., I realized. When she didn't like a person, or was pissed at them, she erected a wall and pretended they didn't exist.

Interesting . . .

Eugene collected Sharpe, pulling him away from Kat and excused them both, briefly explaining they needed to take care of an urgent matter. He also promised to return soon so we could review the will and get started with the day's meetings. His earlier tension was replaced with a twinkle in his eyes and a spring in his step.

Good.

I liked the old guy, even though he was devious and his professional ethics were questionable.

This left Kat standing at 9 o'clock and me at 12 o'clock around the oval conference table. She was still holding her coffee.

"He's broke?" she asked, looking thoughtful.

I nodded. "Yep."

"Alex?"

I nodded. "Yep. Alex and Quinn sent over the specifics yesterday morning. I meant to tell you, but . . ."

She nodded. "Don't worry about it." But then her stare grew hazy, like she was doing math in her head. "Where did the money go?"

"I don't know. His salary is capped, so are his stock options, but it's not like Caravel pays peanuts. He sold all the shares he had months ago, but the cash is nowhere. At least, nowhere Alex could find it. Yet. Your cousin has two mortgages on both his houses."

"Hmm. . ." Her gaze went blurry again. "There's been a problem with the division earnings reports for the last twelve quarters."

"What do you mean?"

"At Caravel." She set her coffee down, looking at me thoughtfully. "We've had no new agents go to market, and spending in R&D is way down—way down—but profits are up."

"Where is the money coming from?"

"Current product sales, which shouldn't be the case because all of our in-house catalogue is out-of-patent with generics available. At least, I think generics are available." Kat frowned, her gaze sliding to the table and resting there. "I should check on that," she murmured.

A knock sounded on the door, followed by a team of assistants appearing with a platter of fancy croissants and pastries, and asking us if we wanted a latte or cappuccino. We didn't. We thanked them. They left.

I sat down, taking the seat next to where she was standing. Placing my coffee on the table, I grabbed one of the fancy croissants. "The way I figure things, Eugene didn't know anything about the frozen assets until just this morning. Obviously, Caleb and Sharpe showing up took him by surprise."

She studied the platter, grabbing a napkin. "Sharpe isn't a bad guy, but he's never considered me a priority client. He doesn't know me. He considers Caravel the main client, even though it's my family's money that pays the firm's retainer, not the company. Caravel has their own legal team in-house. And Caleb is the CEO. So. . ."

"Why would Eugene pick that guy for his partner?"

"He and Eugene founded the firm thirty years ago, and my father is a big reason why they've been so successful. Sharpe goes where the money is, which makes sense. They have a big staff of people here who rely on them for paychecks and Eugene is on his way out the door, ready to retire. He needs to take care of his people." She selected a cheese and cherry danish, licking her fingers after setting it on her napkin.

"You're being very generous to Sharpe, a guy who's been working to have you committed to a mental institution and just froze your assets."

"It's business. One day, I'll be responsible for voting the controlling shares in Caravel and I'll have to make decisions based on what's best for the company, because the people are the company. That's what my father used to say."

"He did? He used to say that to you?"

"No. I've read interviews he gave to magazines and newspapers," she admitted sadly, then sighed. "I think I need to go into the office tomorrow."

"What? Go back to Chicago?"

"No. Here." She glanced at me, a small smile tugging at her mouth. "I have an office at the Caravel headquarters in Boston."

"Oh?" I turned toward her more fully, leaning an elbow on the table, lifting my eyebrows. "Is it a corner office?"

"It is."

"On a high floor?"

"Yes."

"Do you have your own secretary?"

"I don't have an *executive assistant* of my own, no. I use the executive pool when I need help."

"Hmm." My gaze flickered over her. "You're worried about the problems with the reports?"

"Do you think Janie would take a look? If I asked? I mean, I know she just had a baby. But she was honestly the best person we had in the accounting department before they let her go. She's unbelievably amazing. And she knows things, random facts, which help her pick up on discrepancies. I feel like she'd see the pattern I'm missing."

"Why don't you ask someone in Caravel to help?"

"I don't know who I can trust."

"Yeah. Good point. I'm sure Janie would be happy to help."

Kat exhaled, sounding relieved. "Okay. Good. This is a good plan. When they come out next weekend, I'll have her go through them with me."

"Elizabeth, Sandra, and Ashley could also help." I tore off a piece of my croissant. "They might be able to quickly look at your current agent, or drug catalogue—that's what you called it?—and tell you which ones have generics."

"Yes. Good idea. I've been meaning to do this research forever, but with work and school, I've let my concerns about Caravel slide, figuring I just needed more time to learn the ropes. I just thought . . ."

"What?"

Her small smile looked regretful. "I thought I had more time."

"More time?"

"Before my dad died. For some reason, as long as he was alive, even though he was in no shape to run Caravel or vote the family shares, I felt like I had a buffer. I could live my life like I wanted, where I wanted."

I studied her, her gaze now intense, like she was trying to tell me something without saying it. She didn't need to say it, I could put the puzzle pieces together myself.

"You're moving to Boston," I guessed.

Kat chewed on her bottom lip, watching me, maybe hoping for more mind reading.

When I said nothing, she sighed, her attention dropping to her pastry. "That depends."

"On what?"

"On you." Pink spread over her cheeks and she picked at the danish's flaky dough. "I would like to—I would like for us to . . ."

"Yes?" I found myself leaning forward, on the edge of my seat.

"We've done everything backward." Kat brought her thumb to her tongue, licked the icing, her stare coming back to me. "If we were in Chicago, would we live together? Now that the Caleb threat seems to have vanished, do we stay married?"

For some reason, my heart was beating faster. All I knew was, I didn't like the direction she was heading with these questions.

"The Caleb threat hasn't vanished," I hedged, taking a bite of my croissant, chewing to give myself more time, taking a drink of my coffee to give myself even more time.

But, now that I thought about it, my statement was true. Our confrontation just now had been too easy, I'd won too easily. Maybe Caleb's lack of funds had made him sloppy, but he wasn't ready to give up. I was sure of it. I may have cauterized his access to the law firm and legal resources, but that still left him illegal resources.

"I know people. Little shits like Caleb don't give up. They just keep coming and coming, never know when to stop. He's out of money, and he's lost for now, but that just means he's desperate."

She didn't seem surprised by my assessment of her cousin. "So we stay married?"

"Yes. Absolutely. And I think we decide here and now to just shelve that issue indefinitely. You know, just in case. No need to end it, really. At all. Ever." I took another bite of my croissant, washing it down with a big gulp of coffee and watching for her reaction.

Kat smiled a little shy smile, her gaze growing soft, her eyes drawing me in. "Agreed. But then, do we live separately? Or would you . . ."

"Would I?" I prompted.

"Would you consider living, at least part time, in Boston?" She winced, like she was bracing herself for my answer.

"Absolutely." I nodded.

Her gaze searched mine. "And we would live together?"

"I should hope so, we *are* married."

"You know what I mean."

"Yeah, I do." I leaned back in my chair, giving her my serious face. "We can live together and still take things slow."

She was chewing on her lip again. "It'll be hard."

"You have no idea," I mumbled.

Her face split with a smile and she shook her head at me. But then her expression sobered. "I don't want to live in my father's house, in Duxbury. He used to take a helicopter into work."

"Holy shit. You own a helicopter?"

She nodded, looking uncomfortable.

"So who's living there now? At the place in Duxbury?"

"No one. It's been empty since he moved to the care facility. But it's still maintained, just like all the other houses."

"All the other houses," I parroted, letting the lunacy of that statement roll around in my brain.

"Yes." Her features grew stark and she rubbed her forehead. "So many houses. Eugene has the list."

I studied her for a beat. "Where are you thinking in Boston?"

She twisted her lips to the side. "So, I was talking to your mom—"

"We're not living with my mom."

"No. I agree." She grinned. "But maybe on her street?"

I choked. "You want to live down the street from my mom?"

"Yes."

I shook my head. "Can I think about it?"

"Of course. It would be your home, too."

"I guess it would." I rubbed my chin, thinking about that.

My folks lived with my paternal grandparents for their entire marriage, until my father left. My dad's folks left the house to my mother in their will. My ma's parents had sold their house—which had been next door—and moved to Florida seven years ago.

The neighborhood had changed *a lot* in ten years. Homes had been knocked over and two or three townhouses had been placed on a single lot. Managing security for a house was more difficult than an apartment building, too many points of entry. Kat was worth buckets of money and that kind of money attracted serious problems.

"You'll need a security detail," I spoke my thoughts out loud.

"I know." She sounded resigned to and unhappy about it, but at least she agreed. "I was thinking, for at least the next few weeks, until we figure something out, we'll have to move to The Langham. They keep a penthouse open for my family's use and they'll allow Wally."

"You already asked the hotel about Wally?" Warmth suffused my chest at this news. *She's been thinking about this, making plans, including Wally.*

She nodded, her eyes hopeful.

My thoughts drifted to the logistics of running a security detail for her. Quinn and I were out of the private security business mostly, but—

obviously—we'd make an exception for Kat. Also, I needed to start planning on what would happen when the newspapers caught wind of her father's death, which would happen any day now, and all the public interest that was sure to follow.

"I'll need to meet with the hotel people as soon as possible. I assume the penthouse has restricted access? And we'll need to keep the team close by, maybe a floor below, where we can have more control over your safety."

"Agreed. I'll let you handle those details," she said, all professional and shit.

I cocked an eyebrow at her tone. "Oh really? You'll *let* me handle the details?"

Her lips curved into an answering smile. "Security is your area of expertise, so why would I need to be involved? I trust you to handle it and keep me informed if there's anything I need to know."

I snorted, laughing. "Aye-aye, boss."

"Delegation is one of my strengths," she said. I loved the way she was looking at me, like she actually *was* my boss, but she also wanted to get in my pants. "I'm very good at it."

"I bet."

We stared at each other while I wished we were anywhere but here —in my room at home, at our place in Chicago, in the rental car—I didn't care where.

My eyes dropped to that first button and I wondered what she'd do if I reached over and unfastened it, maybe the next few as well. Or what would she say if I asked her to stand so I could hike her skirt up and touch the soft skin of her thighs?

"I wish . . ." she said, which brought my eyes back to hers.

"What?" *Tell me.*

"I wish I didn't have to withdraw from the University of Chicago."

"Oh yeah. Can you transfer your credits to some place out here? Isn't that how it works?"

"Yes. Eventually. I'll call tomorrow, or maybe Friday, and explain the situation. Once things settle down, I'll apply to schools out here." She looked resigned, regretful. "And then there's work."

"You mean Foster?" Foster was the architecture firm where she worked.

"I'll have to turn in my notice. I'll do that on Friday, too. There's no getting around it. I just wish . . ."

When she didn't finish, I prompted, "That you could keep working there?"

"More like, I wish this weren't so sudden. I wish I could phase out over a month, so they would have time to find someone and I could train them."

"Didn't they fire Janie suddenly? Because her ex-boyfriend's father, who was giving Foster business, wanted her gone?"

Kat seemed to consider this. "Yes, they did. But that doesn't mean I feel great about leaving abruptly."

He shrugged. "It's business. They did what they had to do with Janie. You do what you gotta do. Life, work, business goes on, even when great people leave."

"I guess it does. When Janie left, it took months to find a replacement, and then they ended up hiring four people to do her job. But, eventually, she was replaced."

"In business, no one is irreplaceable."

Her eyes came back to mine, sharpened. "The opposite of a family."

"What?"

"In a family, no one is replaceable."

I studied her, not knowing where she was going with this. Was she talking about her father? Or . . . ?

Chewing on her lip, her stare grew increasingly intense until she blurted, "Why is your mother alone? What happened with your father? I see pictures of him all over the house, but aren't they divorced?"

The air was driven from my lungs. I blinked at her, startled. She'd blindsided me.

"I'm sorry." She winced, a concerned frown settling between her eyebrows. "I'm sorry, it's none of my business. I just—"

"My dad, Denis, was in love with this lady. Let's call this lady Linda." I leaned forward, placing my elbows on my knees and glared at the back of my hands. There was never going to be a right time to tell this story, so it might as well be now. "Linda had a baby, let's call the baby Seamus. Linda didn't want Seamus, and she didn't want my pop, so she left Seamus at a fire station when he was something like three months old, and my dad—he's a navy guy—was deployed overseas."

I lifted my eyes to hers, found them thoughtful and interested. "My mom, well, she'd known my dad since forever. He's ten years older than her, but they grew up next door to each other, and she'd been full stop crazy about the guy for years and years. The firefighters where Linda had left Seamus knew my dad, they all went to school together, so they take Seamus to my dad's parents while they try to track down Linda. They can't find her, she's gone, skipped town."

"Seamus is your half-brother."

I nodded, rubbed my face, and then leaned back in my seat, placing my arm along the table, so fucking tired of this story already. "My mom helped my grandparents out from time to time. She starts babysitting Seamus for free, who of course falls in love with her, grows attached, you know? When my dad gets back, his parents don't like the idea of raising their son's illegitimate child, they want him to sign his rights away to the state, put Seamus up for adoption. So my dad, he asks my mom to marry him, to raise his son. She's in love with the guy, in love with his son, and she's only seventeen—a dumb, love-sick kid —so she says yes, and he is so grateful."

She stiffened, a hint of dread in her expression, like she knew what was going to happen next in the story.

"My mom marries my dad when she graduates from high school, adopts Seamus, goes to live with the O'Malley's—my dad's parents— and puts herself through nursing school part time while taking care of his parents and his kid. But he's always so grateful, can't say thank you enough. He buys her presents, nice stuff, and expensive jewelry. Gratitude for miles. She wants more kids. He's deployed, career navy guy, so he's only ever home to get my mom pregnant. Appreciation as far as the eye could see. He gives her everything but his time."

"Then one day, my dad is home for a weekend. Being an asshole teenager, I sneak my father's wallet, planning to lighten him of a few twenty-dollar bills. I open the wallet and what do I find? Pictures of him with a lady who is not my mother, and they look recent."

Kat flinched.

"No pictures of my mom. No pictures of us kids. Just pictures of that lady." My eyes lost focus as I remembered. "I took one photo, 'cause I didn't know who this person was, and asked my grandfather O'Malley about it. He loses his temper—as he was prone to do—and confronts my dad in front of my mom. So there we were, the four of us, my mom crying, and the truth all comes out. I didn't know about Seamus, about any of it, and I didn't know my dad had been running around on my mom the whole time with this lady, but it all comes out. And Grandpa tells my dad he has to choose, he can't keep putting Eleanor and the kids through this."

The taste of coffee and croissant turned sour in my mouth.

"He packed his bags." My stare returned to hers. "And do you know what he said to my mom before he left?"

She shook her head. Her big, brown, beautiful eyes teeming with compassion.

"He said he would always be grateful. But that gratitude wasn't love, and he was tired of trying to force it."

"What a bastard." The words were a breath, like she hadn't meant to speak them aloud.

I smirked, though I didn't find her statement funny so much as painfully true. "Yeah. Well. I found out later his precious Linda died that same year. His parents didn't speak to him, went to their graves disowning him. He's still in the navy and that's all he's got, high up now, an admiral or something."

"You don't know if he's an admiral?"

I shook my head, pushing the croissant away, no longer hungry.

"Was that the last time you saw him?"

"No. I saw him . . ." My eyes moved up and to the right. "I saw him a few years back in Washington, DC. I was there for work and ran into him at a restaurant."

"Did you talk to him?"

I nodded. This part of the story was easy to tell. But, looking back, I'd always had the sense it had happened to someone else. "He approached me, wanted to go somewhere, to talk."

"What did you do?"

"I told him that I'd always be grateful he sent money home to Ma when we were growing up, but that gratitude wasn't the same as love, and I was tired of trying to force it."

She flinched again. "Ouch."

"What the fuck does he care? He's the one who left, he's the one who didn't give a shit."

Kat nodded, her pretty mouth a mournful line. "You're right. He's the one who left."

"Damn straight." I reached for my coffee, but then set it back on the table, feeling restless. "And you want to know the worst part of it?"

"What's that?"

Disgusted, I crossed my arms. "Those pictures of him in the house. She won't let us speak badly of him, sends us down the cellar if we do."

"Do you think she still . . . ?"

"I don't know."

And that was the God's honest truth.

CHAPTER TWENTY-THREE

Sildenafil, sold as the brand name **Viagra™** (among others), is a medication used to treat erectile dysfunction and pulmonary arterial hypertension. It was initially studied for use in hypertension (high blood pressure) and angina pectoris. When the first clinical trials were conducted, male patients presented with a common adverse side effect: marked penile erections.

There is a generic version of Viagra™ available (as of December 2017) via Teva Pharmaceuticals.

THE AMERICAN SOCIETY OF HEALTH-SYSTEM PHARMACISTS

Kat

D AN BEGAN PLAYING footsie with me under the table just after 9:00 PM.

I felt something slide up my leg and jumped. Mr. Stevenson, the VP of estate finance at Brooks and Quail, where many of my family's US-based investments were housed, had been reviewing the loss statements over the last quarter.

"Are you all right?" he asked, looking concerned.

He was on my left side, Dan across from us, Eugene sitting on Mr. Stevenson's other side. The touch—presumably a foot—had come from in front of me on the right.

"Yes. Fine. I apologize, just a sudden cramp." I reached under the table as though to scratch the right side of my leg; in reality I pinched his ankle. "Please continue with the prospectus."

He continued. I planned to send a warning glare to Dan. That plan fled my brain as soon as our gazes connected.

Dan was leaning slightly to one side, looking relaxed, lounging in the chair; his elbow was on the table, his middle and index fingers along the side of his face, his chin propped on his thumb, his ring and pinky fingers just under his lips, one of his eyebrows slightly raised over a smoldering gaze.

He looked like he was issuing me a dare. My heart quickened.

I endeavored to glare at him. He smirked, his stare dropping to my mouth as his tongue licked his bottom lip. Then he drew it into his mouth, his foot coming back to my leg and sliding along the interior. I felt dizzy.

I'm frustrated to admit it, but his distraction techniques were working.

Earlier in the evening, close to 7:00 PM, he'd been sitting next to me. Everything had been fine, perfectly professional all day. We'd made it through the will, an extensive and detailed account of all the properties, bank accounts, offshore holdings, and so forth. But then I'd turned to Dan, planning to ask a question, and found his eyes on the top button of my shirt. His stare was intensely focused, like he wanted to destroy the buttons, or maybe just maim them. .

I asked Dan the question, to which he'd shaken himself, blinked, and responded with, "What was that?"

I asked it again and he'd replied, pragmatically, dispassionately, and objectively. But I immediately missed the way I'd caught him looking at me. On a whim, holding his gaze, I decided to surreptitiously unbutton the top button of my shirt. The smolder hadn't stopped since.

Presently, Mr. Stevenson said, "We have another four hundred statements on the viability of this particular fund I'd like to show you," and I decided I'd had enough.

"Thank you, Mr. Stevenson." I gave him a tight smile, pushing back in my chair. "But I believe that's enough for today."

He glanced from me to Eugene. "I have seventeen more accounts to review."

"Yes. And we'll do so tomorrow at my office downtown. You know the address." I stood and so did everyone else.

"I plan to return to New York tonight," he protested, pointing to the binder he'd brought.

"You'll have to change your plans." I was already gathering my belongings.

"That's not possible. We'll have to make an appointment for later in the month. Should I have my assistant call Mr. Marks's office?"

I stopped organizing my things and stared at Mr. Stevenson, giving him an opportunity to reverse his assertion.

When he didn't, I continued stacking papers. "Mr. Stevenson, you will meet me at my office tomorrow at nine. You knew how long it would take to review these reports. It is your job to plan your meetings with me efficiently, not mine. I will not be expected to conform to your schedule if you and your firm wish to continue managing this portfolio. If you didn't want to stay another day in Boston, then you should have used your time more wisely." Finished organizing my things, I placed the load into my bag and walked around the table towards the wooden double doors. I didn't need to look to know Dan was behind me, and behind Dan was Eugene.

"I'll see you out." I heard Eugene say.

"That won't be necessary." I turned right, toward the elevator. "We know the way. Please ensure Mr. Stevenson knows how to find my office."

Eugene's footsteps fell away, and Dan drew even with my shoulder.

Once we were out of earshot, he took my bag from me and slung it over his shoulder. "You didn't cut that Stevenson guy any slack."

"No. I didn't." I shrugged. "But he makes a lot of money off of my family. Requesting he stay another day isn't asking for something inappropriate. You and I, and Eugene, shouldn't be expected to stay until midnight. That was poor planning on his part."

"Hmm." I felt his eyes on me.

I glanced at him as we approached the elevators. "He works for me, not the other way around."

As soon as I pressed the call button, the doors slid open. I stepped on first. Dan followed and pressed the button for the lobby. The doors shut and he turned to me, crossing his arms, looking as though he was fighting a smile.

"What?" Now I was glaring.

"Nothing." He shook his head, the smile he was fighting morphing into something else as his eyes traveled down the length of me and then back up, his gaze coming to rest on the button I'd undone. "You're just really sexy when you're bossy."

Now I was fighting a smile, and also the heat sliding up my cheeks. "I wasn't bossy."

"You were bossy."

"I was communicating my expectations."

"Bossy." His gaze slowly rose to my lips.

"If I were a man, you would call me assertive."

"If you were a man, I would have called you a bossy motherfucker."

I huffed a laugh, he was cheeky and unbelievable and I loved this about him. "Then call me a bossy motherfucker."

"I can't."

"Why not?"

"Because I'd never call you that name." His gaze came to mine; the earlier teasing and heat were still present, but now tempered with sincerity. "I would never call you any name other than your own."

"You call me Kit-Kat."

"Exactly." He pushed away from the wall of the elevator, reaching for my hand and bringing it to his lips. His voice lowered, "I promise you, if you were any other woman, I would definitely call you a bossy motherfucker."

Somehow he'd made that last sentence sound like a seduction. My heart skipped a beat, my stomach fluttering. I watched and felt him place a sensual kiss on the skin between my middle and index fingers, wicked thoughts dancing behind his expressive eyes.

The elevator dinged, the doors slid open, and he held me transfixed.

"Let's go." He finally said, tilting his head toward the exit. "I'm sure you're tired from a full day of being bossy."

I rolled my eyes and scoffed, mostly to cover the fact that Dan calling me "bossy" twisted my lower belly into warm, velvety knots.

Hand in hand, we walked through an almost empty lobby. The security guard unlocked the door for us and soon we were in the car, driving back to Dan's mom's house. Once we were on our way, his palm settled on my skirt over my knee. I stared out the window, thinking over all the information I'd learned today about the nature and structure of my family's fortune, and feeling the weight of it all.

"What's going on in that sexy, bossy brain of yours?"

Turning toward the windshield, I became acutely aware of his thumb tracing a circle over my knee. Glancing at my leg, I realized Dan had pushed the hem of my skirt up on one side, his fingers now curled over the bare skin of my thigh.

I leaned my elbow on the windowsill and angled my legs toward him. "I'm going to need to assemble a team of people I trust to help me manage our investments."

"You have Eugene."

"That's true." I did have Eugene. "He's loyal, but he keeps secrets. He doesn't trust that I can handle things on my own."

Dan glanced at me, then back to the road, saying nothing, his fingers inching higher on my leg as he slid his palm upward.

"He thinks I need to be protected."

"Yeah. He does."

"How do I prove that I don't need to be coddled?"

Dan seemed to think it over before saying, "Just keep being you. He's smart. He'll figure it out."

A new kind of warmth, which had very little to do with his hand on my leg, uncoiled in my stomach. It had everything to do with this man. This wonderful amazing man.

I love this man.

It wasn't a realization or an *ah-ha* moment. More like, just an acceptance of fact, like knowing myself deep down and acknowledging who I was.

I am Kathleen Caravel-Tyson. I am good at delegating. I'm a little neurotic. I have brown hair and brown eyes. I like cheese too much. I rely on order and routine. I'm in love with Daniel O'Malley.

I trusted him. I trusted him implicitly and explicitly and I couldn't imagine a situation where he'd ever break that trust. I loved him and I trusted him and I was happy.

"Thank you for believing in me," I said before I realized I was speaking.

His smile was small as he lifted an eyebrow, glancing at me again. "Thanks for making it so easy."

* * *

BY THE TIME we'd made it back, my skirt was at my hips, the first three buttons of my shirt were undone, and my heart was racing. Dan's fingers were scant millimeters from the apex of my thighs, his jaw was tight, and he was speeding.

Taking a corner entirely too fast, he finally slowed to pull into the street parking spot across from his mother's three-story house. As soon as he engaged the emergency break and cut the engine, he clicked the button for his seat belt as I undid mine. He helped me—i.e. pulled me —across the center console. I hit my head on the rearview mirror and banged my knee against the cupholder. I didn't care.

Straddling his lap, hungrily seeking his mouth, I rocked against him, shivering at the heavenly feel of his hard against my soft.

A low sound vibrated from his throat, his fingers making quick work of the buttons at the front of my shirt, his mouth trailing hot and hungry kisses down my neck to my chest.

I rocked against him again, wanting—needing—the pressure, the friction. His twelve o'clock shadow scratched the swell of my breast as he pulled down the cup of my bra, tonguing my nipple and groaning.

I dug my fingers into the back of his head, holding him in place as white hot spikes of sensation streaked through me. "We need to—we need to go inside."

But do we? Do we really?

His fingers slid into the back of my underwear, palming my ass, caressing and squeezing. "One more minute. Fuck, does this bra clasp in the front?" He groaned at the discovery.

"Dan," I moaned, his teeth nipping my breast just before he swirled his tongue over the peak, sucking it more completely into his mouth. I couldn't help it, I bore down on him, trying to open myself wider.

"Oh fuck." His hips jerked upward and his breath caught.

"I want you." I didn't think about it, where we were, what I was saying. I wasn't analyzing my breathing, my movements. I didn't even allow myself to take stock of what I was feeling.

I just felt, allowing myself to be mindless.

Dan's forehead came to the valley between my breasts. His hot breath panting and ragged as his hands came to my hips, gripping me, holding me still. "Why are you so fucking perfect? Why do you feel so fucking good?"

Fire in my lungs, I tried to move again, tried to redirect his mouth back to my breast. "Dan."

He held rigid. "Kat, hold still. Please."

"I need you," I said, again without thought. "I want you to make me feel good. I love—"

A string of expletives left his mouth and he leaned his head back and away, his eyes were shut tight. "You were right, we need to stop. We need . . ." he shook his head as though to clear it. "We need to go inside."

"Yessss." I tried grabbing his wrist to force him to move his hand, but he was too strong. He wouldn't budge.

"And take a cold shower."

"Noooo," I groaned, bending to kiss his gorgeous lips, and sucked the bottom one into my mouth. This was the one he'd been teasing me with earlier. I savored it before releasing him with a slow lick.

Now he groaned. "Maybe we'll play a nice, friendly game of Monopoly."

Frustrated—but not really frustrated—I began to laugh, my head falling to his neck.

"We could play something else."

"Strip poker."

He made a choking sound. "You're trying to murder me."

I laughed again, placing a kiss on his neck, and trying to calm my pulse. This was great. He was great. And I felt *great*.

Wrapping my arms around his neck, a wave of gratitude and warm fuzzy feelings flowed through me. "Thank you. Thank you so much. Thank you."

His breathing slowed, his hands loosening their grip and sliding to my arms.

He cleared his throat before asking, "For what?"

"For so much. For everything."

Dan encouraged me to release him and lean back. I did. He held my hands in his and kissed them, one at a time, his attention fixed on my knuckles.

"Let's go inside," he said, letting my hands go, his fingers moving to the buttons of my shirt and fastening them. "Personally, I think this is a good look for you."

I smiled down at him, watching his progress. "My clothes are a mess."

"You're beautiful." He finished with the last button.

"So are you."

Dan lifted his gaze to mine, a small smile on his lips that wasn't quite reflected in his eyes.

"What's wrong?"

He shook his head, his shoulders giving a subtle shrug. "Nothing. I'm hungry, I guess. And I haven't worked out today."

He helped me shift back to my seat and I inspected him. "Do you work out every day?"

"Yes. Every day." Dan rubbed his eyes with the base of his palms. "I like field work better than desk work, so I gotta be in shape. Plus, I like it."

"Have you always worked out? Did you play sports in high school?"

He blinked a few times, staring out the windshield. "I started working out in prison. Never played sports in high school before I dropped out. I hated anything to do with organized socialization or the bullshit rituals." He paused here to exhale a laugh. "Which is ironic because I joined my brother's gang when I was thirteen, and that's how I got these." Dan gestured to wisps of black ink just visible above his collar.

"You got those when you were thirteen?"

"Not all of them. But, yeah, starting when I was thirteen. If you see a guy around here with these kinds of designs around his neck, he's part of my brother's gang." Dan glanced at me, a self-deprecating smile on his handsome features. "I didn't see the similarities when I was a dumbass kid. All I knew was, I wanted to belong to something and be important, respected."

It was quiet. Quiet car, quiet street, quiet neighborhood. But more than that, it was still. I had an odd sense that we were treading water next to each other, as though in a tranquil lake beneath a starry sky, the cadence of silence manifesting as two beating hearts.

I didn't want to break the spell by speaking. But my faith in him, and my trust, told me: this might've been the first of these moments, but it wouldn't be the last.

So I asked the question I'd been wondering for a while. "What did you do when you were part of your brother's gang?"

Dan's chest expanded with a deep breath, his gaze falling away. "Lots of things. But what I was *caught* for doing was armed robbery."

"Will you tell me?"

He nodded, his hand coming to the back of my seat as he angled himself to face me, his attention on my headrest. "We were robbing a house—not the first time—and we thought no one was there. I was smallest, still scrawny at seventeen, so I went in through the basement

345

window. I let them in. Turns out, someone was home. *That* hadn't happened before. The lady came out of her room, catching Seamus by surprise and he shot at her."

"Oh no." I covered my mouth.

"He got her in the arm." Dan itched the back of his neck. "He freaked out, moving like he was going to shoot her again, and I knocked the gun out of his hand. Everyone ran, including him. I picked it up, thinking I didn't want it to be found there with his prints. He'd just been released from jail—armed robbery of a package store caught on camera—and if he were caught again, he'd be up at Chucky's Place for a long time."

"What happened to the woman? Was she okay?"

"She needed stitches and was shaken up." His mouth curved ruefully to the side. "My mom was wicked pissed, she was the one who turned me in."

My mouth dropped open and it took me several seconds before I could form words. "Your *mom* turned you in?"

"Yep. Mrs. Zucker, the lady whose house we robbed, she saw me when I picked up the gun. She recognized me. She called my mom."

"Mrs. Zucker didn't go to the cops?"

"No. She was scared. She thought, if she went to the cops, we'd retaliate."

"That's terrible."

"That's Seamus," he said, as though terrible and Seamus were one and the same. "Anyway, I gave my brother back the gun, but he didn't get rid of it. He put it in his room. So when I got picked up, my mom let them in the house and they found the gun with my prints all over it." He shrugged. "I confessed, said I was alone, served three years of a seven-year sentence and that's that."

"Wow."

"Yeah." His eyes came to mine briefly, but then lost focus again, his voice distant. "And when I got out, there was my brother, saying I'd earned my place, proved myself." An expression of disgust and loathing—whether for Seamus or for himself, I had no idea—claimed his handsome features. "Like what we'd done was no big deal, not just to Mrs. Zucker, but to our mom. To our *family*. Like we should be proud of ourselves, for how tough we were."

"Is Seamus still—"

"As far as I know, he's still running scams." He shook his head, scoffing, his brows drawn together in an angry frown.

"And your mom puts up with it? With him? She turned you in to the police."

He glanced at the ceiling. "If she had evidence against him, she'd turn him in. But she's never going to give up on him, her heart is too soft. She's always going to hope."

"But you don't?"

He breathed out. "I've tried helping him. I've given him money, given him a job. He stole from me, used the money to fund a scam. He's come to me a hundred times, always with the same story, always with a promise to change." He shrugged, avoiding my eyes. "At a certain point, you got to draw a line in the sand."

I studied Dan, the hard line of his jaw, the stark, mournful look in his eyes and realized Seamus had broken Dan's heart.

I was sure of it.

Maybe not all at once, or by doing any one thing. It had happened over a lifetime and it was possible—even though Dan claimed he'd drawn a line in the sand and had given up hope—Seamus was still breaking his heart.

I found myself wanting to punch Seamus in the throat and shove a hot poker up his nose.

Instead, I asked, "So what happened? You didn't go back to your brother. What did you do when you were released?"

His mouth hitched to the side, and his eyes lost some of their melancholy. "Quinn."

"Quinn?"

"Quinn used to do some work for Seamus—and a bunch of other bad guys—managing tech, security, computers, firewalls."

"He provided tech support for criminals?"

"Something like that." Dan rubbed his jaw. "When I got out, he'd quit running scams and was already in Chicago, doing his thing. But he had more business than he could handle. He offered me a job as private security for some senator's son, to start."

"But now you're partners."

"That's right. I told him about some inefficiencies, dead weight—as far as I saw them—and made suggestions for improvement. He promoted me a few times until we became partners. We worked well together, building up the business. He focused more on the tech and investment side and I was the personnel and project guy—scoped the jobs, checked the clients, made the hires, staffed the jobs—that stuff."

As he spoke and his dark mood seemed to lift, his usual matter-of-fact lightheartedness returned.

"Do you like it?"

"What? My job?"

"Yes."

"Yeah, I like it. And I'm good at it." His gaze flickered over me and he lifted an eyebrow, opening his car door. "Why? You planning on offering me a job?"

I laughed, but didn't answer, hiding my expression because the thought had crossed my mind.

He walked around the car to my door as I exited. I pulled my big bag of documents and binders from the back seat and surveyed my clothes, finding myself disheveled.

Actually, I was a mess.

I touched my hair. It was big, wild, and fluffy. I probably looked like I'd been making out with my husband in our rental car.

"Why're you making that face?" He closed my door and reached for my hand, glancing both ways before crossing the street.

"Do you think your mom is home?"

"Maybe. Why?"

"I need to change. I'm . . . rumpled."

"You're gorgeous. I hope you change nothing." He grinned, his gaze moving over me, communicating his appreciation for my untidy appearance. Dan pulled keys from his pocket and began working on the locks, muttering under his breath, "She needs an alarm system."

"She won't get one?"

He shook his head, turning the last deadbolt. "No. She's stubborn, says it's a waste of money, that she'll forget to use it." Pushing into the house, he held the door open for me. "I believe her, because she usually forgets to lock the door. I keep telling her to lock the front door. How hard is it to lock the front door?"

"I keep telling her the same thing," a voice answered.

Dan and I stopped abruptly, spotting Seamus leaning against the wall at the end of the entryway. I heard Dan breathe out a loud, aggravated breath as he walked around me and snagged my hand, shutting the door behind us.

"Not in the mood. We're going to bed. Lock up when you leave."

"I don't have a key." Seamus's eyes were on me as we passed. "And I'm not here for you."

Dan, shoving his keys in his pocket, stopped at the foot of the stairs. "If you don't have a key, how'd you get in?"

Seamus's stare sharpened on me, and he lifted his chin in my direction. "You never told me your name. What should I call you?"

"My name is Kat." I slipped off my shoes, releasing Dan's hand to pick them up.

"You're not going to call her anything, because you're never going to talk to her." Dan glared at his brother; his dark mood had returned.

Now knowing about the brothers' history, Dan's statement didn't strike me as domineering or him ordering me around. He hadn't forgiven his brother and I didn't think it likely he ever would. Not unless Seamus made some serious changes.

As things were, Dan didn't want Seamus to be a part of his life. I understood, respected, and supported his decision.

Turning to Dan, I placed a kiss on his cheek. "Come upstairs. We'll play Monopoly."

"Yeah." He smirked, stealing a kiss. "Let me see this bozo out."

"Kat is short for Kathleen." Seamus pushed away from the wall and the movement drew my attention. His eyes were still on me and something about them, about him, sent a shiver of discomfort racing down my spine.

The room fell silent for a beat, Dan and me watching Seamus as his boots scuffed against the floor on his way to us.

Dan—very, very slowly—placed his hand on my thigh, guiding me behind him. "What do you think you're doing, Seamus?"

"I just want to talk to her. Can't I talk to my sister-in-law? Ask her some questions. Get to know her. Learn all about her hopes and dreams."

I felt Dan go stiff and he stepped more completely in front of me. "You know."

For the first time since we entered, Seamus's eyes left mine. "You married a fucking heiress, Dan. A. Fucking. Heiress. She tell you that? Did she tell you who she is? Do you know how much money this bitch is worth?"

I sucked in a breath, startled by the venom in Seamus's tone. Of course, it was only a matter of time before Seamus found out. But what I didn't understand was why Dan's brother made my past, who I was, sound like a betrayal.

Dan flinched but took a threatening step forward. "You shut your goddamn mouth."

"The bitch is using you."

"You don't know what the fuck you're talking about, and if you call her that one more time, you'll be shitting teeth."

I placed a hand on Dan's shoulder. He shook me off while placing his hand on my hip, gently pushing me back.

Eyes full of defiance, Seamus lifted his left hand to his hip, his right hand slowly sliding behind his back. "You're too fucking stupid to see what's right in front of you and the kind of payday this bitch could—"

I jumped back, covering my mouth with my hands, because Dan punched his brother in the face.

And then he'd punched his brother in the face again, and throat, and side, and kept on punching. For Seamus's part, he landed a few blows, but he'd been caught by surprise.

Also, Dan seemed to be more motivated.

I'd witnessed fights before. I'd been targeted twice when I lived in a tent city west of Chicago; those encounters had resulted in my fair share of bruises, cuts, and cracked ribs. I'd learned to run. At the first sign of trouble, I ran. Always. I was small. I didn't know how to fight. I was always running, sometimes all night. By the time I was incarcerated, running had become a deeply ingrained habit.

That had been a very long time ago. A lifetime ago.

Now, watching the brothers destroy their mother's living room, I didn't run. I couldn't. It was like watching a car accident, or being in one. I was so shocked by what I was seeing, the violence, I couldn't move.

But then Seamus—who was clearly the dirtier, sneakier fighter—reached for the brass lamp on the side table. Dan saw this, and blocked his arm, leaving his right side undefended. Seamus took advantage of the opening and grabbed Dan's throat, forcing Dan to twist back and away.

While this was happening, and before Seamus's fingers could close completely over the lamp, I grabbed my bag of heavy documents, rushed forward, swung it around once, and whacked him square in the face.

Seamus's neck snapped back, he stumbled, tripped over his own feet, and crashed to the ground. His hands came to his nose as he rolled to the side.

"You dumb bitch! You broke my nose!"

Dan moved like he was going to kick his brother in the ribs, but I stepped in front of him, placing my hand on his shoulders and pushing him back.

"They're just names. Please. Please don't. He's not worth it."

Dan wasn't looking at me, he was looking at his brother, his eyes dark with murderous rage. "Get the fuck out of here."

"Or what?"

Dan stepped around me, grabbed the lamp from the table, and advanced on his brother. He yanked, tearing the cord from the wall and ripping the lamp shade from the bulb.

"Dan. Wait. Stop. Please." I reached for his arm, but it was no use.

He didn't shrug me off or push me away, but he was too strong. I might as well have been trying to stop a speeding train.

He crouched behind his brother, taking the chord and wrapping it around Seamus's neck. He pulled.

"Oh fuck," Seamus said just before he couldn't say anything at all.

Yanking him up and back, Dan leaned close to his ear as his older brother kicked and struggled, grasping at his neck.

"Now you listen to me, you worthless piece of shit. You don't talk to her. You don't look at her. You don't think about her. She doesn't exist to you. If I see you near her, if I catch talk that you've said her name, I will find you and not even a fucking UN resolution will keep me from dissecting you alive. Do you understand me?"

Seamus did his best to nod.

Standing suddenly, Dan let his brother drop to the floor with a painful sounding *thunk*. He then moved to Seamus's back while the man was gasping raggedly on the ground. I tensed, bracing for another blow, but Dan merely reached into the back of his brother's pants and retrieved a gun. Then, stepping on Seamus's ankle and placing a knee on the back of his other leg, Dan retrieved a knife and another gun from his boots.

"You come here to kidnap her? Huh?" he asked, wiping the blood from the side of his mouth with his hand and then checking the weapons.

Cold dread slithered over me, down my neck and spine, like a bucket of ice water. I stared at Seamus while he struggled to breathe, and he stared back. His eyes were large with some emotion I couldn't read.

Dan placed the guns on the stairs, then moved back to his brother, patting him down. When he seemed satisfied, he reached into his own back pocket and pulled out his phone.

"Who are you calling?" I asked, holding on to the banister for balance.

"The police," Dan responded flatly, bringing the phone to his ear.

I nodded, wrapping my arms around myself and sitting on the stairs next to the guns and knife.

Dan turned to me, his eyes full of concern. "Hey. Hey—are you okay?"

I nodded again, my shoulders hunching forward. I was cold. So cold. I began shivering. I couldn't stop.

Dan rushed to me, cupping my cheek tenderly. "Kit-Kat, I—Yes, yes. I'd like to report an attempted kidnapping. The perp is still here, but he's incapacitated." Dan paused for a moment, listening to the person on the other side of the call. "Sure, sure. The address is—"

The phone was knocked from his hand before he had a chance to finish because Seamus had brought the lamp down directly on his head.

Dan crumpled to the ground.

I screamed.

Without thinking, I scrambled for the gun, standing on the stairs and flipping off the safety. "Get away from him!"

Seamus stared at me as he stumbled back, dropping the lamp to the floor and showing me his palms.

I stepped around Dan. Perhaps it was stupid, but my first instinct was to protect him, stand between him and his brother. "I swear to God, I will shoot you if you touch him."

Seamus wiped blood from where it was dripping into his eye. "He knew," he rasped. "You told him."

"What?" I shifted my weight back and forth on my feet, not under-standing his meaning. "What are you talking about?"

"The guy said," his voice was rough and he paused, like speaking was painful, and backed up slowly, "he said you were playing him. He said you were using him."

"Who?" My hand was shaking and I forced myself to hold still, bending my elbow, gritting my teeth. "Who said that?"

"Doesn't matter," he said, shaking his head, reaching behind him, presumably for the doorknob.

He opened the door, slowly, and I watched him. His eyes were no longer defiant. If my instincts could be trusted, they looked . . . remorseful. I didn't know what to do. I didn't want to shoot him. But I couldn't let him leave, could I?

Tears blurred my vision and I rolled my lips between my teeth to stay my wobbling chin, taking two steps forward, but to no purpose.

I don't know what to do. What do I do?

"Tell him—" he grimaced, his hand coming to his throat. He paused in the open doorway, looking at me. Just looking.

I blinked away the tears, staring at him.

"Tell him I'm sorry," he whispered.

Leave.

Just leave.

He nodded, making me wonder if I'd spoken my thoughts out loud.

His eyes dropped to some spot behind me.

And then he slipped out the door.

CHAPTER TWENTY-FOUR

U.S. Food, Drug, and Cosmetic Act: Originally passed in 1938, this act subjected new drugs to pre-market safety evaluation for the first time. This required FDA regulators to review both pre-clinical and clinical test results for new drugs.

FDA.GOV

Dan

"..."

"What?"

"..."

"You want to say something, just say it." I glared out the window of the penthouse rather than glare at my phone, watching the ant-sized people below. I followed a guy in a black suit with my eyes as he walked down Pearl Street before turning into the park.

"You're in a bad mood," Quinn said from his side of the call, all matter-of-fact.

I didn't respond.

He was right.

I was in a bad fucking mood.

I'd been in a bad fucking mood for five days, ever since my tirefire shitdumpster of a brother tried to kidnap my wife. Seamus attempting to kidnap someone didn't surprise me. Hell, Seamus attempting to kidnap a billionaire heiress made perfect sense, in its own twisted way.

But, his own brother's *wife*? That was some fucked up shit.

"Yeah. What else is new?" I grumbled finally.

I kept my eyes on the guy in the park. He walked past a bench, stopped, turned around, walked back to the bench and sat on it.

That was weird, right?

No.

It wasn't weird. Since last Wednesday, I'd been seeing threats where none existed and acting like an agitated asshole on the daily. Rubbing my eyes, I shook my head. I needed to get a grip.

When I'd awoken, after Seamus had knocked me over the head with my Grandma O'Malley's favorite lamp, I came face-to-face with a paramedic. My first question was, "Where's Kat?" Once I saw she was okay, my second questions was, "Is he dead?" Because if he wasn't dead, I was going to kill him.

For the record, he wasn't dead and I hadn't killed him.

Yet.

Seamus had disappeared. Kat told me how he'd left, with her holding the gun on him and that piece of shit apologizing as he backed out the door. Apologizing. *What the fuck?*

"You have a concussion, dummy. Why aren't you resting?" Quinn didn't sound upset, and he didn't sound curious. He just sounded like Quinn.

"I have been resting. I'm resting right now."

"You're on a treadmill."

"But I'm not running. I'm walking. I've been stuck in this hotel room since they discharged me from the hospital." My eyes narrowed on the guy in the park again; he looked like he was talking on his phone. "But you know this, so I don't know why I'm telling you this again."

"It's because you need to complain to someone." This came from

Sandra, her voice sounding like she was yelling from the other side of the room. When she spoke again, she was closer to the receiver. "You need to commiserate."

"I do?"

"Yes. You do," she said, sounding reasonable. "You've been through an ordeal. Ordeals require commiseration. You need to talk through your feelings, otherwise PTSD may manifest. So, please, commiserate."

I stared through the window, my eyes now on the skyline. "What? You mean, right now?"

"Yes, Stripper Eyes, right now," Sandra ordered; then I heard her say quieter, like she was whispering, "You can listen if you want, but I'll take it from here."

"Wait." I frowned. "What did you call me?"

"It was a compliment. Accept it in the nature in which it was given."

I shook my head, she was confusing me. "Is Quinn still there?"

"Yeah. I'm here." He paused, cleared his throat, and then added robotically, as though being prompted, "Please commiserate."

I huffed a laugh, imagining Sandra feeding him lines on the other end. Man, it felt good to laugh. It also hurt. My lip was mostly healed, but Seamus had bruised a few of my ribs. He was a dirty fighter and they were still sore.

"Good. Quinn, listen, you all set for this weekend?"

"Why aren't you commiserating?" Sandra asked, her voice taking on the peculiar quality she used when trying to psychoanalyze one of us. "And how is Kat? Has she visited her mother yet?"

"Yeah," I grumbled. "She went Sunday."

"You didn't go with her, did you? I mean, you were resting, right?"

"No."

Kat's visit to her mom was a sore subject for me, put me in a worst mood.

"No to which question? Did you go with her or did you rest?"

"No, I didn't go with her. Yes, I rested." I rolled my eyes, ignoring the pain in my brain at the movement.

357

We were supposed to go visit Kat's mom last Friday. With my hospital stay and everything, the visit had been cancelled. But Kat needed to go see her mom, needed to tell her about her father's death, so she'd gone on Sunday. Without me.

"She should go back soon, next week, when you're better. Make sure she's not avoiding."

I made a face. "Give us a break, Sandra. Things have been nuts."

Honestly, I didn't know if I wanted Kat to go back to see her mom. She'd come back from the facility all sad, her eyes red from crying. Seeing her that way landed like a punch to the gut and I hated it.

"Dan the Security Man—" She sounded like she was getting ready to make a threat.

So I cut in, "Sandra the Shrink, I have fifteen minutes until my ma gets back and she'll shit a kidney if she finds me on the phone. So let me talk to Quinn."

"Fine. But when I see you on Saturday, there *will* be commiseration. Give Kat a hug for me."

"Understood. Now put Quinn back on the line and tell him to take me off speaker."

The phone made a sound, like it was being passed from one person to another, and then Quinn said, "Okay. I'm walking into the other room." What he didn't say, *Away from these nutjobs.*

He didn't need to say it; it was implied by his tone. That also had me smiling.

"You all set for this weekend?" I asked again. "Everyone still coming?"

"Yes. We'll all be there. We're leaving Chicago early, should arrive before ten. Betty made the arrangements for transportation from the airport, so we'll meet you at The Langham."

"Good. That's good." I knew Kat was looking forward to seeing her friends.

They'd offered to come out this past weekend, but with me recovering from a concussion and Kat freaking out about me recovering from a concussion, it wasn't a good time. Also not a good time, Kat not letting me do anything for the past few days other than stay in bed—without her—and rest.

Man, I fucking hated resting. I'd made up my mind, I was never going to retire. Resting was for the dead.

"And you're bringing Wally? How is he?" My eyes sought out the guy in the park again, he was still sitting on the bench talking on his phone.

"Yes, we're bringing Wally. He's good. I think Sandra and Alex are going to get a dog."

"Hey. That's great."

"Yeah." Quinn cleared his throat again. "So, listen, I don't have any new information on Seamus. He's disappeared."

"Disappeared." I closed my eyes, but then quickly reopened them when my balance went wonky on the treadmill. "How is that possible?"

"Alex tracked him as far as Harvard Street. He was on foot. And then he passed into a shadow. He never came out. Our people there haven't seen him since."

"Okay. Fine. I guess . . ." I shook my head, lifting my hand to grip the handle at my side. "I guess that makes sense. No one knows Boston better than him. If he wants to be lost, he'll be lost. Tell me, what's going on with Kat's cousin? Any new movement there?"

"Yes. Did you know Kat sent Janie some financial reports? From Caravel?"

"Yeah. Kat mentioned something about it."

Despite my protests that I was fine, Kat hadn't gone into work until just yesterday. At first, when I'd been taken to the hospital and forced to stay overnight so they could *observe me* or some bullshit, she'd slept in the chair next to my bed. She wouldn't lay with me because she didn't want to jostle my head, she'd said. Then, when I was released, she'd worked from the penthouse at The Langham.

Even worse—not to sound like an asshole ingrate—my ma had taken the last few days off work and stayed with us in the penthouse. Me on one side of the suite, Kat on the other—in a different bedroom—and my ma in the bedroom between us. I didn't know how it was possible, but we'd had less privacy in the penthouse than we'd had at my mother's house. Go figure.

As soon as Kat made it into Caravel on Monday, she'd sent Janie the financial reports. She was still working on getting her hands on the full list of Caravel's drug portfolio. It was taking a while to get the list since the folks in operations were being dickheads (my words, not hers).

I knew all this because that's all we'd been able to discuss, more or less, since my mom was always close by, keeping an eye on me, making sure I didn't do anything *strenuous*. She felt guilty about telling me to make nice with Seamus. That was obvious. She didn't need to, but she did. So she tried to take care of me.

But her guilt had kept me from second base with my wife.

For five days.

We hadn't done anything but kiss like siblings for five fucking days.

But anyway, back to now and Quinn and the financial reports.

"Janie thinks she found something, but she needs more time," he said. "She's hoping to have answers before Friday."

"Anything you can tell me now?"

"I don't really know. She said something about Caravel buying up a bunch of smaller laboratories and companies, starting around the time Caleb Tyson became CEO. She seemed to think this was significant as the source for the extra money."

"What about Caleb's empty bank accounts? Does she have any idea what happened there?"

"No. *Janie* doesn't . . . ." Quinn sounded like he wanted to say more.

"What is it?"

"Marie knows that Kat asked Janie to help."

I waited for him to continue. He didn't. "So?"

"So, Marie was talking to her boyfriend, Matt, about how Kat has concerns with Caravel, but Marie obviously doesn't know the specifics. And you know how Matt is into artificial intelligence stuff?"

"Not really." I didn't know Matt well. I'd only met him once, at the hospital when Janie and Quinn's, and Fiona and Greg's babies had been born.

"He's a big deal in the field, so he knows all this stuff about robotics and all the main players in the industry."

"And?"

"Matt went to school with an AI guy who ended up at Caravel as a research manager after grad school, working on ocular implants that use AI to help people see. It's risky, and Matt said this guy had a lot of difficulty getting approvals for the bench research when he worked at Caravel."

"What's bench research?"

"In this case, I think it means he was using animals before he could use humans. This ocular implant could be a game changer for people who have been born blind, and this guy, Dr. Branson, was let go from Caravel last year. Research and development money in his department was cut back."

"When last year?"

"May."

That caught my interest. Caleb had cashed in his stocks in April.

Quinn continued. "This is the strange part: Dr. Branson received a bunch of money right after he was let go—I mean, he received funding *the very next day*—to continue the research."

"That is strange. Where is he? Is he still in Boston?" Maybe I could stop by his research facility and take a look around.

"No. He's no longer in the US. He was set up with a laboratory and clinical facility in St. Kitts."

I searched my mediocre knowledge of world geography and came up empty. "Where is that?"

"It's a Caribbean island. Janie thinks it makes sense for Dr. Branson to move his research to a small Caribbean island if he was having trouble getting approval from the Food and Drug Administration. Janie says these small islands usually don't have the same 'ethical treatment of human subjects' requirements that the US and other developed nations have."

"You're saying this Dr. Branson moved to a poor country so he could do research on poor people without having to worry about the FDA stopping him?"

Quinn sighed. "That's what it sounds like."

"This is some Dr. Frankenstein shit. So, where did Dr. Branson get the money? I mean, he'd need a lot of money, right?"

"Matt doesn't know. Yet."

"Matt can ask though, right? Is he close with Dr. Frankenstein?" I didn't know how I wanted Quinn to answer this question. On the one hand, if Matt was close with Dr. Frankenstein, I would need to rethink my approval of his relationship with Marie. Marie was good people. She was the best people. She deserved the best kind of person. Exploiting poor people to circumvent the law wasn't cool.

On the other hand, if Matt wasn't close with the guy, then we might not get any answers out of him.

"Matt said he'd ask, but that he and Dr. Branson never got along. He said the guy was always doing everything for the wrong reasons."

"Wrong reasons?"

"Money. Fame. Power."

I grunted. "Sounds like Caleb."

"So, that's it. We have people on Caleb Tyson, watching his movements since you asked for the tail last Thursday, but so far nothing out of the ordinary."

"What's out of the ordinary for a guy like that? Drinking O negative virgin blood instead of B positive?"

Quinn made a small sound, like a laugh. "So far he's gone home, to work, to a few nice restaurants, to the marina in Duxbury. That's it. Alex is running communications surveillance. So far, nothing interesting."

By "communications surveillance," Quinn meant Alex had tapped his phone, hacked his computers and email.

The sound of the penthouse door opening had me halting the treadmill and stepping off. "Oh shit, my mom's back. I gotta go." I strained to listen for her footsteps and whispered, "Message me if Caleb does anything I need to know about or if Seamus resurfaces."

Not waiting for his response, I hung up, walking as quietly as I could to the big chair by the window.

And yes, I know I'm a thirty-something guy who is afraid of his mom's wrath. In my humble opinion, I believe that means she raised me right. Even as an adult, and speaking in general terms, if you're not just a little bit afraid of letting down one or both of your parents, then you must've had shitty parents.

I'm not talking about paralyzing fear—paralyzing fear also means shitty parents—I'm talking about a sliver of worry, a shard of concern. Take my parents, for example. I couldn't care less what my pop thought. He was a shitty parent.

But my ma? That woman had my respect.

Picking up the book I'd left on the side table, *What If?* by Randall Munroe, I snuck a glance out the window at the park before I pretended that I'd been reading the whole time she'd been gone. The guy I'd been watching earlier wasn't there, but clearly my obsessive paranoia was still alive and kicking.

I needed to get it under control, and I would. This wasn't my first concussion, I knew what to expect. I'd be agitated, moody, and paranoid for a few days. Then I'd be much better at the end of a week. By one month, I'd be completely back to normal.

A soft knock sounded and the door slowly swung open. I braced myself for my ma, for her fussing and kissing and cod liver oil, which she believed cured everything but really just gave me the burps. Like I said, she felt guilty.

When I looked up, Kat stood in the doorway.

"Kit-Kat."

"Dan the Security Man." She leaned against the doorframe, her hands behind her back, looking ten kinds of beautiful and, as always, impeccably put together.

Except this time, her clothes looked different. Expensive. *Really* expensive. Gone were her khaki pants with iron creases down the front, brown loafers, white dress shirts, and cardigans in different colors. Instead, she wore a dark blue dress buttoned up the front with pearl buttons, from her neck to her knees, matching blue shoes, and more pearls at her ears and wrist.

Also, as always, I found myself daydreaming about how it would be to disorder the order. Unbutton her dress, kiss off her lipstick, unhook her bra, and fill my hands and mouth with her body and taste.

Kat was twenty-five. Looking the way she did now, meticulously sophisticated, I wouldn't have been able to place her age if I didn't already know. My neck itched, but not because I was feeling guilty. It was the gang tattoos that I wanted to scratch; they felt like dirt on my skin.

I ignored the impulse.

"You're back early," I said. The clock by the bed told me it was only 3:30 PM. God, it was good to see her.

"I thought I'd work from here for a while. How are you?"

I didn't say, *Bored. Missing you. Horny. Missing you. Paranoid. Missing you. In pain. Missing you.*

Instead, opting for, "Well-rested."

Her gaze narrowed, like she didn't believe me.

I listened for a minute. "Ma with you?"

My mother had been gone for almost a half hour after receiving a call from the hotel about something or other, which was why I'd called Quinn and jumped on the treadmill.

"She's getting a massage."

I lifted an eyebrow at that. "A massage?" My whole life, I'd never known my mom to get a massage.

Kat nodded. "And then a facial, pedicure, manicure, body glow scrub, haircut, and blowout."

"Blowout?" Now I lifted both my eyebrows.

She took seven steps into the room. "It's where they use a blow dryer to dry and style your hair."

"Huh." *How about that.* Definitely not what I was thinking.

"What did you think a blowout was?" Kat sat on the edge of the mattress, facing me, and slipped off her shoes.

"Never mind." I stared at her bare feet, my eyes sliding to her calves, knees, and stopping at the hem of her dress. I probably shouldn't admit what I thought a blowout was; plus, we had more important things to discuss. "How long will all that take?"

I watched as she neatly tucked her dark blue heels under the bed, toes in; a small smile on her lips. "A few hours."

A few hours?

A few hours!

Thank you, whoever the patron saint of getting lucky is, assuming there was a patron saint of getting lucky. Maybe it was Saint Jude. That guy was the patron saint of lost causes, which was sometimes the same thing.

I knew we wouldn't be going all the way. We were still on orgasm lockdown, and that was perfectly fine. But I missed the feel of her, her skin, the heat of her body, the way she moved when she was mindless and relaxed with arousal. All I needed was some of that and I'd be happy.

And some listening to her speak. And some making her laugh. And some making her sigh.

Yep. That's what I needed. Just all those things.

So I returned my book to the side table and stood. "Oh. Really?"

"Yes. Really." She also stood, her hands clasped behind her back.

The smile was gone, and in its place was a wide-eyed stare that looked suddenly nervous. I didn't cross to her, figuring she'd be less anxious if she came to me.

"Whatever shall we do?" I tapped my chin with my index finger, keeping my voice light.

She cracked a small grin at that, releasing a nervous laugh and shrugged. "I guess we'll think of something."

Now she was staring again. And not moving.

Okay.

I took a small step forward, testing the waters. She took a small step forward. I took a larger step forward, and she did as well. She swallowed like swallowing wasn't easy, and I noticed her hands were now at her sides, balled into fists.

Hmm.

"How was your day?" I asked, watching her carefully. Today had been her second day going into the office. Caleb had been there both days, but when she got home yesterday she'd said that she hadn't seen him. That was good. I hoped it was a sign he'd planned to back off, but I didn't believe for one minute he was going to.

Which was why our guys Stan and Nicolas had flown out from Chicago last Friday, taking turns as her shadow. Anywhere Kat went outside of the penthouse, she had a full complement of security, but either Stan or Nicolas never left her side. They were the two guys I trusted the most and they'd be with her until I staffed a permanent team and vetted everyone to my satisfaction.

"My day was fine." Her attention dropped to the T-shirt I was wearing and she took a deep breath. "How was your day?"

"Boring." Impatient, I closed the space between us in four steps and bent to kiss her neck.

Kat tilted her head to the side, giving me more access. Fuck, she smelled good, felt amazing, and tasted even better.

"How do you feel?" she asked.

"With my hands." I slid them down her back to her ass, rubbing her backside over the silky fabric of her midnight-colored dress, lifting the skirt slowly.

She huffed a laugh and I felt her smile against my cheek. "I mean, how is your head? And your ribs? Are you still sore?"

"A little." I lifted my fingers to her dress's buttons and unfastened the first, then the second, then the third, watching my progress and seeing she was wearing another bra that clasped in the front.

Fuck, I love this woman.

Automatically, I tensed at the thought and quickly rejected it.

I mean, I did love her. Just like I loved my fellow man and woman. I cared about her *a lot*. But I didn't *love* her. It was too soon, way too soon, for any of those kinds of thoughts. Maybe next year, or the year after, when things between us had settled to a predictable routine, then we could look at each other, set some time aside, and have the discussion.

But not now. Things were too good to muddy the waters with that kind of pressure.

Meanwhile, her hands lifted like she was going to wrap her arms around my neck, but flinched them away at the last minute. Then they lifted like she was going to place her fingers on my chest, but—again—stopped. Her hands fell back to her sides.

I bent to kiss the swell of her breast, wrapping an arm around her waist and groaning as I pulled down the cup of a lacy bra, exposing her sweet nipple.

I sucked on it.

Tongued it.

Licked it.

But then, I stopped.

Because her body was tense. *She* was tense. And when I glanced at her hands, they were once more balled into fists at her sides.

Fuck a duck.

I sighed, louder than I'd intended, and shook my head. She was not turned on and she was not relaxed. Straightening slowly, I righted her bra and brought together the edges of her dress. The wind had left my sails. Because I was an asshole.

I wasn't in the mood to take things slow and be careful with her. I didn't want to do the work necessary to seduce her, keep her preoccupied so she wouldn't tense up or freak out. My brain hurt. Thinking hurt. I didn't want to—I couldn't—think that hard, stay one step ahead, make sure with every touch she was enjoying herself.

I wanted her to relax, but, in summary, I didn't want this to be work.

Leaning away, I let my hands drop and gave her a tight smile. "So . . . Want to play Monopoly?"

She blinked up at me, bewildered. "What?"

"Or checkers?"

Kat, looking absolutely gorgeous, stared at me, giving me the sense she couldn't figure out if I was joking or not. "Right now?"

"Look," I shook my head, suddenly feeling like maybe the doctors were right, maybe I did need a rest. "You know how I feel about you, how badly I want you, right?"

She didn't nod, or speak, or give me any outward sign of her thoughts. She just continued staring at me like I was confusing her, or she was having trouble making sense of my words.

So I kept talking. "You're tense. Really, really tense. I want you, obviously, so much I can't think straight. Which means I need to help you relax and enjoy yourself. I want to make your pleasure my priority. Believe me, it's super high on my priority list. But right now, I'm irritable. Everything irritates me. The color of this carpet irritates me. So, maybe . . ." *I can't fucking believe I'm saying this,* "Maybe we should hold off on doing anything until I'm more myself."

She stared at me for a long moment, then her gaze fell away to the irritatingly colored carpet as she took a step back. Then she breathed out, squeezing her eyes shut.

"I'm sorry," she said, shaking her head, her eyes still closed. Rubbing her forehead, she took another step back. "You're right, I'm tense. I—I couldn't stop thinking about your concussion, and your bruised ribs. I was worried I would hurt you."

"Oh." I frowned at that and felt like a royal dickwad. Sir Dan, his majestic highness of dickery.

Here I was thinking about myself, and here she was worried about me. Maybe I did need to send a prayer to Saint Jude, *that I get my head out of my ass.*

"Oh. Well—"

She cut me off, "But you're right. I'm being selfish."

"No, no—"

"You're recovering from a brain injury."

"Well, yeah. I mean, technically that's true. But—"

"And I can't—I'm incapable of relaxing like a normal person, even in the best of circumstances. I have to be *coaxed* into enjoying myself."

My eyes narrowed on her, because I didn't find that statement to be entirely accurate. "I don't think that's true."

I'd never coaxed her, and I would never coax her. Ever.

Seduction, making an effort, wasn't the same thing as *coaxing.*

Coaxing was trying to convince a person to do something they didn't want to do. If I thought Kat didn't want me, if I thought she wasn't as invested or—and just keeping it real here—hungry to the point of starving to be with me as I was with her, I would never try to convince her otherwise.

Now before you think this is me being unselfish and self-sacrificing, it's not. It's definitely, definitely not. This is me being consistently selfish and self-centered.

I'd seen firsthand how wanting a person who didn't want you, or only wants you for the wrong reasons, leads to devastation and heartbreak. More than anything in my life, I never wanted that for myself. So if I thought for one second the intensity of her desire for me was less than my desire for her, there'd be no coaxing.

I'd be out.

Things between us would be over.

Bam.

Just like that.

I'd promised myself the moment my dad walked out the door, I would *never* be the one left behind with a broken heart. Never going to happen.

Kat exhaled another frustrated breath and continued like she hadn't heard me, "And that's not fair to you. You're healing, and now is not the time for me to thrust my issues upon you."

"Hey, I'm not opposed to thrusting."

Kat laughed lightly, but her eyes told me she was frustrated with herself. "I'm sorry."

"Stop apologizing. Don't let this bring you down. I'm out of it, cranky, paranoid. There's nothing for you to be sorry for."

She pressed her lips together, as though to physically stop herself from apologizing again, and she turned like she was going to leave. I caught her by the wrist.

"Wait a minute, wait." I gently pulled on her arm until she faced me. "Right now, I need time to get better. That's true. But, I guarantee you," bringing her closer, I tucked her hair behind her ear, allowing my fingers to trail along the soft skin of her jaw and neck, "in a few days, when I'm better, it'll be seduction city."

Kat was shaking her head again. "You shouldn't *have to* seduce me. You deserve—"

"Hey." I tugged her forward, kissing her, licking her lips and then deepening the kiss because I wanted to, because I could, and because I knew she liked it.

I felt her relax slowly as the kiss turned from seconds to minutes, her hands came to my shoulders with a light touch, and she kissed me back with all the intensity I'd been craving.

When I was finished, and not a moment before, I leaned back again. This time keeping her close, and lowering my voice to a rumble. "Don't tell me what to do."

"You don't want me to be bossy?" she asked. I was pleased to see the worry behind her eyes was gone, replaced with lightness and teasing. I was also pleased to see her lipstick was smudged and her dress was still open, disheveled.

I tilted my head back and forth as though considering. "Okay. Feel free to tell me what to do." I kissed her nose, and then whispered against her lips, "But never tell me what I deserve, unless it's you."

CHAPTER TWENTY-FIVE

Patent: "A set of exclusive rights granted by a sovereign state to an inventor or assignee for a limited period of time in exchange for detailed public disclosure of an invention."

Wex Legal Dictionary

Drug patents generally last about 20 years from the date of application. Prescription drug patents usually have an exclusivity period that can last 180 days to 7 years.

FDA.gov

Kat

J ANIE TEXTED ME late Friday afternoon.

Janie: *I figured out how Caravel is making record profits. Do you want to talk now? Or have this discussion in person?*

Janie and I had spoken earlier in the week in vague terms about her ideas, but she seemed reluctant to commit to any one theory. She wanted time to thoroughly research both the reports I'd sent and news articles over the last three years specifically relating to acquisitions made by Caravel.

Presently, I was in a meeting with no end in sight, but I was acutely interested in the topic being discussed. Therefore, I returned her text rather than excusing myself from the conference room.

Kat: *Can you call Dan? I'll see him for dinner, he'll fill me in.*

Placing my phone on my lap, I gave my attention to the senior vice-president of Research and Development, currently detailing the lack of funding for major divisions within his purview. I was taking notes, but said nothing. I'd dropped into the meeting unannounced, like all the other random R&D meetings I'd attended since Monday. My goal had been to observe, hoping to get a sense of Caravel's drug discovery agenda.

So far, it seemed like Caravel's current agenda—as mapped out by Caleb—was to maintain the status quo.

Of the meetings I'd attended thus far, this man was giving me the most valuable and comprehensive cataloguing of cuts made to R&D I'd encountered. Additionally, this cataloguing was information no one else had been willing to share with me despite my numerous—official—requests.

I didn't doubt for a moment that Caleb was responsible for the lack of responsiveness by division leaders; Caleb was the CEO after all. As it currently stood, I didn't have voting rights for my own shares, so what motivation did they have to respond to my requests?

However, this vice-president seemed to be at his wit's end. Perhaps he was so frustrated with my cousin, the man was willing to *take one for the team*, as it were. He wasn't directing his comments to me explicitly, but it was clear the man had gone off-script because I was present, implying that severe cutbacks to drug discovery had damaged Caravel's long-term viability.

I agreed with the senior vice-president. If we weren't researching and developing, then what were we doing? What was the point?

Another twenty minutes or so passed, maybe longer. The subject turned to adverse event reporting to the FDA and EMEA. The cell phone on my thigh buzzed, Dan's name flashing across the screen, and my heart gave a flutter and a twist. As quietly and unobtrusively as possible, I left the room, Stan following me out and closing the door carefully behind us.

I accepted the call and brought my phone to my ear. "Hello?"

"Hey. It's me. I'm almost there and I'm bringing dinner, for Stan too."

"Thank you." I glanced over my shoulder to Stan and tilted my head down the long hall which would lead us to the elevator. "We're on our way back to my office and will meet you there."

"Sounds good." I heard the turn indicator click on in his car. "Pulling into the parking garage. Hey, any trouble from Tiny Satan today?"

"No. I haven't seen him." I looked to Stan again and he nodded, indicating he hadn't seen Caleb either.

"Hmm. . ."

"What?"

"It's just, you haven't seen him all week."

"Yes, but he's made his presence known by impeding through subterfuge any and all attempts to gather information. The only way I've been able to get a picture of what's going on here is to attend division meetings unannounced."

"Hmm . . ."

"What? What does *Hmm* mean?"

"He hasn't tried to contact you. He's not taunting you. Stopping the flow of information seems mild in comparison to trying to lock you away. We know he's there, in town, showing up to work every day. Why isn't he trying to torture you? What's he waiting for?"

"Maybe he's given up." Even as I said the words I knew they were a long shot.

"You know that's not true. He's biding his time, waiting . . ." Dan didn't finish his thought. I listened as the light squeaking of tires taking a sharp turn on cement sounded from his side of the call. "Never mind. Listen, I'll see you soon. Like, five minutes soon."

"Sounds good."

We exchanged our goodbyes, and as the call ended, I spotted a few people walking down the hall, moving toward us. Stan shifted to my left and placed his hand on my back, inserting himself between me and the approaching group. This was the type of thing I used to hate when I was a teenager, when my assigned security detail would hover, stand between me and other people.

But now, with Stan, who I knew and liked, I found myself not really noticing enough to care.

I recognized one of the cluster from her picture—Dr. Carlyle—a member of R&D from Dr. Branson's old group, before he'd been downsized. Dr. Branson was the scientist who'd been let go by Caleb's special order and then, according to Marie and Matt, had immediately received funding from some unknown source to continue his work on a small island in the Caribbean.

I'd made it a point to look up Dr. Branson and his team after speaking with Janie this past Wednesday about Marie and Matt's information.

Placing my hand on Stan's arm, I leaned toward him. "Just a second. I want to speak to this woman."

He nodded, looking tense and taking a step back to give me room.

"Excuse me, Dr. Carlyle?" I moved to intercept the woman, offering my hand. "Hi. I'm Kathleen Caravel-Tyson."

The whole group stopped, their eyes going wide as they looked between me and their colleague.

For her part, she seemed mildly surprised, but not awestruck. That was too bad. I would have preferred her to be awestruck.

"Uh, hello. Nice to meet you." She accepted my handshake, giving me a tight smile.

"Can I speak to you for a moment? I'm interested in the work you've been doing on ocular AI. I'm on my way to the elevator and I have,"—I glanced at my cell without really noticing the time—"I have five minutes. I'm pushing the board to double funding for the next six quarters and I'm looking for flagship projects. I'd like your thoughts on the focus of R&D dollars moving forward."

She nodded, now looking more surprised and maybe a little dazed. "Yes. Absolutely."

Stepping away from her colleagues, she glanced to Stan—who stared back at her, expressionless—then came to my side.

"Please," I motioned for her to walk with me, "give me some background on your current project."

Dr. Carlyle glanced at me nervously. "I—since we only have five minutes, I'd prefer to discuss your plans for the new R&D dollars."

"You don't think your current project is worthy of expanded funding?" I searched my memory, struggling to remember to which project she'd been assigned after Dr. Branson's exit.

"No. Currently, I'm working with the ophthalmological regulatory team on obtaining an orphan drug status for a new generic we've acquired. It's pretty straightforward and doesn't require expanded funding, or investigation."

I slowed my steps, wanting to prolong the conversation in order to ask her about Dr. Branson. I noted she seemed to be discouraged by her new assignment.

"Well then, where would you like to focus your energy moving forward? What areas of research have been underfunded—or have lost funding—that, in your estimation, are worthy of investment?" I pasted a calm smile on my features, hoping my method of questioning wasn't too obvious.

Dr. Carlyle glanced at the elevators a few feet away and stopped, turning toward me. "We had a team dedicated to ocular implants last year that was shut down without warning, even though our early results were promising."

Bingo.

"Tell me more." I crossed my arms, studying her.

She proceeded to describe in painfully specific scientific detail Dr.

Branson's ocular AI project. My heart quickened as she spoke and I tried to keep up. The truth was, I didn't understand most of what she was saying, each word contained more syllables and Latin roots than the last.

Her voice raised suddenly—not to a shout, but enough that I could tell she was agitated—and she launched into a tirade, using phrases like, "evidentiary power analysis," and "split-tailed T-tests." I did my best to look thoughtful and not lost, reminding myself that scientists often spoke a different language. Likewise, they usually had no idea that most people didn't know what continuous variables were in reference to a confidence interval estimate.

I had a vague idea, and only because I'd taken research methods last semester on accident.

But then, she said, "The point is, the project was misrepresented. I don't know how or why, but the results our research manager shared with the executive group were completely misleading. He'd left out—"

"Misleading? Why would your research manager mislead the executive group? What was his name?"

"Dr. Branson was the research manager and," she shook her head, looking exasperated, "I don't know. He left out the latest trial information, making it look like we'd stalled and made no progress in the last six months, when in fact, our—"

"Dr. Branson? Which group does he manage now?"

She grimaced. "He left. He was downsized last year."

"Hmm . . ." I nodded thoughtfully. Very, very thoughtfully. "Do you think you can reach out to him? See if he'll speak to me?"

Dr. Carlyle huffed impatiently. "Maybe. But, honestly, he's not critical to the project. I was the PI with the FDA. Actually, co-PI with Dr. Barelvi. We worked with legal to ensure Caravel filed the patent before the project was dropped."

Despite my efforts to hide my surprise, my mouth parted and I blinked at the woman.

If Caravel held the patent, then what the heck was Dr. Branson doing in the Caribbean?

"Could you—are you sure Caravel holds the patent?"

"Yes," she nodded. "Dr. Barelvi and I did the legwork with legal."

"Not Dr. Branson?"

"No." Her hands came to her hips and she gave me a skeptical once-over. "Dr. Branson was only our research manager. It wasn't his research."

CHAPTER TWENTY-SIX

Fiduciary: "An individual in whom another has placed the utmost trust and confidence to manage and protect property or money. The relationship wherein one person has an obligation to act for another's benefit."

Wex Legal Dictionary

Example of a fiduciary: *The CEO of a company is a fiduciary for their company.*

Kat

"DAN IS BRINGING you dinner."

"Good," Stan grumbled, "I'm starving."

I gave him a small smile from where I leaned against the back wall of the elevator. My feet hurt.

We were finally on our way to my office. Stan had texted Dan to let him know we'd be running late. The conversation with Dr. Carlyle had taken more than thirty minutes. I'd learned quite a lot.

"You could've said something if you were so hungry. I could've cut short my discussion with Dr. Carlyle."

He shrugged as the doors opened to the executive level. "No biggie."

We exited the elevator together. "Starving is no biggie?"

He shrugged again, which wasn't a surprise since Stan shrugged a lot, and gave me a rueful grin. "I'm always starving."

"Should I carry food with me?" I teased, scanning my card and reaching for the door handle to my office, which also happened to be my father's old office and the biggest office in the building.

Stan seemed to consider this as he held the door open for me to precede him. "I carry nuts in my pocket."

I was about to suggest I carry a pizza in my purse when Dan's voice interrupted, "Stan, please stop telling my wife where you keep your nuts."

Stan, standing in the doorway, laugh-snorted. "Good one."

Dan, standing next to the conference table, grabbed one of the three plastic bags on the surface and walked to me, a welcoming smile on his features. He brushed a soft kiss against my lips, and my body sighed.

That's right. I experienced a full-body sigh at the sight of him. Everything relaxing, stilling, and yet, at the same time, tensing with anticipatory restlessness. And at the end of the sigh was a single whispered thought.

I love him.

Of course I loved him. He made it so easy.

Gazing and smiling into my eyes, Dan held the bag extended toward his friend. "Get out of here."

"Sure thing." Stan snatched the takeout and disappeared through the door, leaving Dan and I together. Alone. *Yay!*

"How are you feeling?" I asked, enjoying his closeness even though we weren't touching.

"Good. Better."

My smile grew at his answer and relief for him had my body sighing again.

Dan had been in a perpetual bad mood for most of the week, quieter than usual, less prone to smiles and jokes, easily confused, and —sadly—less prone to touching or kissing me. I completely understood. He needed time and space to heal, and I wanted to do everything I could to support him. But seeing how frustrated and unhappy he'd been concerned me.

Yesterday had been better than the previous days. When I arrived at the penthouse and upon his suggestion, we'd curled up on the couch and watched a movie. He'd fallen asleep a half hour into it, so I covered him with a blanket and let him sleep. He'd still been on the couch this morning when I departed for work at 7:30 AM.

"You weren't up yet when I left."

"I slept in, didn't wake up until noon." He laughed at himself, his gaze moving over my face in that way, giving me the impression that he really, really liked looking at me.

"Wow. That's—"

"Something like fourteen hours." Dan's hand slid down my arm until our fingers met. "Are you hungry?"

"Actually, no. Not yet." I wanted to see if I could find the patent information for Dr. Carlyle's project. For that matter, I wanted to fill Dan in on what I'd discovered. "But you should eat if you're hungry."

"Nah. Not really. Ma and I had a late lunch. Do you want me to horrify you with her latest plans for dinner on Sunday?"

I chuckled, allowing him to lead me toward the couch in front of the window.

Since my knitting group and their significant others were flying in for a visit this weekend, Dan's mom had decided to throw a "small family get-together" on Sunday as a way to celebrate our recent marriage. According to Dan, this meant at least fifty to a hundred people, depending on who was working, who was in town, and who was in jail.

"You make it sound like meeting your family is the same as being burned at the stake."

"Except, being burned at the stake is less uncomfortable." He motioned for me to take a seat, and then claimed the spot next to mine, his arm along the back of the sofa, his attention on my hair. "And the people are nicer."

I shook my head at his antics. "Before we talk about Sunday I wanted to check, did Janie call you?"

"Not today."

"Ah, okay. She texted me earlier and I told her to call you. And I need to tell you about a conversation I had just now with one of Caravel's R&D investigators."

"Sure." He fiddled with my hair, twining it around his fingers. "Go for it."

I described my conversation with Dr. Carlyle, pleased to see he looked just as confused as I felt when I got to the part about Caravel holding the patent to the ocular AI device.

"Are you sure?"

"I don't know why she would lie." I crossed my legs, bringing myself closer to Dan. "It should be easy enough to verify."

"Huh." He stared off into space. "Then what is that guy, Dr. Branson, doing in the Caribbean?"

"I don't know." I also stared off into space.

Dan stood abruptly and crossed to my computer. He appeared distracted, still lost in thought as he sat behind my desk.

"What's your password?"

"You want me to give you my password?" I shook my head at him, trying to look serious. "I was told by tech support here never to give out my password."

He rolled his eyes, a reluctant smile on his lips. "Fine. You type it in."

I crossed to him, coming to stand behind the desk so I could type in my password. But mostly, it was an excuse to lean forward across and in front of him, my breast brushing against his shoulder and arm, my behind in the air. Straightening once the computer logged in—half-leaning, half-sitting on the surface of the desk—I smiled sweetly at his expression.

His eyes were narrowed, and hot. "You're good at that."

"What?"

"You know what."

I rolled my lips between my teeth so my smile wouldn't spread and crossed my arms. "What's the plan? What are you looking for?"

"Nothing. I'm going to let Alex look for it." Dan navigated to his Cypher Systems email account and typed out a message, quickly summarizing all I'd learned from Dr. Carlyle and asking Alex to determine who held the patent.

When we were both satisfied, he hit send and leaned back in my chair, once again his eyes losing focus as though he were deep in thought.

I took the opportunity to study him, the color of his cheeks, nose, and forehead; how, even though he was thinking, he felt present in a way that had been lacking for the last week. He wore one of his sleek suits, dark blue, with a vest. His forest green and gold silk tie made his eyes look hazel.

He looked better.

He seemed better.

A lot better.

Earlier in the week, I'd made the mistake of rushing things. I'd arranged for his mother to have a spa day. I'd caught him sending me smoldering looks over the weekend and I thought perhaps a little TKC —touching, kissing, and cuddling—would help.

Plus, I'd missed him. Desperately.

But it was too early.

Yes, his mouth had been on my breast, doing wonderful things that should have felt wonderful, and all I'd felt was frantic, cold detachment. He was still in pain from his concussion and bruised ribs, I realized this as soon as we'd begun kissing, but I didn't know what to do. I tried to relax. I couldn't. I was worried for him and wasn't able to turn my brain off, couldn't disengage enough to feel anything.

Just like old times.

Therefore, other than a few tender kisses, all of which had inspired more heat and longing than my rushed attempt at intimacy, we hadn't been physical since.

The failure had been frustrating, but I did my best to treat the incident like a small setback, one that wasn't likely to repeat. I mean, how often would he have a concussion?

He'd needed to heal.

I'd needed to be patient.

But now . . .

Gone were the dark circles beneath his eyes, the pale sheen to his skin, the thin quality to his lips, and the ever present frown at his forehead. They'd been fading by degrees, slowly. But today, he looked great. So great. So, so, so great. Almost his old self.

His lips weren't at all thin. They were back to their full, gorgeous, luscious, lickable, biteable normal. And I couldn't help but wish he'd unbutton me, like he'd done on Tuesday, and brush those lips over my exposed skin. Unclasp my bra, open my dress, lay me back on the desk and—

"Kat?"

"Hmm?" I blinked at him. Or rather, I blinked his eyes back into focus.

"Did you hear what I said?"

"No. Sorry." Stirring, I forced myself to stop thinking about his lips. "What where you saying?"

He watched me, his gaze intense, probing, as though he were trying to peer inside my brain and discover my most recent thoughts. My neck heated. I said nothing, determined not to rush him again. If he wanted me, he'd have to make the first move.

The barest of smiles tugged his mouth to the side and his eyelids drooped over eyes now darker, hot with intent.

Oh. Well. Okay.

Don't let yourself get too excited.

"Did you know . . ." he paused, his gaze dropping to the front of my dress, and then slowly climbing up to my lips. "I once asked Janie if she thought you'd leave your job at Foster? Come and work for me, as my Betty, at Cypher Systems?"

"You did?" By "my Betty" I knew he was referring to Quinn's longtime executive assistant. Betty was the glue that held that place together, the center of the clock around which everything revolved. She made it all happen, and she did so wearing pearls and a smile.

"Yeah." He leaned back further in my office chair, his hands behind his head.

"Why didn't you?"

"Janie said they needed you too much. That the place would fall apart if you left."

"Well," I shrugged, "I'm gone now. I turned in my notice last Friday."

"Yeah. But I think that's not the only reason she advised me against it."

"Oh? Why else?"

He shrugged lazily, his hands still behind his head, regarding me evenly. "I think she was worried about me."

A little spike of excitement shivered down my spine. "How so?"

Dan paused for a moment, thinking. "Janie didn't know Quinn was her boss until after they got together."

"Yes. I remember when she found out." The hot, spiky sensation lingered, likely because he was still looking at me like I was dessert; I gave into the urge to rub the gathering heat at the back of my neck. "And he wasn't her boss, he was her boss's boss." I gave Dan a pointed look, remembering how upset Janie had been.

"Yeah. And I think it's always kinda pissed her off, that he was her boss—excuse me, her *boss's* boss— and he was making the moves on her."

"But he made moves on her *before* he was her boss."

"And he continued making moves on her even after she was hired. I think that's why she didn't want you working for me." Dan turned in the swivel seat, coming forward and straightening, his hands dropping to his lap as his knee brushed mine.

The look in his eyes sent warmth to my abdomen, lower, the beginnings of a pulsing ache.

"She was worried you'd make a move on me? If you were my boss?" I lifted an eyebrow at him, fighting the instinct to regulate my breathing.

So many thoughts.

But I wouldn't regulate my breathing.

I needed to surrender. I needed to pant if I wanted to pant. I needed to moan if I wanted to moan. I needed to give myself over to sensation and not worry about looking or sounding silly, or disappointing him. I needed to enjoy myself, because I wanted to very, very badly.

And I needed to love him, own it and feel it and not worry. I needed to trust him, that he loved me, that he wouldn't bring me to this edge and let me fall by myself.

He loved me and I loved him and it was time to surrender.

Surrender.

Dan leaned forward, sliding his large hand around my leg, his fingers just below the hem of my skirt at the back of my knee, sending pinpricks of sensation up my leg. "She was worried I wouldn't make a move."

We traded stares for a moment and my heart increased in tempo. I allowed it to quicken, to race, to speed.

When he spoke next, his voice was deeper, huskier. "Late nights with the boss, working closely together, it would've been torture."

"For you? Or for me?" *Was that my voice?* I sounded breathless.

He flashed a quick grin—there and gone in a second—and he dropped his eyes to my stomach, tugging at my leg. I moved where he guided, until I was standing in front of him, my back to the desk, him sitting before me.

"Maybe we would've found ourselves here, like this." His fingers were on my thighs under my skirt, inching it higher and his eyes followed the upward progress as the lace bands of my stockings were revealed.

My breathing had become excited, erratic, and I didn't care because this was what I wanted and I trusted him.

His fingertips trailed a light touch on the back of my legs as he fingered the lace. Dan encouraged me with a subtle movement to lean my bottom on the desk.

Then he made a sound of disapproval, shaking his head. "Mrs. O'Malley."

Warmth engulfed me, spreading over my skin and unfurling low in my belly. This was roleplay. Dr. Kasai had suggested it to me when I'd spoken with her privately last week. But I hadn't mentioned it to Dan, and I hadn't realized I wanted to do it until just now.

I couldn't think. And I didn't want to.

"Is there something wrong, Mr. O'Malley?" I shivered.

Needing to steady myself, the base of my palms came to the edge of the desk on either side of my legs.

His mouth curved upwards into a smirk, and he nudged my knees wider, his knuckles skimming the bare skin above my thigh-highs on either side of my panties.

"You've been making me work late with no overtime pay."

I frowned, studying him, pulled out of the fantasy for a split second by his words.

You've been making me work late . . . making me . . .

My breath hitched and my eyes widened when I realized what he'd done.

I was the boss.

He was the executive assistant.

"I feel like I deserve something for my efforts," his eyes were on my underwear, where my legs were spread.

He licked his lips.

I felt my body tighten, clench.

But I was unable to speak, so lost was I to the moment, greedily anticipating his next move.

Dan lifted his fingers to hook into the waistband of my underwear, tugging it gently, slowly down until my body was revealed to him. Guiding them down my legs, he encouraged me to step out of my underthings, tucking the lace into the pocket of his jacket. He then straightened, his fingers sliding up my calves to my knees, thighs, higher.

"Sit on the desk, Mrs. O'Malley." Dan's searing gaze flickered to mine, white hot intention piercing me. He pushed me gently backwards, wanting me to sit fully on the desk, then moved his hands to my knees and separated them, spreading me to his gaze, insinuating himself between my legs.

Dan bent forward. He trailed featherlight kisses up my inner thigh, making me pant and squirm and moan. I was making a lot of noise, and maybe I sounded silly, but I didn't care. I trusted him.

"Shh . . ." He quieted me and blew against my exposed body at the same time. I shuddered, my hips tilting automatically, offering myself.

I watched as he licked his lips again, wetting them, and then brushed them against my center, making me whimper.

Damn.

Damn.

Torture.

"You want this?"

I nodded my head, it was a jerky movement, ungraceful. My fingers were in his hair now, urging him closer.

He resisted.

"What do you want?"

"Kiss me," I said, not thinking about it.

He kissed me softly, too softly. I whimpered again, the pulsing ache unbearable.

His fingers slid up my thighs, leaving trails of goosebumps and shivers in their wake. His thumbs came to my center, separating me.

"This is my compensation for all my hard work. I'm going to suck you into my mouth, Mrs. O'Malley," he said quietly, darkly, the sound more rumble than voice, the breath of his words hot against my exposed center. "And then, I'm going to fuck this sweet pussy with my tongue."

All the air left my lungs at the sordid decadence of his words, spikes of pleasure-pain erupting along my spine, arms, and torso. My legs began to shake. But before I could react further, he closed the scant inches between us and did just what he promised.

"Oh God, oh god, oh god." I couldn't think. I didn't know who I was, where I was. All I knew was the feel of his mouth devouring me, hungrily lapping, sucking, his luscious lips slippery against my body.

He groaned, the vibrations making me gasp, and I heard myself say, "I love you, don't stop, I love you."

Somehow, one of my legs had been draped over his shoulder. The other was bent at the knee, the heel of my foot on the edge of the desk, my fingers still in his hair, now grabbing fistfuls and pulling.

I had a fleeting thought. I wondered if I was being too rough, if I were hurting him, if his head had recovered, if his chest gave him pain. I hadn't asked him specifically about his injuries. I'd meant to ask, but I hadn't.

But just as the thought occurred to me, another thought eclipsed it, *You can trust him, he will tell you if you need to stop, just like he's done in the past.*

Then the thought, the worry, was gone. Leaving me lost to every wicked and wonderful sensation caused by his mouth, lips, tongue, and teeth.

I felt myself rushing toward completion, the coiling in my center, the hot, heavy weight of my breasts, the bursting stars behind my eyes.

Preventing this didn't occur to me. Stopping him didn't even enter my mind. One moment I was rocking my hips against his mouth, inelegant curses and grunts spilling from my mouth as I begged him to never stop—wanting it harder, wanting him deeper, wanting him inside me—and then I was sighing his name on sharp cries of complete ecstasy. My body bowed, tensed, pulsed, and I shrieked—yes, *shrieked* —my pleasure.

Unable to keep myself upright under the force of it, I swayed backward, wanting to fall forever.

Dan caught me. Standing abruptly, his strong arm reached around my waist and brought me against him. He held me and I clung to him, my fingers tangled in his jacket, feeling like I'd just run a million miles and was now enclosed in a perfect, Dan-scented cloud of awesome.

It took me a while—a long while—to emerge from the blissful fog. When I did I became aware of three things:

1. Dan was placing light, loving kisses on my neck, jaw, and cheeks, as though he were using his lips to feel my skin.

2. His arms were around me, his hands on my waist and back, and everything about the way he held me felt perfect. Absolutely perfect.

3. While I'd been lost to the frenzy of passion, I'd told Dan that I loved him.

It was this last realization that had me tensing, holding my breath, and wondering who was going to win between my racing heart and mind.

He must've felt the shift in me because his lips stalled on my neck, just behind my ear.

Straightening, his arms loosened so he could lean away and catch my gaze. On his face he wore a small, knowing, satisfied smile, and, apparently, our recent tryst had done nothing to bank the simmering desire in his eyes.

"Hey there, Kat."

I stared at him, my mind calming. My heart also slowed, but each beat reverberated like a drum within me, my blood pumping thick and hot.

"Dan."

"Yeah?" He pushed his fingers into my hair, closing his eyes and bending to place an achingly gentle kiss on my mouth.

"Dan," I sucked in a breath, and then blurted, "I love you."

The words were torn from me, from someplace wild and frenzied, and felt so raw and real that my throat burned.

His eyes opened, blinked, and he gazed at me, as though he found me curious. Or maybe he found what I'd said strange.

"What?"

"I love you." I held fast to his jacket, feeling an odd sort of desperation that he know—right now—that I loved him, that I loved him so much, that he was my love.

His eyebrows pulled low as he stared at me. "Uh . . ." Reaching for my hands, he tried to loosen them, force me to release my death grip on his jacket. "Kat," he laughed lightly, though there was no humor in the sound, more like irritation and bewilderment. "While I appreciate the thought, you don't have to say that."

I shook my head, the desperation that he know becoming a rising tide. "I wouldn't—I wouldn't say it if it weren't true. I lov—"

Dan stepped away, shaking his head firmly. "Okay, okay." Now he looked truly perturbed. "Maybe let's talk about this later? When the last few minutes aren't your most recent memory of me."

As I reached for him again, he stepped out of my radius and to the side. After a brief moment of hesitation, where he continued looking perturbed, he walked around the desk and to the conference table.

"Are you hungry?" His voice was higher than normal. He sounded strained.

And now I was confused. I blinked at him, at his back, because it was the only thing he was giving me.

Shaking my head, I slipped off the desk on to wobbly legs, pushing my skirt back over my hips as I watched him open the plastic bags and withdraw plastic takeaway containers.

"I didn't know which kind you wanted, so I got you both," he said, his voice no longer pitched high. He sounded like himself, just . . . distant.

Wait a minute.

Wait a minute, wait a minute, wait a minute, wait a minute, wait a minute.

He didn't believe me. Why didn't he believe me? Had I done something wrong? What had I done wrong? And if I'd done something wrong, why hadn't he told me?

Dread, like a cold hand, slithered up my spine, threatening to close around my throat. I beat it back.

No. You haven't done anything wrong. You trust him, so trust him.

The desk and most of the room was between us when I lifted my voice to a near shout, "I love you."

He tensed, his shoulders bunching, and he placed his hands on the conference table, leaning against it as his head dropped forward. Dan sighed again. It sounded frustrated.

Then he turned, crossing his arms, his chin lifted, and I was not prepared for the remoteness in his gaze. "You just had your first orgasm without alcohol, right?"

"So?" Mimicking his stance, I also crossed my arms, the desperation that he know I loved him became something else, a cold rock in my stomach gradually heating with anger. "So what?"

He shrugged, giving me a little bullshit smile, like I should connect the dots.

"So what?" I asked again, louder this time, sharper.

His eyes narrowed and his jaw ticked, more distance, more frustration. "So, you're not thinking straight. You're confusing what just happened with something deeper."

I flinched, my mouth falling open. I almost looked down at my chest because I was 99.9% sure there would be a handle to a knife sticking out of it.

"I'm not confused." I shook my head, my words more breath than sound.

"Kat . . ."

"I'm not confusing love with lust. This isn't something that *just* happened. I love you. I'm in love with you, I—"

I stopped myself from saying more because he was shaking his head slowly, stubbornly, his eyes on the carpet. "We'll talk about it later."

A stinging swelling ballooned in my chest, clogging my throat, infecting my nose and eyes as I stared at him. A little voice insisted quietly, *Why are you pushing this? You'll still love him tonight, tomorrow, and the day after. Tell him later. Talk about it later. Convince him later.*

But I quickly silenced that voice, speaking my thoughts without thinking, "You want me to convince you? Is that it?"

Dan closed his eyes, rubbing his forehead. "This is gratitude. What you're feeling right now is gratitude. It'll pass." His hand dropped, his eyes opened and crashed into mine. "It's too soon, too early for this kind of stuff."

Once more my mouth fell open. Once more I was gaping at him. Once more I spoke my thoughts as they occurred to me. "You don't . . . you don't." *You don't love me.*

Oh God.

The pain.

"You told me to trust you. You said—you said—"

The pain was sudden and unbearable. The knife in my chest tugged downward, pulling my heart with it until both lay on the floor at his feet.

And do you know what he did?

He laughed.

He huffed a little laugh, this time sounding mildly amused, like I was cute. "Kat—"

I saw red.

How *dare* he laugh.

How fucking dare he!

Unthinkingly, I picked up the nearest object on my desk—I had no idea what, maybe a stapler—and threw it at him. It went wide, missing him by a mile, but it got his attention.

His eyes bulged, he was no longer laughing. "What the hell?"

"Get out." My voice was firm and I meant it. I didn't want to see him.

Looking shocked as hell, he took a step forward, his hand extended like he wanted me to calm down. And that just pissed me off more.

Grabbing objects indiscriminately, I lobbed them at him, eventually reaching for my shoes, coming around the desk to get a better aim and punctuating each item with a loud, "Get. Out. Get. Out. Get. Out!"

"Stop it, what the fuck, Kat? Stop throwing shit at me and listen!" He didn't get out. Instead, he dodged my missiles and moved closer.

When he was very close, I hesitated. I wanted him to leave, but I didn't want to hit him in the head. So I aimed for his chest, catching him in the stomach at close range with some kind of plaque or award of my father's.

Out of ammunition, I turned away to avoid him, but he was strong and fast and, as usual, motivated.

His arms came around me from behind and he pulled me against his chest. I stiffened, closing my eyes and promising myself I wouldn't cry.

"Hey, hey. Calm down."

"Don't tell me to calm down." I thought about elbowing him in the ribs. I dismissed the idea, knowing he might still be sore.

"Okay, okay." His voice was soft. Carefully soft.

It pissed me off.

"Don't use that voice with me."

"What voice?"

"The you-think-I'm-a-crazy-person voice."

He faltered for a second, then growled in my ear, "Well what the fuck kind of voice do I use when you keep throwing office supplies at my head?"

"This voice is fine. Use this voice."

"This is my angry voice."

"Well, this is my angry voice, so I guess they match!"

I heard and felt a low growl vibrate against my back. I felt his exasperated exhale against my neck, before he said, "Can we just—can't we talk about this later? When we've both cooled off?"

"No." The rage was quickly becoming cold resolve. It slid over me much like my heart had slid to the floor, except this didn't hurt. It didn't feel good, but it felt safe.

I couldn't see him, but I knew he was gritting his teeth and rolling his eyes.

"Kat, you can't—"

"Fuck off, Dan."

I felt him flinch, his grip on me loosen, and I seized the opportunity.

Stepping out of his grip, I swiped my underwear from where it was hanging out like a porno pocket square, and searched for my shoes. Finding them on the other side of the conference table, I slipped them on, and moved to the door.

But before I could get it open, he was there, behind me, his big hand holding it closed.

"Where are you going?"

I said nothing. I wouldn't say a single word. It was always the same, when I was this angry with a person, I couldn't speak and, honestly, my blind and soundless rage frightened me.

I felt him, the heat of him, hovering. I saw him, his arm, wrist, and hand. The wedding ring was on his third finger. I closed my eyes.

"Talk to me," he said.

We stood like that for a long time and I felt his struggle, I could hear his ragged breaths. I couldn't do a single thing about it. It was too late. I was too hurt. My brain had disengaged, retreated, and blanked.

I waited.

In this state, I could wait for hours and never be aware of the time passing.

Eventually, his hand slipped away. Dan took a step back.

I opened the door.

I left.

CHAPTER TWENTY-SEVEN

The Nuremberg Code: A set of research ethics principles for human experimentation set as a result of the subsequent Nuremberg trials (war crimes) at the end of the Second World War.

NIH.GOV

Dan

SHELL-SHOCKED. That's what I was.

She'll calm down, she'll get over it, she'll calm down, she'll get over it . . .

Those were the thoughts on repeat in my head, because she had to. She had to get over it. She had to see reason at some point.

Right?

. . . Right?

Right.

I stared at the cement wall beyond my windshield, sitting in my rental car and wondering how and when I'd arrived at this pathetic, sorry-ass moment.

She loves you.

She didn't, though.

Not really.

She might, someday, but not yet. It was too soon. I'd given her one fucking orgasm—and it wasn't even a good orgasm—and now she had all kinds of ideas. She was confused. *Confused.* People don't—they didn't—fall in love this fast. It didn't happen. It wasn't possible.

She'll calm down, she'll get over it, she'll calm down, she'll get over it . . .

I kept seeing her at the exact moment she'd told me she loved me for the first time. Those liquid eyes, drawing me in, wanting me to believe in fairy tales.

I wasn't talking about after I'd gone down on her, I was talking about when I was eating her out and she'd said it, her gaze locked on mine, her cheeks flushed. The words had spilled out of her and had taken me by surprise, but I shrugged it off. People say all kinds of shit when they're about to orgasm, made all kinds of promises. Sex made people nuts.

Her *I love you* had been a figure of speech, that's it.

Or at least, that's what I'd told myself until she'd said it again. And again. And again. Like it was a pitchfork and she was chasing me with it.

Except, it wasn't a pitchfork.

It was a gift.

And what had I done?

Fuck a fucking fuck of fucking ducks.

I bent forward, my forehead coming to the steering wheel. I couldn't breathe. My eyes hurt. My throat was clogged, tight, dry, the worst.

I mean, I could breathe. But also, I couldn't. It felt like I couldn't. It wasn't the shitty feeling in my chest this time, it was something else.

Maybe Ebola, Maybe cancer. Maybe I was dying. I needed to go see a doctor.

She'll calm down, she'll get over it, she'll calm down, she'll get over it . . . she has to.

She has to.

My cell rang and I jumped—no lie—a half foot in the air, hitting my head on the visor of the rental car.

"Fuck!" I growled, reaching for the phone in the console without checking the caller ID and bringing it to my ear, "What?"

A pause, then, "Dan?"

I closed my eyes, letting the back of my head fall to the headrest behind me. "Janie."

"And Quinn," he chimed in.

"Oh, hey." I shook my head, trying to shake off my thoughts and the dread, so much dread, making my chest feel like it was full of burning coals. "What's up?"

"Kat said to call you."

"She did?" That had me perking up. "When? When did she say to call me?"

"She texted a few hours ago, around four." I heard a baby in the background, making a fuss all the sudden, and then Janie answer with a soft, cooing sound.

4:00 PM was before I'd met her for a dinner we hadn't eaten, before I'd tasted the sweetness of her body, before she'd told me that she loved me and I'd . . . *what have I done?*

"I'm going to interpret." This came from Quinn.

"Interpret what?" I was confused, my brain a mess. "The baby?"

"No, jackass. I'm going to interpret for Janie. She's got her hands full, feeding Desmond. Or trying to feed Desmond." He added this last part under his breath.

Janie and the baby sounded further away when Quinn spoke next. "It's about Caravel, and where the profits are coming from."

"Oh." I had to mentally crowbar myself into switching gears. "Janie figured it out?"

"She wants to talk to Kat about it in person tomorrow, just in case she has questions."

That's right. Tomorrow our friends were coming for a visit. Which meant I needed to fix things between Kat and me before tomorrow.

"Can you give me the short story?"

"Yes." He paused, likely because Desmond's cries abruptly

stopped; then he said, like he was distracted, "It's complicated. I didn't know this, but some drugs can't have generics. Meaning the company that develops the original name-brand drug has exclusive rights to make, market, and sell the drug for a long time."

"That makes sense, though. I mean, if I discover a drug, why would I want someone else selling a drug I discovered?" Movement in my rearview mirror snagged my attention, a black SUV pulling into a parking space behind me. I told myself not to look at it, I was just being paranoid. "What's in it for a pharmaceutical company if they can't make money off their discovery? They got to make money somehow."

"Yes, I agree. That makes sense. So most drugs have an exclusive period, which is called being 'under patent' I think, where they can recoup their investment and make money. But once the patent runs out, other companies, laboratories, etcetera, can make generic forms of the drugs. But first, the other companies have to go through the FDA and get approval for the generic version. There's a lot of hoops to jump through, and it's expensive for companies to obtain approval for the generic version."

"So what's the problem? That seems fair." My eyes, moving of their own accord, flickered to the SUV. The engine was still running and the lights were on.

"The problem is, there's not always a big demand for out-of-patent drugs. And that means, some drugs only have one version available and only one company makes it."

"Let me get this straight." I paused, moving my attention back to the benign sight of the cement wall, collecting all the pieces of the info Quinn had dropped on me. "Some drugs—even though they're out-of-patent and anyone can make them if they jump through the hoops of the FDA and spend a bunch of money up front—can only be bought from one company?"

"Exactly." I could almost see Quinn nodding.

"So, what does this have to do with Kat's financial reports?"

"Kat was concerned—Janie said Kat was concerned—about the reduction of funding to research and development at Caravel. She's worried that Caravel hasn't brought any new drugs to market since Caleb took over as CEO."

"That's right. So how is Caravel making money?"

"First, they're selling their name-brand drugs and devices as normal and expected."

I waited for him to continue; when he didn't, I prompted. "Okay. And?"

He made a sound of exasperation. "Caleb has been directing Caravel to acquire the rights to market and sell generics from small companies and laboratories. These are drugs that have been out-of-patent for twenty or thirty years. In a few cases, these drugs have never had a name-brand version, they've never been under a patent, they've been around for forty or fifty years, sometimes longer. He doesn't need to go through the expensive hoops from the FDA, that process has already been done by these smaller companies. These aren't drugs with a high demand, there is no name-brand version. So there's only one source who makes these drugs. Once he's acquired the rights, he's jacking up the prices by five hundred percent or more."

Five hundred percent? "No shit."

"Yes. And patients who need these drugs—most are for rare diseases—have no choice but to pay the cost."

My eyes bugged out. "But if it's for a rare disease, how can he make so much money from them?"

"Do the math. A rare disease affects less than two hundred and fifty thousand people. Thirty different drugs times two hundred thousand people, each needing one dose daily. One pill that used to be a dollar a dose is now sixteen hundred dollars a dose."

"Fuck me." My mouth dropped open. *This fucking guy . . .* This guy was the devil. "How is someone supposed to pay for that?"

Quinn's tone was frustrated. "I don't know. I was too pissed off after Janie explained the reports. I took Desmond for a run in the stroller rather than flying out to Boston and getting arrested for assault."

I thought for a minute, trying to figure out what he meant, but my head was fuzzy. Eventually, I just asked, "Getting arrested for assault?"

"Yes. For beating the shit out of Caleb Tyson."

No one could argue with that.

"Okay, well, at least now we know. Kat is going to be pissed." Immediately, I knew I needed to amend that statement. Kat was already pissed, now she was going to be even more pissed.

"Yeah, and—"

A cry in the background pierced the air; baby Desmond was upset about something.

"Okay, I have to go. See you tomorrow at the hotel." He sounded tired. I almost felt sorry for him.

"Yeah. See you tomorrow. Bye. And good luck."

He made a short sound like a chuckle and we ended the call.

As I sat there in the middle of this giant information dump, I navigated to my phone's recent contacts, finding Kat's immediately. Next to her name was the picture she'd sent me when I was in Australia weeks ago.

She was smiling.

She looked happy.

She loves you.

I was a fucking idiot.

Scrolling past her picture, I tapped on Stan Willis and brought the phone to my ear.

He answered after two rings. "Boss."

"Kat with you?"

"Yeah."

"Where are you?"

"Still at Caravel."

"What's she doing? Can she hear you?"

"No. She's in the executive locker room lounge thing," he cleared his throat, then added haltingly, "She's . . . taking a shower . . . I think."

Of course she is.

Now I was thinking about her in the shower. Great.

"Did she say when she's heading to the hotel?"

"She didn't say anything about going home."

I nodded, a plan forming in my head. "Okay. I'm coming back up. I'll take over your shift."

"You're coming all the way back here?"

"No. I haven't left. I'm just downstairs in the parking garage."

"Okay. Bye, boss."

"Bye." I hung up, staring at the cement wall again, nodding as my plan came together, resolve replacing the rocks in my stomach.

We'd spent two years—two fucking years—with a misunderstanding between us. I didn't want to do that again, not even for two hours.

So what am I going to say?

It was a particular place to be, this limbo. It had me asking myself philosophical questions and thinking things like,

What is love?

And, *How do you know you're in love?*

And, *Why does she think she loves me?*

And, *If this shitty feeling is love, I'm going to be so pissed.*

Because if this shitty feeling was love, if this choking, desperate mix of happiness and pain I felt every time I saw her or thought about her was love, if I'd been in love with her this whole fucking time and I'd been lying to myself and lying to her and wasting time, then I deserved a big, fat fucking punch in the face.

"Crap," I said, shaking my head at myself.

Worst-case scenario, she wouldn't speak to me. But at least I'd be close by in case she changed her mind. Best-case scenario, we would talk things out, she'd help me figure out *my* dysfunction, and we'd end up banging on the couch this time instead of the desk.

Or maybe the shower.

I opened the driver's side door, shut it, turned, and was punched in the face.

Falling back and down, the wind was knocked out of me, not because the punch was strong, but because I'd been caught unawares.

"Stay down," a voice ordered.

I coughed, trying to clear my lungs. In the empty parking spot next to my rental car were three sets of boots. I glanced up, squinting at the owner of the boots who had knocked me down.

"Ricky?"

"Stay down, Danny." This came from a different pair of boots.

I looked over. "John? What the fuck are you guys doing?"

I didn't get up, giving myself a minute to cough and check my jaw. It was fine. I might end up with a bruise, but no biggie. Like I said, the punch hadn't been that hard. Given the similarity of Ricky's build to a brick skyscraper, the fact that my jaw wasn't broken was a miracle.

He'd definitely pulled his punch.

Someone behind me made a grab for my wrist and I pulled it away, turning and glaring. It was Mark.

"What the fuck you doing, Mark?"

These guys. These were some of my brother's guys, all sporting neck tattoos that looked just like mine, all good guys.

Actually.

No.

Not good guys.

Criminals.

But, for criminals, not always bad guys. Just sometimes bad.

"You got to come with us," Ricky said, crossing thick arms over a thicker chest under an even thicker neck.

"I'm not going anywhere with you assholes."

John, the smallest of the group, sighed. "Come on, Danny. Just, fucking cooperate. We're tired. We haven't eaten all fucking day."

"Your blood sugar levels aren't my problem."

Conner, who'd been silent up 'til now, pulled out a cigarette, lit it, and grumbled, "I told you we should have used the taser."

"But then he would have shit his pants," John motioned to my pants. "Look at those pants. Those are nice pants."

"Yeah," I agreed, "I don't want to shit these pants. I like these pants. The pockets are deceptively roomy."

Ricky squatted in front of me, and it was a little like watching a tree bend down. "Danny, you got to come with us. Either we do this the nice way, or we do it the taser-shitting-pants way."

"Why don't you just knock me out?" I glared at the four of them, knowing there was no way I'd be able to successfully fight my way out of this flock of dickbirds. Stalling them, hoping someone would see and call the cops, was my best option.

"Seamus said you had a concussion and not to knock you out," John replied evenly, his attention moving to my torso. "But he said broken ribs were okay."

"That brother of mine, always so thoughtful. What a fucking prince."

Ricky smirked.

John smirked.

Conner took a drag from his cigarette, smirking.

But Mark pulled out a taser and sighed. "That's enough, we got to go. One way or the other, Danny, you're coming with us." He flipped it on. It buzzed. Mark lifted his eyebrows as though ready for my answer. "So what's it going to be?"

CHAPTER TWENTY-EIGHT

Self-Dealing: "The conduct of a trustee, an attorney, a corporate officer, or other fiduciary that consists of taking advantage of his or her position in a transaction and acting for his or her own interests rather than for the interests of the beneficiaries of the trust, the company, or the interests of his or her clients."

Wex Legal Dictionary

Kat

THE RANSOM DEMAND arrived early Saturday morning.

They said I had twenty-four hours to wire three million dollars into an offshore bank account or else—they said—I would never see Dan again.

Wait. I'm getting ahead of myself.

Let me back up.

After our fight Friday night, I left Dan in my office. Stan was just beyond the outer door to the suite and he followed me, thankfully saying nothing as I made my way to the executive lounge.

I felt blank, like an empty piece of paper. This wasn't the first time I'd felt this way, and whenever it happened I did one of three things:

1. Take a long hot bath or shower, or

2. Bury myself in blankets and watch *Doctor Who* until I could smell myself and myself smelled like cheese—but not in a good way, or

3. Watch cry-porn on the internet, where cry-porn is videos that are so sad—or happy/sad—they make you cry buckets. Think videos of military parents returning home and surprising their kids at school; or inspirational videos of a child with cancer who overcomes, beating all the odds; or the first ten minutes of the movie *Up*.

I wasn't ready to watch cry-porn.

I didn't have time for a smelly *Doctor Who* marathon.

Shower it is.

Stan stood guard, loitering in the main lounge area while I had my shower. When I finished, dried and dressed, I didn't feel any better.

I felt sad and . . . vacant.

I decided I would ask Stan to drive me back to the hotel, hoping I wouldn't see Dan, but also hoping I would. Usually, in the past, when I'd been furious with someone, I didn't want to see them at all. I avoided them, their company, mentions of them. I avoided it all until I could gain distance and perspective.

Take my cousin, for example. If I never saw his weasel face again it would be too soon.

However, Eugene—with whom my irritation hadn't fully abated—I was almost ready to interact with him again. Almost.

Dan was different. Not even an hour had passed since our fight and I pined for him. I ached to see him, to touch him, to speak with him even though I didn't know what I would say.

He didn't love me.

Okay.

Fine.

It hurt. Shards-of-glass-shredding-my-skin hurt, but there was nothing I could do about it. Like Dan's mom had said, I couldn't make him feel something he didn't feel. I couldn't force a connection.

The real question was: *where do we go from here?*

I couldn't see a way forward. I didn't want to waste years of my life hoping he'd change his mind. I deserved better, and so did he.

When I finished dressing, I still didn't feel better, but I did feel grimly resolved to my fate.

So when I asked Stan to drive me home and he'd said, "Dan is on his way up," I'd nodded, swallowing the flare of hope and tucking my grim resolve tightly around me. I made tea in the large kitchen, offered some to Stan. He accepted and we waited for Dan.

We talked about Stan's landlady and her weekly pinochle game. We talked about Stan's cousin and her ugly baby; I surmised that was the "ugly baby" he'd been referring to weeks ago. We talked about how he'd come to work for Dan and Quinn—he'd grown up with them in Boston—and how much he liked his job. We talked about how he and Fiona had been training at the same jujitsu studio in Chicago and how she kicked his ass on the regular.

But Dan did not show up.

Fifteen minutes became a half hour. Finally, Stan texted him, asking for a status update, and Dan immediately texted back,

Dan: *Staying with friends in town.*

Dan: *I won't be back tonight.*

Shards of glass.

As Stan escorted me from Caravel, I decided that if I formed a band, I would call it Shards of Glass. And we'd only sing really, really angsty songs about my ex, Dan O'Malley. So many words rhymed with Dan. It was meant to be.

Man. Plan. Fan. Ban. Tan. Lan. Uzbekistan. The songs would basically write themselves.

During the ride to the hotel, I dodged Stan's curious glances in the rearview mirror and expounded my list of rhyming words.

When we arrived at the penthouse, I saw a note from Eleanor. She wrote that she was working a night shift, and then would go home, to her house, afterward to sleep and prepare for the party on Sunday.

This meant I had the penthouse all to myself.

Burrowing under blankets, I pulled up *Doctor Who* in my room and ordered room service. Unsurprisingly, the order consisted mostly of cheese. But—good news—the appetizer platter helped me realize that mascarpone and provolone rhymed, which meant Shards of Glass would definitely be writing a song about cheese.

Distracted, depressed, and dazed, I succumbed to a dreamless sleep sometime between Doctor Who's first adventure with Donna, and the episode afterward, where ghosts of departed loved ones return to earth only to end up being an army threatening world domination.

But when the sound of my phone woke me—several text messages sent back-to-back, a plate of cheese cuddled to my chest, and the last episode of *Doctor Who* season two just finishing on the television—events of the previous evening returned to me.

I winced as the boulder of pain landed and resettled on my chest and checked the clock. It was still early. My alarm wouldn't be going off for another forty-five minutes.

Another chime announced another text message came through, and bleary eyed, I checked my phone. I stared at the messages. I looked up at the wall, wondering if I were still asleep, and then looked back to my phone screen and read the messages again.

Unknown #: *We have your husband. You will wire $3mil within twenty-four hours of this message. If you involve the authorities, you will never see him again. If you don't send the money, you will never see him again. Respond within 10 minutes for proof of life or this message will be sent again.*

I scrolled through my texts, seeing that the message had been sent five times and each time the hour-window decreased by ten minutes. They'd texted me five times. Clarity didn't arrive all at once.

At first, in my sleepy haze, I thought the messages were a joke. I wracked my brain, trying to figure out who we knew with this kind of sick sense of humor. I didn't believe it. It's not that kidnapping and ransom were out of the realm of possibility. Rather, it felt implausible.

I loved him, I told him. He didn't love me. We'd fought. I'd thrown things. He'd gone into town to spend the night with friends.

And then, what? He'd been kidnapped? Who did we know that kidnapped people?

Seamus.

Seamus kidnaps people.

Ice entered my veins. Seamus tried to kidnap Janie two years ago, he'd tried to kidnap me just last week. So . . . *not implausible.*

I gasped.

Confusion gradually became worry, which gradually became panic. The sensation reminded me of videos I'd watched on YouTube of tsunamis, how the water level rises slowly at first, and then higher, higher, higher, faster, faster, faster.

"Oh God." I covered my mouth, staring at the screen of my phone just as a repeat of the message appeared, ten minutes subtracted. I dropped it to the bed and stood, backing away, my mind racing.

What do I do?

"Wait," I said to no one, closing my eyes, telling myself to get a grip. "Quinn."

Rushing forward, I grabbed my phone, found Quinn's number, and dialed it.

"Pick up, pick up, pick up." Pacing the room, I pulled my hand through my hair, about to scream when Quinn finally answered on the third ring.

"We're just boarding the flight."

"Quinn. Dan has been kidnapped. He didn't come home last night. I woke up and there were messages on my phone with a countdown every ten minutes and I—"

"Stop. Calm down. Take a deep breath." His voice was granite hard. "Start at the beginning."

"What's the beginning?"

He didn't answer right away, giving me the impression he was multitasking. "Fiona and Alex are listening. Tell us about the last time you saw him, that's the beginning."

"Okay. Okay." I regulated my breathing, still pacing, and forced myself to focus while I filled them in on the last twelve hours.

Obviously, I left out the sexy times in my office and the fight that followed, but I told them all about Dr. Carlyle, how I'd left the office, how Dan had texted Stan about taking over my security for the evening, how he never showed up, how he'd texted Stan again to say he was going out with friends and wouldn't be home, and how I'd awoken to the threatening messages on my phone.

"I think it's Seamus. I think he took him."

There was a pause, and then Quinn said, "It's a possibility we won't rule out."

"What do I do? Do I call? Do I get proof of life?"

"No, not yet," Fiona answered immediately. "The timetable worries me, twenty-four hours. Once they give you proof of life, whoever they are might not feel Dan is worth the trouble of keeping alive. Do you want to involve the FBI?"

"Is there time for that?" Quinn asked in return.

"I have the money," I volunteered, biting my thumbnail. "Couldn't I just pay the ransom?"

"That's an option," Fiona's voice was steady, soothing. "We'll need to talk to Stan Willis ASAP, so we'll call him next. He was the last one to speak with Dan, correct?"

"Yes. That's right."

"Get the money ready." This came from Quinn. "I've known Seamus a long time. If it is him, we know money is his driving force. I doubt he'd seriously hurt Dan, but you should have the money ready."

"But what if it isn't him?" I asked, sitting on the bed and wrapping my arm around my middle. "What if it's my cousin?" I didn't finish my thought, which was: *Caleb is desperate and I believe capable of seriously hurting Dan.* "He was furious when he left the lawyer's office. But he's been so quiet since. He could have been planning this for a week."

"We have a team following him," Quinn reminded us all. "I'll check in after we talk to Stan."

"Okay," *Oh God, oh God, oh God, please let Dan be okay.* "Do I—do I tell Eleanor? Do I tell his mom? Do I call the police?"

"No. Don't tell Eleanor. There's no reason to worry her unnecessarily." Quinn's voice was firm. "Tell no one."

"Kat, I'm going to hack your phone once we hang up," Alex spoke for the first time, "see if I can figure anything out about the number that's been texting you."

"Don't respond to the kidnapper's text until we get there." I heard Fiona take a deep breath. "We'll be at the hotel in three hours and I'm confident we'll know more by then."

"Okay. I won't."

Three hours.

Three hours.

What the heck was I going to do for three hours?

"Last night, did you talk to Dan after he and I hung up? Did he tell you about what Janie found in Caravel's financial reports?" Quinn asked.

"No. You must've spoken to him after we—after I saw him."

"In just a minute, I'm going to hand the phone to Janie. She'll fill you in on what she found while Alex, Fiona, and I call Stan."

"There's something else you should know." This came from Alex. "I looked up that patent information Dan sent over last night involving Dr. Carlyle. It is held by Caravel, for now, but they're selling it to a venture capital firm."

"What? Why?"

"According to bank records, this venture capital firm is the same one who is funding Dr. Branson's research in the Caribbean. I also found that Caleb is a major investor in the firm. But Caleb Tyson isn't just the main investor in the firm," Alex paused, and if I didn't know him better I would've assumed the pause was for dramatic emphasis, because he said, "Caleb Tyson is the *only* investor in the firm. He's selling the patent to himself."

"That weasel bastard," I said and thought at the same time. "Can he be arrested for that?"

"No. You can't be arrested for self-dealing." Greg, Fiona's husband, cut in. He must've been listening to the conversation. "Sorry to butt in, but CEOs self-dealing is not illegal. It happens all the time."

"But isn't he defrauding shareholders?" Fiona asked her husband. "Isn't he committing fraud?"

"Not technically," Greg answered. "Actually, not unless you can prove that he falsified reports to the board."

I rubbed my forehead. "We can talk about this later. Quinn, you need to call Stan. Text me when you know anything."

"I will," he promised.

"Let me get Janie," I heard Alex say.

A welling of frustration made my throat tight and uncomfortable. My gut told me Caleb was behind Dan's kidnapping. My mind began playing through scenarios, bargaining with an imaginary Caleb.

Maybe if I willingly divorced Dan and signed over guardianship to my cousin, he'd let Dan go.

Or maybe if I could find evidence that Caleb falsified reports to the board, he'd let Dan go.

Or maybe if I find Caleb, tie him up, and threaten to tweeze all of his body hair—one hair at a time—he'd let Dan go.

"Kat." Quinn's voice cut through my sadistic reflections.

"Yes?"

He paused, as though considering his words. When he spoke, his voice was deep and his tone was stark, "Dan is family to me. He's my brother. *Nothing* is going to happen to him."

I closed my eyes, nodding, wanting desperately to believe him.

But if Caleb had Dan, there was nothing Quinn or I or anyone else could do to keep him safe.

CHAPTER TWENTY-NINE

Medicare Prescription Drug, Improvement, and Modernization Act: Law passed by US Congress in 2003 which makes it illegal for the US government/Medicare to negotiate drug prices with pharmaceutical companies.

Congress.gov

Dan

TURNS OUT GETTING tased doesn't make you shit your pants. At least, Mark didn't shit his pants when I tased him.

Regardless, he was still pissed at me.

Long story short, as they marched me to their SUV in the parking garage of Caravel Pharmaceuticals, I tried to give them the slip. I failed, but Mark got tased, Conner earned himself three loose teeth, John was going to have a new scar above his right eye, but Ricky walked away without a scratch.

The big guy had been the one to finally subdue, cuff, duct tape, and carry me to the car. And so here we were, at some piece of shit warehouse turned man cave, twelve hours later. No sign of my brother, yet.

"He's on his way. Should be here soon." Ricky was trying to feed me pancakes. "And remember, when he gets here, you need to act like we've knocked you out, like you're passed out."

I didn't want pancakes and I definitely didn't want someone spoon-feeding me pancakes while my hands were cuffed behind my back, my arms were duct-taped to my sides, and my ankles were zip-tied to a metal chair unless that someone was Kat, we were both naked, and it was her kink.

So I glared at nothing, keeping my mouth shut, and thought about Kat (and kink).

"Come on. Eat. They're good. I know you like pancakes," Ricky poked at my lips with the fork, so I murdered him with my eyes.

He sighed, like he was disappointed, and sat back in his chair. "You gotta eat."

"You know who made good pancakes?" Conner asked this from his place on a ratty old orange couch. He hadn't wanted pancakes either on account of his loose teeth.

"Who?" John looked up from his breakfast through his left eye, his right eye now swollen completely shut.

"Paul the Plum."

"Why do they call him Paul the Plum?" Ricky asked, finally letting the fork drop away from my mouth.

I tried to zone them out, and it was easy whenever I remembered the sight of Kat on that desk, wearing those stockings, her underwear in my pocket, her legs spread, her fingers in my hair. . .

But then I'd get a hard on, and I'd have to push the images from my mind lest Ricky think my stiffy had anything to do with his fork of pancakes.

Conner took a drag from his cigarette, squinting as the smoke drifted past his eyes. "The only way he could cum was from a Lucky Stranger."

I'd had a lot of time to think about Kat—her smile, her laugh, her bossiness, her starched shirts—and I'd had a lot of time to think about what an idiot I'd been to believe I was in limbo, to believe I didn't love her.

Such an idiot.

And this was my penance, sitting here with these fuckwits listening to their dumbfuck conversations about shit that didn't matter.

"What? What's that?" John's left eye swiveled between me and Conner, like I would fucking know what a Lucky Stranger was.

I glowered at him. "Don't look at me. I don't know what the fuck he's talking about."

"Yeah. You know." Conner held up his hand. "When you purposefully put your hand to sleep and then jerk off, making it feel like someone else is doing it. Lucky Stranger."

"Why would I know that?" I grumbled through clenched teeth. This was such a waste of time.

Conner ignored me. "Get it?"

John sneered. "I thought that was called the Scary Uncle."

I gave John a dirty look. "Don't call it that! What the fuck is a matter with you?"

"I knew a guy who could only cum with a Wilmington Deluxe," Ricky put in, he and Conner sharing a glance.

"What's that?" John gave Ricky the side-eye.

Ricky shook his head. "You don't want to know."

And that conversation, ladies and gentlemen, was my last twelve hours in a nutshell.

Mark's phone ringing cut off the conversation and everyone tensed. Conner sat up from where he was sitting on the couch and all the guys watched in anticipation as Mark brought the phone to his ear.

"Hey." Mark looked at me, his eyes narrowing into slits. "Yeah . . . Yeah . . . Yeah. . . Yeah. . . Yeah. Okay. We'll be ready."

Then he hung up.

"Breakfast time is over," he said, walking towards me, stopping to pick up duct tape and a black hood on his way. He pulled out a length of tape.

I didn't struggle as he taped my mouth. Nor did I put up a fight when he put the hood over my head. It had little eyeholes, so I watched the other guys spring into action, picking up their dirty dishes and carrying them away, like the sight of pancakes would be shameful.

They left the rest of the mess, beer bottles scattering the floor, pizza boxes in the corner, drug paraphernalia all over the place.

But maple fucking syrup? EVERYBODY PANCAKE!

"You got to hold still." Ricky bent close to my ear, tilting and arranging my head against the wall, like it was resting there. "We've knocked you out."

They'd been telling me this—that I was going to have to hold still and, no matter what happened, act like I'd been knocked out—since I arrived, but they refused to explain why.

Soon the guys had taken their positions—Mark by the entrance and Ricky, Conner, and John hovering in the doorway to an attached room —and were on high alert. It wasn't long before the sound of a car pulling up followed by feet on gravel had them all sharing meaningful looks.

Then the voices, more meaningful looks.

Then the door opening, more meaningful looks.

I swear, even with the black hood partially obscuring my vision, I could see it was a soap opera in here with all the meaningful looks.

And then finally, the big man made his entrance.

Ricky, Conner, and John hid, making themselves silent and scarce.

Seamus stopped by the door, conferring quietly with Mark, his eyes swinging to me. He didn't look surprised to see me, but then I didn't expect him to look surprised. For my part, I didn't move. I figured I would bide my time, making a move if the situation called for it.

Whatever this was about, eventually Seamus would let me go. He'd have to. Or else he'd have to answer to Ma.

But then a second guy appeared right behind Seamus and I almost forgot to hold still.

Caleb.

Caleb *fucking* Tyson.

The fury boiled over and I had trouble reminding myself that I was all tied up. Even if I fought against these restraints, it would do nothing. That's not true, it would show I wasn't knocked out and it would show how much I hated this guy. What good would that do? He'd probably get a kick out of seeing me struggle.

So I breathed out through my nose and I waited.

"Now you see him," Seamus gestured to my slumped form as the pair of assholes walked further into the space. "You want me to take off the hood?"

"No. It's him. I recognize trash when I see it."

Seamus cleared his throat, then rubbed the back of his hand across his nose—and that meant he was irritated. He only ever rubbed his hand over his nose when he was irritated.

But when he spoke, his voice was calm. "We've sent the message to your cousin, but she hasn't responded."

"She'll respond. She'll want proof of life before she sends the money." Caleb wrinkled his nose at me like I was a pile of skidmarked underwear, and then tilted his head towards Mark. "And it's just you two?"

"Yeah. I told you, I run a tight operation. No need to include more guys when Mark and I can handle it."

Caleb leaned closer to Seamus, lowering his voice, "And your man Mark is trustworthy?"

"Absolutely. Won't breathe a word, especially after he gets his cut of the ransom."

Ransom.

Fucking Seamus!

Caleb nodded, stepping away. "You'll have your half when the job is finished."

"What do you want us to do with him? After she sends the cash?" Seamus asked, gaining back the step Caleb had taken.

I started, blinking my disbelief. Seamus's question shocked the hell out of me. My brother was a worthless piece of shit, but I'd never known him to take orders from anyone except our ma. Ever.

Ever.

And now he was asking Caleb for his opinion? Or rather, asking him for direction on what to do? Nah. This wasn't right. Something was up.

"I told you before, I don't care how you do it." Tiny Satan glanced around the warehouse, sounding agitated.

Seamus studied Caleb for a minute, like he was thinking through a puzzle. "Why do you want him dead so much?"

Caleb's glare moved over Seamus, and then settled on me. His eyes sharpened with menace and a rage, I imagine a vein or two was probably popping out of his forehead.

"He's in the way."

"You're talking about Caravel? You want those shares your cousin owns?"

"Caravel can crash and burn, I don't give a shit about Caravel. And soon no one else will either, when it's insolvent and the stock price is in the toilet."

"So what's the deal? Why not take the ransom money and run?"

Caleb scoffed at Seamus, tugging on his cuff links. "Please. Three million won't last me a year."

"You mean one point five."

"What?" Caleb snapped.

"One point five. Your take is half."

"Oh, right. The point is, I need him gone and my loony cunt of a cousin committed—where she belongs. They're in the way."

"How are they in the way?"

Tiny Satan's glare moved back to Seamus. Then he turned, strolling back to the exit like he didn't have a care in the world and calling over his shoulder, "None of your fucking business. You do your part, and I'll do mine. When it's over, you'll get your half."

Seamus, hands in his pockets, watched the man go. He held still, like he was waiting for something. A vehicle started, and I listened as it pulled away, eventually fading into the distance.

Once it was quiet again, Seamus called out, "I told you fucking assholes not to knock him out."

Ricky appeared in the doorway to the adjacent room—right behind him were Conner and John—and walked over to me. "He's not knocked out, he's holding still."

When Ricky removed my hood, I took a deep breath, tilting my neck to one side to stretch it.

Seamus, his eyes moving over me, smirked. "Get that fucking tape off his mouth."

"I'll do it." Mark hurried over, apparently not wanting to miss another chance to yank the duct tape from my face.

He did it, slower than necessary, drawing it out. When he was done he winked at me. "That's for the taser."

"Are we even?" I asked, stretching my lips. "Or do I have to watch you give yourself a Lucky Stranger?"

Now Mark smirked, shaking his head like he thought I was funny, and walked away.

My attention returned to my brother. He was watching me, a happy but small smile curving his mouth and behind his eyes.

"You hear all that?" he asked, like he was pleased with himself.

"Yeah." I nodded, giving him a once-over. "You planning to kill me?"

His smile dropped. "What the fuck is wrong with you? Asking me shit like that?"

"I'm not going to sugarcoat it, assface. What do I look like? Willy Wonka?"

He sputtered for a moment, and then hollered at me, "You're my brother, dipshit. I'm not killing my goddamn brother." Seamus turned, grabbed a chair and dragged it over to where I was sitting. "I fucking swear to Christ, you're so fucking stupid sometimes."

I waited until he'd sat down before speaking. "Are you going to untie me?"

"Not yet. Not until you listen. Then I'll untie you."

"Fine. Talk."

Seamus studied me for a beat, then launched into it. "This is what happened. So, that rich fuckstain? Caleb Tyson? He comes to me last week, tells me he's Kathleen Caravel-Tyson's cousin and she's crazy. She needs to be committed and he's worried about you. She's got a psycho mother, locked up in a hospital somewhere, and she's a danger to my brother."

"How is Kat a danger to me?"

He held his hands up. "I'm just telling you what Tyson told me. He says that he had a court order to be her guardian, so she tricked you into marrying her. He also said, if she inherited, she'd be worth billions. But she was safer locked away, then she wouldn't be a danger to you. He also said, if anything happened to her, he'd pay a ransom to get her back."

"He just . . . tossed that out there? Like, 'Hey. My cousin is a loony bitch, but I'd pay a ransom to get her back.'"

Seamus squirmed. "When you put it like that, it makes me sound like a marblehead for believing him."

I blinked at my brother's use of the word *marblehead.* According to him, I was a dipshit, Caleb Tyson was a fuckstain, but he was a wee little adorable marblehead.

This fucking guy.

"You realize everything he said was bullshit, right?" I asked, wanting to make sure he and I were on the same page about Kat's cousin.

"She's not worth billions?"

"No. That part is true. The rest is bullshit."

"Yeah. I know that now. But why would I doubt him then?"

"You didn't want to doubt him. All you saw were the dollar signs."

Seamus ignored me, like I hadn't spoken. "He was slick, convincing. I thought I was doing you a favor. I thought you didn't know who she was, that she'd pulled one over."

"So you, what? Went to the house last week to save me? Or to kidnap her?"

He shrugged. "Both. I figured you wouldn't mind me taking her off your hands. Caleb would pay a ransom, I'd be all set up, you'd divorce her, she'd go to an institution. Everybody wins."

"Everybody wins, huh?"

Seamus rolled his eyes, turning his head to shout to Ricky, "You got any more pancakes?"

My attention snagged on the purple and green bruises around his neck. I didn't feel remorse about putting them there. I'd done what I had to do to keep Kat safe, but sometimes I still wished Seamus wasn't such a corrupt piece of shit. Even now, tied up in his warehouse club-house, I still wished he was just my brother.

"Kidnapping me was stupid."

Seamus gave me the side-eye, his eyebrows ticking higher on his forehead. "Oh yeah? Why?"

"Because Quinn."

He seemed to think this over, his eyes growing smaller with the effort required to use his brain. "You think he's gonna find us?"

"My guess is, he already knows where I am, and he's gonna come in here any minute and shoot you."

Seamus crossed his arms, giving me a look like he knew a secret. "You don't know your wife."

"What?" I snapped.

"That woman you married, she's not going to let Quinn come in here, guns blazing. She's not going to take the chance that you might get hurt in the cross fire. She'll pay the ransom."

I frowned at my brother, peering at him, saying nothing, because he was probably right. Guilt flared again, so much fucking guilt, along with the image of her throwing a stapler at the wall behind me. I'd hurt her. Thinking about Kat hurt made it feel like I had a two-ton weight on my chest.

"That woman loves you. That woman is crazy about you. I saw it the first night, when she was walking back to the table after you two were smooching. After talking to Tyson, I thought maybe she was just plain crazy, but I was wrong." He paused here to rub his chin, his stare moving beyond me. "When I knocked you out, you should have seen her. If I'd made one wrong move, she was going to blow my head off, shoot me dead in my own mother's house. That, brother, is true love."

"Am I finished listening?"

"Not yet." Seamus pulled out his phone, pressed a few buttons, and then showed me the screen. "This is the message Caleb has been sending Kat since seven this morning."

I read the threatening text, unsurprised. "I already figured out that I'm being ransomed."

"Caleb thinks you are."

Examining my brother, I turned my head slightly to the side, sending him a disbelieving look. "What does that mean?"

Seamus's attention was back on his phone and he was tapping through screens until the sound of a recording filled the silence.

Caleb: *"She'll respond. She'll want proof of life before she sends the money. And it's just you two?"*

Seamus: *"Yeah. I told you, I run a tight operation. No need to include more guys when Mark and I can handle it."*

Caleb: *"And your man Mark is trustworthy?"*

Seamus: *"Absolutely. Won't breathe a word, especially after he gets his cut of the ransom."*

Caleb: *"You'll have your half when the job is finished."*

Seamus stopped the recording, giving me a satisfied smirk. "Consider it a wedding present."

I didn't try to disguise my shock, mostly because I didn't think I'd be able to. "You . . . recorded that? You recorded Caleb?"

"Yeah." His grin widened. "When I figured out Kat wasn't playing you, and you tried to beat the shit out of me—"

"Hey. You come in the house with two guns and a knife, planning to kidnap my wife. Did you think I wouldn't see the Glock tucked in the back of your pants?"

"I didn't draw it, did I?"

That gave me pause. "Why didn't you?"

"I'm not drawing a gun on you," came Seamus's stern answer; he looked serious, earnest in a way he seldom did. Clearing his throat, he asked, "So why didn't you use the gun on me? When you found it, why didn't you point it at me to keep me from getting up?"

Glaring at him, flexing my jaw, I stalled.

The truth was, I had no idea. I should've, and usually I would've if he'd been anyone else, but I didn't.

Eventually, I muttered, "Go fuck yourself."

He smiled. "That's what I thought."

"Whatever," I rolled my eyes, my knee bouncing for some reason. "What—specifically—happened after you hit me over the head?"

"That wife of yours, she grabbed the Glock, stepped between you and me, and started screaming for me to back off, to not touch you. Like I said, I swear, I thought she was going to shoot me. She was pissed, like, if I gave you a funny look she was going to snap my dick off and feed it to Bark Wahlberg as a snack."

I smirked at that, proud of her for some reason. "Yeah, well. Don't piss off the wife."

"Tell me about it," he sighed, then chuckled, then sighed again. "I tried to apologize, but—you know—my throat didn't exactly work. So I left. Then, last weekend, I tracked Tyson down to his marina in Duxbury and we had a little chat. He admitted he'd been trying to use me to get what he wanted—his cousin out of the way—so he made an alternate offer."

"Which was?"

"I pick you up, Kat wires a ransom, then I kill you, and he and I split the payday."

"And you accepted?"

"Yeah," Seamus widened his eyes on me, like my question was stupid. "Yeah, I accepted. If I didn't do it, he was going to find someone else. So I played along, to keep you and Kat safe."

"Played along." I studied my brother, watching his big-eyed act of innocence, like he was swooping in and saving the day for Kat and me.

Nope.

I didn't buy it.

I knew my brother.

I believed him when he said he didn't want to kill me. I believed him when he told me why he hadn't pulled his gun. I even believed him when he said he'd taken the job so Caleb wouldn't offer it to someone else.

But not for one second did I believe he was doing this out of the kindness of his heart.

"What's in it for you?"

He blinked at me, looking stunned. "Pardon me?"

"You can take that pardon and shove it up your ass. What's in it for you?"

Seamus shook his head, his eyes flickering over me like he was disappointed.

In me.

Don't everyone die laughing at once.

"Nothing, Danny. Nothing is in it for me. I recorded things so you could put that Tyson shitbag in jail. I took the job to keep you safe. I organized my guys to bring you here. I even made sure they didn't knock you out, 'cause I know you got that concussion."

Nope.

Still didn't buy it.

I glared at my brother, waiting for the other shoe to drop.

He stared back, still wearing his mantel of angelic intentions.

And then his phone rang. He sighed, glancing at it, his eyebrows ticking up on his forehead. "It's Kat."

"Kat's calling you?"

"It's probably for you." Seamus swiped to answer, then held the phone to my ear.

Glaring at my brother, I listened as Kat's soft, sweet voice said, "Hello?"

I blinked, winced. That shitty feeling, now an old friend, detonated in my chest.

God, I miss her.

"Kit-Kat."

"Oh God." She made a sound like a sob, like she was holding in tears, and the sound made me want to smash everything in Boston. "Are you okay?" she asked, her voice breaking.

"I'm fine." I had to clear my throat, it was tight, but I wanted to reassure her. "I'm not hurt. I'm totally fine. I—"

Before I could say anything else, Seamus took the phone away. My eyes cut to his and I watched as he ended the call, a small smirk of triumph on his features.

And then he laughed, like he couldn't help himself.

And then he turned, still laughing, and called to me over his shoulder, "Thanks, Danny. Thank you for providing proof of life."

CHAPTER THIRTY

Weinberger Kidnapping: One-month-old Peter Weinberger was kidnapped from his suburban home in Long Island on July 4, 1956. The kidnapping resulted in new legislation—signed by President Eisenhower—that reduced the FBI's waiting period in kidnapping cases from 7 days to 24 hours.

FBI.GOV

Kat

THANK GOD FOR knitting.

And knitters.

And yarn.

I was at the end of my tether, and everything was unraveling (no pun intended).

At some point over the last hour, Ashley had forced my work-in-progress into my hands and said, "Knit."

It was a scarf, a simple pattern, no counting or stitch markers required. The yarn was variegated, so the beauty of the finished object would be in the array of colors, not in the intricacy of the pattern.

I knitted. As I knitted, my brain quieted, breathing became easier, and my thoughts began to focus on plotting my revenge.

Wait. Sorry.

I'm getting ahead of myself.

Let me back up.

I spent the three hours waiting for my friends to arrive by calling my personal banker and requesting he prepare a wire transfer, dated today, for three million dollars. Then I combed through Caravel's financial records, division financial reports, and efficacy findings for in-progress R&D projects.

I discovered that Caleb had been systematically shutting down projects at Caravel, culling scientists and staff, and then supporting those projects privately through his venture capital firm. He'd been stealing research from Caravel and siphoning it into his own companies for two years.

Irate didn't begin to describe how I felt.

I wasn't going to tweeze his body hair, that would be too good for him. I was going to cover him with honey and put him in a box of fire ants.

Quinn texted me halfway through the flight with both good news and bad news.

The good news: they knew where Dan was being held. They also knew that Seamus's men had abducted him.

The bad news: Seamus and Caleb were working together.

According to Quinn, camera footage in the parking garage of Caravel headquarters showed four men taking Dan and forcing him into the back of a black SUV. He'd tried to escape at one point, but he'd been overpowered by one of the men who, according to Alex, looked like a giant.

Quinn recognized the guys in the video as belonging to Seamus's crew. Quinn also said they hadn't knocked Dan out, which went a long way to alleviating my fears about the kidnappers reinjuring or aggravating his recent concussion.

Alex had tracked the SUV as far as the warehouse district, and then he'd lost it. However, tracking the vehicle had become a moot point, as the team following Caleb for over a week alerted Quinn to a meeting between my cousin and Seamus.

The security team followed Caleb and Seamus into the warehouse district, where—presumably—Dan was being held.

When Quinn's plane finally landed and everyone was gathered in Quinn and Janie's suite at the hotel, we were all in agreement that Seamus wouldn't seriously hurt Dan. Therefore, Fiona had me make the proof of life call.

And so, I did.

It had been terrifying and overwhelming and truncated. Immediately afterward, Seamus—or Caleb—sent a new text:

Unknown #: You have nineteen hours for the $3mil to transfer into this account. Text this number when you have done as instructed. Once we confirm the money has been received, we will tell you where to find your husband. If you alert the authorities or take any action other than as instructed, you will never see your husband again.

"This is bullshit." Quinn growled at the phone. "Standard kidnapping procedure in the US uses an honest broker intermediary to deliver the money."

Wally, clearly agitated by Quinn's mood, let out a bark. I reached out to him and scratched his ears, tears welling behind my eyes. I forced them back.

"Standard kidnapping procedure?" Elizabeth, who was sitting with me, lifted an eyebrow at Quinn.

Nico of all people responded, "Yes. And usually the honest broker is provided by the insurance company managing the K&R insurance policy."

"What?" Elizabeth squinted at her husband like he was speaking Greek.

"K&R is Kidnapping and Ransom." Quinn said flatly. "Most people worth over a certain amount have a K&R insurance policy in the US. The insurance company typically provides the honest broker intermediary at the time of exchange. In foreign ransom cases," his gazed flickered to Greg, "it's completely different."

"Maybe let's get back to Dan instead of standard operating procedure for kidnappers." Greg suggested dryly, sending Quinn a pointed look. "What's the plan?"

Everyone looked at me, but I couldn't speak.

My lungs on fire, my brain a storm of panic and doubt, I retreated into myself, my imagination holding my words hostage with worst-case scenarios.

I needed him safe. I needed to see him again so I could . . . so I could . . . *damn it.*

"Give her a minute." Elizabeth wrapped an arm around my shoulders, pulling me into a hug. Wally whined, jumping up on the couch like he wanted to get on my lap.

That's when Ashley ransacked my purse and handed me the knitting. I always carried knitting. Always.

Ten minutes later, Wally at my feet, my mind was clearer, now absorbed in plotting revenge schemes against my cousin.

And that brings us to the present.

"Are you ready to review options?"

I glanced up from my project and found Alex crouching in front of me, petting Wally. His blue eyes were gentle and sympathetic. Elizabeth was on one side of me, Sandra was on the other, and they were sitting very close, as though to provide a warm, protective cocoon of support.

"I am." I nodded. "I am ready to discuss options."

I felt Sandra's hand on my shoulder, drawing my attention to her. "When you're finished discussing options, we should spend some time commiserating."

Commiserating was Sandra's code word for *please allow me to help you deal with your feelings.*

"Sounds good," I said, and I meant it. I had so many thoughts, fears, and feelings about what was happening, I felt like—any minute —I would shatter. "Commiseration sounds good."

But first, Dan.

And then, revenge.

Her hand dropped away from my shoulder and I stood. Wally also stood, as did Alex. After a moment's hesitation, he offered me his elbow.

I glanced between him and his arm, not quite sure what to make of the gesture.

"Here," he said, giving me a pained expression, making me think he was a little embarrassed. "Obviously, you can walk on your own. But I thought you might want someone to lean on. I know I would if I were you."

I returned his smile with a grateful one and slipped my hand into the crook of his arm. "Thanks, Alex."

"You're welcome, Kat," he said, his deep voice soothing.

He walked me over to where Quinn, Fiona, and Greg—who was holding his sleeping, infant daughter—were gathered around the high countertop of the suite's wet bar, speaking in hushed tones. Wally followed behind, bumping my leg with his nose every few steps. When they saw us approach, they all straightened and waited for us to join them.

Fiona studied me, a concerned expression pulling her eyebrows together. "I'm not going to ask if you're okay, because I know something of what you're feeling. Instead, we're going to jump right to the point, okay?"

I nodded. "Yes. Please."

Gathering a deep breath, she began, "Here are the options: Quinn's team goes into the warehouse and tries to extract Dan."

"No." I ignored the frustrated scowl on Quinn's face and shook my head vehemently. "I can't take the risk that he'd be hurt in the cross fire. Next option."

"We contact the police,"—Fiona looked to Quinn, who seemed to tense even further—"and bring them up to speed, relying on their resources to extract Dan."

"No." I rejected that plan as well. "For the same reason as before, plus Dan said he's related to several people on the force. We don't need this turning into a circus."

"I agree with Kat on this one." Quinn lifted his chin towards me. "He is related to a lot of guys here. However, our goal is to get Dan back safely, as soon as possible. The police's goal will be to get Dan back, but they'll also be focused on capturing those responsible. As far as I'm concerned, capturing Seamus and Caleb is low priority to Dan's safety."

"Agreed," everyone said in unison.

"But at some point," Quinn addressed this comment to me, "we'll need to call the police, even if we only do it once Dan is safe."

"Okay. Fine," I agreed, then to Fiona, I said, "Next option?"

"You pay the ransom," Fiona sounded resigned, "and trust Seamus to let him go."

"But it's not just up to Seamus, is it?" I knew my voice was high and tight, belying the panic I felt, but I didn't care how I sounded. "Caleb and Seamus are working together. Seamus wants the money, but what does Caleb want?"

"What if you don't pay the ransom?" Greg asked. "You could use the financial records from Caleb's venture capital firm to force him to cooperate."

"I thought you said self-dealing isn't criminal." I glanced between Fiona and Greg.

"I'm not a lawyer. I only know what I've read in the news about CEOs and self-dealing, but in some cases it can be," Greg explained gently.

"Like insider trading?" Alex asked.

"Actually, no. In the US, insider trading—where a company's officers and directors buy or sell stock with insider knowledge—isn't illegal as long as they follow reporting rules to the SEC. But in all cases, if shareholders are impacted by the self-dealing, the shareholders can file a lawsuit. You could threaten a shareholder lawsuit for fraud as leverage, to force him to release Dan unharmed. He'd definitely be fired as CEO of Caravel."

"What if we did both?" Fiona looked to me. "What if you approach Caleb and threaten a lawsuit, which would force him to back off, and also pay the ransom? Seamus should be happy with the payout, and Caleb's hands will be tied."

"I can send Caleb images of the bank statements." Alex turned to me. "You don't even have to talk to him."

"So we blackmail Caleb and bribe Seamus in order to force them to release someone they're holding hostage. Great." Quinn's voice held not a small amount of sarcasm. "This is so fucking backwards."

"Three million dollars." Greg's statement brought my gaze to him. "Do you have three million in liquid assets on hand?"

I nodded. "Yes. I have more than that locally. I've already called my banker and told him to prepare the wire transfer. He has the account number, he just needs me to make the call."

Fiona looked at Alex, Alex looked at Greg, Greg looked at Quinn.

And Quinn looked at me. "I'll go in with a team," he offered. "We know where he is, I can get him out."

I shook my head before he'd finished speaking. "No. Absolutely not. You and Janie just had a baby. Think of Desmond. And, I'm sorry, but I can't take the risk that Dan would get shot or killed or—" my voice failed me again and I choked on a sob, covering my mouth with my hand as the worst-case scenario flashed vividly through my mind.

Alex turned me to him, wrapping me in a tight hug. Perhaps I was beyond caring; or perhaps I was losing my mind; or perhaps being with Dan over these last weeks had fundamentally changed me, because I held on to Alex.

My instinct wasn't to shrink from his support, but rather to cling to it.

* * *

Alex sent Caleb the images along with a message demanding that he release Dan or else the board would find out about his self-dealing.

I called my banker and had the three million dollars transferred.

Fiona, using my phone, messaged the kidnappers and let them know the money had been sent.

Alex rigged a device to my cell so that any call received would be recorded and traced.

Nico ordered room service for everyone and handed me a plate of cheese when it arrived. *<3 Nico <3*

And then we waited.

We waited in near silence.

It was very weird.

Some of us knit. Some of us held babies. Some of us changed baby diapers. Picking up on the mood, Wally did a lot of huffing and pacing. Alex and Drew took Wally on a walk. Lots of people gave me hugs. I couldn't stop imagining the worst. No matter what I did or how I endeavored to distract myself, my brain kept going back there, showing me images of everything that could possibly go wrong.

And then, almost five hours after Alex had sent the images to Caleb, my cousin called me. Taking a deep breath, I accepted the call, putting him on speaker so everyone could hear.

"You think you're very clever."

I hadn't spoken more than ten words directly to Caleb in over three years. My instinct was to stay silent. But I couldn't. Not this time.

"Why are you calling me?" I asked.

"You know why." He was being evasive, vague, which was extremely out of character for my cousin. I assumed that meant he knew he was being recorded.

"Are you calling to negotiate?" I asked.

"Have you made the payment?"

That gave me pause. I looked at Quinn and Fiona; they were also confused.

"Didn't you receive my text message?" I asked, and then promptly muted our side of the call, whispering to the group, "Why doesn't Caleb know I've made the ransom payment? If he and Seamus are working together, wouldn't he already know?"

Quinn's phone buzzed and, dazed, he pulled it out of his pocket, frowning at his screen. He flinched back, like he was surprised, and huffed a laugh, muttering, "Unfuckingbelievable."

Meanwhile, Caleb was monologuing. "You sent no text. Stalling and lying will not yield the results you want, nor will your attempts at blackmail. Where are you going to tell people you found these documents? How are you going to explain accessing protected information? You can't. Being in possession of these documents means you've done something illegal. These are inadmissible because they were obtained illegally, you stupid cunt." His voice became a shout, "Soon you'll be locked up, where you belong. I'm calling your bluff. I'm—"

We didn't get to find out what Caleb was about to say because Quinn hung up on him.

"Shitbag." Quinn issued my phone an irritated look. Then, turning a miniscule smile on the rest of us—which, for Quinn, was a huge grin —he said, "Dan's safe."

I gaped at him. We all gaped at him.

"What?" someone said. It might have been me.

"Dan's safe." Quinn lifted his voice so that everyone—even Drew and Ashley, and Nico and Elizabeth in the living room—could hear. "Once the money hit Seamus's bank account, Seamus's guys brought Dan back here, dropped him off in Kat's penthouse, and called Stan. Stan is with Dan now, up in your suite."

What?

I continued to gape at him.

Quinn, meanwhile, was holding his phone to his ear, listening to something. "Seamus also sent a recording . . ."

Elizabeth walked over to me and pulled me into a hug while Nico stood on my left, rubbing my back. "Thank God he's okay. Do you want me to walk you up there?"

"We're all going." Quinn—still holding his phone to his ear—was already hustling to the exit, Wally at his heels; the dog's tail wagged like he knew what had just happened.

My feet were rooted, too afraid to move. I couldn't believe it. I couldn't allow myself to believe it was over.

Please be real.

What if I were imagining this? If I moved, then the illusion might disappear. Dan might still be in danger.

Please. Please be real.

Quinn opened the door and then paused, turning, holding it open with a booted foot and motioning for me to hurry. "Kat," he said sharply, "Let's go."

CHAPTER THIRTY-ONE

Hemp Rope: Providing superior strength, braided rope helps benefit from reduced stretch characteristics, making this one of the most secure natural rope options available for Shibari and bondage enthusiasts seeking the highest quality in secure bondage rope.

AMAZON DOT COM PRODUCT PAGE FOR SHIBARI 100% NATURAL
HEMP ROPE

Dan

"JUST USE A knife." I rolled my eyes.

"I don't have a knife." Stan was squinting at the rope binding my feet to the bed, his tongue poking out between his lips on one side while he concentrated on trying to—unsuccessfully—untie the knot.

The problem was, Ricky was a fisherman's son. He knew how to tie a real wizdinger of a knot.

He and Conner had placed me on the bed, already tied up, and then used more rope to bind my legs and hands to the base of the bed frame in an intricate knot contraption.

"How did they get you into the hotel and up here without anyone seeing?" Stan sounded distracted.

"You remember Ricky? Well, his sister works here."

"Oh yeah. She was nice."

"She probably doesn't work here anymore, after this afternoon. She's probably long gone. They brought me up in one of those big, stupid laundry carts, covered me with sheets."

"You were tied up the whole time?"

"Yeah. And gagged and blindfolded, like you found me when you got here." I flexed and stretched my jaw, knowing I would never take breathing for granted again.

Stan huffed, straightening from the knot. "I can't undo this. I don't even understand how this kind of knot is possible. It's witchcraft."

"Then use a fucking knife."

He scratched his head. "I think I'll use a knife. I'll be right back."

At just that moment, I heard the penthouse door open, followed by the sounds of people and footsteps. My heart jumped against my ribs and I craned my neck to see.

"Dan?" Quinn called. "Where are you?"

Stan strolled to the doorway of the bedroom, throwing his thumb over his shoulder. "He's in here, but he's all tied up. Anyone have a knife?"

Wally galloped in, running through Stan's legs.

"Wally!" I called to him, grinning at my awesome dog as he jumped on the bed. But then he started licking my face, which made me laugh 'cause I couldn't get away. I tried turning my head and he just bounded to the other side, still licking my face. Which meant I had my eyes closed and my lips rolled between my teeth when he was finally pulled away.

Hands came to my cheeks.

I opened my eyes.

BAM.

There she was.

"Kat."

She filled my vision, leaning over me, her chin wobbling, her eyes shining with emotion. She took a breath, then another, then a third before speaking.

"Are you okay?"

"Yeah." I let my eyes move over her, finding solace in the familiar landscape of her gorgeous face. The shitty feeling was back and I embraced it. Actually, I tackle-hugged it. "I'm actually fine."

"How is your head?" Her fingers tentatively moved through my hair. "Did they—"

"No. They didn't knock me out. Just . . . There were ten of them. Maybe twenty. All with guns, semiautomatics. Seamus really brought out the heavy artillery," I lied. Right there on the spot.

Yeah. I lied. I didn't want her to know I'd been overpowered by four idiots with a single taser. So sue me.

Don't give me that look. You would've lied, too.

Kat stared at my face, her brow wrinkling with confusion.

I heard someone clear their throat from behind her in a way that made me think they were trying not to laugh.

"You dumbfuck." This was Quinn. He strolled forward, presumably so I could see him, but maintained a solid four feet between him and the bed. "Your mother doesn't know what happened. We didn't tell her. We're leaving you now." Then to Kat, he said, "I'll call my contact at the Boston PD and get the ball rolling on reporting all this. Message if you need anything—*anything*—we'll be just downstairs."

"Thank you." She nodded, then turned to look over her shoulder. "Thank you all."

That's when my eyes moved to the door and I realized everyone— and I do mean *everyone*—was standing just inside the doorway.

"Glad you're safe, Dan." Janie passed baby Desmond to Quinn and grinned at me. "The average ransom demand is two million dollars, so you should feel pretty good about your life's monetary worth."

Leaving me with that fascinating tidbit, Janie and Quinn left.

"Do you need me to examine you?" Elizabeth offered, frowning as her eyes moved over me. "How's your head? Those ropes are going to leave a mark."

"I'm fine. Really. The worst thing they did was tie me up."

"You're getting hemp rope from Christmas," Nico said, capturing his wife's hand and tugging her out of the room, calling out, "See you tomorrow."

"I'm glad you're okay." Sandra used her index and middle fingers to point at her own eyes, and then used them to point at us. "And I shall find you both tomorrow for some commiseration. Got it?"

"Hey. Thanks for watching Wally," I said, giving her a grateful smile.

Wally wagged his tail at the sound of his name, did a little dance around the carpet, and then settled on the rug leading into the bathroom.

"No problem, Chachi." Alex placed his hands on Sandra's shoulders, gave me a devious little smirk, and turned Sandra toward the living room.

That fucking kid.

"Do you need help with the rope?" Drew was sliding a knife out of his boot.

"I'll take it." Kat stood and Drew placed it handle first in her outstretched palm. "Thank you."

"Y'all let us know if you need anything. Cheese, or a different kind of cheese, or cheese pie, or cheesecake. Just let us know." Ashley made her offer to Kat, giving her a squeeze on the shoulder just before she and Drew left.

"Who tied those knots?" Greg, arms crossed, was studying Ricky's handiwork from a distance. "Those are impressive knots."

"Come on," Fiona shifted their infant daughter to her other shoulder, then pushed on Greg to guide him from the room. "I'm sure Dan will fill you in tomorrow, maybe teach you a thing or two so you don't have to learn it on the streets." Then to me, she said, "Glad you're back and safe."

Marie gave me a little wave as Fiona and Greg walked past. "We're so happy you're okay." Her gaze shifted to Kat. "Both of you."

"Where's your guy?" I asked, craning my neck to see if he was around, and relieved to find he wasn't. Since I didn't know the guy very well, it would have been fifty shades of awkward for him to see me like this.

"Matt is flying out tonight—I guess right now—he'll be here for the party tomorrow. Oh, wait, will there be a party tomorrow?"

Kat stiffened, and started shaking her head, so I spoke over her before she had a chance to answer. "Of course there'll be a party tomorrow. And after, you ladies are supposed to knit at my mom's house. She's so frickin' excited about it."

Marie grinned, but her eyes were sympathetic. "Are you sure? You've just been kidnapped." She chuckled a little, probably at the lunacy of the entire situation.

"Get out of here, I'm fine. We'll see you tomorrow."

With one more smile for both of us, and a reminder to call if we needed anything, Marie turned and left. I heard the penthouse door open, close, and then silence.

My eyes moved to Kat. She was standing at the foot of the bed, holding the knife Drew had given her, and was looking at me. Her lovely face held no expression.

"Hey," I said, the ache in my chest flowing outward to my arms and fingers. Or maybe the ropes were cutting off my circulation. "Are you going to cut me loose?"

I wished she'd say something.

I wished she'd come closer.

I wished she'd cut these ropes so I could touch her and kiss her and tell her how much I loved her. I loved her so fucking much, part of me thought maybe I wouldn't be able to last another ten minutes without her in my arms. My heart would give out. I'd die. BAM. Kaput. The end.

She continued to watch me, like she was thinking about cutting me loose, but hadn't yet made up her mind.

"Kat?"

"Are you really okay?" she asked, sounding worried.

"Honestly? Yes." I rolled my eyes at myself, admitting, "And there were only four guys and a taser, no guns. Sorry I lied."

The side of her mouth curved upward, but then flattened again.

She took a deep breath, walked to the table by the bed and placed the knife on it. As she did this, her expression grew cold. "Aren't you going to thank me?"

I stared at her, then glanced at the knife, my lips parting in confusion. "Thank you . . .?"

"For paying the ransom." Now she sounded pissed.

I flinched, her words landing like a slap.

Is she mad about having to pay the ransom?

Now we were wearing matching frowns. "You want me to thank you for paying the ransom?"

"You must feel grateful."

I glared at her, unable to believe what I was hearing. This was not the reunion I'd imagined.

"I wonder," Kat tapped her chin theatrically, "how will I ever know whether your feelings for me are real, or because of gratitude?"

Gratitude? What the fuck is she—

. . .

. . .

. . .

Oh.

Gratitude.

Right.

I'm the asshole.

I closed my eyes, breathing out a rueful laugh. She was a smart one, this wife of mine.

"Well-played."

She also laughed, but it sounded bitter. "That's it?"

Her angry tone had me peeking through one eye.

"That's all I get? *Well-played?*" She sounded slightly hysterical. "I thought you were going die. I thought," she took a breath, like she had to, "I thought Caleb was going to have you killed. You said I could trust you."

"You can trust me. Me being held for ransom doesn't mean you can't trust me."

"That's not what I'm talking about!" She spun away, throwing her hands in the air and then pulling them through her hair.

In the corner of my eye I noticed that the volume of her voice caught Wally's attention. He lifted his head, glancing between the two of us.

But then the sound of a choking sob coming from Kat meant that she had my full attention. I strained against the rope, needing to get to her, needing to pull her into my arms and kiss the fuck out of her.

"Will you please cut me loose?"

She turned halfway, giving me her profile. "Maybe I should."

It took me a second to realize she wasn't talking about the ropes, and in the next second my stomach dropped, like someone had cut a hole in my abdomen. In fact, it felt like they were still cutting the hole, the pain was so bad.

"Don't you say that." I choked on the words, my throat clogged with emotion. I cleared it, and said firmly, "There's no cutting me loose from you. We're—we're it."

She glanced at me, hurt and accusation in her eyes. "I trusted you."

"You can still trust me."

"I can't." Her face crumpled and she shook her head. "Because you don't trust me."

"Of course I trust you. I trust you more than any—"

"You didn't believe me when I told you that I loved you."

That had my mouth snapping shut and us trading glares again, because she was right.

"You don't trust that I love you because," her expression cleared and I could see she was working to maintain her composure. When she spoke next, her voice had firmed. "Because you think—some part of you thinks—maybe, maybe I'm only with you because of gratitude."

My chest rose and fell with a deep breath. What could I say? She was right. About everything.

So say that.

"You're right."

Kat continued to glare, saying nothing, like she expected me to continue.

"What can I say? You're right. That's what I thought. I was a dumbass. You're right."

"That's what you *thought*. What does that mean?"

I tugged on the bindings holding my arms and growled, frustrated. She was so close. She was right fucking there. And I couldn't touch her.

Kat's eyes flickered to my straining arms. Maybe she could read my thoughts, or maybe she took pity on me. Whatever it was, she came back to the bed and sat next to me.

Horrible and wonderful barbs of heat burst outward as she approached, making it hard to breathe.

"Kat," I said, "You gotta untie me. I need to touch you."

Christ. I sound like a junkie.

But something about it, the words or my tone, had her eyes turning soft. "Dan, I love you. And I need you to believe me. I know you don't feel the same, but—"

"Are you fucking kidding me with this? Of course I love you. I love you. *I love you.*"

She reared back, blinking like my words were a bucket of water to the face, or something was in her eyes. "Wh-what?"

"I'm in love with you. You're my fucking—fucking *sunshine*. My goddamn everything. You're the center of my whole fucking universe. I'd give up swearing for you, I swear. If you asked, I'd never say the word *fuck* ever again, that's how much I love you. I love you more than fuck, so that's a whole fuckavalot."

During my tirade, Kat's expression changed a few times. At first, she was shocked, and then confused, and then she laughed, and then her face crumpled again and she hid it behind her hands, her shoulders shaking.

I watched her, trying to figure out if she was happy or sad. "Kat?"

She shook her head.

"Are you crying? Or laughing?"

Her hands fell away and she lunged at me, saying, "Both," just before her lips landed on mine.

As much as I could, as much as the restraints would allow, I chased her mouth, needing more of her. I was so hungry for the taste of her, I was starving. I'd been dying, wasting away, and everything about this woman fed every part of me.

Her hands were on my body, pulling my shirt up, her fingers on my stomach reminding me again that I couldn't move. I winced as the rope dug into my wrists, rubbing the skin that was already raw.

"Oh, I'm sorry." She pulled back suddenly, jumping from the bed and picking up the knife. "I'm sorry. That must hurt."

"Stop saying you're sorry and, please, cut the rope."

She gave me an apologetic smile and worked on cutting the first tight strand holding me down to the bed. "I think if I cut these two, you'll be free of the bed. But I still need to get the ones holding your legs and arms together."

Once the two main lines were cut, she carefully sliced through those that held my ankles together, her eyes on her work.

"I need a shower. I have Wally slobber all over my face and I stink." I said, knowing it was true, but grimacing at my thoughtlessness.

Real nice, Dan. Real smooth. You just told the woman you love her, and then announce that you stink. Romantic of the year award.

I was about to apologize when she moved to straddle me, reaching for my wrists, and saying quietly, "Maybe I could join you."

I blinked at her. "What?"

"In the shower. Maybe we could . . ." She swallowed, her neck and cheeks growing a fantastic shade of pink.

"Okay," I said, nodding a lot.

Not going to lie, just the thought of Kat, me, shower, naked made me dizzy. It also made my dick hard, which was likely the reason for me being dizzy. Also likely, Kat felt this new development, seeing as how she was sitting on my lap and a small, knowing smile curved her mouth, the blush receding.

As soon as my wrists were free, she darted away to the bathroom, pulling her shirt off as she went and calling over her shoulder, "I'll start the water."

I scrambled to free myself from the last of the tangles and then stood, getting my bearings.

Once I found my balance, I yanked off my shoes and socks. Tugging off my shirt, tripping over my pants, I paused just outside the door.

Thumbs hooked in my boxers, I stared at the sight before me. All the air left my lungs and I didn't dare blink.

She was naked.

In the glass shower.

And she was wet. *Wet all over.*

Her back to the spray, her chin tilted up, her eyes closed, her arms lifted, her hands in her hair.

At some point in my life, I must've done something really fucking awesome to deserve this moment.

Sliding off my last piece of clothing, I didn't take my eyes from her as I shut the door on Wally and walked across the bathroom to the shower.

Don't get me wrong, I loved my dog, but I didn't want to share her with anyone right now.

I opened the glass door, my mouth watering, and she opened her eyes. Kat half-blinked, her arms moving slowly to her sides as she looked at me. Then her stare moved to my neck, my chest, stomach, hips, lower.

I didn't move, it was only fair. I'd taken my time, memorizing every detail, watching her. She deserved no less, if she wanted it.

"You're beautiful," she said on a breath, the sound almost lost to the noise of the shower.

"I'm yours," I said, not knowing I was going to say it before it came out, and thinking immediately after how stupid I sounded.

I should have said she was beautiful. I should have said she was gorgeous, perfect, flawless, a fucking goddess, lust and desire personified.

Before I could, her eyes came back to mine and the look she was giving me . . . well, let's just say, maybe I wasn't so stupid after all.

Oh, fuck it.

I reached for her. Her skin was hot and slippery beneath my hands. Perfect. We met under the water, her arms coming around my neck, her breasts slick against my chest, and I think I groaned into her mouth. Like the greedy bastard I was, I pressed her against the wall, and feasted on her stunning body. I bit her neck, her chest, shoulder, and my hands were just as insatiable, consuming and memorizing the softness of her hips, ass, thighs, the bend of her waist, the lush fullness of her exquisite tits.

That's right.

Exquisite. Tits.

I wanted to smother myself, inhale her, suffocate on her skin. I couldn't get enough. My heart thought I was running a sprint, and my dick—which had made itself right at home sliding and pressing against the wet hot of her bare stomach—thought we were about to fuck.

Sorry for all the dick status updates, but my wood was important to the action here, and I didn't want to leave anything out. I wanted to commit to memory every single second.

We needed to slow down, I needed to slow down. But I wasn't thinking with my brain.

I bent my forehead to hers, taking a breather, even as my fingers—moving with a mind of their own—found her tight nipple and gave a tug, the sound she made sent a gratifying, piercing heat down my spine.

Kat gasped, her fingers kneading my backside. Her mouth chased mine, coming to my neck when I held myself away. A hand slid up my back, around my side, fingertips against the ridges of my stomach, moving lower.

I caught her hand. "Wait."

"Dan." She pushed her breast into my other hand, moving in that lithe way. Rocking restlessly against me, like her body was searching for mine. "Touch me."

One of my hands slid lower while the other held her wrist over her head, against the tile wall. I bent to take her breast in my mouth, groaning at the sweetness of it, of her. She widened her legs, her breath hitching, the nails of her free hand digging into the back of my head.

But I hesitated sealing the deal; not because I was uncertain, but because I was a greedy fuck and wanted to hear her beg.

"Dan."

My name sounded urgent. She tilted her hips. I pressed the base of my palm against her lower stomach, my fingers teasing her opening without touching where she needed.

"Dan!"

"Mmm?" I swirled my tongue around her nipple, waiting . . . waiting . . .

"Please!" Her voice was high, tight, needy.

It did things to me.

My dick pulsed, ached. Without meaning to, my hips gave a jerk and I was pressing myself mindlessly against her hip.

That's right. I was humping her leg. But whatcha gonna do? It felt great. And she moaned, so I knew she didn't mind.

"Dan. Touch me. Please, please, please." Kat was breathing hard, excited. I released her wrist. Her nails digging into my skin a punishment for my delay.

"I want you," I said, sliding a finger into her, separating her, tracing a circle around the spot where she wanted me. "I need you. I want inside you."

She whimpered, such a sexy sound, her nails scratching down my back, her legs shaking. "Yes."

"How badly do you want me?" I baited, biting and kissing a path up her neck, sliding my cock between her legs, slick against her clit, nudging her entrance, whispering in her ear, "You're so fucking sexy like this, hot and wet."

I leaned back to capture her mouth, giving her another stroke down below. She shivered, her nails digging into my hips.

I ended the kiss with a slow lick of her lips, wanting to remind her of my mouth on other places. "I thought about you all day, on your desk last night," another sliding stroke, another shiver, "your skirt hiked up. How you opened your legs for me—"

A gasp.

"How much you liked it when my mouth was on you, eating your—"

She covered my mouth with hers, groaning, her hands coming to my shoulders and pushing me back, back, back, beneath and past the spray of the shower, until my knees connected with a ledge.

"Sit down," she ordered, pushing, her hand sliding down my body to wrap around my cock.

She stroked.

I shuddered.

And then I sat the fuck down.

Her eyes on mine, she climbed on my lap, straddling me, her knees on either side of my hips, the friction of her breasts slick and hot against my skin.

I grabbed two handfuls of her ass, but not to guide her, oh no. Not that. She gripped me, stroking, her body open and hovering, but making no move.

"Do you like being teased?"

I grunted, my fingers digging into her hips, and tried to keep my voice even as I said, "Was I teasing you?"

Her eyes narrowed and she tilted my cock towards my stomach, treating it like a slip-n-slide for her clit.

"Oh fuck." My head fell back, connected with the wall of the shower, and I lost my damn mind.

"You're so sexy like this," she echoed my earlier words, sucking on my neck, grinding against me. "Tell me what you want."

"Fuck me."

"Nicely."

"Fuck me nicely."

She laughed, low and husky, but then she did.

She positioned herself above me. She slid down, taking me in, her breath catching, her eyelashes fluttering shut, her nails leaving new marks on my shoulders.

"Dan."

"Kit-Kat."

"I love you."

"I fucking love you, too."

She laughed, but then her forehead wrinkled as she set the pace, the slow, slow, slow pace.

A groan wrenched from me.

Sadist.

She was a sadist.

I'd married a sadist.

. . . I can deal with that.

Little sighs, little moans, little high-pitched cries of pleasure. But I didn't want these sounds. I mean, yeah. They were sexy as hell. I liked them. A lot.

But I couldn't stop thinking about the sounds she'd made when I'd eaten her out. The deep grunts, the cursing, like she was possessed, like she couldn't hear herself, like nothing mattered and she didn't care one fuck about anything but how great she felt in the moment.

Her lip had curled. I wanted to see her lip curl.

So I gave her a minute to do her thing, liking my view of her swaying tits in my face, equally hating and loving how slowly she was bouncing on my dick, and then I took over.

I stood and she held on. I carried her the short distance to the wall and used it as leverage, propping her up.

Now, can we just pause here and take a moment to appreciate how difficult this is? I mean, she's on my lap, making me crazy, and I pick her up—with my cock *still inside her*—and carry Kat to the wall. I deserved a gold fucking medal for technique, and she deserved a platinum one for her balance and strength, 'cause I definitely wasn't the only one making this happen.

Her eyes flew open and captured mine. I spread her wide and thrust, setting a quicker tempo, making sure every quick slide was friction where she needed it.

"Oh, Dan, oh, Dan, oh, Dan!"

It sounded like a cheer. Like she was a cheerleader. And us having sex was a super exciting touchdown pass.

Her body bowed, everything tense and tight, and she grunted,

452

cussed, her lip curling. It wasn't a pretty face, and it wasn't tidy, or neat, or thoughtful, or controlled, or graceful.

But in this moment, it was a gorgeous, messy, perfect, inelegantly sexy face. It was her O face and I loved it.

She pulsed, shuddered, shrieked as though possessed. Her hips moved instinctively, greedy, searching, demanding.

It was all I needed.

I'm not going to say I exploded inside her, because I pulled out and exploded against her stomach. Now I'm fully aware pulling out isn't an effective form of birth control, but in our mindlessness to devour each other, it was the best we had. Clearly, she hadn't been thinking about it.

But still, big fucking *kaboom*. The earth shook, the angels sang, the heavens opened. St. Pete tossed me a high-five. He might've winked— dirty old bird—and I might've also forgotten my name.

When I came to, Kat was wrapped around me. Legs around my hips, arms around my shoulders, head buried in my neck, and she was breathing like I was breathing. Like we were going to die.

And I had two thoughts:

One, *I love her.*

So I said, "I love you." And I kissed her shoulder. Why her shoulder? I don't know. I just really loved her shoulder. And her neck, chin, ears. Everything.

Two, *I want to do it again.*

So I asked, "We got any Gatorade?"

CHAPTER THIRTY-TWO

New drug research and approval facts (USA):
1) The overall success rate for drugs moving from early stage Phase I clinical trials to FDA approval is about one in 10 (10%).

REUTERS

2) The average drug can take anywhere from 8 - 18 years from pre-clinical (development) to clinical (phase 1, 2, and 3) to FDA approval.
3) The average cost to bring a drug to market: Phase 1 $15.2 million; Phase 2 $23.4 million; Phase 3 $86.5 million (total = $125.1 million)

FDA.GOV

Kat

A SLANTED SUNBEAM spilled across the carpet and the corner of the bed. Sounds from the city were faraway, only permeating the quiet when I held my breath and strained to listen. Cuddled beneath fluffy, warm covers that smelled like soap and clean cotton, I watched Dan sleep while I swallowed past a lump of rising self-recrimination.

We'd made love in the shower. After, we'd touched and kissed in the dark, learning each other's bodies by heart. I'd fallen asleep content, happy, feeling hopeful. In the light of day, as I relived our frenzied moments, remorse replaced contentment.

I'd completely forgotten about birth control.

I'd been irresponsible.

I'd been thoughtless.

That's not true. I hadn't been thoughtless. I'd been thinking, but only about myself. Only about how great he felt, and how much I wanted him, and how loving him felt like freedom from fear and anxiety, and that freedom was just as inebriating as alcohol and drugs.

I'd been fortunate enough to escape my days of substance abuse without the encumbrance of addiction. I knew I was lucky. Some scientists believe, though as far as I knew it hadn't yet been conclusively proven, a combination of genes are responsible for addiction vulnerability. If I'd been born with those genes—a luck of the draw, a roll of the dice—perhaps I wouldn't have had the strength to change my life.

Or maybe I did have those genes. But instead of drugs and alcohol, my addiction was right in front of me.

Dan slept like a stone, strong even in his stillness. He lay facing me, his back to the window. The sunbeam touched the crown of his head and shoulders, giving the illusion that he, and not the sun, was the source of the light.

My gaze glanced over his crooked nose, the fringe of dark lashes against his cheeks, the grainy stubble of his jaw, the line of his lips at once luscious and stubborn.

He's so beautiful.

My heart swelled and a quiet battle persisted within me.

Abruptly, Dan frowned, his body quaking, and he sucked in a short breath. He opened his eyes and I tucked my hands beneath my chin to keep from touching him.

"Hey," he said, squinting at me, then the room, then the bed. "We're at the hotel."

I nodded, saying nothing as I studied the way his body moved as he turned, the stretch and pull of his muscles, the details of the ink on the plateau of his chest, the slope of his sides.

"Kat?"

My eyes darted to his. "Yes?"

Dan studied me for a second before he lifted an eyebrow, a mischievous smirk on his wonderful mouth. "Like anything you see?"

"Everything. Too much," I lamented, and perhaps that was the problem.

"What time is it?" He propped himself up on his elbow, the side of his face resting in his hand.

"Just past nine. We need to be at your mom's house by ten thirty." I searched his face, finding a light bruise at his jaw I hadn't noticed before, his stubble had mostly hidden it. "Your jaw—" I reached out, not touching the spot but tracing around it. "They did hurt you."

Dan made a sound like *pshaw*, catching my fingers and bringing them to his lips. "Nah. Ricky pulled his punch. No biggie." Dan yawned, his eyes sobering as they moved between mine. "There's something I want to talk to you about."

"Go ahead. But there's something I want to discuss with you, too."

"You wanna go first?"

I shook my head; I was still gathering my thoughts. "No. You go first."

"Okay." He inspected me, but then eventually said, "We need to talk about security."

"Security?"

"Yeah. Seeing how easily Seamus's crew could get in and out of here made me realize we can't stay."

He had a good point. "What are you thinking?"

"You're not going to like it."

"Go ahead." I braced myself.

"What about your family's place in Duxbury?"

Staring at him, I felt myself frown. "You're right, I don't like it."

"When we were at Eugene's office, going over the properties, it's the one that makes the most sense. It's nearby, gated, secluded on several acres, you got those guard dogs, the helicopter. You'd be skipping Boston traffic. Any security upgrades should be easy to handle, and it has a panic room on every floor."

"Panic room," I scoffed, laughing without humor. "Great."

"Just think about it. We'll stay here for another week, increase the security, but after that we've got to go." Dan placed a kiss on my hand again, looking equal parts sympathetic and matter-of-fact. "Now you. What did you want to talk about?"

Taking a deep breath, I pulled my hand from his and sat up, holding the sheet to my chest. "We need to talk about birth control."

He grinned, scratching his neck. "Yeah. I guess neither of us were really thinking about it last night."

I gaped at him. "That's it?"

"What?"

"You're not more upset? What if I'm pregnant?"

Dan seemed surprised by my outburst. "You don't want kids?"

"That's not the point."

"Then what is the point?"

"We haven't talked about it. What if you don't want kids?"

"I do want kids."

"But what if you didn't? And I did. And I got pregnant, and then you were unhappy, and—"

"Hey. Slow down. Why are you twisting yourself up about this? If you're pregnant, you're pregnant."

"That's easy for you to say, you don't have to carry the child for nine months."

His eyes moved between mine, narrowed. "So you don't want kids?"

I groaned, shaking my head. "I *do* want kids, just not right now."

"Okay." He nodded, like the matter was settled. "Sounds good. Kids later."

"But that's not my point. I—we—acted irresponsibly and recklessly. We need a birth control plan."

"Okay." He nodded some more. "Sounds good. How do you feel about condoms? You like condoms?"

"The birth control plan isn't the point either."

He exhaled a huge breath. "Then what is the point?"

I glared at him. "The recklessness! The recklessness is the point. We can't be reckless like that."

"About birth control?" He squinted his eyes again, like he was having trouble following.

"About anything."

Dan stared at me for a few seconds, and then his eyes lost focus as they moved around the room. "Uh . . . okay. But,"—he sat up, pushing his back against the pillows behind him—"sometimes people are thoughtless, and they make mistakes. I mean, yeah, ideally, let's do our best to be responsible. However, no one is perfect. That's why we have the concept of consequences and forgiveness. Forgiveness doesn't mean there's no consequences, it just means we accept and deal with the consequences, and then we move forward."

My heart was racing and I didn't know why, but before I could catch the words, I blurted, "I think I'm addicted to you."

He blinked at me, unhurried and still a little sleepy, a slow smile claiming his lips. "Thank you. The feeling is mutual."

I moved to him, bringing the sheet with me, and climbed on his lap. His hands settled on my hips, one above the sheet, the other below it.

"Dan." I needed to make my point. "I'm worried that, when we're together, when we're . . ."

"Making *l-o-o-o-ve*," he provided, using that deep voice of his, lifting a sly eyebrow. The backs of his fingers beneath the sheet brushed against my bare skin, moving higher to fondle my breast.

I clutched the blanket tighter, trying to ignore the sensations ignited by his touch, but not wanting to stop him either. "Yes. When we're making love, I'm completely uninhibited."

He smiled, looking pleased. But when I didn't continue, he frowned. "Is that a problem? I mean, isn't that the point?"

Closing my eyes, my forehead came to his shoulder and I groaned. "I guess it is. But, in my experience, those kinds of blissful highs don't come without a devastating low. I worry about, what happens when we fight? I'll still want you. Will I bend on or be thoughtless about something important to me because I crave being with you? Or I'm worried about you? You see what I mean?" I shook my head, not even certain of my own point. "I guess, what happens if the recklessness I feel when I'm with you becomes carelessness in other parts of my life?"

I felt the beat of his pulse next to my cheek, the stubble of his jaw along my neck, the heat and strength of his body against me. I inhaled him, the moment and the feeling, loving our closeness entirely too much.

At length, he guided me back so he could look at me. "That's probably going to happen."

Before I could speak, he continued, "It's already happened to me. When Seamus came into my ma's house that night, when we came back from the day at Eugene's office, I was careless when I turned my back on him, even though I'd taken his weapons. But I was worried about you, and so I was thinking about you. Not him."

A pragmatic smile tugged at the corner of his mouth. "You're going to bend, and so am I. We're going to compromise, negotiate, and distract each other. Being together means our priorities are going to change. That's what happens when you make space for another person. Comfort zones will be *stretched*."

I couldn't help but laugh at how he said the last part, like it was a promise.

"Kit-Kat," he began gently, "I think having Everest-sized highs and Marianas Trench-deep lows is just a part of life. But you can't have one without the other." Dan pushed my hair from my cheek, tucking it behind my ear, his fingers lingering on my neck before tracing along the bare skin of my chest.

Dan's gaze followed his hands as he hooked a finger in the bedsheet and tugged, exposing my breasts.

His eyes heated and he leaned forward, holding me up while my hands automatically came to his shoulders for balance.

He placed a soft, wet kiss at the center of my chest and murmured, "If you numb yourself to the valley," his lips feathered across my breast, moving to its center, "you won't be able to recognize the peak."

* * *

DAN'S KIDNAPPING was the best kept secret at the party on Sunday.

What wasn't a secret?

Dan's oldest sister Mary owned a pink vibrator that went off in her purse while she was in a parent-teacher conference for her kindergartener and she said it was a bomb rather than admitting to the nun that it was a sex toy.

I couldn't recall a time I'd laughed so hard, or so freely, ever. The story had everyone gathered laughing, even Quinn.

"So, I guess I learned my lesson." Mary took a sip from her beer.

"I'm so afraid to ask." Matt, Marie's boyfriend, wiped his tears of laughter.

"Don't leave the batteries in the vibrator." Mary shrugged. "Obviously."

"Not 'Don't take a vibrator to my kid's school'? That's not the lesson?" Dan gave his sister a look that was equal parts teasing and indulgent.

She scoffed at him. "What if I need it?"

He closed his eyes, shaking his head.

"What if I'm walking to the art classroom and I—"

Dan's eyes flew open and he covered her mouth. "Stop talking."

She laughed silently, her shoulders shaking, staring at him.

When he dropped his hand, she blurted the rest of her question, "— AND I WANT A FIVE KNUCKLE SHUFFLE!"

Dan covered her mouth again and now they were both laughing, staring at each other, him trying to give her the evil eye. The effect was ruined by his barely suppressed laughter, and my snorts of laughter, and Marie's guffaws.

They were too freaking cute. Seeing the love, respect, and admiration between them warmed my heart. I loved how they teased each other and made each other laugh so easily. I glanced at Marie and she glanced at me, and a little voice reminded me that this is what I had with her, and Janie, and Sandra. It's what I had with my friends.

Eventually, he released his sister and she wagged her eyebrows. "Ah well, doesn't matter. We're moving before Christmas, so she won't be going to that school anymore anyway."

"Where're you moving?"

Mary sighed tiredly. "Dale wants to move us to Cowhampshire."

"Ah jeez. That's beat. Sorry." Dan placed his arm around my back, drawing me close to his side, and I leaned against him. He'd been doing this all day, finding reasons to touch me and hold me since we woke up this morning.

He'd found me in the bathroom after our discussion, brushing my teeth. I'd been debating on what to do about Caleb, how best to annihilate him, when Dan slid an arm around my middle and began devouring my neck. Then his fingers were in my hair, pulling it, angling my head to expose more of my skin. Then his hand around my waist moved into my shirt, and well . . . you know.

"It's not that bad." Mary sounded like she was trying to convince herself. "At least the house is big."

"Where exactly?" Quinn asked.

"Down east." She shrugged, giving her eyes a half roll.

Dan scratched his jaw. "Oh. That's not too far. They got a Dunks?"

"Uh, *yeah*. I'm not moving anywhere I can't get my coffee."

"I feel you." He smirked. "We're actually looking at moving to Boston."

"Get out!" Mary grinned at us both. "Well that's great, back in the neighborhood, huh?"

"That's the plan." Dan returned his sister's smile. "We're looking for a house right around here."

"Where you living now? Renting a place?" Mary took another gulp of her beer.

"Nah. Kat's got a place we'll stay in temporarily."

"Where is it?" She looked at me.

"Duxbury. It's south of Boston, on the shore."

Mary let out a low whistle, glancing at her brother while Dan seemed to brace himself.

"Look at you, Danny. No more Nantrashbasket or Marsh Vegas for you. Moving on up to Deluxebury."

He grunted, shaking his head, fighting a smile.

I laughed. "Deluxebury. That's hilarious."

"Don't encourage her," Dan leaned close to me, like he was telling me a secret, but kept his eyes on his sister and whispered loudly, "I once told her she could borrow my pink vibrator and she had a field day."

Mary smacked him in the arm.

Everyone laughed.

Again.

The best.

Over the course of the afternoon, we drifted from the kitchen to the dining room to the deck. There was always someone new to meet, always a new story about Dan growing up.

A Red Sox game was on in the family room, and a radio broadcasted the game in the backyard, providing background noise and a soundtrack for the party. At intervals, everyone—it seemed—would either cheer or groan, depending on who got a hit, who was safe, or who was out.

Most of the people present were relatives, some were neighbors, some were work friends of Eleanor's, and everyone brought something.

Even Uncle Eugene brought something when he showed up late in the afternoon, a cottage cheese pie, which was my favorite.

"Thank you." I accepted the pie while Dan sent me a look that said *be nice* over Eugene's shoulder.

"You're welcome." His eyes moved over me, as though making a mental list or tally. "How are you?"

"I'm good." I gave him a hard look and decided it was time to set him straight. "You can't lie to me anymore."

Nodding thoughtfully, he leaned against the kitchen counter, crossing his arms; he was the only person in a suit and stuck out like a sore thumb. Everyone else was wearing Red Sox or Patriots apparel, jeans, and sneakers.

"Okay," he finally conceded. "I won't."

"I need to be able to trust you because I am going to need your help. I want my voting shares back immediately."

He continued to study me. "You think you're ready?"

"I have to be." I stepped closer to him. "Caleb has been sabotaging Caravel for two years, maybe longer. I have to save it."

Eugene looked surprised, and a little doubtful, so I looked to Dan and motioned for him to come over.

He did, glancing between us. "What's up?"

"We need to fill him in."

Dan seemed mildly surprised, but nodded. "Okay. You want me to find Janie?"

"Who's Janie?"

I touched Eugene's elbow and tilted my head toward the kitchen exit. "She's a friend of mine who figured out in three days what no one else has been able to piece together in three years. Come on, Dan will get her."

I guided him to the study, stopping along the way to greet people and introduce him. For simplicity's sake, I called him "my Uncle Eugene." Everyone seemed to accept this, and with acceptance came hugs and "welcome to the family" and questions about his team loyalty.

Dan's Uncle Zip looked him over, his eyes narrowing suspiciously, and said, "You look like you're a Yankees fan. Are you a Yankees fan?"

Eugene responded with a succinct, "Go Sox," and Zip let him pass.

Janie and Dan were already in the study when we arrived, and my friend wasted no time filling in Eugene on what she'd uncovered from the division financial reports. He listened attentively, grimacing when I filled in the rest of the blanks about Caleb's self-dealing, but interrupted me when I suggested that we should pursue a shareholder lawsuit.

"No. This is illegal. He's stealing trade secrets, disallowed by the Uniform Trade Secrets Act. What he's doing constitutes obtaining patents by improper means. He'll go to jail." Eugene stopped short of rubbing his hands together.

"So then, here's the question," I glanced between Eugene and Janie, "How do we make this information public with the least amount of damage to Caravel and without incriminating ourselves?"

My lawyer's eyes grew impossibly shrewd. "You have a friend who's a journalist, correct?"

"Yes. Marie Harris."

"What does she know so far? About Caleb?"

I tried to remember where Marie had been the day prior and what —if anything—she'd heard. "Other than Dan being kidnapped, I don't think she knows much about what happened yesterday. She stayed in the living room mostly." *Almost like she was doing her best to keep herself in the dark.* "Before that, she and her boyfriend uncovered some information for us about Dr. Branson, but she doesn't know that Dr. Branson's research in the Caribbean was funded by Caleb. We never brought her in the loop on that."

"You also have a friend who is good at hacking, I think?" Eugene's gaze cut to Dan.

Dan shrugged noncommittally. "We might."

"Have your hacker friend find the offshore law offices handling Caleb's companies' paperwork and filings, it'll be more damning than financial records, and less likely to raise the interest of the SEC. Give the documents—anonymously—to the International Consortium of Investigative Journalists."

Janie gasped. "Of course! The Panama and Paradise Papers. That's genius."

Eugene nodded, sending her a slight, but impressed, smile of approval.

"What are the Panama and Paradise Papers?" Dan glanced between Janie and Eugene.

Janie looked frustrated, like she had so much to say and no time to say it. "It's a long story, but basically the International Consortium of Investigative Journalists received a bunch of documents anonymously originating from law firms that focus on offshore dealings, nicknamed the 'Offshore Magic Circle.' You can look this all up on Wikipedia. Anyway, the documents have brought down a few government leaders, people in the Dominican Republic protested, the Prime Minister of Iceland resigned."

"Have your journalist friend keep an eye out for the documents.

She can report on Caleb's self-dealing. Have her be the one to suggest a lawsuit for fraud against shareholders in addition to pointing out the obvious illegality of his actions."

"What about the jacked up prices on generics?" I crossed my arms, giving Eugene a hard look. "I can't continue to allow that."

He nodded. "We'll go to the board together. Share prices will drop, but Caravel has enough cash on hand to weather the storm."

"And they'll be better in the long run." Dan smoothed his hand down my back, giving me a kiss on my shoulder.

After answering a few more of his questions, our impromptu meeting dispersed. As we left the study, Eugene was cornered by Uncle Zip, asking him what he thought the Yankees's chances were this year, apparently still suspicious of his loyalty to the Sox.

Luckily, Eleanor rescued Eugene, asking for his help in the kitchen, and Dan introduced me to more relatives.

Everyone was really nice except for a few people who were cranky, giving me the impression that being polite wasn't in their nature. However, nice or not, they made it clear that I was part of the family.

More than once throughout the day, I found my throat clogged with a strange wave of emotion, and I'd have to blink against stinging in my eyes and nose.

I would regulate my breathing, smile, and the emotions would pass. Dan seemed to pick up on these ebbs and flows, stepping into a lag in conversation, making a joke, giving me a kiss, or even pulling me away to someplace private for a quick hug and shared *I love yous*.

We were on our way back from one such private embrace when Dan stiffened and took a step back.

"Ah God, it's Aunt Meg." Dan turned, as though to block me from her view.

"What? What's wrong?" I whispered, trying to see around his shoulder.

"Don't drink when she speaks," he whispered urgently.

"Why not?" I searched his eyes.

"She buries the lead."

"Buries the lead?"

466

"Daniel Patrick, there you are."

He stiffened again. "Too late." Pasting on a smile, he turned, revealing a dainty, lovely, sweet looking woman who might've been over one hundred years old. "Aunt Meg."

"Let me kiss you."

She did, and left two red lipstick marks on his cheeks, giving me the impression she'd just applied a new layer.

"And who is this?" She turned her gaze to me, giving me a friendly smile.

"This is, uh, Kathleen."

She extended a hand and I gave it a gentle shake.

"So nice to meet you," she said.

"Thank you," I said, meaning it.

"Welcome to the family."

"Thank you, I—"

"We're so happy to see Daniel finally settling down with a nice girl, you have no idea how much his mother wants more grandchildren. And it's about time one of these boys did something for their mother."

"Aunt Meg—"

"But they're good boys, more or less. I remember one time, I think Daniel was just about three, and Seamus must've been almost ten or eleven. My Harriet was out in the garden and there was your husband, holding the basket for her. So sweet."

I smiled at the older woman, bringing my glass to my lips for a sip of water. Dan caught my wrist, forestalling my drink. I glanced to him while Meg continued her story and he gave me a severe look, shaking his head then tilting it back towards his aunt.

"They picked carrots out of the garden that day, zucchini too. I think she made zucchini bread, a few loaves and, you know your ma,"—Meg gave Dan's cheek a soft, affectionate pat—"she had you boys take the vegetables around to the neighbors. And that's how Seamus discovered Mr. Cleary's dead body."

I choked on air, my eyes bugging out, and I began to cough.

"Yep. I remember that day." Dan rubbed his hand down my back to my bottom, giving it a surreptitious little pat. "Poor Mr. Cleary."

CHAPTER THIRTY-THREE

Ravelry: a community site, an organizational tool, and a yarn & pattern database for knitters and crocheters. You should join.

RAVELRY.COM

Kat

KNIT NIGHT WAS in full swing.

All of the guests, family members, and friends had departed, leaving just us knit night ladies, our significant others, and Dan's mom Eleanor. Surprisingly, Eugene had been one of the last to leave. He'd stayed and helped Eleanor pick up, lingering with her in the backyard past 8:00 PM.

When Eugene left, Dan came up behind me in the kitchen and placed a kiss on my neck. "So, you and your uncle made up?"

Condensing the leftover appetizers to one platter, I shook my head. "We have a truce."

"But you don't forgive him?" Dan leaned to the side, catching my eyes.

"He didn't ask for forgiveness."

Dan made a sound in the back of his throat, coming to my side, his hand sliding down my back to rest on my bottom. "You can still forgive someone even if they don't ask for forgiveness. Forgiveness is about you not holding on to other people's shit."

Before I could respond to this bit of wisdom, Quinn walked into the kitchen.

"What's up?" Dan lifted his chin toward Quinn.

Unsurprisingly, Dan didn't remove his hand from my bottom. Instead, he slowly rubbed my backside, and then shifted his arm so that it draped along my back.

"I have something you should both hear." Quinn's eyes were on Dan as he pulled out his phone, navigated to an audio file, and pressed play.

I listened as a conversation between Seamus and Caleb played over the phone's speaker, my mouth dropping when I realized it was extremely incriminating for both Dan's brother and my cousin.

"They're discussing Dan's kidnapping." Outrage and residual fear rose to tighten my throat. "They were going to kill him."

Dan shook his head, ending the recording. "I was there for that conversation. I was never in any real danger."

Quinn and I listened as Dan explained what had happened.

"So . . . Caleb wanted you dead, and Seamus wanted the money," I recapped. "But Seamus double-crossed Caleb."

"Seems like it." Dan nodded, kissing my shoulder. "Like I said, I wasn't in any real danger, but Seamus was hoping you wouldn't know that."

"So she would pay the ransom," Quinn filled in. "And Seamus got away with the money."

Dan rolled his eyes. "He'll be back. He's like my mailman."

When Dan didn't continue, or offer an explanation for his analogy, Quinn and I shared a look.

Eventually, I asked, "How is he like your mailman?"

"He always comes back and brings bad news."

I chuckled while Quinn stared at this friend, clearly not impressed with the joke.

"So, what's the plan? You giving this to the cops?"

"I called my contact at the Boston PD last night, but I didn't tell him about the tape or about Caleb." Quinn moved his slightly unsettling gaze to me. "You can use this tape to blackmail your cousin. It was obtained legally and will definitely convict him, especially if Dan was there in the room. Tell Caleb you want those patents returned, and for him to leave Caravel quietly. That'll keep your company out of the news, stock prices high, and you can make internal changes without anyone knowing what happened. Seamus took the money, he can take the fall for the kidnapping."

I held my breath, my mind racing, looking between Quinn and his phone.

It sounded too good to be true: my cousin out of the picture, Caravel safe and intact.

And yet . . .

I shook my head, remembering something Eugene had brought up earlier in the day. "What about Marie?"

Dan and Quinn shared a quick look, and Dan asked, "What about Marie?"

"She knows about the kidnapping. Do you really think she didn't pick up on some newsworthy details? Like Caravel's price-hike ono generics, or about Dr. Branson and his sinister research in the Caribbean?"

Quinn frowned, crossing his arms. "I didn't consider that."

I shook my head. "No. I can't hide what happened. It all has to come out. I'm not going to be responsible for a cover-up. That's how my cousin does things. Stock prices will drop, yes. I know that. I think Caravel can weather the storm. And, I believe Caleb deserves to pay for what he's done. Publicly. If I don't do something now, he'll just . . . turn into *my* mailman. I'll never be free of him."

"Most of your wealth is tied to the stock price of Caravel," Quinn reminded me. "You might lose everything."

"I won't lose everything. I have plenty of investments elsewhere," I reasoned, even though the thought of Caravel in jeopardy *felt* like losing everything.

Dan's hand came to the space between my shoulder blades and he rubbed. "What does it matter if you gain the whole world, but never get revenge on your dickface cousin in the process?"

I huffed a little laugh, but then immediately sobered. "I just hope…"

"What?"

Twisting my lips to the side, I admitted, "I just hope Marie doesn't write a story about what she saw, what she witnessed when Dan was taken. How I—how I handled it." I swallowed past a growing tightness. "It's her job to report the news. What happened to us *is* news. But it was also something I consider private, personal, and none of anyone's business."

Dan made a soft sound in the back of his throat. "She wouldn't do that. Marie isn't like that."

"Marie isn't like what?"

We all turned our attention to the speaker of the question, who also happened to be the subject of the question.

Quinn stiffened, looking conflicted. Dan straightened, looking unconcerned. And I met Marie's stare evenly.

Well, there's no time like the present.

"Hey, guys," I turned to Dan, kissing him on the cheek. "Give us a minute?"

"Sure." He gave me a pointed look, as though to say, *This is Marie, we trust her.*

I nodded. He grabbed the tray of appetizers. I patted his bottom as he left and noticed Marie grin at my maneuver.

Once Quinn and Dan were gone, I started, "So, Marie—"

"Did you try my lemon drops? Is that what you all were talking about?" She ventured further into the kitchen, a fretful expression on her face as she whispered, "No one is drinking them. Why isn't anyone drinking them?"

I grimaced before I could catch the impulse, because I'd tried her lemon drops earlier and they were terrible.

"What? What is that face? Why are you making that face?"

"Marie."

472

"You can tell me the truth," she took a deep breath, like she was bracing herself.

Studying my friend, I couldn't help but smile. No one had told her the truth about the lemon drops because everyone liked her so much. But as the evening wore on, it was very likely someone—probably Sandra or Elizabeth—would let it slip that her version of the beloved cocktail was disgusting. Since I was just about to ask Marie something that might potentially damage our friendship, I wasn't going to be the one to admit her lemon drops tasted like lemon-scented dishwater.

"I need to ask you something."

"About the lemon drops?"

"No. It's not about the lemon drops. Marie . . ." I hesitated, because my heart unexpectedly hurt.

Yes, I needed to know whether she was going to write a story on Dan's kidnapping—or anything else about me—but I didn't want to know. I didn't want our friendship to change.

But deep down, I recognized that it already had, and not just because I would be moving to Boston. Our friendship would change because I was now in a position of power and authority.

Fundamentally, Marie's job was to hold people in authority accountable.

So I asked, "Are you planning to write a news story about Dan's kidnapping?"

Her smile faded and her blue gaze sharpened. I imagined she was giving me a look that mirrored my own.

She asked, "Have you ever heard of The Journalist's Creed?"

"No."

A tight smile pulled at her lips but didn't make it to her eyes. "It was written by Walter Williams in 1914, and it's a good summary of how I view my job and the role of journalists. In summary, I believe in clear thinking and clear statements, accuracy and fairness. I believe that I should write only what I absolutely believe to be true. I also believe that any suppression of the news, for any consideration other than the welfare of society, is indefensible."

I nodded, sharing a weighted look with my friend, not allowing my stomach to drop even though I knew this—her job and my position—would be a barrier between us. In my role at Caravel, I may not always be able to weigh the welfare of society over the welfare of my employees. The most I could hope for was that society and Caravel would, more often than not, share common goals.

She took a deep breath and continued, "Furthermore, I believe the supreme test of good journalism is the measure of its public service. Therefore, no." Her gaze softened. "I will not be writing a story about Dan's kidnapping. Or, for that matter, about my personal relationship with either of you."

I breathed out, feeling the relief in my bones. "Thank you."

"Don't thank me," she said, her tone suddenly exacting and harsh. "I consider Dan's kidnapping salacious, but I do not consider it news. In fact, publishing it would detract from important, actual news, distract the public from what matters. Sure, it would sell a lot of papers —heiress husband kidnapped by brother—but how does that serve public interest? It doesn't. It's garbage journalism, *infotainment*. It's a cheap way to make a buck. However . . ."

She took a deep breath, her stare looking solemn, maybe even a little regretful. "I will be researching Dr. Branson, what he's been doing in St. Kitts, and Caravel's role—if any. That story is in the public interest. He's experimenting on a vulnerable population in order to avoid US law. I wish I could say I'm sorry, but I'm not. The public deserves to know, even if it hurts your company."

"I understand." I nodded, my heart still hurting, but not as much.

Things would never be the same between us from this moment forward, but I was determined to salvage our friendship. Not knowing Marie would never be an option. Life had changed, shifted, moved, and grown for all of us, but that didn't mean we couldn't change with it.

People aren't static creatures, so why should their relationships be?

"I would never ask you to apologize for having professional ethics," I continued, reaching out, and tangled our fingers together. "But . . . I will ask you to apologize for the lemon drops. You're never allowed to make anything but tequila drinks ever again."

She laughed, squinting at me. "My lemon drops are just fine. You're a lemon drop snob."

"It tastes like lemon-scented dishwater."

She laughed harder, tugging me back toward the family room where everyone was gathered. "Fine, oh ye mistress of lemon drop greatness, show me your superior cocktail ways."

I grinned at her.

She grinned back.

Marie gave me hope.

Despite the changes and challenges on the horizon and down the road—for all of us—I didn't doubt that everyone in this tight-knit family we'd chosen would continue to *try*. We would always love each other, and we would always support each other.

And that was enough.

* * *

"This place doesn't look like a mental institution," Dan mumbled, turning his head from side to side as he inspected the fountain on our left leading to a wide, picturesque grassy lawn. "This place looks more like a fancy hotel. Or a spa."

I smirked at the murky expression on his features. "What did you expect? People walking around in straightjackets?"

He shrugged. "More crows."

"Crows?"

"Yeah. I don't know." He looked adorably flustered by his admission. "Don't ask, it makes no sense. I don't know why I expected crows. I'm an asshole."

"You are not an asshole."

"Sometimes I am," he mumbled, scratching his neck.

I scoffed at him, but said nothing. He was being silly.

We walked hand in hand through the outside walkway, toward the wing where my mother was housed. I reflected on how grateful I was that we'd been able to take the day off to do this.

The last few weeks had been hectic. Our friends had departed on the Monday morning after the party. Plans were made to keep our normal, run-of-the-mill knit nights on Tuesdays, where both Ashley and I would join via in video conference.

The rest of that Monday afternoon had been taken up with the aftermath of Dan's kidnapping. Eugene and two other lawyers from his firm were present while Dan and I were questioned by the police. The rope burns on Dan's wrists were photographed and entered into evidence.

Seamus was still at large, but we told them everything. We left nothing out except anything related to Caleb's venture capital firm's bank statements. Since Alex had obtained them by hacking various financial institutions, we decided it was best not to bring them up.

But we did share the audio recording Seamus had sent to Stan, where Seamus and Caleb had discussed Dan's kidnapping. The recording, plus Dan's sworn affidavit, were enough to arrest Caleb.

The very next day, accounts of Caleb's violation of the Uniform Trade Secrets Act hit the news. Just like Eugene had suggested, Alex had sent offshore legal documentation to the International Consortium of Investigative Journalists. They'd run the story. The scandal was huge.

Two days later, the media caught wind of Dan's kidnapping and Caleb's role. Soon, the whole country was swept up in the twisted tale of Caleb Tyson and his attempts to bring down the pharmaceutical giant, his illegal dealings, and his attempt to kidnap Dan.

Naturally, gossip magazines were paying a premium for pictures of Dan and me, separate or together. But soon, it was everyone. Every news outlet was running the story of the heiress who married the ex-felon from the wrong side of the tracks and how she'd paid his ransom.

Eleanor was harassed on her way to work and dogged outside of her house. She agreed to move in with us—at the Duxbury estate—until things settled down. Even so, all the family and neighbors I'd met during the party were interviewed. The most shocking revelation to come out of the family interviews was that—according to Dan's Uncle Zip—my Uncle Eugene was a Yankees fan.

The first couple of days at the Duxbury estate had been difficult. It was so big, so ridiculously big, it felt lonely. But after the media became insatiable, the big house grew to be a sanctuary, a place to avoid prying eyes and paparazzi.

And, yes, I took a helicopter into work almost every day. Eleanor also took it, using the helipad at the hospital and cracking herself up whenever anyone asked how her commute had been.

At Caravel, an emergency board meeting was called, Caleb was removed as CEO, and our chief operating officer was asked to step into the position temporarily until we could find a replacement. During the same meeting, I presented my findings related to the division earnings reports and asserted that I would be voting the controlling shares from that point forward.

No one voiced opposition. Apparently, no one wanted to get in my way after what had happened to my cousin.

Today, over two weeks later, was the first day we'd had an opportunity to break away from the craziness. I'd called my therapist in the morning and we'd had a good session, but we both agreed I needed to find a doctor local to Boston. She offered to help me find someone suitable and trustworthy.

I'd also called Steven and made him a job offer. I'd given Quinn a heads-up about my plan and he'd grudgingly given me his blessing to reach out to Steven. Maybe Quinn wouldn't be too happy with me if Steven accepted, but I needed someone I could trust in charge of finance at Caravel.

After that, I'd called Ms. Opal and offered her a job as well, as my personal executive assistant. She agreed on the spot.

Once all my calls were made, and Dan was finished with his work for the morning, I suggested we visit my mother. Dan hadn't met her yet and I was overdue for a visit. Work had been stressful. Caravel's stock was down—way down—but not as low as we'd originally forecasted. With Caleb arraigned and bail withheld, I was breathing easier than I had in months.

And so presently, I turned my thoughts to Dan and his statement about crows. "Are you an Edgar Allan Poe fan?"

His brown eyes slid to mine, narrowing like I'd said something suspicious. "How do you know that?"

"Maybe your assumption that there would be crows has something to do with Edgar Allan Poe's poem, "The Raven." A man goes slowly mad while a bird says, 'Nevermore.' Classic literature is full of alarming depictions of mental illness. Have you read *Jane Eyre?*"

"No." Dan was looking increasingly uncomfortable.

"The villain—or the victim, depending on who you're talking to— of the story is the main male character's first wife. She's 'mad,' but he didn't know that when they married. He keeps her locked away in a tower until she eventually burns it down."

"Yeah. I'd burn some shit down too if my husband locked me in a tower. That guy sounds like an asshole." Dan held the door open for me.

I thought about his statement for a minute, then shrugged. "Maybe, but I don't think so. It's convenient to judge people—and fictional characters—through the lens of present-day knowledge and values. But, if you think about it, it's also ridiculous. Do we judge people in the middle ages for not understanding combustion engines until the seventeen hundreds? No. Knowledge about any subject has to build over time."

"Hmm . . ." Dan marinated in my words and we walked down the bright, sunny hallway. "By that logic, one day people will look back at us, at our generation, and think of us as primitive, unenlightened shit-for-brains."

I chuckled as we approached my mother's building. "Probably. On that note, there's likely plenty of people in our own generation right now who would consider you and I primitive and unenlightened."

"Bah," he waved this statement away. "Those people are shit-for-brains."

I laughed harder, squeezing his hand.

"But seriously." The look he sent me was slightly perturbed. "No one can know everything, understand *everything*. People gotta make mistakes, make assumptions, learn. And they need the space to do it without being condemned. So . . ." his expression cleared and he pulled me to a stop. "Thank you, for giving me the space to learn from my mistakes."

How could I not smile at that? How could I not kiss him? *Impossible.*

So I did.

My heart tugged towards him as we separated and continued on our way, walking to the heavy security door. I pressed the call button and waited, a sudden flutter of nervousness igniting in my belly.

I hope she likes him.

Almost immediately, one of my mother's personal nurses appeared, opening the door. "Kathleen, good to see you."

She ushered us in and I turned to Dan. "This is Becky. She's with my mother during the weekdays."

They exchanged a short greeting and Becky motioned us forward. "She's in the sunroom today."

"How is she?"

Becky hesitated, then said, "She's okay. She had a good day yesterday, sat in a chair, but today has been harder."

I thanked her for the update, and then let Becky walk ahead as Dan slowed our steps, tugging on my hand.

When Becky was several lengths in front of us, Dan leaned in and whispered, "I thought you said your mom is . . . that she's catatonic."

I nodded. "She is. She's been diagnosed with a very severe case of catatonic schizophrenia. Sometimes she is manic and moves around. But usually, she's still."

"Does she ever respond to you? Ever talk to you?"

I glanced down the hall to where Becky had disappeared. "No. She hasn't spoken to me or acknowledged me since I was eight." I breathed through a familiar twinge of sadness that had once felt like a mountain.

"But not all people with catatonic schizophrenia are like that?"

"It depends on the severity. Sometimes it can be treated with medication and psychotherapy, but it isn't what would be considered curable. It's a chronic disorder, and her case is very, very severe. It's also very unusual. Medication hasn't helped."

Feeling Dan's stare on me, I looked at him. He appeared to be a little panicked.

"I really am an asshole. I should've done some research before I came."

Giving him a reassuring smile, I pulled him down the hall. "We've been a little busy, in case you've forgotten. I'd say you get a pass. Besides, there's nothing to be afraid of or nervous about."

He swallowed, looking like he wasn't too sure.

We turned the corner and passed through a door into the sunroom. I spotted my mother immediately. She was lying on the floor in the corner. The top half of her body was turned toward the door, the other half was twisted toward the wall. She was wearing white scrubs, and they'd recently given her a haircut.

Becky was in a chair by the door, painting a portrait of a child on a medium-sized canvas. The nurse gave us a nod as we entered.

I studied Dan's reaction as he looked at my mother, curiosity getting the better of me. His brown eyes moved over her motionless body for a long moment. She stared in our general direction, but her eyes were unfocused.

"She looks like you," he said softly, his hand tightening on mine. "She looks like she could be your sister."

"Thank you," I said, and I meant it. I'd always considered my mother beautiful. "Dan, this is my mom, Rebekah. Mom, this is Dan. He's . . . we're married."

My mother didn't move, didn't speak, just stared forward. I hadn't expected any different.

So I did what I always did when I visited. Releasing his hand, I walked to the middle of the room and sat on a small sofa. And then I talked to her.

"We met a few years ago, and I liked him a lot. Wouldn't you know it, he was also fond of me." I sent Dan a grin over my shoulder, which he returned like he couldn't help himself. His eyes were round with wonder, but I also spotted a small wrinkle of concern between his eyebrows.

Gathering a deep breath, I shifted my gaze back to my mother.

"Dan and I had a misunderstanding that kept us apart for a while. But, don't worry, we worked it out."

* * *

OUR VISIT LASTED ABOUT AN HOUR. Dan hadn't said much at first, but once I'd coaxed him to the couch and pulled him into my narrative about our relationship, he loosened up and began talking.

Becky cautioned me not to approach my mother today, since she'd been manic earlier in the morning, so I didn't. We said our goodbyes, and I promised to visit again soon.

"I'll come, too," Dan said to her. "Maybe I'll bring my mom."

I hid my smile behind the curtain of my hair and we left.

I felt lighter as we drove away, as I usually did after each of my visits.

We were almost to the county road when Dan asked distractedly, "The whole building is for your mother?"

I sighed. "Yes. My father had it built. He used to stay there, with her, so it was kind of like his house." "This was before or after he got Alzheimer's?"

"Before. When I was at boarding school."

Dan nodded, still distracted, like he was assembling a puzzle in his brain.

Abruptly, he asked, "When did you start visiting her?"

"Uh . . ." I watched the scenery pass beyond the windshield, trying to figure out where best to start. "So, honestly, my mother—seeing my mother—was one of the main reasons I decided to change my life."

I felt Dan's gaze flicker to me. "What happened?"

"I was exhausted. In Chicago, I was running all the time, never knowing where I was going to sleep, or if I was going to eat. I'd made it back here, to Boston, and was couch surfing, but I was tired—so tired—of everything. So one day, I decided I wanted to see her."

I tucked my hair behind my ears, the memory still vivid. "I showed up and used my old student ID. They let me see her, and it was like . . ." I turned to him. "I felt like she could hear me. Maybe she can, maybe she can't. But I *feel* like she can. I told her everything, it all came out, and I felt so ashamed of who I'd become. She'd loved me so, so much. I remember that, when I was younger, and I was letting her down."

"Kat—"

"As I was leaving, I was walking past the outpatient recreation room. There were a bunch of people there, playing board games. I didn't want to go back to the place I was staying, so I sat down at a table and played checkers with this woman I'd never met. Her name was Delilah, she was forty-three, and she had schizophrenia."

"Like your mom?"

I hesitated. "Yes and no. My mom was originally diagnosed with paranoid type schizophrenia. It has now become catatonic. Delilah has paranoid type, but she received treatment early."

"So, if you receive treatment early—like cancer—it can get better?"

"Not necessarily. Every case of schizophrenia is as different as the person who has it. There are four main types and—similar to cancer— each has a spectrum of severity."

"Huh." Dan thought about this briefly before saying, "My mother had cancer."

"What?" A spike of dread pierced my chest.

"Yeah. Breast cancer. Stage two. It was before my parents divorced. I used to hold her hair while she puked, before it all fell out."

"I—I'm so sorry."

He waved away my concern. "Nah. Don't be. She's fine now, been in remission for—jeez—almost twenty years."

I released the tense breath I'd been holding, realizing this news had sent my heart racing with fear. I'd just met Eleanor, but I loved her already. I wasn't ready to lose her. The reflexive nature of my reaction to this news also made me realize that all disorders and diseases could sound frightening when the details are unknown.

Fear of the unknown, not a revolutionary or novel concept.

"Anyway, I get what you mean about severity." Dan's hands flexed on the steering wheel. "She had stage two and that wasn't great. Some people have it worse, some people have it better. When it's worse, it's scary."

"It is scary," I agreed. "Illness is a reminder that we don't really have any control. And I understand why people find schizophrenia frightening, believe me, I get it. Hallucinations, delusions, it's difficult to imagine having a mind that is not fully your own, just like it's difficult to imagine having cancer, where your body isn't fully your own. But people living with paranoid type often experience less dysfunction than people living with other subtypes. They're often able to live, work, and care for themselves. And yet, almost every depiction you find in books or movies make people living with paranoid schizophrenia the villains. Can you imagine if books and movies did the same thing to people with cancer?"

Dan made a surprised sound and he blinked, rubbing his jaw. "I'd never thought about it that way."

I continued, feeling impassioned by the subject, "It's so frustrating to me, because when I visit my mom, I usually go to the rec room and play board games with the outpatient group. They're not villains, or frightening. That's not who they are."

"Who are they?"

"They're smart, interesting, funny, sweet, beautiful, creative, logical—so many things other than their diagnosis. But take a person on the street and ask them about schizophrenia, and it's the bad guy in a slasher film. Or the crazy wife in the tower. I guess I'm frustrated because a mental illness diagnosis is a lazy scapegoat. And portraying all people living with mental disorders—all people living with schizophrenia—as one extreme, evil archetype is irresponsible."

"Here, here. Well said."

My gaze moved to Dan and I studied him. "Are you tired of my soapbox yet?"

"No. But I am curious, what was it—about playing checkers with that woman—that changed your perspective on everything? What about playing checkers had you wanting to make a change?"

"It wasn't the checkers. It was her. I looked at Delilah and I realized that if one day I started exhibiting symptoms of schizophrenia, my life would not be over."

"Ah." He nodded, like the puzzle pieces of me and my past had suddenly clicked into place.

"I'd thought for so long that I would *become* a schizophrenic, and if I *was* a schizophrenic, that's all I would ever be. But a person doesn't become their diagnosis. Your mom isn't breast cancer, you don't become cancer. You live with cancer. So often, we think of a person living with mental illness as their mental illness, and that's unfair. A person is never their diagnosis, not even my mom. Delilah showed me that. She lives—and has lived—a full life. She has a husband. They travel. She's a photographer, an artist. She tells the funniest knock-knock jokes I've ever heard. She takes her meds every day, but still has hallucinations from time to time. She is not schizophrenic. She lives with schizophrenia."

"So," I sighed, shrugging. "That's my story. I came back a few times to visit my mom, and I was drawn to the others here. I made friends. Once I figured out that I'd been basing my decisions on misinformation and the fallacies of a fourteen-year-old brain, I decided I had to make a change. I was unhappy. So I went back to Chicago, turned myself into the police, and you know the rest."

"I guess I do." His attention moved between me and the road. Dan opened his mouth, then closed it.

"What? What is it?"

"Do you still worry? That you'll start showing signs?"

"Every day." I smiled, though my eyes stung as I made the admission. "There's not a day that goes by where I don't question myself, a choice I made, something I saw out of the corner of my eye, something I heard. My father was so convinced that I would become my mother, I think he convinced me, too."

Dan sighed, shaking his head. "That's beat."

"If it happens, it happens. And I'll know what to do. And I'll still live my life. And I'll still try to make a difference."

He reached for my hand and placed a kiss on the back of my knuckles. "You're tough. I love that about you."

"Sometimes I don't feel tough."

"That's why you have me." He tightened his hold on my hand.

"Why? So you can be tough for me?"

"Who? Me? Nah. I'm just a big softie." He made a surprised face, and then frowned his extreme disagreement. His expressions were theatrical and they made me smile.

We drove in silence for several minutes, and it was another of those peaceful moments. Quiet car, quiet street, quiet neighborhood. But more than that, it was still. Instead of treading water next to each other in a tranquil lake beneath a starry sky, I imagined we were lying in a field, holding hands beneath puffy summer clouds, the rhythm of two beating hearts becoming one.

"You have me so I will know you," he said suddenly, kissing my hand again. His words spoken against my fingers were just above a whisper, and the quiet intimacy gave me the sense he was speaking to himself just as much as he was speaking to me. "So I can remind you of how tough you are, how good, strong, and capable. Because, when you love someone, that's what you do. Because you'll do the same for me."

EPILOGUE

Dan

"ALL I'M SAYING is, Catholics are basically already Jewish. I mean, we have the Old Testament, right? And you pay retail for some things, like commandments, I think you have something like six hundred, whereas we have ten. And we pay retail for other things, like penance."

Kat stared at my reflection in the mirror we were both using, the only one in the master bedroom. Since arriving in Chicago three days ago, we were staying in Janie and Quinn's old penthouse apartment at the East Randolph Street Property.

There was another mirror in the bathroom, but I'd been meaning to bring this topic up for weeks and we never seemed to have time to talk about it. So I'd hijacked her while she was finishing up her makeup.

"What are you talking about?" She tilted her head to the side. "You want to convert?"

"Not necessarily. I'm just saying, you all have Yom Kippur, one day for penance. We have Lent, forty days. Plus, Jesus was Jewish. If Judaism was good enough for Jesus . . ." I shrugged. The way I saw it, Jesus being Jewish made my entire case for me.

Finishing up with her eye makeup, she turned away from the mirror and crossed her arms. "What is the point to this conversation? What is it you're asking for?"

Fuck a duck.

I gave her a disgruntled look. She was forcing my hand. She wanted me to get to the point. I hated it when she did that. I had so many good points lined up before *the* point.

Watching her reaction carefully, I said, "Getting married."

She blinked twice. "Getting married?"

"That's right."

"Dan, my love, we *are* married. We've been married for fifteen years." She walked closer to me and lowered her voice like she was going to tell me a secret. "I don't know if you know this, but we have three kids."

"Very funny." I craned my neck to watch my fingers in the mirror as I tried to tie a Windsor knot at my neck. "I was just thinking, wouldn't it be nice to do it right?"

"Right?"

"Stomping on the glass, the canopy, getting carried around in chairs." My eyes flickered over her body. "A white dress for you, a tuxedo for me."

At the suggestion of a tuxedo for me, her brow cleared and finally, *finally,* she looked interested.

I should have led with the tuxedo.

In retrospect, I should have known the idea of a tuxedo would get her going. Sometimes I thought the only reason Caravel hosted so many black-tie events was so she could get me in—and out of—a tuxedo. Not that I was complaining.

As far as I was concerned, Kat earned as many black-tie events as she wanted. She'd taken a big risk when she exposed her cousin all those years ago, she'd opened her family's company up to hostile takeovers, lawsuits, fraud claims, and she'd weathered the storm like a champ. Now Caravel was better than before, stronger, a leader in research and development rather than a bottom-feeder that chased profits, like some of her competitors.

To say I was proud of her would be a big fucking understatement.

"You want to have a traditional Jewish wedding?" She didn't look surprised, more like curious.

"Yeah. Why not? The kids would love it. They're going to Jewish school, makes sense."

Her eyes narrowed, like she was suspicious. "Did Rebekah put you up to this?" Rebekah being our oldest by two minutes, just before her sister Eleanor had made her grand entrance.

"What? No." I scoffed. "Rebekah didn't put me up to this."

Rebekah had put me up to this.

To clarify, it had been her idea—at first—but the more I thought about it, the more I wanted to make it happen. It had all started two months ago when Rebekah came home from a friend's house and asked to see our wedding album. I told her we didn't have one. This led to all kinds of questions, like:

"Did you love mom when you married her? If so, why didn't you want to take pictures to remember the day?"

And,

"What about your kids? Didn't you ever think your children would want to see the photos?"

In case you haven't picked up on it yet, Rebekah was basically my mother come back to life.

I thought about showing my daughter the video we had of the wedding, but decided against it after giving it another watch. Man, I never got tired of watching that video.

Presently, Kat didn't look convinced, doubt warred with a confused smile as she checked her watch. "Can we talk about it later? Jack's concert is in an hour and DJ hasn't taken his bath yet."

That was no surprise. Our youngest hated baths. He was basically Pig-Pen from Charlie Brown, just with a bigger dust cloud.

"Fine. I'll give Danny a bath, and you think about your husband's genius idea."

"I can give him a bath."

"No. It's fine. Plus, Eleanor needs you to do her hair again."

"What's wrong with her hair?"

"Do I know?" I shrugged, starting over again with the tie. "I braided it, but she said she likes the way you do it better."

Kat chuckled and so did I, because our daughter Eleanor was very particular. About everything. And judged people harshly based on their fandom associations.

#Reylo4Ever

Closing the distance between us, Kat leaned forward, giving me a kiss while her hand came right to the front of my pants. I straightened, my eyes swinging to her as she stroked me over my zipper.

"Well, hello Mrs. O'Malley." I let the knot sit unfinished at my neck and put my hands on her body, sliding them down to her waist.

I missed her.

Before the family trip to Chicago, she'd been gone on a two-week business thing to China. And before that, she'd been gone for five days to Dubai. When the kids didn't have school over the summer, we all went with her. Just like, if I had a trip, everyone went with me.

But Kat and I agreed, we wanted the kids at a good school during the year, where they could make friends and live in a house that felt like a home. That meant, one of us was at home every day. We never took trips at the same time. This wasn't always easy, but when something is important to you, you prioritize it. We could, so we did.

"I want you. Tonight," she said, her gaze dropping to my lips.

"You shall have me. Tonight. Several times, if you wish."

Her grin widened and she sighed wistfully, moving like she was going to leave. I held her in place.

We weren't running late yet, and that was a miracle. I knew I shouldn't mess up her makeup, or pull her hair, or stick my hand up her dress, especially since we actually had a chance to make it to the venue on time. But I'd never been very good at doing what I should.

So I hitched up her skirt.

Her eyes widened and she caught my hands. "Dan."

"Why wait 'til tonight?" I bent my lips to her jaw, gave her a little bite.

She sighed again, angling her head back. "We'll be late."

"No we won't." I kissed her neck. "We'll be quick."

"You're never quick." She laughed, then another sigh as I palmed her still exquisite tits over the thin, silky fabric of her dress.

"But *you* can be quick." Trailing my fingers down her sides, I lifted the hem of her dress.

Her breath caught. "Don't you dare wrinkle this dress," she said, her hands gripping my shoulders, making no move to stop me.

"I need to taste you." I pressed my tongue flat against the sensitive inch beneath her ear, slowly licking, my fingers rubbing her over her little cotton underwear.

Let me stop right here, because I know what you're thinking, *Cotton underwear?* But you don't understand. This underwear was so fucking soft and comfortable, it was like wearing a cloud. I'd had some boxers made of the same material after I'd felt it. Janie had bought Kat a ton of pairs after she'd had the twins. I couldn't sing its praises highly enough. *And so breathable!*

That said, I wanted it off of her body right fucking now.

I hooked my thumb in the waistband and tugged. "One taste."

She breathed out, like she was feverish, but managed to say, "Fine, if I can have one taste of you."

My hand stalled and I thought about that. She meant what she said, I'd get one taste of her, and then she'd take me into her mouth like a popsicle for one, hot, wet, slow suck.

My wife is a sadist.

And I'm still okay with that.

Before I could answer, a little voice somewhere down the hall asked, "Can I use superglue to put an eyelash back on my eye?" and we both stiffened, our eyes wide and panicked.

"I'll get it."

"You get it."

We said in unison, and we were off.

Sadism and sexy times would have to wait until later.

* * *

JACK'S CONCERT WAS INCREDIBLE. He was only in town for one performance, on his way to Italy, and we felt lucky we got to see him play.

Greg and Fiona's oldest kid had more musical talent in his pinky finger than all three hundred members of my entire extended family combined, even though my sister Colleen considered herself a singer.

She was not a singer. Getting drunk at a pub in Ireland and singing "Danny Boy" a cappella to a rousing round of applause does not make you a singer. You sing "Danny Boy" anywhere in Ireland, they applaud you. It's a thing. Look it up.

Anyway, we weren't late to the concert, despite DJ's best efforts. But he was impossible to stay mad at; the kid was five and his favorite joke was, *beware of atoms, they make up everything,* followed by a ten-minute lecture on the nature of matter and a disclaimer about whether atoms made up antimatter. And then he'd fart.

The day after the concert, since it was Sunday, we all made the trek to Greg and Fiona's home in South Shore. Their place was great. A huge, triple decker brick house built in 1915 with a workshop out back, and a nice big yard for the kids.

Of course, their youngest was now fifteen, so mostly I was thinking of my kids when I said the backyard was nice. Long story short, we would be here all day.

When we arrived, Greg was out back telling one of his big fish stories to a rapt audience that consisted of Alex, Matt, Drew—who was manning the barbecue—Nico, Quinn, Desmond, and some kid, maybe sixteen or seventeen, that I didn't recognize.

Kat went inside to visit with her knitting ladies while I stayed outside to keep an eye on the kids. Mostly, I was keeping an eye on DJ, making sure he didn't roll himself in the mud. *Covers my scent,* he'd say.

I swear, this kid.

I turned my attention to Greg's story.

"She considered the raccoon to be *her* raccoon?" Matt looked totally confused as he asked Greg this question.

Greg took a swig from his beer. "Mmm. That's right. But you have to understand, where I lived, this woman was a crackhead. It was a three-story complex with one big, shared backyard. Ms. Jenner—"

"The crackhead?" Alex sought to clarify.

"Yes. Though I doubt she listed, *Ms. Jenner, Crackhead*, on her resume. Anyway, as I was saying, Ms. Jenner considered the raccoon to be her raccoon. So when she came home on one fateful morning at three AM and found the raccoon on the second floor balcony, well . . . she was displeased."

"What did she do?" Drew asked, but the way he asked gave me the impression he was afraid to find out.

"She put out a bag of sugar at first, in an attempt to lure the animal."

"Sugar?" Nico glanced at Drew. "Just a little bag of sugar?"

"No. A five-pound bag. The raccoon was not impressed. She then used found objects in the yard to build a stairway of sorts to the second balcony. This is when I was awoken. She'd fallen off a garbage can, causing a ruckus outside my window."

"Was she okay?" Quinn asked.

"As well as can be expected, given it was three AM and she was a crackhead in deep despair over the appropriation of her beloved raccoon. But let me finish the story. When I came outside—mind you, I was sixteen, newly arrived from Mayfair—I found Ms. Jenner setting up the garbage can again in an effort to climb up to the second floor balcony. Immediately, I realized her error."

Quinn and Alex traded looks and I asked, "You stopped her from climbing?"

"No. Certainly not. I realized she'd been trying to climb on the garbage can without a lid. She was attempting to balance herself just on the rim. I flipped it over for her and held the base so she could use a hula hoop to reach the raccoon."

This was the best and the worst story I'd ever heard, and I couldn't wait to find out how it ended. "Did it work?"

"It didn't. The raccoon climbed down the waterspout, grabbed a handful of sugar, and made off into the night like the little ninja bandit that it was. Meanwhile, the owner of the second story unit became enraged, jumped down from the balcony wielding a katana, and bit Ms. Jenner on the kneecap."

"The kneecap?" Nico asked, as though the placement of the bite was the strangest part of the story.

Alex seemed to be the only one who didn't look confused.

"What are the chances of trying to trap a wild animal, and being bit by your sword-wielding neighbor instead?" Matt asked Drew.

The big man shrugged.

I answered, "In Boston, pretty high."

This earned me some laughs.

"Hey, Dan." Matt pointed at me with his beer. "Are you and Kat still coming to Marie's birthday party?"

"Yeah. Kat has already pulled our Hogwarts robes out of the attic."

"I still can't believe you're a Hufflepuff." Nico clinked his beer against mine. "Marie and I were the only Hufflepuffs until you took the test."

"Was anyone surprised to find out Kat was a Slytherin?" Alex asked the group, grinning at me. "For the record, I was not."

"That's because you're a Slytherin. You people recognize each other." Greg grabbed another beer, popping off the top.

"*You people*? What are you talking about? You're a Slytherin." Quinn gave Greg an irritated look and then shook his head, mumbling to himself, "Why are we having this conversation? What are we, ten?"

Greg ignored Quinn's mumbled statement, saying, "I'm allowed to call myself *you people*. Prerogative of the pejorative."

"Hey guys!"

We all turned towards the sound of the voice, finding Fiona and Janie leaning out of the kitchen window. "Where are the kids?"

Now we all turned towards the lawn, finding the backyard empty.

Meanwhile, Greg called back to his wife, "They're in the workshop, probably. Don't worry, Jack and Ava are supervising."

I'd never say it out loud, but his assurances didn't do much to ease my mind. I felt like every day since DJ had been born I'd been one step ahead of him from blowing up the neighborhood.

Fiona looked like she wanted to push the issue, but before she could, I volunteered, "I'll check on them." Then to the guys I said, "I'll be right back, just want to put eyes on the boy."

Quinn set his beer down. "I'll come with. I haven't seen Natalie in a while."

As we walked to the workshop, I heard the unknown teenager ask Drew about a huge, nasty-looking scar on his arm, and Desmond say proudly, "Oh, that? Drew got that from a black bear."

Quinn and I traded a look, both of us laughing as we walked away.

"Hey." I tossed my thumb over my shoulder. "Who is that kid? The one who just asked Drew about his bear scar."

Quinn rubbed his hand over his face, like either the question or the answer made him tired. "That's Ava's boyfriend."

I stopped, needing a minute, and then began walking again. "Ava, as in *the youngest* of Fiona and Greg's kids, has a boyfriend?"

"Yeah, don't get me started." Quinn rubbed his face. "Desmond has been acting like a shithead since he found out."

"Why would Desmond care if . . ." I glanced at Quinn.

He lifted an eyebrow.

"Oh!" I laughed. "That's beat. Poor Desmond."

"He'll get over it."

"I don't know." I thought about the very first moment I'd laid eyes on Kat and how I'd not been able to move past her in those two wasted years before we were thrown into an inconvenient marriage. And Desmond had known Ava his whole life. "Are they even old enough for this kind of stuff?"

"Dummy, they're fifteen."

"So?"

Quinn shook his head, saying nothing.

Upon walking into the workshop, we smelled a faint odor. A chemical sort of smell. If I had to describe it, I'd say it was a fragrant bouquet of rose hips, cedar, metal vapor, a drop of chlorine, and a touch of cancer.

Glancing around, I spotted my kids by the entrance, stacking smooth, sanded wooden blocks to make a tower. Most of the young kids were also messing with the play blocks. But I also spotted the origin of the smell.

"What the f—" Quinn and I both started to say, and stopped

ourselves in unison. Children were present. I'd had to curtail my colorful language when Eleanor's first word turned out to be *fuck*. Before you ask, yes. Kat wrote it down in her baby book.

Our voices must've carried, because Jack—who'd been facing the action with his arms crossed—twisted at the waist.

I waved him over. "Hey Jack, come over here."

He did, jogging the few feet. "What's up?"

"Is . . ." I glanced behind him again, making sure my eyes weren't deceiving me. Sure enough, at the far end of the workshop, where the big garage-style door stood open for ventilation, was Ava in a Speedglas helmet leaning over Rose—Elizabeth and Nico's oldest—who was also in a Speedglas helmet. Rose's helmet was kid-sized.

"Is Rose welding?"

Jack nodded. "Yes."

"These fumes can't be good for the kids." I motioned to the little ones by the door where we were standing.

"That's why we have the big fans, see?" Jack pointed to two big shop fans blowing air out of the workshop. "And we opened the workshop door."

Quinn and I looked at each other before he asked, "Does her dad know she's welding?"

Jack blinked at Quinn, his expression blank. "If she doesn't learn to weld here, she'll just learn it on the streets."

I lifted an eyebrow at the kid. "Street welding? That's a thing?"

"Very dangerous. An epidemic sweeping the nation," he said, completely straight-faced.

I snorted a laugh. *This fucking kid.* Just like his dad.

Kat: Meanwhile...

"**WHAT ARE YOU** knitting?"

I turned my work and held it up so Sandra could see.

"Oh! It's that poncho by Olive Knits, isn't it? I love the color." Sandra used her thumb and forefinger to feel the texture of the yarn. "So soft."

"Thank you. I found this indie dyer online, Highland Handmades, and her superwash merino is my favorite."

"Is this worsted weight?" Ashley picked up the label next to me and then gasped happily. "It is worsted! I love it."

"This green is my favorite." Sandra was petting the two additional balls of yarn in my knitting bag. "Does she have any left?"

"Sadly, no. I bought her out."

Sandra's eyes narrowed. "Do you have any extra?"

I shifted my knitting bag closer to my side and out of her reach. "Go fondle your own fiber, Sandra."

Elizabeth, who was sitting on my left curled up next to me, began to shake with silent laughter.

Janie held up the ball she was using for her crochet project. "Here. You can stick your finger in my ball. But I warn you, it's acrylic."

Sandra made a face like Janie's yarn was made of cockroaches, Ashley gave a little shiver of revulsion, while Fiona laughed. "You two are terrible. These hats are for infants. Acrylic is a great yarn for baby hats."

Fiona was on her seventeenth baby hat for the year, Grace— Fiona's oldest daughter—was on her twentieth, and Janie was on her twenty-sixth. Natalie, Janie and Quinn's youngest, had been born prematurely. Janie had gone nuts for the first few weeks, feeling like she couldn't do anything while her infant daughter was in the NICU, so Fiona had suggested we all crochet and knit infant hats for the hospital.

Now, whenever any of us were in between projects or had just about 100 yards of worsted weight yarn to use, we knit a baby hat.

"Okay," Sandra stood and walked to the center of the room, "I want to ask everyone's opinion about something."

"Great." Ashley tried to hide her smirk behind a pained sounding sigh.

"Here we go." Marie rolled her lips between her teeth, clearly fighting to keep her face straight.

"I can't wait!" Grace set her knitting down and skootched to the end of her seat, looking up at Sandra with excitement.

Sandra placed her hands on her hips, glaring at each of us. "You don't even know what I'm going to say."

"You know," Elizabeth sighed sadly, "Rose wants to learn how to knit soon. So we might not get a chance to have these 'Sandra' conversations for much longer."

"Is it about edible condoms? Because we've already covered that." Ashley's voice was perfectly flat.

"But was it covered in enough detail?" Elizabeth gave Sandra an encouraging look. "Because, if memory serves, Sandra only made it through the fruits and vegetable flavors."

"And sex robots." Fiona shook her head. "Don't forget about the sex robots."

"Did I miss that one?" Grace asked her mother.

"It was before you started knitting," she answered, then under her breath added, "thank God."

"That was Marie, not me." Sandra pointed at Marie.

Marie chuckled, admitting sheepishly, "That was me."

"Okay, fine, out with it." Ashley waved her hand in the air impatiently, "What is it this time? Sex cruises?"

"They have those?" Elizabeth sat up.

Marie shook her head, like she was disappointed in Elizabeth's lack of knowledge about sex cruises. "Of course they have those. This *is* the United States."

"Holy crap! It's none of that." Sandra issued Marie an irritated look.

"Okay. Fine." Fiona set down her knitting and turned a patient gaze to Sandra. "We're sorry."

Sandra lifted her nose, and then gave Fiona a small head-nod of acknowledgement. "Thank you."

"Now what would you like to discuss?" I asked.

Sandra cleared her throat, gathered a deep inhale, and then asked the group, "Are any of you lovely ladies familiar with the concept of nocturnal orgasms?"

The End

ABOUT THE AUTHOR

Penny Reid lives in Seattle, Washington with her husband, three kids, and an inordinate amount of yarn. She used to spend her days writing federal grant proposals as a biomedical researcher, but now she writes books.

Published in 2018, 'Marriage of Inconvenience' is Penny's 17th novel.

Come find me-
Mailing list signup: http://pennyreid.ninja/newsletter/ (get exclusive stories, sneak peeks, and pictures of cats knitting hats)
Facebook: http://www.facebook.com/PennyReidWriter
Instagram: https://www.instagram.com/reidromance/
Goodreads: http://www.goodreads.com/ReidRomance
Email: pennreid@gmail.com ...hey, you! Email me ;-)
Blog: http://pennyreid.ninja
Twitter: https://twitter.com/ReidRomance
Ravelry: http://www.ravelry.com/people/ReidRomance (if you crochet or knit...!)

Read on for:
Penny Reid's **Booklist** (current and planned publications)

OTHER BOOKS BY PENNY REID

Knitting in the City Series

(Contemporary Romantic Comedy)

Neanderthal Seeks Human: A Smart Romance (#1)

Neanderthal Marries Human: A Smarter Romance (#1.5)

Friends without Benefits: An Unrequited Romance (#2)

Love Hacked: A Reluctant Romance (#3)

Beauty and the Mustache: A Philosophical Romance (#4)

Ninja at First Sight (#4.75)

Happily Ever Ninja: A Married Romance (#5)

Dating-ish: A Humanoid Romance (#6)

Marriage of Inconvenience (#7)

Winston Brothers Series

(Contemporary Romantic Comedy, spinoff of *Beauty and the Mustache*)

Truth or Beard (#1)

Grin and Beard It (#2)

Beard Science (#3)

Beard in Mind (#4)

Dr. Strange Beard (#5, coming 2018)

Beard with Me (#5.5, coming 2019)

Beard Necessities (#6, coming 2019)

Hypothesis Series

(New Adult Romantic Comedy)

Elements of Chemistry: ATTRACTION, HEAT, and CAPTURE (#1)

Laws of Physics: MOTION, SPACE, and TIME (#2, coming 2018)

Fundamentals of Biology: STRUCTURE, EVOLUTION, and GROWTH (#3, coming 2019)

Irish Players (Rugby) Series – by L.H. Cosway and Penny Reid

(Contemporary Sports Romance)

The Hooker and the Hermit (#1)

The Pixie and the Player (#2)

The Cad and the Co-ed (#3)